A sampling of praise for the work of
ELIZABETH CUNNINGHAM

The Return of the Goddess
"Cunningham gracefully crosses the borders of plausibility into a
luminous metaphysical realm."
-*Publishers Weekly*

The Wild Mother
"Captivating archetypal characters dramatize the everyday magic
of self-discovery. A beguiling tour de force."
-*Publishers Weekly*

How to Spin Gold
"After the Goddess invented writing, She gave the tools and the
imagination to Elizabeth Cunningham and said, 'Daughter, write my
stories.' Surely Elizabeth is Her—and our—best storyteller today."
-*Goodreads* by Barbara Ardinger, Ph.D.,
author of *A Woman's Book of Rituals & Celebrations*

Magdalen Rising
"Smart and earthy...richly imaginative...the epitome of the storyteller's art."
-*St Louis Dispatch*, one of "The Year's Best Books"

The Passion of Mary Magdalen
"Lavish and lusty...Cunningham's Celtic Magdalene is as hot
in the mouth as Irish Whiskey."
-*Beliefnet*, one of the year's heretical beach books.

"Cunningham weaves Hebrew scripture, Celtic and Egyptian
mythology, and early Chrisitan legend into a nearly seamless whole,
creating an unforgettable fifth Gospel..."
-*Library Journal*

Bright Dark Madonna
"Scholarship, whimsey and delectable fiction so close to fact, it's tempting to believe Maeve's story wholesale."
-*Huffington Post*

Red-Robed Priestess
"Cunningham, a storyteller as crafty as J.K. Rowling, ends the Maeve Chronicles befittingly and beautifully, with a fourth novel as fully fruited as the first. "
-*Publishers Weekly*

"This final episode in The Maeve Chronicles, for all its carefully recreated battle and bloodshed, lingers in the mind equally for its introspection and revelation. *Red-robed Priestess* offers a welcome examination of the ties of love and the conflicts of loyalty on an intimate as well as epic level." -John L. Murphy, DeVry University

Murder at the Rummage Sale
"Cunningham deftly weaves in aspects of postwar life (many of the characters are still overcoming the trauma of WWII), theological stances including Anglo-Catholic mystic and Social Gospel breast-beater, and lush descriptions of food and nature."
-*Publishers Weekly*

"*Murder at the Rummage Sale* is a mystery novel with a style and depth of thought that offers not only the fun of figuring out "Who Dun It" but also gorgeous prose and poetic phrasing which is not so commonly found in the mystery genre."
-Judith Shaw, *Feminism and Religion*

All the Perils of This Night
"Elizabeth Cunningham has taken the small town cast from *Murder At The Rummage Sale*, and brought them to a story that is not only on a much larger stage--London in the 1960's, but also to a world that is far darker, more disturbing, with a young woman's life and soul in the balance. Remarkable book."
-Rachel Pollack, author of *The Beatrix Gates*

"A smart and twisted literary thriller, one of the best of the year. I dare you to read the first few pages and then try to put this book down!"
-Steve Hamilton, Edgar-winning author of *Dead Man Running*

My Life as a Prayer: A Multifaith Memoir
"*My Life as a Prayer* is a wise and careful religious memoir written by a sympathetic contemporary religious seeker—a prayerful touch point amid a world of difficulties."
-*Foreword Reviews*

Also by
ELIZABETH CUNNINGHAM

NOVELS

The Return of the Goddess
The Wild Mother
How to Spin Gold
Murder at the Rummage Sale
All the Perils of This Night
The Book of Madge (a graphic novel)

The Maeve Chronicles
Magdalen Rising: The Beginning
The Passion of Mary Magdalen
Bright Dark Madonna
Red-Robed Priestess

POETRY

Small Bird
Wild Mercy
So Ecstasy Can Find You
Tell Me the Story Again

NONFICTION

My Life as a Prayer: A Multifaith Memoir

MUSICAL WORK

MaevenSong: A Musical Odyssey Through The Maeve Chronicles

OVER THE EDGE OF THE WORLD

a novel by

Elizabeth Cunningham

BriarRose Books

BriarRose Books
NEW PALTZ, NEW YORK

Library of Congress Control Number: to come

Printed in the United States of America.

ISBN: 978-1-944190-18-7 (Hard Cover)
ISBN: 978-1-944190-19-4 (Soft Cover)
ISBN: 978-1-944190-20-0 (E-Book)
ISBN: 978-1-944190-21-7 (Audio Book)

Over the Edge of the World by Elizabeth Cunningham

Cover and Book Design by Glen M. Edelstein, Hudson Valley Book Design
BriarRose Logo by David Budd

To My Three
Darshann, Julian, and Marina

CONTENTS

OVER THE EDGE OF THE WORLD

BEFORE
THE BEGINNING
AND
AFTER THE END

The Grannies

"Granny Rose, are you the oldest, oldest, oldest, oldest in the world?"
Jack, the youngest of a long line of Jacks, asks the question, as he often does. It is the hour between day and night, when the sky and the sea tantalize the beauty singers with subtle changes, always and never the same. It is the time when stars are shy, glimmering, brightening, fading before darkness gives them the courage to shine. The children have all been fed, the babies are in their cradles, rocked by the breeze, the ones that are not resting on their mothers' breasts. Some of the parents have slipped away to have time alone with each other or just to be fully alone; some are adding wood to the fire that warms me, and some are settling down in the circle gathering around me. They were once children, too. They are children still, holding their own children in the hour of the story that the youngest Jack has begun.

"I may be the oldest person in the world," I begin, "but I am not the oldest, oldest, oldest, oldest."

"Who is, Granny Rose, who is?"

"Granny Sweep!" shouts a scrappy girl, the youngest Sal.

"Granny Spark!"

"Granny Dirt!"

"Granny Brine!"

Voice after young voice shouts. And for a moment I forget where I am in this world we never knew existed, this place I would give my life, what's left of it, to protect. The world even the grannies had forgotten in their exile, or most of them had. I see the secret tower, the cracked window that gave me my first taste and scent of wind and rain.

"Grannies," the children beg. "Tell about the grannies."

"Once long ago," I begin.

"When you were a child?"

Longer. Before I was born, before my mother was born, or her mother…
And I tell what I remember, a story that is always and never the same:

Once long ago there was a world, and it was the only world any of us knew.
In each corner of this world lived a granny, even though people had forgotten
who the grannies were, even though the grannies themselves had forgotten.

Granny Sweep lived high on a pinnacle with sheer sides. She did not
know how she had come to be there. There was no path leading up or
down. But it was all right, because on the top of this pinnacle there was a
meadow big enough for her sheep, goats, and chickens, as well as one old
cow who was almost as old as Granny Sweep but still gave milk. (And, of
course, a cat named Puss.) When the cow said *moo*, Granny Sweep knew
she was saying *moon*, for when the cow was young and full of leaps and
kicks, she had jumped over the moon and landed on the pinnacle, where she
intended to live out her days. At least Moo-n, as Granny Sweep called the
cow, knew how she had arrived on the pinnacle. The goats boasted that they
had climbed carrying the sheep on their backs; the chickens, who were not
even eggs at the time, had heard that they floated there on high seas in their
wooden coop, which they lived in still.

There was only one creature who came and went, now shadowing
the whole pinnacle, now a speck faraway in the sky until she disappeared
altogether into the clouds or the blue. That was the raven Nightwing,
Granny Sweep's oldest friend, her informer and confidante.

At the edge of the meadow grew an orchard of apple and pear, hickory
and walnut trees, and one old wind-twisted oak. There was a thicket of
blackberries that grew along the edges of the precipice and pricked Granny
Sweep awake if she went sleepwalking at night, which she sometimes did,
for she had dreadful nightmares. (I will tell you about those another time.)

"You always say that, Granny Rose," says Sal, "but you never do."

I nod to acknowledge the truth of Sal's accusation, and then go on.

Granny Sweep had a cistern for catching rainwater spiked with stars, sun, and moon. When she was not outdoors, which she was most of the time, she lived in a little house made of stones, sticks, turf, and grass. Because it was round and low to the ground it did not get swept away on the winds that blew almost all the time, sometimes from one direction, sometimes another, and sometimes around and around.

Granny Sweep had a broom. She swept her little house every day, even though the floor was made of dirt. She lived so close to the sky, she swept that too, swept clouds that had gotten stuck on the pinnacle, swept the cobwebs or what she thought were cobwebs from the night sky. Granny Sweep had tricky eyes, maybe because the wind made them water or dust caught in them. Sometimes it was hard for her to see, especially out of her right eye, but with her left eye, her wind eye, she could see all the way to the edge of the world. She could see small things, too: bees in the hearts of roses, tears catching light. She could see right inside a person's heart, inside their dreams.

Even though she could see over the highest of walls into ramshackle hovels and piecemeal gardens, she could not see inside the vast dome at the center of the walled enclosure. In the daytime the dome reflected the sun; in the night the moon and stars. No matter how she widened or narrowed her wind eye, she could not get past the huge, smooth, glaring dome. It troubled her. She sometimes wondered if that dome hid her own secrets from her— who she was, how she had arrived at her high pinnacle, or what she was to do about anything.

"Did she ever find out what was inside the dome?" Jack asks as he always did.

Not yet, not for a long time. We have not come to that part yet.

"Her hair comes next," Sal reminds him, giving me a reprieve.

Granny Sweep had beautiful hair the color of moonlight spilled on the sea, the color of high clouds in a high wind. Most of the time she kept her hair in two long braids wound around and around her head. You see, Granny Sweep never cut her hair. She believed one day her braids would be long enough to reach to the bottom of the pinnacle. Long enough for someone to climb up to visit her.

"Who?"

Two children, I remember silently, with bare, blistered feet, running, running . . .

When the moon was full, I go on, she would unbraid her hair, pull out the flowers and twigs she had woven into it. These she threw into the fire, and the smoke smelled sweet, like a spring garden no matter what time of year, and she would comb and comb her hair with a comb made of bone.

"Whose bones?" someone wants to know.

Granny Sweep did not know. She had always had this comb, since before she could remember, and she did not remember before. On full-moon nights, when the wind was strong, the star spiders would spin their webs and come to admire the threads of Granny Sweep's hair.

"And they told her not to sweep away their webs!" says Sal.

They did. In exchange for her promise, they taught her something no one else knows, something only Granny Sweep knows how to do.

"How to weave a web with the wind!" all the children shout.

Yes, I say, an invisible web, more invisible than the finest spider's web. No one can see it, and no one but Granny Sweep can sweep it away. And no one but Granny Sweep can weave it again. And again. And again. She weaves it still, I say, as a soft, warm breeze wraps around us. Just like the spiders weave their webs in the sky and in the grass, where you can see them in the morning, shining with dew like stars.

The babies sigh in their sleep; the younger children are closing their eyes. The older ones are fighting to stay awake, using their fingers to prop their eyes open.

"More!" demands Jack, determined to stay awake. "Tell what happened next."

I will tell you more about the grannies tomorrow, children. Sleep now.

"We don't want to sleep," says Sal. "We might have nightmares. Like Granny Sweep."

Ah, children, I say silently, *that is why I haven't told what happened next. What happened to the first Jack and Sal, what happened to Briar.* (For me, there is only one Briar.)

"The nightmares are over," I say firmly, and I hope it is true. It must be true.

"But you said you would tell."

"Not yet," I say. "When it's time."

"I want to see Granny Sweep," says Jack.

"Go to sleep. Dream and maybe she will come to you."

As she once came to me, I do not say.

Tomorrow, I promise, tomorrow I will tell you about Granny Spark.

The children bed down in hammocks and tree houses, heads tucked under a mother or father's arms, or all tumbled together with brothers and sisters in warm heaps, twined arms and legs a nest, furred and feathered ones all part of the heap. Forgotten for a moment, almost unseen in the shadows I gather around me, I get to my feet. I can hear the creaks of my old worn joints; skin so thin, when I stand in the moonlight my bones shine. I walk out of our camp down to the shore, where I will walk till I can walk no more, keeping sleep at bay a little while.

I remember the nightmares, all the nightmares, the grannies' nightmares and my own. They visit me, not every night, but often, so I don't forget.

✳   ✳   ✳

The night is chilly. We gather around the fire. There is enough wood here, so that we can have fire made by wood, not just dung, though I have never minded that form of fuel. We never take more wood than we need. We consult the forest before we cut a tree, and we don't even take all the dead trees. Birds favor them as lookouts and for the insects that make their homes there.

The fire is blazing now, crackling and hissing, so loud that for once the children are quiet, their eyes wide and some of their mouths, too, as they gaze at what has always been and will be a wonder: the sun come down to the earth. And of course the sparks fly up, racing the smoke, the highest sparks mingling with the stars.

Then the fire gentles, whistles, whispers, as if it too is waiting for a story.

"Granny Spark," Jack prompts. "You promised, Granny Rose. Tell about Granny Spark."

"Is she as old as you?" a little girl asks.

"Older," I say.

"How old? How old?" they demand.

"Older than the stars."

"So old she forgot who she was?" Sal asks, and then declares at once, "Like Granny Sweep forgot."

"That's right," I say. "Granny Spark lived deep in the forest. She could not remember how she had come to be there."

"Could she get out?"

They always ask this question. Because, unlike Granny Sweep, who did not know how to climb down from her precipice, Granny Spark could have left the forest. And once did—but I have not yet told that part of the story.

"She could, but she didn't want to," Jack says.

The forest was her home, I go on, and her hiding place, and she was happy there. In the summer she lived high in the treetops.

"In a tree house, like our tree houses."

Very like. And in the winter she made a cozy home for herself among the roots.

"With the rabbits and badgers and bears."

Yes, Granny Spark was friends with all the forest creatures and with anyone, animal or human, who needed to hide.

"Who did they hide from?"

"Bad people," says Jack. "The people who wanted to burn down forests and cut down all the trees."

I am quiet for a moment. We haven't come to the part of the story about what happened before. Or what the people ran away from after. Or what would happen to the people if they were found, or to the forest itself.

The forest where Granny Spark lived was a magic forest, I tell them. You see, it was the last forest left in that world. Whenever people who wanted to cut down the trees came too close, Granny Spark would sing this song to the trees.

up trees, make your roots strong legs and swift feet
up and away to find new earth, dark and sweet
away, away over the dry and thirsty ground
to a place near or far where we cannot be found

And the trees would hear her, and their great roots would stir, and the whole forest would move, like a cloud shadow over the earth, or a wave over the sea, leaving not a trace, confounding anyone who tried to follow. Such was the magic of the forest, such was the magic of Granny Spark.

"And did the people go too and the bears?" the children wonder.

The bears and the newts, the owls and the squirrels, the deer and the wood thrush.

"The snakes," someone shouts, "and the porcupines!"

While the children go on with the litany of creatures, I fall silent for a moment, not adding out loud: rogues and whores, moonshiners and fiddlers, smugglers and bards, wolves and hunger.

"And Moo-n," shouts a little girl. "And the chickens."

"Moo-n lives with Granny Sweep," Sal says. "Granny Spark didn't have a cow or chickens or sheep or any farm animals, did she, Granny Rose?"

"What did she eat?" The children are rightly concerned with practicalities.

Granny Spark and the creatures ate what the forest gave them to eat: roots, berries, nuts, mushrooms, ferns.

"And sometimes they ate each other," says Jack.

Some of the children are worried, but this is Jack's way. To insist that magical stories be real.

They did not eat others of their own kind, I assure them. But yes, sometimes wolves ate rabbits and deer. Sometimes the people did, too. And the owls ate mice. The bears scooped fish from the stream and larvae from the hives of wild bees. Granny Spark made it into a rhyme.

come to the feast, you're welcome to dine
sing hey for the honey spooled on a spoon
I'll be your dinner and you'll be mine
merry the sparks that lick at the moon

"Tell about Granny Spark's hair," Sal prompts me.

She was very, very old, I remind them. Most of the time her hair looked like smoke, it even smelled like smoke, sweet cedar or hickory smoke. But when she laughed or when she got angry, her hair turned red as fire, sparks flew from it, and people followed her around with a pail of water so that her sparks did not land on dry leaves or pine needles and start a forest fire.

"Did they ever throw water on her head?"

Sometimes they had to, and Granny Spark would snort and stamp and bellow. But then she would laugh, more gently, and call for the fiddlers. She would dance until her hair was dry again and floated all around her.

"Did Granny Spark comb her hair?"

Granny Spark also had a comb made of bone, just like Granny Sweep. When the full moon rose as the sun set, the comb would gleam and hum. Everyone, all the animals and people, would gather round as Granny Spark pulled the comb through her tangled hair. And while she combed it, her hair would change color, all the colors that you see in a fire, not just orange but green and blue, purple and gold, red and black. When she was done, she'd hold the comb up and the birds would come and take strands for their nests.

"Did they teach her magic, like the star spiders taught Granny Sweep?"

The trees taught her magic.

"What, what did they teach her?"

What fire is, where it comes from, where it lives.

"What is fire?" the children shout.

"Fire is fire," some shout back.

Their voices rise, the flames rise, the sparks fly.

And then they die back.

Look, children, I say. Listen.

Because they are sleepy, they do as I say. We all gaze into the fire, where we can glimpse in the flames the green of new leaves, the blue of the sky, the colors of dusk. The sound holds the rhythms of all rhymes, the crackle and pop of surprise.

"I want to see Granny Spark," says Jack.

They know what I will say next.

"Go to sleep. Dream and maybe she will come to you."

"What if the nightmares come?" whispers Sal.

The nightmares are over, I want to say. But I look in her eyes, and I see that maybe they are not. Soon I will have to tell them more, but not tonight.

"Find your beds, children, snuggle down deep in your soft cozy dens. You are safe, you are safe."

It is true, isn't it? Can it be true?

"Tomorrow I will tell you about Granny Dirt."

I leave the children in their mothers' arms or their fathers' and walk down to the shore again. Even though it is almost dark, I dare to climb a rock, an old rock, that was once liquid fire, pockmarked with memories of its journey from mountain to sea. I feel the smoothness and roughness through the thick calluses of my old bare feet. I sit down on the rock and watch the night turn soft with darkness, sharp with stars. So strange to remember that once upon a time I had never touched a rock, never seen a flame. Did not know that fire burned in the sky.

I wrap my cloak around me, find a hollow in the rock that seems to hold the memory of heat. I close my eyes, willing to risk the nightmares if need be.

✳ ✳ ✳

The next evening after supper, I keep my promise to the children.

"Why is Granny Dirt called Granny Dirt?" some child faithfully asks.

"Dirt is dirty!" comes the chorus from children whose hands are stained and sticky with the juice of berries, their mouths mustached with cream. For yes, though we have a forest, we also have goats and a cow. Granny Dirt's story is always told with dessert.

"Dirt is dirty!" they shout again and again.

"Granny Dirt is dirty."

"Is not! Is too!"

"Granny Rose, how old is Granny Dirt?" someone remembers to ask.

As old as dirt, maybe older.

"So old she forgot who she was," comes the ritual refrain.

"But Granny Rose, how old is dirt?"

Older than the oldest, dirtiest feet, I answer. Older than the oldest, toughest shoe.

"Tell about the shoe," the children clamor.

They never tire of hearing this story, although it makes no sense, *because* it makes no sense.

Granny Dirt lived in a shoe.

"What kind of shoe?" the children ask, although they themselves, due to the sheer luck of where we live, go barefoot most of the time.

It was not a dainty dance slipper, I begin. It was the kind of shoe a farmer would wear, with a thick sole to keep out the damp of the dew, a shoe that could walk through a muddy field and keep a foot dry. The kind of shoe that went right up over an ankle to the shin, a shoe that could be laced up tight or loosened.

"What about the roof?" Jack always asks. He knows but he wants to make sure I explain. "How did Granny Dirt keep the rain out?"

Granny Dirt was very clever, I assure them. She not only had laces up the shoe but also a thatched roof at the top. When it looked like rain was coming, her children would climb up the shoe, grab hold of lace, and jump down, and the boot would close up tight. The laces were very springy, you see, so the children never got hurt.

Then come the cries of, "I want to live in a shoe. I want to swing on the laces."

"But how did they get back inside the shoe, when the rain started?" asks Sal.

Easy, I say. Each little lace hole had a little door, and they would all find the way in and snuggle down in one of the bunks built into the wall. And there was also a door in the arch of the shoe.

"It must have been a big shoe," says Jack.

Oh yes, oh my yes, a very big shoe. They say it was once a seven-league boot worn by a giant when giants still walked the earth.

A long discussion of giants follows: speculation about where they went, and if they will come back, and what to do to avoid being stepped on by one. I lean back against a tree, content to let the children follow this loose thread in the story.

"Where's the other shoe?" someone always asks, drawing me back in.

No one knows, I answer.

"Not even Granny Dirt?"

She might know, but she never told.

"She probably forgot," someone says, "because she was so old."

It was a big shoe, I go on with the story, but when all the children were inside, it was very crowded. If you came upon the shoe when it was raining, you might have thought a foot was trying to wriggle out of it, that it wanted to dance, or run barefoot in the rain.

"How many children did Granny Dirt have?"

She never tried to count them, I say. They never stayed still long enough.

I did not give them the answer you may have heard in the rhyme of your world: so many children she didn't know what to do. Because Granny Dirt did know what to do, and given half a chance, enough sun, enough rain, she did it.

"Why did she have so many children? Where were their mamas? Didn't they have any daddies?"

I never know how to answer. How to tell about a world where mothers sometimes went hungry to feed their children, where most children never knew their fathers? So I close my eyes; the children wait, quietly at first. Then they start to fidget and fuss.

Well, in that time, I say, in that world, when the grannies had forgotten who they were, forgotten everything, except the nightmares, not everyone was safe.

"Like we are. We are safe, aren't we?"

Yes. I sigh the word. But in that world some people had to run away and hide.

"In Granny Spark's forest?"

Some of them, yes. Mothers would come with their children to Granny Dirt. Granny Dirt had magic. Granny Dirt knew how to make food grow out of dirt.

"Like we do!" the children chorus.

They shout the names of the foods they know, the food they learn to grow from the time they are tiny: turnips, leeks, beets, rutabagas, onions, apples, grapes, pomegranates, barley, oats.

That's right. Granny Dirt taught all the children, who taught all their children, so they would always have enough to eat. And Granny Dirt had another magic that kept the children safe.

"Safe from the bad people," says Sal.

"Did the shoe run away, like Granny Spark's forest?"

This is the part that the children love best.

When the people hunters came, Granny Dirt brought all the children inside, and turned the dirt around the shoe to mud.

"And the shoe shrank," Jack can never contain himself, "and no one saw anything but an old shoe in the mud."

The children are silent here, their eyes round as their open mouths, imagining themselves safe and tiny in the shrunken shoe.

"And then the shoe got big again!" one child reassures the others.

Yes, I say, and the laces loosened, and the children burst out of the shoe to play and to help Granny Dirt in the garden.

"Tell about her hair," says Sal.

Granny Dirt's hair was thick and black, just a little darker than her brown skin, with just a little silver like the first frost. It hung down in long ropes that sometimes wriggled and danced.

"Like snakes!" the children shout.

Like snakes. You see, Granny Dirt's hair was alive.

"Did she have a comb?"

Yes, she had a comb, made of bone, like Granny Sweep and Granny Spark. When she combed her hair, the comb would go deep and dig into her beautiful darkness. Her hair smelled good, like dirt that's damp and warmed with the sun. When she combed her hair in the heat of the day or in the summer, you never knew what good things might tumble around her feet.

"Eggplants, watermelon, plums, red peppers."

The children keep the list going, while their mothers and fathers begin to wipe their sticky fingers and mouths. The smaller children curl in their parents' laps.

"I want to see Granny Dirt," says Sal.

I answer, in your dreams. Maybe she will come to you in your dreams.

The younger children are carried to bed, but the older children get up and run off into the dusk to play games of chasing and escape, danger and hiding. They screech and laugh, because they are safe.

For now they are safe.

I tiptoe away from the circle, from the play, to walk the shore where the sea foam, bright in the twilight, seeks my toes.

Tell them the truth, tell them, the white foaming wave rushes in; the truth, the sea pulls back into darkness. Tell them the truth. Tell them. The truth.

✳ ✳ ✳

"Granny Brine," says Jack, his voice deeper than usual, almost not a child's voice, almost like a bell, a bell buoy, I think. Even though we are too far away from that distant shore Granny Brine once paced, I hear the bones rattle, the bells ringing in the rise and fall of the waves.

We have waited for the story of Granny Brine, as we always do, till the right time of the moon, full, rising, its light making a path the children long to follow to the round rim of the world. We've come to the shore and made a fire of driftwood. The wind is damp. Now and then a cloud covers the moon, a few drops of rain spatter our faces, hiss on the burning wood. A freshwater stream makes a ribbon across the sand. The beach roses lend their sweetness to the salt, the red ones disappearing into the dark, the white ones catching the moonlight.

Granny Brine was old, I begin.

"How old?" they chant.

As old as the sea, maybe older.

"So old she forgot who she was?"

Yes, but maybe she tried harder than the others to remember.

"Why?" asks more than one child.

"Because," says Sal—she would be whispering if she didn't have to speak over the wind—"Because she remembered the nightmares. Even in the daytime."

The nightmares are over now, I say.

The truth, tell them the truth, say the waves rising and ebbing on the shore.

"Where was Granny Brine's house?" asks one of the youngest ones, who may not have heard the stories before, but now knows that where the grannies live begins the story.

Granny Brine lived on a sailing ship. Many times Granny Brine sailed beyond the curve of the world and back again, beyond and back again, farther and farther each time, but always back again.

"But she didn't fall off?" the children ask in unison.

No, she didn't fall off. That was how she kept herself a secret—because she knew the secret. But she always came back to the shore at the bottom of the world.

Granny Brine had a parrot named Captain who could talk to birds and animals in their own language. She had a crew of monkeys who loved to climb and swing from the rigging. Wherever she went, she made friends with dolphins and whales, seals and even sharks. I am sure you can guess what she ate.

"Fish!" the children cry.

Yes, fish from the sea and also, when the tide was right, she came ashore and dug for clams and mussels. She also ate seaweed, which she made into a soup, a briny soup.

"Seaweed soup!" the children shout.

"Did the monkeys like seaweed soup?"

Not especially, I say. Whenever Granny Brine went ashore, they would find nut trees and fruit trees. They were very clever. They would stand in a row and toss the food from the tree to the shore to the rowboat that would carry them back to the ship. Granny Brine also loved to follow the freshwater rivulets and rivers deep into the mountains, to waterfalls and pools. She would fill canteens with fresh cool water to take back to the ship, water that tasted of moss and stars. On the ship she also had barrels to catch rainwater, just as Granny Sweep did on her pinnacle.

"Tell about her hair."

Granny Brine had shiny blue-black skin that would change color with the weather and the light. Her hair was green-black, long and slippery.

"Seaweed hair!" the children chant.

"And did she have a comb, too?"

Oh yes, she had a comb made of bone, like all the other grannies. In fact, she was the one who made the combs. And when she combed her hair, barnacles and seashells would spin into the air and clatter onto the deck of the ship. Seagulls and cormorants from miles around would gather and the air would be filled with their cries.

"Did the birds teach her?" Jack demands. "Like the star spiders taught Granny Sweep?"

Everything taught her, I say, the birds, the fish, the moon, the tides. Everything kept her secrets.

"Tell, Granny Rose," says Jack. "Tell Granny Brine's secrets."

I fall silent and for a rare moment the children do, too, hardly breathing, like that moment just when the tides change. In and out, breath and tide, remembering, forgetting.

If I tell, it won't be secret anymore.

"Granny Brine doesn't need her secrets now," reasons Sal.

Maybe not, I say, but I need my secrets, for now, for just a little while.

"I want to see Granny Brine."

In your dreams, I say as I always do. She may come to you in your dreams.

"But they might be nightmares," says Jack. "I don't want to see Granny Brine in a nightmare."

The nightmares are over, children, I say.

The rain starts to fall. The children's parents gather them up and carry them away to dry beds. I pull my cloak over my head and listen to fire the sputter. And I remember, I remember the edge of the world, miles high, disappearing into cloud at the top and into fog below, mist that shrouded a gleaming temple of bone.

Granny Brine's secrets.

My secrets.

❋　　❋　　❋

It's raining harder. The fire is sputtering out. Come with me if you want to hear the story. Just a little way down the shore there's a cave hollowed out of a cliff, not deep. But it's enough to shelter from the rain and the wind. I know, I know. You are not children, and this is not a children's story. You don't live in my world, a land of make-believe and nursery rhyme. A map with no key, a promontory no one can climb up or down, a forest with feet, a shoe than can house unnumbered children, a ship beyond the edge of the world. No need to believe it exists. Yet I will go on telling the story, to you or to no one. (No, Noone cannot hear me; he never could.)

Listen, if you are curious, if you are willing, listen . . .

The Nightmares

Granny Sweep's nightmares begin with the wind howling round and round, finding its way into the cracks of her hovel, the cracks of her mind, whirling her back in time, whirling her out of form. Now she is nothing but a force carrying everything before it, uprooting trees, houses, whole cities, blotting out sky with waves of water, tossing huge balls of fire.

Make an end of it, an end, she wails. I've been choked and poisoned, and I have choked and poisoned. I eat dust. I bring deluge. I can't breathe, I've lost my breath, I've lost your breath, you've lost my breath. No more breath.

This nightmare goes on and on, it blackens the sun and stars and moon, obliterating time, the memory of night or day, the scent of the earth. Except in moments impossible to predict or hold. Then back to turmoil.

Make an end of it, an end.

The nightmare ends in a calm that is another kind of nightmare. In a huge world that has a sky that is not a sky, a world where air goes slowly round and round the same paths, dead air. Sometimes, only sometimes, she can find her way out, to a place filled with the smoke of dung fires, babies crying, people shouting.

And, between dark and dawn, a song, women's voices singing.

Granny Sweep wakes from the nightmare exhausted. For comfort, she rests her head against Moo-n's warm flank as she milks her.

Granny Spark's nightmares begin with a roar, her head exploding into fire. The sun and stars falling down, the earth erupting with fire. The sky nothing but flame and smoke, the earth nothing but flame and ash. Sometimes the screams of trees, herds of animals, people, birds cut through the roar. There is nothing she cannot consume, nothing is ever enough. Exhilarating, terrifying, both.

The burning, the pain, the pain, the burning, the loss, the release.

Make an end of it, make an end. There is nothing left, even fire dies, peace falls fine and bitter as ash, thick as smoke—no, not peace. Death.

Make an end of it, an end.

And then the other nightmare: the empty echoing world, light without sun, warmth without flame. Sun and moon, stars and night, appear and disappear, circling in a never-changing sky that is no sky. What is the way into this world, what is the way out?

There is no way but down, down, into darkness lit with greenish lamps, the clammy heat of sweat on bodies, explosions in blackness, as if the sky itself wants to escape, as if the sun wants to be born again. Then silence, except for the fall of pickaxes, the light stillborn.

Granny Spark wakes chilled, drenched in cold sweat. It will take hours by the fire for her to feel warm again.

✳ ✳ ✳

Granny Dirt's nightmares begin with shaking, her body pulled apart, mountains flattened, chasms opened. She is the withering of roots and the shriveling of shoots and leaves; she is drowned, swept away, or left to rot.

Make an end of it, an end. I am deserted, I am desert. Wind, flood, fire, you leave me with nothing, as nothing.

Make an end of it, an end.

For Granny Dirt, too, there is another part of the nightmare. A huge world with no dirt, with no bare feet. In this world she does not exist, and yet she senses herself below, beyond. How to find herself?

Find the cracks, follow the stench of dung, the sound of women crying out in labor, children crying for food, for milk. She must find them, she must find them.

Granny Dirt wakes in tears. For comfort she gathers the babies, the children, as many as she can hold in her lap, more.

Granny Brine's nightmares begin with rocking so violent there is no up or down, only rolling, crashing, smashing, splintering. It doesn't matter, whatever it is, there is no holding back. She swallows land, houses, sea creatures, land creatures all mixed together; the sky, too, is water, billows and sheets of water, birds drowning on the wing.

Make an end of it, an end, let me go, let me rock myself to sleep, everything, everyone, to deep sleep, fathoms of death.

Then she is gone, where has she gone, leaving a wrecked, parched world in her wake.

Make an end of it, an end.

Her nightmare also changes. She is locked up, imprisoned, behind walls. A pretty little bit of her flows through channels, rises in a bouquet of fountains. There is no sky anymore, no clouds. She looks and looks for a way out.

A crack in a wall, here, there. Wherever she gets out, a woman with a bowl, a beast with a tongue, a bird hovers, a butterfly.

Granny Brine wakes with tears on her face. She drinks them. There is no comfort for her. If she is near enough to the shore, she takes a small boat and searches for bones at the bottom of the world.

And so my children—I've decided to call you that, even though you may be grown, even though you live in another world that is wakening to its own nightmares—these are mere glimpses of the dreams that troubled the grannies' nights, that made them fitful and forgetful by day. In the story

I am telling you, the grannies were exiles and prisoners both, even though they did not yet know it. For they had forgotten who they were, what they had done, what had been done to them.

In the time long ago, when the grannies' nightmares were not just dreams, many living things died. And even those who survived thought the world was coming to an end. Some wished it would. Make an end, make an end.

Yet there was another for whom the world, or *a* world, was only beginning. He had been hard at work in secret, with his magicians and minions, building a world with no sky, a world where there was no dirt, a world where water flowed where it was directed, where air never gave way to wind. When this world was ready, he brought the first families, the founding families, inside, and left the rest not quite to their fate, those desperate ones pounding at the gates that would never open to them, surrounded by high outer walls that would never let them out into the wide, desolate world beyond.

And remember, children. I may be the oldest living person in the world. *Rose knows, Rose knows.* You will hear that chorus many times. And what I don't know, I will—I must—imagine.

Noone Everlasting

He sat in front of the fire in the fireplace, built for atmosphere. It had no chimney, because the fire made no smoke, but rather consumed and renewed itself. It was an undying fire, an immortal fire, one of his first perfections. He himself would be—no, not his last perfection, for soon, very soon, there would be no more last or first. There would be only the everlasting. For those who earned it. He had not yet decided how to decide who had and had not merited unending life. There was no rush. He had time. He had timelessness. He had, or would have, eternity.

He had put in a long day, as usual. He would not say he was tired, though sometimes his colleagues could be tedious in their necessary delusions and enthusiasms. Fatigue was for those outside of the world he had created. Soon those wretched outsiders would no longer be needed. Everything necessary would exist inside a world that would expand and expand until there was nothing else. A drop of water was singular, self-contained until it merged with others, becoming one continuous element. So it would be with his world, the only world.

He picked up his glass, such a clear crystal it would almost be invisible but for the golden elixir it held. He took a sip and felt the liquid flow directly into his veins. Digestion, too, would soon be eliminated. Eliminate elimination. He smiled at his cleverness. Some of the first families (who would one day no longer be the first families, but the only families) did not yet grasp the scope of his vision. They still cherished antiquated beliefs in dynasty. They still imagined immortality lay in progeny. Really they were not so different—just a little cleaner and more orderly—than the primitive riffraff outside, who lived corralled between the dome and the high unclimbable wall. Yes, corralled like livestock.

The woman--he had long since stopped calling her mother—giving birth in that hovel, the horrible sounds and smells. They took him to see her body, and the body of the hideous stillborn creature that killed her, held in the crook of her cold arm.

Soon he would eliminate memory, too. There would be no need for it any longer. Though this memory had set him on his course. Outside, under a sky that spit rain, hurled lightning, standing in a muddy pasture that stank of dung, into a wind that howled and stung, he had shouted a vow.

When I am king, there will be no more death.

Of course, he did not call himself a king now. That would be unnecessarily crude and self-important. It would draw attention that he did not want. He had been a boy then, but if he were to make the vow now (he did not need to make it, he was fulfilling it now) he would say, *when I rule*. But maybe even *rule* was too simple a concept. He envisioned, he created, he orchestrated. He ruled over and under where few could see. His rule was invisible and invincible.

Those who wanted power and pomp, the first families with their vast wealth, had titles: king; vice king (oh, there were a lot of those); queen; queen-in-waiting; minister of this, that, and the other; masters; mistresses; first ladies (no second ones, he'd noticed). And they had their uses. They quelled any uprisings and seditions outside the dome, and any intrigues inside it. They enjoyed the drama of crime and punishment, the rare and thrilling banishment of traitors over the edge of the world .

Yes, that edge gave him an edge. He had seen it once—or had he only dreamed it? It didn't matter now. It was vivid in his mind, the only mind that mattered. Far below were clouds and below that . . . nothing. People who fell or were thrown over the edge never stopped falling. Who could say if they were alive or dead? Everyone inside and outside the dome lived in terror of that endless falling into endless nothing. Everyone except himself.

And, perhaps, his chief magician. If there was anything he feared . . .

No, Noone feared no one.

But he didn't like the man's eyes, his opaque eyes. Were they depthless or bottomless? *Damn it, man, blink!* he had wanted to shout more than once. The chief magician never did.

"I am a mere technician," the magician would assure Noone (did he sense Noone's unease? that would not do!), his voice as expressionless as his eyes, neither high nor low. "I do not exist except as your dream, to bring your dreams into being."

Really, there was no need to fear someone he had imagined.

(Had he also imagined the man's subterranean chamber, his hissing vats, his endless experiments? What of the tunnels where the outsiders toiled to mine the magic that fueled his world, the beautiful world that would soon be without end, without an edge . . .)

It was just a matter of time before time became timelessness.

Noone drained the glass that would refill itself, stood up abruptly, satisfied that nothing creaked or ached. No one knew how old he was. Soon Noone would not know either. Such numbers would not be relevant. He left his quiet chamber (whose location was known only to a very few) and walked down a corridor to his porthole (you could call it a spyhole, but he didn't). He had created the most magnificent vessel in the world, a vessel that *was* a world. And every night before sleep (sleep that he would soon no longer need), he liked to survey it through this secret opening that would take his gaze wherever in his world he liked.

His sky was not a cold, remote, merciless thing, but a work of wonder and beauty—not a ceiling, but something that moved and spun. The stars and planets, sunrises and sunsets here more perfect than any outside. There were vast cities made of shining glass, precious stone. Water flowed where it was meant to flow, never flooding. Fountains sparkled. There were parks and gardens and pleasure palaces and people (he liked to watch them promenade, almost gliding rather than walking, all of them beautiful), just enough people, who all knew their place, who all had more than enough. Who were safe as long as they did not question (could not question) an authority they scarcely knew existed.

And when he had his nightly fill of these glories, he did something he would have considered odd and even perverse if he had considered it. But he didn't. If he had, he might have felt disdain for what had become a compulsion. He walked up the corridor, around and around to a section of wall that looked no different than any other. Sometimes it stayed that way and he would suddenly shake himself as if he had been sleepwalking, and go back to his chamber. But sometimes (unless it was a dream—whose dream? how dare anyone dream such a thing) the wall would open or dissolve onto a spiral staircase. (Had he designed it? He must have, but he could not remember.) Up and up he climbed, to a round room with window that looked out onto a sky uncreated by him, out into a cold wind, into a dark night alive with smoke and the din of people below, shouting, fighting, yowling, mating, sobbing, singing.

This was his nightmare, not the endless nothing over the edge of the world. Soon he would put himself—and them—out of their misery, a misery he felt so acutely he could not bear it, would not bear it. He looked beyond the high walls that kept out an even more desolate world (a world, if he were truthful—and he was—that the first families had laid to waste with their greed. Waste, waste, soon there would be no more waste, no more rubbish heaps.) The sky, so inferior to the one he'd made, lowered over that empty expanse, parched now where once it had flooded, when it was not on fire.

Beyond the wall, beyond the wasteland, the edge of the world. As he extended his gaze farther and farther, the cacophony below receded. All he could hear was a roar. Was it the wind? Was it fire? Was it rain? The earth crashing open?

"Stop!" he shouted. "I vanquished you! I rule you. Stop!"

They obeyed. Of course they did. And the wailing and howling also ceased.

Then, in the stillness, he heard singing.

over the edge of the world I go
over the edge of the world I fly

He put his hands over his ears and closed his eyes. But the singing only got clearer. Children's voices; three children dancing, singing—on a rubbish heap!

over the edge of the world we go
over the edge of the world we fly

He opened his eyes. Something brilliant and searingly blue hurtled past the window, flew over the wall, on and on to the edge of the world.

over the edge of the world I go...

Noone turned and fled. He did look back at the gap in the wall. He did not know it sealed itself seamlessly behind him, as if it had never been there. He kept running until he was safely inside his chamber, where he collapsed and let his breath catch up with him. He took a long drink from his refilling glass.

Then he rang for the chief magician.

The chief magician did not answer Noone's summons. Not that night. The chief magician was. . .indisposed. So the magician's bodyguards explained, soothing Noone as best they could, smoothing his bed (whatever the old man claimed, he was tired), helping him into it, fluttering and hovering until he succumbed to their ministrations.

"Tomorrow, tomorrow," they echoed each other as they tiptoed away.

(How could such huge grotesqueries move so soundlessly? Whose idea were they anyway?)

"Sure thing."

"First thing."

"Tomorrow."

PART ONE

Outside World

I had not yet been born that night I just imagined for you. Imagined for myself. Many things happened before I came into this story—or I would not be here, the oldest storyteller left. Now I will tell you my mother's story, not only as she told it to me, but as I imagine it. In the stories she wasn't my mother yet. So really, it is not my mother's story. It is Briar's story.

To those of you who are intrigued by the world inside the dome, its phantasmagorical perfection, my apologies. I will be giving you only rare glimpses.

For now, come outside with me, to the world between the dome and the unclimbable wall, where people lived crowded together in leaky shelters made of whatever discarded materials they could find. There were chickens that belonged to everyone and no one, their eggs fought over, but just as often shared. (Chickens were illegal, as were the scruffy garden patches.) The outsiders who labored in the mines and the fields, or the kitchens and the laundries, of the insiders were meant to be totally dependent on rations, which is to say scraps and castoffs from the insiders. If the Guard discovered gardens or roosts, or other contraband stores or livestock, or huts that were too sturdy or comfortable, they were under orders to destroy them. Sometimes the Guard did, sometimes they turned a blind eye, and more often they never found the roosts, or they looked into an alley and saw only dust and weeds. For outsiders had their own cunning and magic.

Outside world was noisy: feral dogs and cats yowling and yipping; rats scrabbling and fighting; fugitive cows lowing (harder to conceal, but not impossible); babies squalling; people laughing or quarreling; and always someone coughing or spitting--all punctuated by sudden silences and heavy footfalls when the Guard patrolled. It was strong-smelling, too: dung fires; food spicy and smoked to make meager and often rotting meat palatable; noxious gasses from the mines, latrines, and heaps of rubbish discarded by the insiders. Outside world was mostly gray, a layer of dust from the mines coating everything, cloaking the sky, choking the lungs. When it rained, everything turned to mud. The outsiders' clothes and skin were also covered with a thin layer of ash. Cold outside was very cold, and hot, very hot.

But every now and then a fresh wind cleared the clouds, lifted the dust, made it dance in the air, where it caught the light. Then, if you squinted, you could see the dust was made of tiny crystals, with rainbows trapped inside. For a moment the people shone, too, their skin and hair brown, black, and gold, with hints of fiery red, their faded clothes for a moment bright with shiny threads, dancing on the breeze, inviting people's feet to follow.

In the deep of night, outside world quieted. Then the stars and the moon came out, their reflections caught in the smooth surface of the dome. I like to think the celestial bodies did not despise the narrow alleys, patchy gardens, or makeshift hovels, and found a way to cast their lovely light on people who had scant shelter from the sky.

In the darkest, coldest hour before the stars dimmed, certain women rose from their beds. In every part of outside world, they threaded their way through the streets, past the mine yards, past the glassed-in fields of crops for insiders only, past the doors to the laundries, and the gates to the dungeons. And as they walked they sang.

come the sorrow, come the pain
come the sun, come the rain
come the toiling all day long

come the night, come the dawn
beauty will go on, go on, beauty will go on

After a while, words turned into wordlessness. Their voices came from everywhere, from nowhere, high and piercing, as if stars sang, and also low and flowing as underground rivers, their harmonies sweet, with moments of haunting dissonance. They were singing to the rubbish heaps and to the sky, to the wasteland beyond the wall, to the moon, to the sun that would rise. They sang beauty distilled from dreams. They sang blue rivers of milk from breasts. They sang till the break of heartbreak.

No one knew who the beauty singers were, or they pretended not to know. Their singing was considered seditious. If a beauty singer was caught, she could be banished over the edge of the world. Every day the Guard came out to hunt them down. And every day, the beauty singers eluded them. Some say they turned into flocks of birds that scattered over the sky. Some say they *were* birds.

Then, when their songs gave way to the distant cry of birds or the closeness of a rooster crowing, someone's mother or daughter, sister or auntie or granny would reappear, pulling back threadbare covers, stirring banked fires into flame under cauldrons, feeding chickens with pilfered grain. And another day began.

One morning, just before daybreak, a beauty singer wailed a note so wild, the wind moaned in answer, and the sky blazed beyond the wall. Two women flew to her and hurried her away as far as you could get from the dome, near a vast, impenetrable patch of briars. And there a baby girl was born.

If Briar ever had another name, she never told me what it was. Her earliest memory was of crawling into the briar patch. Whether she was only a baby who crawled everywhere or whether she got down on her hands and knees to find her way in, she was not sure. From the beginning, the briars made way for her, and she passed without a scratch deep into their hidden, untouched world. She would lie on her back and look up at roses, the kind of roses that scent the air with spicy sweetness, blown-open roses full of golden pollen and rich nectar. Briar at first did not distinguish the flowers from the bees. She only knew the whole briar patch hummed, the roses trembled and the petals drifted down and fell on her face, softer than her mother's kiss.

A kiss Briar, as a very young child, waited for each dawn.

"Don't get up till I wake you," her mother told her every night.

But Briar could not help waking when her mother wrapped her in an extra blanket, still warm and scented from her body, and slipped away. Briar would tiptoe to the doorway and follow the sound of her mother's voice, weaving with the other voices, longing but not daring to follow. When the rooster crowed, Briar would scurry back to bed, squeezing her eyes tight shut. Soon her mother would bend over her and give her a kiss. In that moment, before her mother left to work all day, Briar felt safe, wrapped in her mother's hidden sweetness.

Briar, like most children, had no known father. The grown men lived in their own camps near the mine—the ones, at least, who had not been recruited into the Guard. The mothers disappeared all day into their own labors, leaving the children to look after the animals, garden patches, and each other. No matter their duties—foraging and playing in the rubbish heaps, toting barely weaned babies or dragging along straggling toddlers— all the children, large and small, excelled in running wild and dodging the Guard. The quicker they were, the more hiding places they knew, the longer they could escape whatever fate would finally snatch them up.

Briar barely noticed that she had no siblings. She was just one of a mass of children, except when she ducked into the briar patch, where even the meanest bullies never followed. The mothers came home at dusk. Word went around: who had food, who had fuel? Everyone who could brought something for whoever had a fire going under a pot. Sometimes weary women fell asleep where they sat, children tumbling around them until their mothers claimed them, scooping them up and bedding them down in whatever shelter they called their own.

There were often children no one claimed. They went from fire to fire, waiting to be fed. They slept under the overhang of any hut that had one, or braved the rats and burrowed into the rubbish heaps for warmth.

One night, when Briar was about five years old, her mother lingered at the evening fire till after the other women had left. Only a lone girl, about Briar's age, remained, staring into the embers. Briar had seen the girl before, sifting through the rubbish heap, but she had not noticed how her dark eyes caught the light, or how her uncombed hair tangled with the night.

Briar's mother got up and banked the fire, then she turned and spoke to the girl.

"Child," said Briar's mother, "have you lost your mama?"

The girl didn't answer; she crouched, digging into the dirt with a rusty blade of a broken knife. She was too young to say: *my mama was one of the rebels*.

Briar's mother must have guessed. This latest uprising had been led mostly by women with weapons smuggled from the mine. Rumor had it one woman's children had been stolen and disappeared inside. Only a few fighters survived to be taken into the bowels of inside world, tortured and tried, then wheeled out on a platform called the Seat of Judgment. Here, sentences were passed down. Floggings and hangings were commonplace, and could even be called merciful, compared to being thrown over the edge of the world, falling through endless nothingness forever, no air, no light, no life, no death.

The child looked up, glancing at Briar's mother but fixing her eyes on Briar.

"My mama is flying!" whispered the girl, then she shouted. "She is flying!"

Briar didn't know then what she meant, but she knew the girl was shouting to keep herself from crying. She knew the girl's mother had left her behind. She felt her own tears starting, her own terrified wail rising.

Briar's mother knew what to do. Holding Briar's hand, she knelt beside the girl.

"What is your name, child?"

The girl shook her head and glared. Then she stood up, crossing her arms across her chest, face to face with Briar.

"Sal!" she said, as if she had just made up her mind and dared anyone to contradict her.

Briar's mother rose and took Sal's hand.

"Briar, Sal," she said. "Come along, it's time for bed."

That is how Sal came to be Briar's more-than-sister, more-than-friend. They looked nothing alike; they were nothing alike. Sal always short, dark and bristling, outspoken. Briar, despite her prickly name, sweet and secretive, hair the color of dark honey, falling over her shoulders as softly as petals. Yet they were each other's mirrors. Each knew herself only through the other.

✳   ✳   ✳

Now Briar wasn't just part of a herd, she was part of a pair. She and Sal went everywhere together, hand in hand, sometimes with other children, sometimes on their own, ranging from the briar patch to the steps of the dome. A year passed, two, they were seven, then eight, almost at the dangerous age.

Like all outside children, Briar and Sal were fascinated by the insiders who sometimes took heavily guarded tours of outside world. The children would trail them, ducking in and out of alleys, trying not to be seen or daring each other to run out into plain view. No matter what color the insiders were (and most were white), they had a paleness and a smoothness to their faces that Briar found frightening. They did not seem real. But Briar did wish she could touch their clothes. Their garments looked softer than the softest fur of a kitten, billowing as clouds on a rare fine day. (Great care had to be taken laundering these clothes, Briar's mother told them. "And the water," she would always sigh. "You've never seen so much clean water wasted.")

One day Briar and Sal saw a woman, she must have been a princess or a queen. Her dress shimmered with tiny jewels. She stood, flanked by soldiers of the Guard, on the steps that led down from inside to outside world. Her hair was long and the color of sunlight on snow. Her blue dress, half night-sky and half sky-blue, fell in folds to her feet. She wore a crown on her head that had golden rays reaching to the sky. Briar was tempted to creep out of her hiding place to touch the lady's skirt. But Sal, usually the bolder of the two, held tight to her arm.

"No way, girl, no way."

As Briar and Sal watched, they saw the lady's eyes widen. She raised an arm as if to shield her face from something, a blow, though no one threatened her, and the day was dull and overcast. Then a gust of wind found its way down the twisted streets. Almost as if it was looking for her, wanting to touch her as much as Briar did, the wind reached the lady.

Briar had never seen anything so beautiful as the lady's shining hair lifted by the wind, cloud and sunlight at once, and her skirt lifted too so that Briar could see the jewels sewn all along the seams. Briar's mouth dropped open in wonder.

The lady's mouth opened in a scream. Her beautiful serene face contorted in terror.

"She's gonna shit her drawers," said Sal, who loved to be crude. "Inside bitch."

"Shh," hissed Briar. "Do you want to be thrown over the edge of—Briar stopped, afraid of the answer, but for once Sal heeded her. They both watched in fascination as the lady turned and ran back up the steps, falling once as she stumbled on her beautiful gown.

"Her shoes," Sal breathed. "You could kill someone with those."

The shoes appeared to be made of silver, with tall heels like knives.

Two guards rushed to help her up, and the gates to inside world swung open. Briar got a brief glimpse of vast space. Then the gates closed again in that eerie way. They could feel the ground shudder under their feet with the swinging weight, but the doors never made a sound.

One of the guard stepped forward, brandishing a spear.

"Show's over," he barked. For he must have known the children of outside world from miles around were hiding and watching. After all, he had once been one of them. The guard took one more step in their direction, and they all scampered away, swift and sure as the rats who were their constant companions and rivals for the best bits on the rubbish heaps.

Giddy with the sight of the inside lady's fright, Briar and Sal ran faster, holding hands. For the sheer pleasure of their sure feet on ground they knew by heart, they ran all the way to the briar patch. They crawled through one of the tunnels, and then came to the place deep inside where they could lie on their backs looking up through the tangle of thorns to the gray sky that threatened a storm.

Sal was the only person Briar had ever brought with her into the patch. At first the briars had grabbed at Sal, tangling with her hair, grazing her skin. After a time, they let her pass as long as Briar led the way. Sal liked the briar patch, but for different reasons than Briar, who felt safe there as she did nowhere else. Sal relished a feeling of danger.

"This place is haunted," Sal insisted. "Did you hear that?"

"It's only the bees humming," Briar would say.

"No, someone, some *thing* is humming with them."

"Are you scared?" Briar would ask, just the tiniest hint of scorn in her voice.

"Of course not!" Sal would say. "I'm not scared of anything."

But then in a little while, she might whisper, "Did you see that?"

"See what?"

"That black shape, gliding through the briar patch."

"It's only a shadow," Briar would say. "Wing shadow."

"Can't be," Sal would insist. "It's cloudy. It's always cloudy. You can't have shadows when it's cloudy."

They would lie quietly, looking and listening, breathing the sweetness of the roses. Then Sal would offer what she would consider her irrefutable proof.

"You know the briar patch is haunted, Briar. If it wasn't they would have torn it up. They wouldn't let us have it."

"Who wouldn't?"

"Them, the insiders."

"Well, I'm glad it's haunted then. I'm glad they're scared."

Briar didn't have the words for it then, but she knew. This was her place. This was beauty. Beauty was real, real as the song the beauty singers sang at dawn. Beauty went on and on and on, for when she was in the briar patch it seemed to go on forever.

The day they saw the glittering inside lady, the roses were just passing their first bloom; only a few bees lingered.

"Why do you think she was so afraid?" Briar asked.

"Who?" Sal had already forgotten. She was reaching up to the roses, trying to touch one without dislodging a petal.

"The princess."

"Bitch," Sal corrected.

"You call everyone a bitch," Briar said.

"Not everyone. Besides, I got other words." Sal collected them from the miners as they passed through the streets on their way to work. "How about we call her Twat. Twat never felt the wind before. Scared her crapless."

"Never felt the wind," Briar mused.

"Yeah, didn't you know? No wind in inside world."

"No wind," Briar chanted, "no rain, no cold, no heat, no pain."

As she spoke the words, the first drops began to fall, fat and luscious. Briar and Sal opened their mouths, thirstily drinking the rain. *Never waste one drop of rain*, the mothers and aunties and grannies told everyone over and over again. The two girls laughed out loud when the drops fell on their faces.

One and One Becomes Three

Now I must tell you about Jack. Remember, children, there is always a Jack.

Jack was neither the tallest boy nor the strongest. Some of the bigger boys tried to bully him, as they bullied others less able to defend themselves. In Briar's first memory of Jack, a story she told me over and over, Jack outran three larger boys who were chasing him and brandishing sticks. Jack had caught them snatching a scrap of bread away from an old woman. He knocked the bread out of their hands and then turned and ran, providing a diversion as the old woman retrieved her bit of food. Briar and Sal, scrambling to the top of a roof to be out of the way of the skirmish, watched as the boys backed Jack into an alley. Just when it looked as though the bullies would beat Jack to a bloody pulp, he somersaulted into the air and landed on a wall above the boys. There he danced a jig. By then other children had gathered, finding perches. Jack's pursuers were so enraged they hurled their sticks at him. He caught one, then the other, tossing them into the air, so he could catch the third. And he began to juggle the sticks.

Cheering broke out on all sides, a cheering so joyful that even the bullies got caught up in it. Jack danced on, the sticks spinning, from rooftop to rooftop, all the children following after him as best they could.

"I shall marry that boy," declared Sal as she and Briar jumped down from the shack to join the throng following Jack. "And you shall, too!"

"We both will!" agreed Briar.

They were all of eight years old, and in truth marriage in outside world was as rare as clean running water. It was a story children told each other, encouraged by the oldest grannies who remembered life without walls, long, long ago, when people had weddings and other festivals.

Briar and Sal began to spend more time at the nearby rubbish pile, a place dominated by boys who fought each other for who would be king of the heap. More and more often, Jack won the title—and the followers and enemies that went with it. Sal was increasingly preoccupied with how they would get Jack to take notice of them, surrounded as he always was by swarms of children. Even the rats and the pigeons followed him. Every now and then, the bullies would pick a fight with him or pick on someone small or weak to see what Jack would do, what ingenious way he would best them.

"If we got the bullies to beat us up or steal from us, Jack would come and rescue us," Briar proposed.

"He's rescued plenty of girls. It's just what he does," said Sal. "He takes no notice of them once he's saved them. Besides, I don't want to be rescued. I don't need to be rescued. I am as strong as any boy!"

Then Sal had what she, at least, considered a brilliant idea.

"We will challenge him."

"Why would we do that?" wondered Briar. "Jack is the best king of the heap there ever was. He even lets people take turns being king for a day."

"That's right," said Sal, "he *lets* them. And he lets *them* be king. Boys. I want to be queen, and I don't want him to let me be queen. I want to win. I want to be the real queen of the mountain."

Briar was speechless, as if Sal had aimed a blow at her solar plexus and knocked the wind out of her.

"But we can't!" was all she could think to say.

"Why not?"

"We're not as good as he is. We don't know how to fight."

"We can fight him both together. Like we do everything together."

Briar stared hard at Sal. They were night and day to each other, sun and moon. What one did, the other reflected back. But this time—

"No!" Briar surprised them both.

"No?" Sal was surprised.

"Don't you see, Sal? If we both fought him at the same time, we'd be just like the bullies, ganging up."

Sal considered this logical point.

"Well, then," Sal conceded, "to be fair, we'll take turns fighting him. First me, then you."

"He'll win easily."

"Then we'll just fight him again. The next day and the next day."

"For how long?"

"Until we win."

"We? Won't one of us win and not the other?"

"We," said Sal firmly. "We'll be queens together."

✳   ✳   ✳

They began their campaign the very next day. An unusually fine day in outside world. There had been rain the night before, enough to catch in pots and barrels. Now the sun shone freely, its light glancing off the vast dome that covered inside world, making it seem like a fallen sun. Flocks of pigeons fluttered up into the light. There were enough places to sunbathe for all the alley cats; they didn't have to fight over them. Even the rats paused in their scurrying and lifted their snouts and gleaming teeth to the light. The rain-freshened, sun-warmed air; a fresh breeze prevailed over the stink of latrines.

The children swarmed the rubbish heaps, laughing and shrieking when their feet sank in deeper than usual, making a game of rolling down, heedless of the filth that covered them. Jack stood astride the biggest heap, occasionally scrambling down to mediate a dispute, making sure everyone got some small treasure or scrap.

Sal and Briar stood at the bottom, watching for a while, summoning their nerve, or at least Briar was; Sal's nerve never deserted her.

"All right," said Sal. "Let's go."

Holding hands, they climbed the hill all the way to the top. At first Jack did not notice them. He was busy swinging and tossing a group of small children who'd come to him for a game. When the last of the children tumbled down hill, he turned to see the two girls, standing before him, Briar with her arms folded across her chest, Sal with her fists at the ready.

"We have come to fight you!"

"One at a time," Briar hastened to add.

"I could fight you both at once, if I wanted to." Jack simply stated the truth. "But why would I want to? You've never done me any harm. Besides, you're girls."

"Ho! So you noticed!" said Sal. "I say, it's high time there was a queen of the mountain. You've been king long enough . . . Jackass!"

Briar turned red. Sal was going too far. She called him the name the bullies used when they taunted him. But Jack appeared to take no offense. He just stood there, eyes golden and gleaming in a dark face, even darker with dirt. He had a gap-tooth grin, where one of his milk teeth (they were all that young) had fallen out.

"Well, if you want to be queen," Jack said kindly, "go ahead. I don't mind."

That was too much for Sal. Without warning, she swung her fist at Jack, who dodged the blow nimbly, and the next one and the next. Enraged, Sal hurled herself at Jack and managed to knock him down. They rolled and wrestled, quickly attracting a crowd of children, who cheered and jeered with equal glee. It did not take Jack long to twist Sal's arms behind her. She struggled mightily but to no effect.

"You win," Sal finally conceded.

Jack loosed her arms. For a moment Briar was afraid it was just a trick, and Sal would attack him again. Instead she just nodded to Briar.

"Your turn."

Briar remembers gazing at Jack, noticing how the sun glinted on his hair. She forgot about fighting as she tried to decide what color it was. Brown, not gold, no orange, with sparks of blue and green, like fire.

"Go on," urged Sal.

Briar saw Jack waver, thinking it could be all over, he could refuse to fight, just let her go. She wavered right back. Why would she want to hit this boy, this agile, beautiful boy, whose rags hung on him like robes. He was a king, for real, a king.

"Queens!" Sal shouted. "Queens together!"

Jack looked from Briar to Sal and back to Briar again. Did he understand at such a young age that kindness could be cruel?

"Come on then, queenie, show me what you got. Fight me, go on, fight me."

And somehow Briar did. She aimed a kick at his leg, and with beginner's luck, knocked him off balance.

"Jump on him!" urged Sal, giving her a shove.

Briar fell more than jumped, and now it was her turn to wrestle and roll. She liked how strong he felt, how sure, and how, despite spending his days sorting rubbish, he smelled like an oat cake.

Finally she ended up flat on her back, with Jack pinning her arms to the ground. The sun overhead fired his hair, and his brown eyes glinted almost as blue as the sky. She wouldn't have minded staying there for a while, but everyone around them roared for action.

"Do you give up?" he asked.

Briar did not know why she didn't say yes. She meant to. Really, she was only trying to get up, and somehow her knee collided with his groin. He grunted and rolled off her, getting to his feet. He reached down his hand to help her up. As soon as she was on her feet, his fist found her nose. Tears blinded her, but she swung back, so hard that when Jack dodged her blow, she fell and landed on her hands and knees. Jack quickly flattened her, his knee in her back.

"I give up," she mumbled into the dirt, not sure he could hear her. "I give up."

And then he lifted her back to her feet and turned her round to face him. Sal came to stand beside her, taking her hand.

"Hail, queens," said Jack, making a bow.

"We aren't queens yet," said Sal. "We didn't win. We'll be back tomorrow, King Jack."

✳ ✳ ✳

Sal and Briar returned to fight Jack day after day. It became a ritual spectacle attended by other children and the stray elders that had managed to dodge the Guard, for the old and the sickly, if caught, were routinely tossed over the wall. The pigeons settled on rooftops; the rats paused in their scurrying. Jack never displayed any rancor, and even coached his rivals, who began to gain some skill. The other children learned, too, and started to spar and tumble and leap. Days and moons passed. Jack had not been bested.

"What does it matter if we win?" Briar said to Sal when they lay resting in the briar patch. "Who cares if we're queens?"

"We have to become queens," Sal insisted. "Or he can't marry us."

Briar did not care about fighting. But she did want to marry Jack.

"All right," said Briar, "tomorrow I will beat him."

"Ha!" said Sal, who loved to fight. "Or I will."

Briar felt a qualm, a stray cloud over sun.

"But we will be queens together, no matter who wins," she said, not quite asking.

"Queens together!" Sal lifted her fist into the air, and knocked a loose petal off a rose.

Briar felt ashamed of her doubts.

All the same, the next day, Briar fought with more determination than she ever had before. In the midst of the fight, she felt herself in two places at once: inside her body that lunged and dodged, parried and punched; and outside her body, as if she were the light or the air. She saw it was a beautiful thing, the dance she and Jack made together, as if they had wings or hooves or shining horns. And she fought on for the sheer joy of it. Till she had Jack pinned to the ground, winded, her knee on his back, his strong arms twisted and held in her grip.

There was a roaring all around her, voices, bird cries, wind.

Then a silence came up out of the ground, and fell at the same time.

"You win," Jack said, still breathless, and then more strongly. "You win!"

Briar loosed Jack and rose to her feet. She turned to Sal. Her eyes were bright with tears. Sad or glad, Briar didn't know.

"Sal!" she said, as if calling her from a longer distance. "Sal, we're queens. Queens together."

And she took Sal's hand. Then as Jack stood up, Sal and Briar each took one of his hands. The cheers rose again and the three began to dance in a circle at the top of the heap. Then the three of them dropped hands and turned out toward the crowd of children. In a moment everyone had hold of someone else's hand. Someone found an old pot in the heap and struck up a rhythm. And everyone danced together round and round, up and down the rubbish heap.

Soon a song sprang up:

over the edge of the world we go
over the edge of the world we fly
queens and kings
when we have wings
we all have wings
over the edge of the world we go
queens and kings, queens and kings

Noone

From the vast depths of inside world, where sound and light and air were perfectly filtered, where people spoke in murmurs and moved with scarcely a footfall, Noone sensed a disturbance.

"Excuse me," he said to the ministers, who were in the middle of some dull and discreet report. About plumbing, he believed. "I shall return presently."

Wherever he meant to go, he found himself making his way up and up, where no one else ever ventured, where he never ventured, except in his nightmare journeys. He was only going to prove it wasn't real, he told himself, since he couldn't seem to stop. Of course it wasn't real. He trailed his hands over the smooth, cool walls of his perfectly sealed world, smooth and serene as his mind. Then—

The wall wavered, and spiraling stairs appeared, shimmering, winding, irresistible . . .

Turn around, he told himself, as he kept going. *It is just a mirage.*

At the top of the stairs he found himself in the round room with an open window. Light and air assaulted him. He crossed the room, determined to close the window that could not, did not, exist in his world.

over the edge of the world we go
over the edge of the world we fly
queens and kings
when we have wings
we all have wings

over the edge of the world we go
queens and kings, queens and kings

Who was singing? Who dared to sing such a song? He leaned out the window, forcing himself to look down into the disturbance. It was children. Just children, chanting, swarming the dung heap, rats, refuse. They were refuse. What did they have to sing about?

over the edge of the world we go
over the edge of the world we fly
queens and kings
when we have wings
we all have wings
over the edge of the world we go
queens and kings, queens and kings

How was it he could suddenly feel mud between his toes, smell the stink of the rot, how was it he held the hand of another child, jerked and danced with the rest? Following that dark boy with the red-brown-gold flare of hair and the two girls on either side of him. Then he heard himself whispering, chanting with them.

over the edge of the world we go
over the edge of the world we fly
queens and kings
when we have wings
we all have wings
over the edge of the world we go
queens and kings, queens and kings

(Yes, children, that is the first time Noone heard the song, but not the last, not the last).

"No!" his whimpered, then he shouted. "No!"

The voices receded. The terrible tactile vision vanished. The children below were no more than ants on an anthill. (Still, he would set a watch on them, those three.) As he made to close the window, a wind rose and roared around his ears. He staggered backwards, then fought his way forward again, slamming the window shut with such force that the glass cracked.

Never mind, he told himself as he ran down the vanishing stairs. The window did not, would not, could not exist.

Granny Sweep

"Ouch!"

Granny Sweep put her hand over her eye where the window had crashed shut on it. The wind moaned and circled around the promontory as if it ached, too. This was the first time her sight had found an opening into the shining, blinding dome.

And she knew she had seen that man more than once. That old, old man.

Then her certainty gave way to confusion. He had not been an old man then, but a grubby little boy, filthy face runnelled with tears. How did he come to have that long white beard, those spidery limbs, that cobwebbed face?

"Father Time," she said aloud. That's who the old man was, who the little boy had turned into. "Father Time, you are running out of time. Give me back my memory!"

She had no idea what she meant by that, but she resolved to keep watch over the world she could not see. And the world she could see, over the high wall. The roses, the rats, the rubbish heap, the children.

"Dance, children, sing," she said out loud.

And words came to her, and she sang too, dancing in a circle, her arms flung wide.

over the edge of the world we go
over the edge of the world we fly

In one direction, Granny Sweep saw iridescent birds fly like sparks from the dark forest. In another direction a shoe tapped its toe and kept time with the tune. And far away, across the wide, empty world, a ship tossed, and on the shore, bones rattled in the wind.

Briar, Sal, and Jack: The Three

After Sal and Briar became queens, they went everywhere with Jack. The three ruled over the rubbish heap in the mornings, and in the afternoons they named other kings and queens to take their places, ones they were sure would be fair. If the bullies were hanging around and menacing anyone, Jack, Sal, and Briar taunted them, leading them on a chase away from the rubbish heap. Of course the bullies hardly ever caught them, or, if they did, they were sorry afterwards. The queens and king ranged all over outside world. Nimble Jack, as people hailed him, had friends and enemies everywhere.

✳　✳　✳

"Clear on this end," said Sal from one end of the alley where they'd hidden, as they often did, from a roaming patrol of the Guard.

"On this end, too," confirmed Briar.

Jack was hidden in a near-empty rain barrel. Boys his age were already being snatched up and sent to the mines, where their small size was an advantage. Few of them ever lived to be full-grown men. Sal and Briar, not quite at the dangerous age for girls, often acted as lookouts.

"You know," said Jack, hoisting himself up and out, "if all the people from all over outside world got together, we could knock down the gates and take over inside world."

The two girls turned from their posts. All three sat down for a moment to catch their breath in the relative cool and shade.

"Why would we want to do that?" Sal said, with her usual scorn for all things inside.

Briar thought of the jewels and the dresses, light as air, shining like raindrops caught in the sun. She remembered the glimpse of the huge space inside that made outside world seem small and cramped.

"Because," Jack answered Sal, "the insiders have all the water. They've got all the food. They've got all our lives. To use up and throw away."

Jack had never sounded so serious before. Briar looked at Sal and then at Jack, feeling afraid and brave at the same time, the way she had when she and Sal had challenged Jack.

"We play at being king and queens," said Jack, "but we rule over nothing but a rubbish heap."

Briar did not know what to say, so she listened. It was quieter at midday than most other times, with all the grown folks at work. The footsteps of the patrol had faded. She could hear chickens in the next lot, clucking pensively and scratching at the dirt. From the now-distant rubbish heap came the faint shouts of younger children, now and then, the more piercing wail of a baby.

"Speak for yourself, make-pretend King Jack," Sal huffed. "I for one am a real queen. I don't want to rule over inside world. It's nothing but a bigger, fancier rubbish heap, a prettier prison."

Still, Briar thought, she would like to see it. Her mother worked in the laundries, on the same underground level as the dungeons. But some people worked as servants. They brought home—or stole, Sal said—odd trinkets and delicacies to share or sell. If the Guard caught them, they were publicly flogged unless they could pay a bribe.

"What *do* you want to rule then, real Queen Sal?" Jack challenged her.

Briar looked from one to the other. Their intensity excited her and frightened her.

"Everything," declared Sal, flinging out her arms, grazing her knuckles on the rough walls. "I want out there, beyond the wall, all the way to the edge of the world."

Jack shook his head, then looked down at the ground. Briar could not see his face, only his black curls with their hint of red dulled in the shadow of the alley. He was drawing with his finger in the dirt, but she could not see what he was making.

"Don't you know?" said Jack. "They ruined all that a long time ago. That's why they made inside world. There's nothing out there but desert and death. They took everything. It's all inside now. That's why we have to fight them."

"No, I don't know," insisted Sal. "And you don't know, either. You haven't been there. None of us have been out there."

"The old people have gone there." Briar spoke at last, her voice as shaky as she felt. And maybe the beauty singers, she wanted to say, their voices rising with the birds into a dawn ablaze with color.

"Only before they die," said Jack, looking up from his scrawl. She could see it now: a miniature dome surrounded by what she guessed must be the wall.

Everyone had seen the roundups of people too old or sick or injured to work. The huge gates, unbarred only for this purpose, swinging open. The guards forcing the sorry crowd into the empty expanse. A traitor's death might be better, Briar thought. Flung over the edge of the world. Maybe falling really did feel like flying. Maybe it was. Surely it was better than crawling over the bare, cracked earth she'd caught sight of when the old and infirm staggered through the gates.

"Maybe some of them lived," Sal argued. "And there might be a way to tunnel out through the mines. And maybe," she lowered her voice, "maybe some of the people being marched to the edge escaped."

They were all silent for a moment, pondering the possibilities. A black shadow passed over the alley, so low they could hear the rush of wings. Then they heard a cry, raucous, not quiet human, not quite laughter. It came from the sky and grew fainter and farther away. Over the wall. Out there.

"Let's find a way to climb the wall," said Sal, "and at least we can look over."

"Let's!" agreed Jack, springing to his feet. "They want us to believe it's unclimbable, but we are queens and king."

King Jack was back!

"Follow me," said Queen Briar; for all at once, she knew exactly what to do.

✳   ✳   ✳

As she led them through the maze of streets and hidden vegetable patches, out and out, away from the dome, it dawned on Briar that since she'd become a queen, she hadn't gone to the briar patch much, not with Sal or even by herself. They'd been too busy roaming with Jack, fighting all comers, running and hiding from the Guard. But what better place to hide than the briar patch, her secret home since she could crawl?

Would the briar patch remember her? Would it let her back in?

When she caught the scent of roses on the breeze and heard the hum of bees, her worries fell away. She was hardly aware of Sal and Jack behind her, running to keep up with her sure, effortless pace. She was going to her own place, a place inside, outside, and beyond. There was an opening, a green arc, a faint shadow, a glimmer of light. She dropped to her knees and crawled in.

"It's all right," she heard Sal tell Jack—Jack who could somersault into the sky, leap from one rooftop to another, but had never, to her knowledge, crawled. "Briar knows the way."

Briar led them in as deep as she had ever gone, to the little clearing where she and Sal had lain on their backs looking at the sky, tasting the rain. Now the three of them sat cross-legged, their knees touching, the sweet scent and the hum of the bees lulling them.

"Now what, Briar?" said Sal at last.

"How far to the wall?" Jack asked.

Briar had never been that far. She looked around. The tangle of briars ahead looked impenetrable. A shadow passed through the briar, cloud or wing, unimpeded by the sharp thorns. The bees went on with their song, tuneless and intent. Briar thought she heard a new sound, a lower drone, a whisper of words. She listened intently, as the hum of the bees thrummed with a rhythm.

briars sharp and roses sweet
make a way for hands and feet

It took her a moment to realize the voice speaking these words was her own. She was singing. Jack and Sal gazed at her with a kind of awe. Then she saw why: with a green, rasping whisper, the briars parted. Still singing, Briar led Jack and Sal on deeper, farther. At last they came to the wall, so smooth in the rest of outside world and always under watch. But here, the roots and branches of the briars had made cracks and crevices as they climbed toward the sun. Here the walls hummed where the bees made hives.

Then they saw an old woman, or the shadow or an old woman. Afterwards, Briar, Sal, and Jack could never remember or agree on what had happened. Had she handed them a piece of honeycomb? All they could remember—and taste for days afterwards—was sweetness on their fingers, sweetness made of air, light, a drop of rain or a rose petal.

briars tall and briars low
find a way for hand and toe

A voice whispered. Or maybe it was only a breeze. Briar sang the words over the drone of the bees.

briars low and briars tall
show the way to climb the wall

Handholds and footholds appeared. Up and up they climbed. And then, there they were, Briar, Sal, and Jack, on top of the wall, on their knees. The wall they had thought was high in and of itself, sat atop cliffs that were even higher.

"Maybe this *is* the edge of the world," said Briar through chattering teeth.

"No," said Jack. "No, it's not. Remember where the gates are? Where they drive the old people and prisoners out? There's no cliff there, just a flat plain."

Briar felt dizzy, looking toward the ground that seemed farther away than the sky.

"Don't look down," said Jack. "Look out."

None of them had ever seen such a vastness—no hovels, no walls.

"It *is* empty," said Sal, her voice quavering. Maybe she was thinking of her mother marching across that emptiness, her hands bound behind her, no shelter from sun or wind, heat or cold. "Where is the edge of the world ?" Sal almost sobbed.

"It's farther than we can see," said Jack. "But look, there's something."

Sal and Briar looked where he pointed. Up out of the nothingness rose a pinnacle, high enough to leave the dry dust of the desert far below, and touch the blue of the sky.

"If we stand up, we can look all around," said Jack.

Slowly, their knees shaking, they got to their feet. The top of the wall was just wide enough that they wouldn't fall off if they were careful. Slowly, slowly, hardly moving their feet, they turned in place, looking in every direction.

"What is that darkness over there?" Sal asked.

"Might be the shadow of a cloud," said Jack.

But for once there were no clouds. The sky was blue and endless.

"It seems like it's moving, but I don't think it is," said Briar.

"At least it's something," said Sal. "Something there."

When they turned and looked in the opposite direction, they saw a band of green snaking through the emptiness toward what was too far away for them to recognize as an old muddy shoe. When they faced their own walled world and the great dome of inside world, they could see nothing beyond. They could see nothing much at all, blinded by the reflection of light. Then the air shifted, and the breeze stiffened.

"It smells like salt," said Jack.

"Shh! Listen," said Sal. "Do you hear the rattling, do you hear the moaning?"

"Bells," said Briar. "I hear bells."

Then they all heard a sound that they knew only too well: the blare of a siren that went off whenever there was a disturbance, from someone opening a sealed spigot to steal water to someone starting a riot. The siren went from a single blare to a shifting, blasting code that directed the guards to the location of the crime.

"They've spotted us," said Jack. "We've got to get down."

"Down where?" said Sal.

For a moment, the three of them looked over the wall. The siren blasted again, and without another word, they began climbing back down to the briar patch.

(And if they had gone over, children, I would not be telling you this story now. No one knows how that other story would have turned out, or if there would have been a story at all.)

At least we'll be safe in the briar patch, Briar thought, with every hand- and foothold. *They'll never find us in the briar patch. We will be safe. Together always, the three of us. Safe.*

But when they got down to the ground, they could hear the baying of dogs, the shouts of the guards as they hacked at the briars.

"Bloody dung buckets! That's the third blade broken!"

"I told you this place is cursed."

"Yeah? Tell that to the chief. Orders is orders."

Briar, Sal, and Jack pressed themselves against the wall. Where could they go? Not up, not down, not in, not out, not over. And then they heard a sound louder than the commotion of guards. Bees humming, bees swarming. And threaded through the sound, a voice, singing.

closer, sweeter, deeper
deeper, sweeter, closer
fear no sting, come in
come in, sweeter, closer, deeper

And the old woman, or the shadow of the woman, or the translucent wings, or the bees themselves, gathered the children into the hive.

(Whenever my mother came to this part of the story, it was a story no longer. I was not in her lap or cuddled next to her, trying to imagine a world I had never seen, a world with wind, rain, sun, sky, however crowded and filthy the streets. Maybe, because I had lived enclosed all my life, the hive felt like my own place. I was there with them. I remembered what they could not, the terrible dreams, the beautiful ones, the sweetness, the warmth, the whir of wings, the dark.)

When they woke in the briar patch, just before dawn, new roses in bloom, petals fallen all around them, the thorny stars beginning to dim, the Guard and the dogs had gone. Even the bees slept.

Then the voices rose.

honey in the stone, rose in the dawn
beauty will go on, go on
world without edge, world without end
beauty will go on, go on, beauty will go on

Briar listened to the voices she had heard all her life. (How could the day begin without them? No day could begin without them.) But today she knew a voice was missing. Hers.

"One day, I am going to be a beauty singer," Briar said so softly she did not know whether or not she spoke aloud.

Sal and Jack made no answer. Briar looked from one to the other. They, too, listened intently to the beauty singers, as if they, too, had never heard them before.

We are together, Briar told herself. *Safe together, we three forever.*

over the edge of the world we go
over the edge of the world we fly

Briar sang, or she thought she sang, but the others did not join her.

"Time to go," said Jack.

"Lead the way, Briar," said Sal.

And the three of them crept out of the briar patch without a single scratch.

Noone

They were in his head again, the bees, the voices, singing. How did they get in? How could be keep them out?

He woke sweating, disgusted by his body's involuntary response to some terror he thought he had banished long since.

There now, there now. The rosy light that had no outside source crept up the perfect wall. Only *he* made beauty. He was the master of beauty.

They could not escape next time. He would have those three rounded up once and for all. When he did, he would send them all over the edge of the world.

Grannies

Granny Sweep stood perilously close to the edge of her pinnacle. Oh, what did it matter if she fell over She was light as thistledown, surely she would float on the wind, maybe then she would find whatever it was she was looking for. She could not remember what that was, just as she could not remember the dreams, dark, sweet, and terrifying, that had kept her half-awake all night. But if she floated away, if she fell, who would milk Moo-n, who would feed the chickens and Puss? A spider spun down on an invisible thread and swung on the breeze. Behind her the sun rose and cast a shadow that pointed to dome world, but did not quite touch it. A spark of blackness dove into the long shadow and disappeared; soon, Nightwing landed on her shoulder.

"What news, Nightwing, what news?"

"They are safe," the raven said. "For now, safe." And she made her beautiful, liquid, clicking sounds.

"Who is safe?" asked Granny Sweep. For she could not remember.

"Use your spy eye, you silly old woman, see for yourself."

And Granny Sweep sent her sight out on the wind, over the wall, into the tangle of briars and roses, humming with bees. She followed a faint trail to the edge. There they were, the three children, racing from the patch to the alley, safe, still safe.

"They are safe." Granny Spark woke with those words on her lips, as the sun sought her out in the hollow among the roots of her favorite sleeping tree.

But she did not know who *they* were. What had she dreamed? She could not remember. Nothing but her body tingling and humming as if she were a hive. "They are safe," she said again.

For now.

Who said that? Were the trees trying to warn her? Was it time to move again? Granny Spark got up, climbed out of the hollow, and swung herself into the branches of the huge old beech. Higher and higher she climbed. She scanned the emptiness for danger, armies, men with axes. She could see nothing but that strange narrow peak, poking rudely (so she always thought) at the sky.

The wind shifted, the leaves shivered. She caught a fleeting whiff of salt and roses, overpowered by the smell of oats and honey from below. Then came the reassuring sound of hearty laughter.

"Come down, old girl." Her lovers had made breakfast for her.

"They are safe, we are safe," she said aloud.

For now.

Granny Dirt woke from a terrible dream.

Lost, she'd lost them. That's all she could remember.

"Children, children!" she cried. They were all bursting out of the shoe as they did every morning. "Wait, I need to count you."

Granny Dirt, climbed through the undone laces of the shoe. "Stay still."

But the children did not, they could not. There was no counting them. Some of the other mothers came to stand with Granny Dirt on the toe of the shoe.

"It's all right," they told her. "They're safe. They're all safe."

For now.

Granny Brine lay on the deck of her ship, still tossing in her dreams. Roses climbing a wall, roses climbing a cliff. She looked up and up into the cloud. She could almost never see the top. But the mist brightened, gold and rose. Soon, behind her, the dark sea would blaze blue. The shore would stay dark till midday, the bones ghostly till they bleached in the light.

The air shifted; the bones rattled and groaned.

We are beyond danger.

We are safe.

Forever.

Safe.

PART TWO

Inside World

Rose

Children, it is time for me to tell you my story, the beginning at least, before I tell you what happened to Briar, Sal, and Jack. Their story, strange as it may be, is probably more familiar to you, maybe more credible than mine. Listen, imagine, if you can, if you will.

I have early memories of being all alone.

I was very small, maybe only just learning to crawl. I suppose I could be left alone, because the room was completely safe. No objects I could swallow or cut myself on, nothing I could climb that was precarious, no landing that would not be soft. I was inside inside world, so deep inside, only three other people knew I existed. They came to feed me and tend me and change my soiled clothes. But much of the time I was alone. The light glowed and shifted, traveling up to the ceiling and down, but it came from nowhere; I was neither too hot nor too cold. For company I had my own fascinating fingers and toes. The only sounds I heard, I made. I cooed, I gurgled. I

61

suppose I cried, but I didn't like that sound—the sound of loneliness. So I didn't make it often.

It is good that I had no idea of time, for if I had, I would have waited, endlessly, achingly for what did happen—I know now it must have been every day, at the end of the day, whatever day or night meant.

A door would open—I call it a door, but it was more like a veil parting or water breaking when a fish leaps or a stone falls, sudden yet seamless. He would come in. He had a severe face with a slim mustache that made his frown even more pronounced. Then they would follow, the two towering ones I called "the aunties" when I had language. And wonderful things would happen. The aunties would peel away the man's harsh face, revealing a woman's, young, gentle, smiling. When they removed the stiff vestments and constraining clothes, they wrapped her in a loose robe. Then the woman would hold out her arms to me. I would crawl, later toddle, and then run to her. She would bend down and scoop me up.

I would settle each evening into the softness of her lap, my head nestled on her breast. Every night before bed she told me stories of Briar, Sal, and Jack. Then she would sing me to sleep. I can feel the heaviness of my eyes closing. The perfect stars and moon that wheeled across the rounded ceiling of the room gave way to dreams of things I had never seen.

At first I did not know that the Briar in the stories was the one who told the stories, the one whose magical transformation from a strange man into my mama was the high point of each day. One night I was drifting off, she said softly, "And that is why I named you Rose, for roses in the briar patch. I am the Briar, and you are my Rose."

And my aunties, who sat close by, leaning against each other, let out such gusty sighs I could almost imagine what wind might be like.

My aunties loved to play--not just to play games with me, which they did, but play with me, as if I were their toy, their living doll. One or the other, or occasionally both, would come to check on me during the day.

As I grew from an infant into a little girl, they never tired of brushing or braiding my hair, dressing me in different clothes (from their magic closet, a place where they could disappear for hours. Our rooms were really just an antechamber for the closet). Sometimes they had stories that accompanied the costumes. I was shepherd girl, mermaid, princess, pirate. I had crowns and jewels fashioned of paper chains and a vast assortment of buttons.

My aunties were tall and very strong. They delighted in swinging me and tossing me back and forth, so that I spun and sometimes somersaulted in the air. They were my flying trapeze, and I was their circus star (not that any of us had ever seen a circus, except in storybooks). I could always tell the difference between them, although my mother explained to me that they were called "identical twins," and most people could not distinguish one from the other (unless they wore different wigs, but since they shared everything, you couldn't always tell by their hair). Their faces were different, the way faces are different in a mirror. But even without that subtle visual cue, their scents distinguished them. Auntie Aloe Vera had a sort of damp fragrance. Or I would have said it was damp and fragrant, like early spring, if I had ever been outside. Auntie Vinda Lou smelled spicy, faintly sweet but also hot. Hot coals, seeds sizzling and cracking, not that I had ever experienced such things then. Yet I recognized and distinguished the differences between them.

Their temperaments were also distinct. Auntie Aloe wept easily and freely. Though I had cried my own tears and though, of course, I had seen water running from a tap, I marveled at Auntie Aloe's tears.

"If they weren't salty, they could make a desert bloom," Auntie Vinda would say, fond and sarcastic at the same time. "Or at least fill up a cistern. She's a natural wonder."

Sometimes I would hold out my hands, just to feel Auntie Aloe's tears fall on my palms, enough tears to make a small pool. I had never seen or felt rain. I did not understand at first that Auntie Aloe cried because she was sad. And maybe she wasn't only sad.

"Why do you cry so much?" I asked her one day.

"Somebody's got to," she would say. "Other people don't have the time—or the talent. Sister won't."

They always called each other sister.

"Somebody's got to dry all those tears," said Auntie Vinda. "Otherwise everything will molder and mildew. Somebody's got to breathe fire around here."

And she would open her mouth and make a roaring sound. Though I never saw actual flames come out, the air would shimmer with heat. I could almost, but not quite, imagine the bright burning thing they recalled as "sun."

My aunties, who were older (and, they claimed, wiser and also more foolish) than my mother, had also been born outside.

"Now mind you," Auntie Vinda said, "we can barely remember a thing about it. Not like your mother; she was outside for much longer. We were barely your age when we were taken inside."

"Taken from our mother." Auntie Aloe would start to cry.

"We were boys then," put in Auntie Vinda.

"I was never a boy!" Auntie Aloe would sniff.

"Freaks. We were freaks," Auntie Vera would insist. "You Know Who wanted to experiment on us."

But I did not know who, and it was hard to imagine my huge aunts as children, boys or girls. Not that I knew what a boy was, for that matter. Or, apart from myself, a child.

"Hush, sister," Auntie Aloe would always say. "Rose is too young to hear about such things."

"Let's play tag," Auntie Vinda would say before I could begin to think how to ask all the questions I wanted to ask.

And we would race around the room that now had furniture we could crash into, or topple over, till we ended laughing in a heap.

Then one of them would say, "Mercy, sister, look at the time."

How they looked at it, I have no idea.

"That meeting is almost over."

And they would kiss me goodbye and disappear through the veils or the door or the opening that would close after them. No matter how closely I clung to them or how I hurled myself after them, I could not break through the wall.

✳   ✳   ✳

My mother was soft and also strong in a different way than my aunties. If I had ever smelled sun-warmed earth or stone, if I had ever smelled green living things, I would have thought she smelled like that.

"Why can't the aunties play with me all day?"

And why can't you? I wanted to ask her, but didn't. What happened to my mother during what we called the "day" was too strange for my mind to touch or for my tongue to turn into words. I snuggled deeper into her arms for comfort.

"I am sure they would rather play all day," said my mother. "But they have jobs to do, work."

"What do they do?"

"They are guards."

"Outside guards?" I was surprised. "They said they hardly remember outside. And the guards outside are mean."

For hadn't my mother told me stories about how all the outside children hid from the Guard?

"No, not outside guards," my mother said. "Inside guards. Bodyguards."

"What is a bodyguard?"

My mother didn't answer right away.

"What body do they guard?" I persisted.

"Mine," she said quietly.

I pulled myself a little apart from her and reached up to put my hands on her face, pulling at it just a little, to reassure myself that it would not come off. Not like the other face, the one that scared me.

"Why?"

"It's a secret, little Rose," she said. "I am a secret. You know that."

I did know, but I didn't understand.

"I am a secret, too," I said, for so I had been told.

"Yes, you are a secret. My best secret."

"Why?" I asked again, though I knew she wouldn't answer, and she didn't.

Instead, she said, "Did I ever tell you why I named you Rose?"

By then she had told me many, many times, but I knew she wanted to tell me again, so I just snuggled close and listened.

"When I was a little girl, not even as big as you, I would crawl into the briar patch . . ."

And she would go on describing the prickly thorns, how after a while it seemed they came to know her and would part for her, letting her deep, deep into the thicket. She would tell about the roses, how some of them were red, some white, some pink, all sweet, with yellow pollen-dusted centers where the bees hummed all day and sometimes even on moonlit nights . . . .

I would fall asleep and into dreams that became more and more vivid. I felt the heat of the sun, the prickle of thorns, the strange hard softness of the bare earth, the bees humming, as if they had found their way right inside me.

honey in the stone, rose in the dawn
beauty will go on, go on
world without edge, world without end
beauty will go on, go on, beauty will go on

All my days began with my mother's voice singing and the light rising on the walls of our small world, my small world, before she went out every day to her other life, a life that baffled me more and more as I grew older and began to form questions that went unanswered.

Every day my aunties carefully dressed my mother in a dark, constraining suit of clothes, and over that, a stiff robe embroidered and trimmed with gold. Then they sat her down in front of the three-way mirror at their makeup table and put on the face, more than what you would call a mask, that made her unrecognizable to me. Her hair, which she let fall loose at night, was tucked up into a wig of short dark hair. For important meetings, whatever they were, the man she became wore a pointed black hat embroidered with jewels meant to connote stars.

The aunties went through a transformation of sorts, too, changing from beribboned nightgowns and caps into elaborate under-and-over costumes.

The stuffed their massive legs into tight stockings and helped each other lace up corsets which made their bosoms balloon. They also covered their graying hair, not with hats, but with complicated wigs that made them even taller as they wound their new hair up in turrets. They jostled each other for the best seat before the mirror and painted their faces with iridescent color on their cheeks and all around their eyes. I was not allowed to hug them and kiss them after their morning toilette, though almost every day they forgot and scooped me up into their arms, leaving me smudged with colors and oils and scents.

Then all three of them would go forth wherever they went, leaving me to my toys and storybooks, paper and pencils and watercolor paints. It was my aunties who taught me to read the words in the books. I liked the stories and the pictures, especially the ones about Jack. I wondered why Jack didn't have a magic bean or a golden goose in any of my mother's stories. If he could climb to a castle in the clouds on a beanstalk, why not the unclimbable wall? And, I had even more pressing concerns than that.

"Where are the stories of Briar and Sal? Where are the pictures of them?"

I did not know that my mother, like other outsiders, had never learned to read. I understand now that one of the ways my aunties guarded my mother was by reading documents to her and for her. They had learned to read when they were taken (or abducted) inside at a young age.

"I suppose no one knows those stories but me," my mother would say. "Shall I tell you how Briar and Sal became queens?"

And I would listen again—and again. So far, all my mother's stories had ended with the bee woman hiding them in the hive, and their waking together in the briar patch to the beautiful dawn. Safe. I still did not know what happened after that.

"Where are Sal and Jack now?" I would ask.

"I will tell you when you're older," she would promise.

"I *am* older," I would insist.

"Not old enough," my mother would say.

I did not know exactly what "older" was. My mother was older than me, my aunties were older than my mother. Did they get older every day? Or did only children get older? My mother and aunties stayed the same size and shape, but I didn't. I grew out of and into new clothes. The aunties made marks of my changing height on the wall. Were growing up and growing old the same thing?

"Just tell me where they are," I would plead.

As if in answer (but not quite), she would sing:

over the edge of the world we go
over the edge of the world we fly
queens and kings
when we have wings
we all have wings
over the edge of the world we go
queens and kings, queens and kings

"Hush now," she would always say. "No more questions. Go to sleep."

And I would dream of the edge of the world . The sky was full of stars, not the flat stars on the ceiling. Stars like my aunties' jewels, but huge. And I would fly among them, searching for Sal and Jack.

＊　＊　＊

In the middle of the day, that is, when the lights were brightest, one, the other, or both of my aunties would come and bring me a picnic. That's what they called it. They would spread out a table cloth on the floor, though we had a table. And they'd open a basket and take out bread and jam and sometimes hardboiled eggs.

"These eggs were laid by chickens," they would marvel.

"Chickens from outside world," I always specified.

"Yes, yes. Do you remember chickens, sister? Do you remember the sounds they made?"

And then the aunties would imitate chickens, not only the sounds, but the movements of chickens scratching in the dirt for feed. Auntie Vinda would pretend to lay an egg. When I was little, I would laugh and imitate them to their great delight. But one day, I just sat, solemn, unmoved.

"I want to go outside," I stated when the aunties had stopped clowning and clucking.

I looked around the glowing round room that was my whole world, and it occurred to me that it was shaped like an egg. I had spent hours pondering what the aunties had once explained to me. Eggs, if not eaten as eggs, contained baby chicks who grew too big for the egg and cracked it open. The chicks grew up to be chickens. And chickens laid more eggs. I covered page after page of drawing paper trying to illustrate this mystery for myself. And once, when I was drawing an egg, I drew not a chick, but a child inside. Me.

"Yes, I suppose you do want to go outside," Auntie Aloe sighed a damp sigh.

"We miss it," admitted Auntie Vinda. "Some things, sometimes. But not other things."

"Like what?" I demanded.

"Being hungry."

"Being dirty."

"Flea bites."

"Rat bites."

"Being bullied."

"Being beaten."

"Being . . ."

"Shh, that's enough, sister."

I stared at them. None of these things had ever happened to me. My mother's stories skimmed over these harsher, uglier aspects of outside world. She filled my imagination with rose petals, honey bees, a girl who was her best friend, a boy who could turn somersaults in the air.

"What about inside world?" I demanded. "Where you go every day to guard my mother's body?"

They exchanged glances, raising eyebrows in a kind of twin code only they understood.

"What is it like?"

More eyebrow exchanges, a frown, a few sighs.

"It is like this room, only bigger," Auntie Aloe finally answered.

"Very big," added Auntie Vinda. "Lots of corridors, chambers, even houses and villages where people live. It is a whole world."

"A whole world inside."

"No wind, no rain, no sky."

I remembered my mother's story of the woman in the beautiful gown on the steps of outside world, terrified by a gust of wind. She had never felt wind.

And neither had I.

I want to go outside, I did not say again, knowing it was no use.

"Why can't I go see inside world if I am already inside inside world?"

I already knew the answer. I was a secret. But I didn't know why. It was hard for me to grasp what a secret was. I had no secrets of my own. Not yet.

More gusty sighs from my aunties, the heat and the damp colliding and almost creating weather.

"Are there other children in inside world?" I asked, not for the first time.

It was hard to imagine my aunties as children. Even then, they'd had each other. And my mother had Sal and Jack. Had. *We three will always be together*. That's what she had believed. But I was alone. I had never seen another child except in storybooks.

"There are other children," said Auntie Aloe cautiously.

"At least for now," Auntie Vinda said.

"Hush, sister."

"What do you mean?" I wanted to know. "Will they go over the edge of the world?"

"What edge of the world?" said Auntie Aloe.

"Who told you about the edge of the world?" demanded Auntie Vinda.

You did, I did not say. I'd heard my aunties, and sometimes my mother, whispering about it at night when they thought I was asleep. I did not want them to know I listened.

"It's in my mother's song," I said instead. "Over the edge of the world we go."

More communication by eyebrow, with a little nose twitching as well.

"No, no, of course they won't!" said Auntie Vinda.

"They will grow up. That's all she meant," Auntie Aloe assured me.

"And they may be the last batch," added Auntie Vinda.

"Hush, sister," said Auntie Aloe.

More secrets. What did they mean by a batch, the last batch?

"Will I grow up?" I asked instead.

A fine mist filled the room and began to swirl in slow circles. It became a fog so thick I could not see my aunties, who had begun to sob—both of them.

"Aunties? Aunties!"

They got hold of themselves, and the air cleared, as the bright light in the room began to soften. My aunties were tall, but not tall enough to crack open the ceiling of this room.

"Yes, darling," said Auntie Aloe, "you will grow up."

"That's why we are guarding you, precious," said Auntie Vinda, "keeping you secret and safe. You and your precious mama."

"But mama goes into inside world, and so do you. Why don't you just make me a mask, or a different face like mama's? Why can't you guard my body, too?"

The aunties looked at each other and spoke for a long time in their silent language.

"Come on!" Auntie Vinda said. "It's time for a rumpus."

And even though I was not a little child anymore, my aunties were still strong enough to toss me into the air.

"I want to turn somersaults in the air, like Jack!" I cried, getting caught up in the excitement.

"Up you go then!"

And I tumbled up almost high enough to kick the ceiling. Maybe someday I would kick it and crack it open like an egg. And I would keep kicking and cracking until I could see the sky, the real sky, the outside sky.

In the meantime, I began to pay closer attention to the comings and goings (you could almost say appearances and disappearances) of my mother and my aunties. There were double doors to my aunties' sacred closet (it was their place of worship!), and a door to what they called the WC. (All things watery happened there.) But the way from our chambers into inside world did not open and close. There were no hinges, no keyhole I could peer through, no crack underneath. Though the wall appeared smooth once they'd left, it would not have been accurate to say that they walked through walls. Somehow the wall made way for them. But not for me. I had run my hands over and over the wall, leaned all my weight against it, made running and jumping leaps at it, attempted to somersault through it. Sometimes I brought my blankets over and curled up and went to sleep beside the wall, only to be awakened by an auntie tripping over me when she returned.

I had never seen a waterfall or a veil or even a window curtain, but the wall turned into something you could part if you knew how. I spent more and more time pondering walls, especially the unclimbable wall that Briar, Jack, and Sal had managed to climb. Briar had sung a rhyme to help them find hand- and footholds. They had stood atop the wall gazing at out there. And then somehow they had been hidden inside the hive, hidden in the wall. Walls kept people in and out, safe or confined, like me. If I could get to the other side of a wall, who knew what might happen?

After hours of trying to make the wall open for me, I would give up, temporarily. Then I would read a book, or play with my dolls (ragdolls named Jack, Sal, and Briar, of course). Or I would take out my paper, pencils, and paints. I made pictures to go with my mother's stories. I would paint the briar patch and blotchy roses that would spill off the edges of the paper onto the table. (No one ever scolded me for making a mess.) I copied the illustrations of Jack, but it was hard to draw a somersault to my satisfaction. Sal and Briar I had to imagine. Two little girls, streaks of color, hand in hand, who always looked like they were flying.

One day I found myself drawing hair so long it would not stay on the page, and it was so white it did not show on the paper. I stood up and looked around the room at all the smooth walls where the light rose and fell every day. There was plenty of room to paint whatever I wanted, as big as I wanted. Maybe you are not allowed to paint on the wall, children, but no one had ever told me I could not. I was alone. This was my world, my only world, inside inside. These were my walls, the smooth inside of my shell.

I felt a pounding in my heart and a pounding in my feet. I was inside the dream Briar could not remember. I was inside my dream. I began humming, humming with the hive. I picked up my biggest paintbrush and began to paint the walls.

Was it a dream, children? How could a child like me paint figures larger than life, figures that came to life? I did not know who they were then— they didn't know themselves!—but there they were surrounding me, the old woman with long white hair floating on the wind, the old woman ablaze amidst dark green branches, the old woman brown as the dirt I'd never seen, her hair, her hands, her feet, a garden, and the one who stood on the pitching deck of a ship, who filled the room with salt and sweetness, clanging bells and bones. The ones Briar had dreamed and forgotten, the ones I remembered. I had brought them to life. They danced in a circle around me. I spun in a circle, and as I spun I sang my own variation of my mother's songs.

> *honey in the stone, rose in the dawn*
> *over the edge of the world I go*
> *over the edge of the world I fly*
> *world without end, beauty will go on*
> *honey in the stone, rose in the dawn*

I danced and sang till, breathless and dizzy, I collapsed on the floor. That's when I saw it: the wall wasn't solid anymore. It wavered like the air when Auntie Vinda breathed fire, or when Auntie Aloe made mist. A curtain, a waterfall, a way through the wall.

I got to my feet, I didn't hesitate; the way opened or I opened the way, I went.

When I turned and saw that the wall had closed behind me, I did feel afraid, but only for a moment. If I just stayed where I was, my mother or my aunties would come and open the way back in. For now I was outside in inside world, and my first sight of it was disappointing. I was in a winding corridor, narrower than our room, but with the same light that did not seem to come from anywhere. In one direction, the corridor sloped slightly downward, and in the other direction, it sloped upward. Of course I had never been on floors that sloped. After a while I could not resist taking a few experimental steps first one way, then another, to see what it felt like. There was a pull to the downward direction that made me want to run. So I gave in to the urge, running faster and faster, telling myself I could always retrace my steps.

I don't know how far I went, how many twists and turns I followed, but at last I came out to a platform and inside world opened up and out before me into a space so vast it was hard to believe there could be any more world than this. How could the sky be any higher or wider than the dome above me, where stars and moons and suns crossed and circled at different speeds? Below me, I saw what I recognized from picture books as castles and villages, fountains and canals. And there were wide promenades where people moved and murmured. I wanted to go down there and become one of that mass of people, more people than I had ever imagined could exist. How could outside world be any bigger or more beautiful? Why wouldn't everyone want to come inside?

I gazed and gazed, so intent on taking in the marvels below I did not notice that someone was watching me, coming closer to me on feet that made no sound, for the corridor was covered in carpet thicker than what I would one day know as grass or moss. And then a hand grasped my shoulder—or it could have been a claw. It was like no other touch I had known. I turned and gaped.

You must remember, I had only seen three other people in my life (or four if you count the face of the strange man), and none of them looked like this one: a man with a long forked beard and black eyes that looked like the beaded eyes on my dolls. I had never seen someone so old. Not outside my story books. He looked like a picture of Father Time come to life-- but Father Time never looked so fierce and frightening.

"What are you doing here, little girl?" he demanded. If I had ever heard a door squeak on its rusty hinges, I might have said his voice sounded like that. "How did you get here?"

I opened my mouth, but no words came out.

"Who are you?" he demanded.

You are a secret, I heard my mother's voice in my head, *my best secret.*

I knew I could not, must not, tell.

"Surely you have a name or at least a pod number."

I shook my head.

"Speak, girl."

"I am no one," I whispered.

"What's that? What did you say?"

"I am no one."

He stared at me, his bristling white eyebrows rising, then falling, furrowing into a frown that took over his whole face.

"No one," he muttered, "Noone. So am I. Come with me."

✳ ✳ ✳

I do not know how long or how far I followed him. Down stairways, through streets crowded with people who blocked my view, past a raised platform where a man in rich blue robes with a crown on his head was talking on and on while people laughed or cheered and applauded. I had heard my aunties clap their hands before, but this sound was deafening.

"Pompous fool!" the old man muttered. "But a necessary diversion."

The old man stopped at a number of doors that opened onto a long low building. I could hear shrill voices inside. Children! Somehow I knew they were, though I had never seen another child. I half hoped, half dreaded he would leave me here.

"Is this child one of yours?" He thrust me forward.

"No, sir," said the woman who'd answered. She was dressed all in dark blue, her hair pulled tightly back, so that her eyes looked as though they could not close. "We've just taken inventory. I assure you, none of the batch is missing."

My guide—or captor—pulled me on, stopping now and then to make inquiries of passersby, but of course no one recognized me. I remember best the fountains and pools where many-colored fish darted and swam. I wanted to touch the water, but he dragged me up more stairs and narrower corridors to a small round room, which we entered through a door that he closed behind us. An actual door, not a wall. I did not know then that doors could lock. Inside the room I saw something orange and alive, glowing and leaping. I stared and took a step toward it.

"Have you never seen fire before?" he asked.

I shook my head.

"Then perhaps you have not infiltrated from outside world, as I was beginning to suspect. There you would have huddled next to fires, paltry fires, fueled by dung, the kind that must be fed or they burn out. Not like this fire. This fire will never die. That much I have accomplished."

I kept my gaze on the fire, not just orange but green and blue, flickering in and out.

"Come, you shall sit beside the fire, while I summon my chief magician."

He finally loosed his grip and fetched a chair from across the room. I could have climbed into it, but he lifted me, and set me there as if I were a doll. My legs did not quite touch the floor. He picked up a bell and rang it once. The sound was so sharp and so loud, I could feel it in my bones. It went on and on. When it finally ceased, he pulled up a chair opposite mine, his legs long and spindly, I would have said like a spider's, if I had ever seen one.

"Do you know about outside world?"

I didn't nod or shake my head yes or no. For I knew nothing of outside world, except in my mother's stories.

"Don't they teach you about it in pod?"

I remained silent.

"No matter. One day there will be no outside world. Inside world will reach all the way to the edge of the world—perhaps beyond."

I just stared at him, trying to imagine an inside world without end, a world that would not crash over the edge, a world that could fly.

"If you will not answer questions, ask me one," he said, his brows as lively and crackling as the fire. "I insist, or I will tell my chief magician to take you down to the dark place—or perhaps to cast you out."

He meant to frighten me, I guessed, but all at once I felt braver, bolder, like Jack when he somersaulted out of the bully's reach.

"How old are you?" I ventured.

He scowled again, then stroked his long white beard.

"I am immortal."

I did not know what "immortal" meant, but I thought it must be very old.

"Are you Father Time?"

He leaned toward me, his face too close. I could see blood vessels sticking out on his forehead. I could feel his breath on my face, dry, but not hot like Auntie Vinda's.

"What do you know about Father Time, little girl? Who told you about Father Time?"

I could not tell him about my storybooks, about the secret room I had lived in all my life, or my mother's stories of Sal and Jack and Briar.

You are a secret, my best secret.

"Who told you?"

Before I could answer, a knock came on the door.

The old man leaned back again.

"Enter," he commanded.

The door opened, and there he was. The man who was and was not my mother. And following close behind him, my aunties.

You might think I would have felt relieved to see them, but in fact I felt more afraid. Not afraid that they would be angry with me, or even that I had put us all in danger, which surely I had. I had seen my mother's other face before and understood it was a mask. Now it seemed real, more real than all the memories of my short, confined life. The chief magician looked at me with no recognition. If not for a brief flash from Auntie Vinda's eyes and a momentary welling in Auntie Aloe's, I would have thought I did not exist at all, or that everything that had gone before was a strange dream. And now I was awake with no idea who I was, and no one to tell me.

"How may I serve you, Noone?" asked the chief magician.

In storybooks important people were called Lord and Sir and King. It sounded as though the magician had called him "no one." How could he be no one?

"I found this child wondering unattended where no child should be. No teacher claimed her for a pod. No one recognizes her. There is a whiff of the outside about her, though she is not ragged or unwashed. I suspect her of infiltration. She cannot or will not give an account of herself. Can you?"

The chief magician regarded me again, coldly, speculatively. I stared back, making my eyes wide and hard so that the tears would dry before they could fall.

"I cannot," the chief magician spoke at length. "But I assure you I will find out where she came from and send her back. I will see to it that she troubles you no more."

You are my secret, my best secret.

I could just hear a whisper of my mother's voice in the carefully chosen words.

"Is that wise?" Noone demanded. "If she is someone's tool, if she has been sent to spy or is from the outside, if she is an agent of corruption or disruption, surely it would be best to keep her confined, to keep her under observation."

The chief magician bowed. "As you wish. I will keep her confined and under close observation. Now, if you will permit me."

The chief magician reached out his hand for me. I wanted to leap from the chair and run to him, and at the same time something in me inexplicably shrank back.

"Ah," said Noone. "You prefer to stay with me?"

Oh no oh no oh no.

"The chief magician can be a bit forbidding, but he'll not harm you, child."

He turned to the man, who stood still, his hand motionless.

"Do not harm this one. Observation only."

And then he rose, lifted me from the chair, depositing me before the chief magician.

"I shall see you again, child. I've taken an odd fancy to you."

"Say thank you to Noone," admonished Auntie Vinda, and I gave a start.

No one? Thank no one?

"Show that whoever raised you taught you manners," added Auntie Aloe.

Noone. That was his name. And that was the name I had given when he asked me to tell him who I was. That had made a bond between us.

"Thank you, Noone," I managed.

And the chief magician took hold of my hand with his hand, which was my mother's and not my mother's.

✳ ✳ ✳

I walked for what seemed like hours, the chief magician holding my hand in a grip that almost hurt. I don't know if the intent was to disorient me or to avoid the open, public places. We stuck to winding, windowless corridors. After a while, I felt like I was sleepwalking, and maybe I was. At some point one of the aunties, Aloe by the scent of her, picked me up in her strong arms and carried me.

I woke up in my own bed in the room (which seemed so tiny now) where I had spent my life. The walls had their dim nighttime glow, and the room was filled with an eerie sound. If I had ever heard coyotes howl I might have thought a pack howled at the moon. Really it was sadder than that, and held a note of wind and rain. I sat up in bed and looked around. I saw them in silhouette, my huge aunties and my mother, her hair loosed as she rocked back and forth.

Keening. I know the word now. Keening.

"Hush," said Auntie Vinda. "She's awake."

The silence was even more strange and sorrowful than the sound had been. I couldn't bear it.

"Mama," I whispered, I whimpered, "Mama."

And then I was in her arms, my own sobs muffled by her soft body.

"You're not him, you're not him, you're really not him," I said over and over.

She just held me and rocked me, and the aunties moved closer, encircling us both. At last my mother took my shoulders and held me a little apart from her, so that she could see my face.

"How did you get out, Rose?" she asked, her voice sharp under the softness.

I pulled away from her and stood up, looking around at the walls. Maybe it was the dim light, but I could see no trace of my crude paintings or the huge dancing figures they had become.

"Why did you take them away?" I turned to my mother and my aunties.

"Take what away?" they all spoke over one another.

"I painted. I painted on the wall. Was that . . . bad?"

Bad was not something I knew much about, though I had heard the word in stories. Until that day I would never have connected it with myself or considered that my mother and aunties could ever be anything but delighted with me. But now I had seen the cold eyes of the chief magician, felt the painful grip of his hand. Maybe I had done something horribly wrong, something that made my mother and my aunties weep.

"What did you paint, Rose?"

Didn't they already know? Weren't they the ones who had washed the drawings off or covered them over?

"You must tell me, Rose."

I opened my mouth to describe the paintings, like the ones in the dream inside the hive, how the paintings came alive, how I danced with them and sang. Then I closed it again. I wasn't sure I wanted to tell. I wanted my own secret. I had found my way out through the wall, even if I wasn't sure exactly how I did it. If I told, they would make sure I never got out again.

I will keep her confined and under close observation, the chief magician had said.

My mother had said.

What if I didn't want to be confined and observed? *I am a secret, my best secret.*

I shook my head, not defiantly, just slowly.

"The child is exhausted," said Auntie Aloe.

"And delirious," added Auntie Vinda. "There are no drawings on the wall. She must have dreamed it."

"She's dreaming awake," said Auntie Aloe.

Had it all been a dream, all of it? The dancing figures, Father Time. I looked at the walls again and glimpsed a shadow of something moving. I heard a rattling of shells and bones, and then felt soft air washing over my face, similar to the way my mother described the wind.

"We must give her bread and honey, honey and warm milk, and put her to bed."

"But how did she get out? We must find out how she got out," my mother persisted. "We might not be so lucky next time."

So I *had* gotten out. It was not a dream.

"Hush, Briar," said Auntie Vinda, while Auntie Aloe brought me the honeyed milk and bread.

"One of us will stay with her tomorrow."

"And tomorrow and tomorrow and tomorrow."

"We won't let her out of our sight."

Keep her under close observation.

As soon as I finished my milk and bread, I was tucked into bed. But somehow I stayed awake, even with my eyes closed. I could hear them waiting until they believed I was asleep.

"It's time," said Auntie Vinda.

"Yes, it's time to tell her what happened."

"To you and Sal and Jack."

"But I don't know. I don't even know."

My mother's voice was so sad. I almost got up and went to her.

"You know enough," said one auntie.

"Enough to warn her," said the other.

"She's so young, she's too young," my mother protested. "She's not ready to hear such things."

"You mean you're not ready to tell her," said Auntie Aloe. "You're afraid to tell her."

I couldn't hear my mother's answer.
"It's time," said Auntie Vinda, and Auntie Aloe echoed, "It's time."
I went to sleep with those words echoing inside me.
It's time, it's time, it's time.

Grannies Dreaming

Granny Sweep rolls over in her sleep, deeper into her dream.

She does not know where she is; she does not know who she is.

What is this small, round, windowless place, full of the sounds of breath and sorrow, like the softest wind, like air just before it stills? And who are those shadows on the wall? Is it her shadow? But there is more than one, swaying, reaching.

Granny Spark rolls over in her sleep, deeper into her dream.

She does not know where she is, she does not know who she is.

How has her room among the roots become so smooth? Who is here with her? She can hear them breathing, creaking, the way trees do. Their breath fans her sparks into light. She can almost see them, old women like herself, not like herself, flickering, now there, now gone.

Granny Dirt rolls over in her sleep, deeper into her dream.

She does not know where she is, she does not know who she is.

The walls of this place are smooth, curved. It is too warm here to be a root cellar or a mushroom cave. Who is casting huge shadows in this lightless place? Do they have hands? Can she touch them?

Wait! Look! There is a child sleeping, dreaming. A child not safely tucked into the shoe.

✳   ✳   ✳

Granny Brine rolls over in her sleep, deeper into her dream.

She does not know where she is, she does not know who she is, but she misses the roll and pitch of the ship.

What is this place with air as still as held breath, and walls as smooth as the inside of a shell? They glow faintly. There are others here. The others are here. She does not know what she means by that.

Sisters, she tries to speak, *sisters*, but her voice is too far away.

✳   ✳   ✳

Deep in the grannies' dreams, a sleeping child wakes and sits up, her eyes sweep the room, like a wind, a flame, a quake, a wave.

Who are you? they ask.

Who am I? they ask.

Who are we?

The child knows.

The child, the child, the child, the child, they echo each other.

We must find her.

She must find us.

We must free her.

She must free us.

Noone's nightmare

That child, that child.

He woke up in a sweat.(He thought he had eliminated sweat; soon, soon he would need no body, nobody.) The smooth sheer sheets had tied themselves in knots, tied him in knots. He'd been having nightmares: smooth walls, huge menacing beings he could not see, only their shadows, insubstantial, beyond his reach.

That child, that child.

He should not have let the chief magician take her away. He should have kept her himself, kept her until he found out who she was.

She could not be no one.

He was the only Noone.

Grannies Waking

Granny Sweep woke up. The cock was crowing, the cow was bellowing. She stepped out of her hut, and looked over the world, what there was left of it, what she could see. She turned to the dome world.

Had it gotten bigger in the night?

Why couldn't she see inside, why couldn't she see?

Granny Spark woke up in her warm bed among the roots, pleased to see her newest lover snuggled beside her. She stretched, and she felt the roots of the forest stretch, too.

Is it time to get up, the trees murmur, *time to go farther away? Has anyone seen us?*

Granny Spark's dream flickered and dimmed, flickered and dimmed. What had she seen? Who had seen her?

Granny Dirt woke up to the din of the children, playing inside and outside the old shoe. Someone swung on the laces and the crockery tumbled off the shelf. A woman moaned. Another one in labor.

She had so much to do. So many children. She didn't know what to do. No, she did know, she always had, but now—

One child, alone in the bed, she remembered, one child who knew what she did not.

Granny Brine woke up and almost went back to sleep to the sound of the wind and the waves. She could just sail beyond, beyond the curved edge, over the edge . . . why didn't she go? There was a reason, a reason.

Seagulls screamed. Captain swore at them.

She rolled out of her hammock and scrambled on deck. The sun was rising over the invisible heights of the cliff. Fog and mist boiled below. The bell buoys rang. Though she couldn't see them, she could hear the temple of bones rattling on the shore.

She could not leave, not yet. There was something she needed to know.

There was someone who knew.

PART THREE

What happened to Briar, Sal, and Jack

My mother might have been right that I was not ready to hear what had happened to her and to Sal and to Jack, what she knew and what she didn't know. *(How could I have been ready?)* And yet my aunties were also right; I had to know. I already knew too much and not enough. They all wanted to keep me safe. I now had some inkling from what.

None of us knew, or would admit, that staying safe might not be possible, but we should have known it would be impossible for things to go on forever as they were.

I am no longer certain what my mother told me and what I imagined on my own. She would tell me things, but when she wasn't with me, I dreamed and daydreamed. Briar, Sal, and Jack were my living storybook, and I inhabited their story all the more deeply, because my own story had stalled. As if someone had bookmarked it, put it away on the shelf, and forgotten it.

In the story, as my mother told it or as I dreamed it, Sal one day took Briar's hand and whispered, "Let's slip away from Jack and hide for a while."

"Why?" Briar wondered.

"There's something I want to show you. There's something I want to ask you. Just you."

And after all, in the beginning, before Jack, it had been just the two of them. Sal and Briar led Jack on a merry chase. At first it felt like just another of their games. But around one twist or turn or another, they left Jack behind. Or maybe he let them go. Maybe he had to dodge the Guard again. There was a new danger to Jack now that he'd shot up. Too tall to be a miner, too dangerous to be left on the loose. Just right, if they caught him soon enough, to be a guard.

It was usually Briar who led the way into the thicket, but today Sal pulled her in, following one path, then another, so quickly that even Briar wasn't sure where they were going.

At last Sal stopped in one of the hollows where they could stand upright. Without a word, Sal unbuttoned her blouse.

"Go on." Sal gestured for Briar to do the same.

"Why?"

"We've got to look," said Sal. "We've got to know."

When they were bared to the waist, they gazed at each other in wonder—and dismay.

"You've got them," Sal made it sound like accusation. "They're bigger than mine."

Briar looked at Sal's brown breasts, the darker nipples that made her think of rosebuds, just before they blossomed. So small, so . . . secret. Briar looked down at her own breasts. They were bigger, rolling away to some unknown edge, like the land she had glimpsed when they climbed to the top of the wall.

"Yours will grow," Briar reassured Sal.

They always shared everything; they were always the same, queens together forever.

"No!" Sal almost shouted, then she looked around, afraid someone might have heard, but they were deep in the briar patch, the din of outside world as far away as it could be, distant enough that they could hear the bees.

"No," Sal said again, her voice low but still urgent. "I am not going to let them. I am not going to have them. They will ruin my plan."

"What plan?"

Sal didn't answer. Instead, she took off her skirt, already tattered, and started tearing it into strips.

"What are you doing?" asked Briar, not sure if she should tear her own skirt.

It was always Sal who started things.

"You'll see," said Sal, intent on her task.

When she had finished tearing her skirt, she began to wrap the strips tightly around her breasts.

"Help me bind them, Briar."

Her breasts, smaller than doves.

When they were done, Sal crawled by herself into a low tunnel in the briar patch. Before Briar could follow, Sal returned, clutching a small bundle of what turned out to be old and tattered boys' clothes. She pulled a tunic over her head, then cast aside the remnants of her skirt and put on leggings instead.

"Why do you want to look like a—" began Briar.

"Wait," said Sal, "I'm not done."

Sal crawled back into the briars and emerged with what looked like a curved knife (not that Briar had seen many knives). Outsiders were allowed no weapons. Tools for miners were confiscated at the end of each shift. No one chopped wood. Outsiders burned dried dung from cows kept for milk. The only animals they ate were chickens, which could be killed by wringing their necks. Of course people tried to fashion weapons from whatever they could: old pails, three-legged stools. One of the chief jobs of the Guard was to keep the outsiders unarmed.

"Where did you get that knife?" Briar asked.

And how did you keep it a secret, why did you keep it a secret from me? she did not say aloud.

"It's a cutlass," Sal said.

And as she spoke the strange word, Briar almost remembered a dream, salty air, the roar of something other than wind.

"Where did you get it?"

"It's mine," was all she said. "I found it. I don't remember where."

For a moment Sal sounded confused. Did she smell the salt too?

"It was all rusty. I polished it; I sharpened it. I'll show you."

She yanked a lock of her hair and hacked it off and kept hacking until her hair was short and bristly. Her long, dark, snaky braids lay on the ground, looking as though they might spring to life.

"There!" Sal said, defiant and exultant at once.

She did not look like a girl anymore. She did not look like a boy either. She looked like something wild and fierce. Dangerous. She held out the cutlass to Briar, who looked from the blade to Sal.

"Now you," urged Sal. Sal, who had always been her more-than sister, her double, her twin.

"But why, Sal?"

And why, she wondered, did she even ask? Why not just follow Sal's lead, as she always had? It would be easy to cut her hair. She had only two braids, soft and slippery, brown, red, or gold, depending on the light. Sal sighed and lowered her weapon.

"You're too pretty, Briar. Look at you!"

But she couldn't, of course. She had never seen a mirror, though now and then they'd gazed into puddles or rain buckets. Sal had always been her mirror.

"What do you mean, pretty?" Briar demanded, almost angrily.

"I mean *you!*" Sal gestured, shaking her head. "You with your shiny hair, with roses in your cheeks."

No, Briar wanted to say, *no. I look like you, brown and quick, eyes dark and bright as night.*

"So pretty, they'll take you. They'll force you inside. Not the inside where you get to be a maid, mopping floors and working the laundry for the fine ladies who are scared of the wind. The other inside."

The inside where no one came out again. She did not know what went on there; she bet Sal didn't either, but the mothers and grandmothers whispered about it. Some tried to hide their daughters. And their sons, too.

"Now you've got those," Sal pointed to Briar's breasts, "the color of cream."

Self-conscious. Briar pulled on her blouse.

"Next, you'll get the blood. I've already had mine once."

Sal had gotten her blood? And not told Briar? Heat flooded her cheeks, shame: she hadn't told Sal about her blood, either.

"Me, too, Sal," Briar told her. "I've had mine, too."

No more secrets now. They were the same again. Nothing had to change. But Sal went on as if she hadn't heard.

"You know what happens when the blood comes? Even if they don't force you inside, some outside man will take you, then you'll have babies. That's what the blood means, Briar. Do you know that? And everything will just go on and on, nothing will change."

Of course she knew. They had both grown up witnessing the women's lives around them. Babies being born, sometimes dying or left to die. Sometimes mothers died, too, or were cast out like Sal's mother. Life and death all mixed up together on a great rubbish heap.

"Unless . . ." Sal gestured to her short hair, her flattened breasts.

"But it's just as bad to be a boy," Briar protested. "They'll force you into the Guard or more likely, because you're small, they'll send you to the mines."

Sal was quiet for a moment, keeping her eyes fixed on Briar's face.

"That's my plan," she said at last.

"What plan?"

Another secret. The clothes she'd hidden in the briar patch, the cutlass, and now a plan. Sal held out the cutlass to her again, and Briar understood it was a condition. If she wanted to be part of Sal's plan, she would have to cut her hair and make herself into a boy.

"What about Jack?" Briar asked, suddenly jealous. "Does he know your plan?"

And what if Sal and Jack left her behind? Became two instead of three, leaving her as one, alone? She couldn't bear it. Just as she was about to take the cutlass, Sal spoke again.

"You know my plan, Briar."

"No, I don't," she began.

But she did, though it had hardly seemed a plan, more like a guess or a dare. "There might be a way to tunnel out through the mines," Sal had said the day they climbed to the top of the wall to gaze at the vast, desolate emptiness that led to the edge of the world. Where Sal's mother had gone, where so many had gone.

"Do you mean," Briar began, "do you mean you're planning . . . to go to the mines? You *want* to go to the mines?"

Sal continued to hold her gaze, her eyes dark, cavernous, as if she had already gone down, deep, far.

"The question is, Briar, will you come with me?"

Briar closed her eyes, shutting out Sal's intensity. Another memory overcame her: waking at dawn in the briar patch after the night none of them had ever mentioned, the sweetness, the hum of bees, the dreams that flickered and fled. Then the song, the voices of the stars melting into light.

honey in the stone, rose in the dawn
beauty will go on, go on
world without edge, world without end
beauty will go on, go on, beauty will go on

"Sal!" Briar called her name as if she were a long way off. "Oh, Sal."
Then she opened her eyes, and there was her friend.

"You don't have to say it, I know," Sal said, her voice harsh and gentle at once. "I've known all along. You're going to be a beauty singer. You *want* to be a beauty singer. It's all you've ever wanted."

"But not without you," Briar cried. "I'd rather—"

"You'd rather, what? Go to the mines? No, Briar. No, you wouldn't. Maybe I'll hear you when I'm deep in the tunnels. I'll think of you, spending your life running and hiding until you're caught, and if you're caught—"

Sal's voice broke.

"Running, hiding," Briar tried to make light, to hold back her own tears. "No one better at that than me."

Except you, Sal, she did not say aloud. *Except Jack*.

Just then they heard a rustling in the briar patch. They crouched down, ready to crawl deeper into the thicket, and then there was Jack, dropping to the ground beside them, as if he had fallen from somewhere, even though he must have tunneled through the thickets, just as they had, maybe following their trail.

"Sorry to interrupt. I know you two were trying to give me the slip," he said without rancor. "The Guard almost got me this time. They will one day."

"Oh, Jack!" Briar and Sal said at once.

"Not to worry," said Jack. "It's all part of my plan."

Another plan, another terrible plan. They wouldn't need these awful plans, if only...if only they could climb the wall again, find a way over, the three of them.

"Jack," Briar began, "do you remember—"

"Sal!" said Jack before she could go on. "What did you do to your hair? How will I be able to pull it now?"

They all laughed. Such a relief to laugh. For a moment it felt like they were children again, wrestling on the dung heap, the dangers of the dangerous age far in the future. They were children still. In a moment, they were all on the ground, rolling around, tickling and mock-punching, till they lay back and looked at the sky. The sun would set soon, but now the clouds were still bright, pink, edged with gold. They used to tell each other stories about the land of the clouds, how they might climb there on a magical vine.

"Do you remember," said Briar again, "the day we climbed the wall? Why don't we try again?"

No one spoke for a moment.

"Do you remember the sirens?" said Sal.

"And the guards and the dogs?" added Jack.

"I remember the bee woman," Briar said. "She kept us safe."

"Safe," said Sal. "Safe in the briar patch."

A breeze stirred, the briars rasped; a few rose petals drifted down to their faces.

"But what if this time," Briar persisted, "we went over the wall?"

"When we have wings," Jack sang softly, "when we all have wings. But we don't, Briar. We don't have wings. We could as easily go over the edge of the world."

"Still. There might be a way down, there might—"

"And there might not. It's a long way to fall."

"But at least we'd all be together. Forever."

Her voice was lost in a sudden huge buzzing, not just a workaday buzzing, bees busy in the blossoms. This buzzing was so loud it was more like a roaring. They looked up. A cloud hung over them, eclipsing the sky, a dark cloud of bees in the air just over the briar patch, just over their heads. And then the swarm rose higher, light catching their wings, their shape shifting just the way cloud shapes shifted. For a moment the bees looked like a huge woman, dancing, swimming, flying into the sky. A voice sang, or thousands of voices that were somehow one.

> *the bees know what will be*
> *their thousand eyes know how to see*
> *the bees know what is to come,*
> *the secret's hidden in their hum*

Then the swarm disappeared over the wall, taking their wild song with them.

"Hush," said Jack, though none of them had spoken. "Look."

In the last light, they saw a shadow against the wall, the old bee woman, a few bees, or their shadows still circling her head.

"Go on, little sisters," the bee woman whispered, or maybe it was just the rasping of the briars in the breeze, "follow your queen."

And the last few bees lifted into the light.

"Where are they going?" asked Sal.

"Why are they going?" asked Jack.

"Can't we go too?" asked Briar.

"When you have wings," sang the woman as her shadow dissolved into shadow. "When you all have wings, queens and kings."

Then there was only her voice, soft and fading with the light:

west of the sun
east of the moon
south of the night
north of the noon
world without edge
world without end

"Is it a sign?" they whispered to each other. "It's a sign."

"Let's stay here tonight."

"Tomorrow at first light, we'll find a way."

They all moved closer together, arms around each other, making their own sweet hive.

Noone Knows

He knows where they are, the three, the three he has marked since they incited a riot of joy on the dung heap. For days or weeks, or even years, he has forgotten about them. Now he has them in his second sight. They are not children anymore. They are too old to be playing hide-and-seek. They are plotting something. He will put an end to it, he will put an end to them, before it's too late.

One and One and One makes One

My mother didn't tell me about that night, not in so many words, but I know. I have dreamed it many times since I became old enough to understand.

It is a beautiful night, warm and fragrant. The star-spiders spin their webs in the sky. The three friends nest, nestle, the same as birds, rabbits, soft warm animals. I don't know who starts the kissing. It doesn't matter. There is a first kiss, like a first star, and then another and another until there is a firmament of kisses. Their clothing is little more than rags, gray ashes over hot coals. Heat. They all burn with it. There are hands on skin. There are legs and arms, woven together. There are fingers exploring, inside and outside, outside and in. There are cries and sighs. Outside goes in and in and in again. The three became one.

As one they fall asleep, too tired and sated to dream.

They woke to the smell of smoke. Birds fluttered frantically into the false dawn.

They saw the flames coming toward them, leaping and weaving through the briar patch.

"Run!" one of them shouted.

But they knew better than anyone they couldn't run. They couldn't stand. They had to crawl through the tunnels while the flames were stopped by nothing.

"Which way is out?" cried another.

And then Briar was Briar again.

"This way," she said, "hurry!"

She led them into a tunnel where, if they crouched, they could run. The crackling of flames grew louder. Just when they thought they might be overtaken, a breeze rose and blew the flame back. A cloud came out of nowhere and settled over them, a mist, a fog, rain. They were nearly out. They could hear the people shouting and babies crying. Then so close it must have been only a few feet away, they heard someone saying, "There's three of them. That's the orders. Take all three. They went in together, they'll come out together."

We three, we must always be together, we three.

"We've got to separate," whispered Jack. "I'm going to go back a bit; the fire's slowed. You two go on, but come out alone in different places."

"No," Briar said. "No!"

"It's our only chance." He gave her a shove. "Go!"

"Come on, Briar," Sal called, already ahead, the wind and the rain making her sound farther away.

Briar crawled after her. On and on. The light from the fire grew fainter, the black cloud was tinged with pink. They could hear the sound of footfalls now, the clinking of chains, and a rhythmic moaning song.

don't know, don't know, got to go, got to go
don't know why, why, oh why, got to dig until I die

Briar fell against Sal, who had stopped still.

"It's time, Briar, this is my chance. Don't follow me. Keep going."

"No," she said again.

Her lips were stopped with Sal's kiss, and then Sal was gone. Briar could hear Sal's voice, low and gravelly, pretending to be a man, but still Sal's voice.

don't know why, why, oh why, got to dig until I die.

Briar could hardly see through sweat, rain, tears, but she crawled on. The birds started singing, the drops on the briars caught the first light, and then she heard them.

another night is gone, come the fire, come the rain
come cruelty, come pain, another night is gone

Briar tore her way out and ran toward the singing. When she caught up with the singers, they gathered her into their midst.

come the night, come the dawn
beauty will go on, go on, beauty will go on

Grannies Dreaming and Waking

She faces a fire burning out of control. It is about to overtake three people.

No! she says. Go back!

She bellows her command, her voice loud, louder than the roar of the flames.

Eyes flash and flare at her. She knows those eyes, but the fire falls back, sputtering and hissing as a rain begins to fall.

Granny Sweep woke to the smell of smoke, her eyes stung with it, the scent hung in her hair, clung to her clothes, bringing back her dream. Was it a dream? She got out of bed and stepped into the cool, dawn air, heavy with smoke and damp and a hint of roses. She climbed to her lookout and sent her vision out to black smoke still hanging over dome world, blinding her flying eye.

"Where are they?" she asked, not knowing who or what she meant.

Then with a familiar rush of air, Nightwing circled and landed on the lookout railing.

"Call back your sight," the raven said. "Look to the orchard."

Her sight clear again, Granny Sweep watched as a dark shape lifted into the gathering light. It looked like a woman dancing, her hair streaming like a comet. It hummed with a thousand voices that was one voice. Before she could catch the tune, what she suddenly knew as a huge swarm of bees flew away into the emptiness.

How dare you, she howls, *how dare you steal my power!*

Someone is forcing her, against her will, against her timing. She is raging. Little things scamper about her feet, mice, rabbits. Birds and bats fly up, and three people run away. Are they the ones who interfered with her? They can't escape her. She will catch them; she will make them tell.

Go back! A huge woman blocks her way. A huge woman made of wind and moonlight.

Granny Spark woke rubbing her soot and cinders out of her eyes. Her nightmares had followed her into waking. She leaped from her bed and banged her head on a root. Then she heard a roaring sound. Fire! Fire in her tree. She scrambled outside, steam rising from her head. The tree was not burning, it was buzzing, humming with a thousand voices that were one voice. Over the trees a shifting shape danced, thousands of tiny wing shining in the first rays of light.

One of her bear friends came to stand beside her, lifting his snout and joining the song. Before she could catch the tune, a huge swarm of bees lifted from the tree and disappeared into the pale blue above the dark green.

Ashes, ashes, turning into black mud.

She knows, she is the only one who knows what is left when everything is gone, when green is only a charred shadow on a wall. Tears are falling, smoke is rising, feet running, hearts pounding. Where are they going?

Children, she calls, *children, come home.*

Granny Dirt woke to the sound of her own voice. Soon she was covered in children and babies, all pulling at her.

"Granny, Granny, Granny," they shouted, their voices sweet, their fingers sticky. "Get up, get up, get up."

She stepped out of the boot into the muddy yard. Was that a cloud overhead? It was shaped like a woman dancing, a woman with roots for feet and a tangled garden of hair. But why was it humming, a thousand tiny voices, one voice? The children began to sing along. Before she could catch the tune, the swarm of bees flew away, the rising sun casting its shadow on the ground.

There's a storm sweeping in over the sea, a huge storm, sky high, without end. She rides the storm, clouds carry her. She is not afraid to fall, she must fall. Water and fire meet like a kiss, the sweetest kiss, this dying so gentle, so meant to be.

For a moment she sees them, she is one with them.

Her sisters.

Then the shouting starts, the sorrow begins. All at once, then one by one by one, three people flee.

Granny Brine woke to her ship rocking on storm swells. Would the sun rise today? Such a long way to the edge of the world, through the smoke and strife of her dream.

"Help!" Captain squawked from the deck. "Don't go any closer, silly primates."

Granny Brine went to her deck and saw her parrot cowering on his perch, and the monkeys climbing the rigging to the crow's nest. A cloud hung over it, a dark cloud shaped like a woman dancing, her hair rising and falling, humming with a thousand voices that were one voice. Granny Brine caught the tune, and she found herself singing words from long ago, from a time before lost memory.

west of the sun
east of the moon
south of the night
north of the noon
world without edge
world without end

A rare wind blew over the edge of the world, carrying the scent of smoke and roses. The swarm of bees spiraled and caught the invisible current. Granny Brine watched as they flew toward the dark curve where the last stars still lingered. She knew where they were going; she knew what they would find there.

On the shore behind her the bones rattled; the bells rang.

For her part, she would wait.

Noone and the Chief Magician

"They were not found," the chief magician reported.

Noone was back in his room. He had seen the fire, he had ordered the fire. He had watched it spread over the briars that should have been destroyed long ago. (For so long—how long?—the briar patch had fallen out of his vision, out of his memory.)

"How is that possible?" Noone demanded. "How did the fire fail to flush them out?"

"The rain, I fear, the rain gave them respite."

A chill crept over Noone's skin, prickled his skull, a breeze that ought not to exist interfered with his beard. Them. They were still against him; they were always against him. They had stolen a corner of the walled world for themselves. *They* were the ones who had hidden it from his sight.

"You were supposed to control the weather!" Noone informed him.

He scrutinized the magician. The man's eyes appeared to have no pupils. There was something unnatural about him. But that was why he had chosen him as magician. Artifice over nature.

"We took every care to confine the fire to the briars, but the weather outside has always been out of control," said the chief magician calmly. "That is why we created inside world."

"We?"

"You," the chief magician corrected himself. "Your genius. I am but your humble servant."

Not humble enough, Noone did not say aloud. He still needed this man. For now. He would give him the benefit of the doubt. For now.

"If they were not found, they must have perished in the fire."

Noone had watched it spread and leap, a many-tongued monster. The rain had only slowed the fire. Then it had flared again. The briar patch was destroyed, not one bramble left.

"The ashes are being searched for remains."

"But say they escaped the fire, how is it possible that they were missed?"

There was a silence; Noone let it lengthen.

"The Guard did not see them, sir. They were told to look for three young people. They found none."

"Who gave that description?" Noone glared at the magician. He could feel his own eyes burning, hot and cold at once. "Answer!"

"I did," said the magician, still unperturbed. "Two girls, one boy. The boy, as I'm sure you are aware, is notorious. Nimble Jack. The Guard has been on his trail for some time."

"Girl, boy, girl," muttered Noone. "That's not what matters. Ring around the rosy, ring leaders. Joy, unseemly joy."

The chief magician eyed him without looking at him. Noone felt unnerved. Was he raving? Again? Not that the chief magician ever said so. His gaze just slithered sideways.

"Permit me," the chief magician said after a moment.

Did Noone have a choice?

"You are permitted. For now."

"We will find them, sir. The Guard will search hovel to hovel, dung heap to dung heap. There will be no place for them to hide. The ground of the burnt patch will be poisoned and covered over. If any one or all three attempt to lead an insurrection, it will be put down; they will be caught. When they are, may I suggest the ultimate penalty?"

Over edge of the world. Living death.

Noone had instituted the punishment himself, instilled terror of it in everyone, inside and outside.

over the edge of the world we go

Noone could hear their voices singing, clear as day, clear as that day when he spied them on the rubbish heap.

over the edge of the world we go
over the edge of the world we fly
queens and kings
when we have wings
we all have wings
over the edge of the world we go
queens and kings, queens and kings

"Stop!" He put his hands over his ears. "Stop them!"

The silence still rang with their voices.

"Sir?"

The chief magician gave him that opaque look again, his voice filled with concern, or feigned concerned. How dare he insinuate . . . what?

"No, we will keep them here," Noone ordered. "We will find out what they are made of."

The chief magician bowed.

"If I may suggest . . . "

You may not. Noone stopped himself. He still needed the man. For now.

"For that purpose, we need only one of them."

"Then go find him. Go find her. Go!"

The magician bowed and left Noone alone. Alone in his room, alone in his great, cavernous mind. Alone with what he would not acknowledge as fear.

They were out there. Conspiring against him.

The terrible old women.

Briar, Beauty Singer

Every dawn now, Briar sang beauty. It was what she had wanted, or thought she wanted. Was that the real reason she had not cut her hair and made herself into a boy? Had she wanted her own beauty? But she had never even known she was pretty till Sal insisted on it. And her beauty, if she had it, meant nothing to her now. The beauty singers cloaked themselves in tatters and shadows, gray as the grayest song birds. They made themselves as invisible as possible.

Now that she was one of them, Briar felt like an imposter. She could no longer see the beauty they sang; she did not believe in it. She saw rats, far sleeker and fatter than the babies they sometimes bit. She saw old people starving to death, hiding in corners and shadows from the Guard so they wouldn't be forced beyond the wall. There were others who put themselves in the way of the Guard, begging for death. She saw children playing on the rubbish heaps just as she and Sal and Jack once had. Now she did not see hidden treasure in a magic mountain. She saw only mud and slop tossed out by the people of inside world, so they wouldn't have to smell their own stink.

She did not want to wake in the dark and the cold to sing, but her mother and the other women were at once ruthless and tender, shaking her awake, hauling her to her feet, but also holding her hand, finding moments to stop and give her a quick hug. No one praised her voice. They didn't need to. She could hear it, almost as if it wasn't hers, as if she were listening indifferently from far away. Her voice was beautiful, but drew no attention to itself, blending with the other voices as if it had always been part of the song, the song that went on with or without her, and would remain after she had gone.

Gone? Where would she go? Where could she go? It was Jack and Sal who had gone, and she did not know how to follow them. Maybe it was not too late to cut her hair and search for Sal in the mines. Or, if she could pass as a boy, maybe she could join the Guard, find Jack, if that's what had happened to him. It must have. If he was still free, where was he? Why hadn't he shown himself to her?

The world was ugly and empty without Sal and Jack, and she was lonely, even though she was rarely alone. It took her awhile to realize it, but the women, the secret beauty singers, were always somewhere nearby. Were they protecting her, keeping her prisoner—or both?

At dawn, when they sang through the streets, they kept her in their midst, even though she, like the rest of them, was veiled. During the day, one or more of them stayed near her in the vast flat fields of grain or the crowded animal pens—all food produced for inside world. Sometimes she worked in the kitchens or the laundries, the underground places of inside world. She had never ventured into the upper regions, not even with beauty singers who went on errands there, or who cleaned the streets and houses of inside world. Only a few women workers had permanent assignments. The rest were rounded up daily by the Guard and taken to where they were needed. The guards had all once been brothers and sons to the people they now marched or menaced. Their eyes, to a man, were eerily empty. Everyone outside knew: recruits were tortured and brainwashed, forced to forget everything and everyone they once knew.

Not Jack, Briar whispered to herself, *he would never forget*.

It's my plan, Jack had said.

One dreary morning, when even the sky was bereft of light and color, Briar got a glimpse of him. She was standing with the other women, waiting for the day's work assignment. A formation of guards came to a halt, ready to take selected workers to their stations. And there was Jack at the end of the line, his red-glinting hair, shorn; his dark skin, almost colorless. Even stranger was his stillness. She had never seen him so still. His heavy boots must have been weights holding him down; otherwise surely he would jump to the nearest rooftop, leap as if he might sprout wings any minute.

It's all part of my plan.

Was his uniform just a disguise, like Sal with her bound breasts, or Briar with her veil? Or had they all three, each one, lost themselves, become who they had to be?

She needed to see Jack's eyes to know.

An older guard called Briar and some of the other women out of the crowd without telling them where they were heading. They would find out when they got there. They began to move, the guards surrounding the women in a square formation. Holding her breath, slipping away from the beauty singers who hissed at her to stay close, Briar dropped back until she was walking next to Jack. From under her cloak, so that no one could see her turning her head, she looked at him. She still could not see his eyes; they were trained straight ahead.

Jack, she cried silently, *Jack*. It would be dangerous to call his name out loud. He showed not the slightest awareness of her. Then she felt a sharp jab in her back.

"Move along. No straggling."

Not Jack's voice. Not Jack's.

One of the beauty singers reached back for her hand and pulled her into their midst. She walked on, tears blinding her, but she did not need to see to go nowhere. Yet on the back of her head she felt the lightest touch. As if sunlight had found a way through the thick clouds to shine for a moment, just on her.

Jack's eyes, Jack.

Briar decided then and there, she had to do something. Sal and Jack had always had plans, full of danger and risk, plans that never included her, or that she had never risked. She supposed being a beauty singer was also dangerous, carrying the penalty of death. But unlike Jack and Sal, she was with people who loved her and protected her.

And would still love her, even if she gave them the slip.

✳   ✳   ✳

One night, when Briar's mother and the other women were sound asleep, worn out from a long day's work, Briar got up. She had scrounged scraps of hard cheese and bits of gristle to quiet any dogs she encountered. As much as she had prepared, she didn't really have a plan, only an ache and a longing, only a need she had not named. But her feet knew what she wanted and they took her soundlessly through the alleys, twisting this way and that, in then out and out, till she came at last to the end of the alleys and stood staring at the wall.

It looked higher than it ever had before, as if it would shut out the highest reach of sky. But the moon was higher still, its stark light exposing the wall and the charred remains of the briar patch, echoes of the twisting branches in charcoal at the base. The living briar would not grow again; the patch was being paved. Some of the stone was already laid, and more was stacked and ready for tomorrow's labor.

Somewhere, somewhere in that hard emptiness, she and Jack and Sal had lain tangled together under the tangled briars. On a night like this one with a full moon, bees would go on gathering sweetness. Briar closed her eyes, her memories so vivid, she could smell the roses. She could taste their tongues meeting for the first time, feel their shy hands growing sure. Had their own fire started the fire? For this memory ended in flame and smoke...

She opened her eyes again and let them climb the wall. Was that a shadow she saw? A crack in the wall, the remnant of a vine? What if she could find a way up, what if there was a way down the other side? Briar left the shelter of the alleys and began to tiptoe across the expanse to the wall, seeing her shadow stretching before her. Exposed, she had never been so exposed. She had always run from alley to briar, flanked by her friends. Since then she'd been in a thicket of women. Now here she was out in the open on the hard stones, under the moon's hard gaze. But she had to find out if that shadow in the wall mapped the way.

By the time she heard the sound of marching feet, it was too late to retreat to the alleys; she froze where she was, her shadow huge against the wall. Then the feet stopped.

"Who goes there?" a male voice called. "Who goes there?"

She dared not turn around. She dared not breathe. She stared at the moonlit wall. Her shadow did not look human. She could be a stick, a leafless tree. Then a wind lifted and huge shadows rose against the wall, shadows that swayed and danced, shadows of swirling hair.

"It's only clouds," said a voice. A beloved voice. "Clouds passing over the moon. But I will go and have a look if you like, Captain."

He did know her, he did. He must.

"Ghosts," came a couple of voices.

"You don't want to go any closer."

"Them that was burned in the fire. Ghosts."

"There's nothing there," said the captain sharply. "And that's an order."

He had ordered the ghosts not to exist, and they didn't. There were no ghosts. They were alive. She and Jack were alive. Sal must be, too. She must.

"March," barked the captain.

Behind her she heard the sound of heavy-booted feet moving off. She wanted so badly to follow. But her feet stayed where they were, as if they had sent roots down. Maybe they had, maybe she was turning into a briar. She closed her eyes. The wind stilled, the air was sweet. When she opened her eyes again, the huge clouds were gone, as if they had never been. Her own spindly shadow pointed toward the shadow in the wall, or the vine, or the ghost of a vine. At last she moved toward it.

It was a crack, a small crack, twisting upward like the vine that must have made it. She explored it with her fingers, looking for irregularities that might support a hand or foot. If only they had climbed over that day, searched for a way down, or maybe just flung themselves into the air. Maybe it was not too late. Maybe there was still a chance. They could be three again. They could be free.

Back at their shack, Briar did not see her mother sitting outside waiting for her; the embers of the dung fire had been carefully covered to hold the heat. The glaring moon had slipped behind the dome. Even the dogs and the drunks slept. She was about to lift the blanket that covered the door when she heard a voice cold as the night.

"You, girl."

It took her moment to recognize the voice as her mother's. Why would she call her "girl"? As if she didn't know her.

"Mama, it's me. I just—"

She stopped herself. She had never lied to her mother. She'd never had to. Her mother rarely asked questions.

"I know who you are," her mother said. "But you, you don't know who I am."

Briar turned and saw her mother, sitting straight-backed by the embers, a slender column of darkness.

"Sit with me," her mother said. "You owe me that much for giving you life, for keeping you alive as long as I could."

Briar sat down facing her, though neither of them could see each other's faces. What did her mother mean that Briar did not know her?

"I may not be able to much longer," her mother went on.

"Mama," Briar cried out. "You're not . . . Are you sick?"

She hadn't thought of anything happening to her mother. She hadn't thought of her mother at all.

"Hush," said her mother, not so loud. "Come. Sit close to me."

Briar did as she was told. Her mother put her arm around her, enclosing them both in her blanket.

"Don't fret, child," said her mother in a low voice, "I am not the one who is going."

How did her mother know what she had barely begun to think herself?

"Someone has to stay," her mother went on. "Someone has to take care of the children left behind. Someone has to go on singing. While the other ones make plans . . . "

And die.

Did her mother actually say that, or was it the scrabbling of a rat's feet, the hiss of an ember going out?

"While the other ones make plans," said her mother again.

And fly.

Briar didn't know she had spoken aloud, but her mother answered.

"Maybe so, Briar. It may be so. I hope someday to know."

Her mother sounded so far away, Briar suddenly felt scared. She leaned closer to her mother and laid her head on her heart.

"Who are you, Mama? Tell me who are you."

"Silly girl," her mother said, stroking her hair. "I am your mother. I am Sal's mother, even Jack's. I miss them, too. I'm the mother."

What comfort it was to hear her mother speak their names. Her mother would keep them safe. Somehow her mother would keep them all safe.

"I know you're our mother," said Briar. "But . . . you said I didn't know who you are. Who are you?"

Briar sat up and looked at her mother, the outline of her face just visible in the ember glow.

"Have you watched the starlings fly up at dawn when we sing, how they disappear when they turn on the wing?"

"Yes," whispered Briar.

"That's me."

Briar did not understand what she meant. But she never forgot her mother's words.

Neither did I.

Briar needed to find Sal. The more she thought about it, the surer she was that Jack was still Jack. Maybe just being where the briars used to grow had brought back his memory, brought him back to himself. He had known she was there. He had done what he could to protect her. She had to tell Sal; she had to persuade her, they still had a chance. Together.

Only a very few of the miners went home at night to their families as such. It was a reward for being trustworthy—or for being a snitch, reporting any slacking or disaffection among the other workers, preventing rebellion or conspiracy. The rest of the miners were kept in a guarded camp, where they dulled their misery with drink or with women supplied by the Guard. The beauty singers, all the wives and mothers and older women, warned Briar and the other girls to stay far away from the miners' camp and not to wander alone by night or by day where they would be easy prey for the Guard. Of course it wasn't always necessary for the women to be forced to go to the camp. Some went to see sweethearts or for the drink or to get extra rations for their children. The easiest way and the safest, if there was such a thing as safety, was to go in as part of a group of women.

Not long after her excursion to the wall, Briar slipped away from the circle of women around the fire. She turned at the edge of the light and looked at her mother. Did her mother see her? Did she know where she was going? Briar almost wished her mother would call her back, although Briar also knew she would not answer such a call. Maybe her mother knew, too. For a moment she looked in Briar's direction, her face without expression, and then she looked away.

Briar stepped into the darkness, making her way through the streets in the direction of the camp, guided by the sounds of carousing, shouting, and drunken singing. When she neared the entrance where two guards stood watch, she ducked into a deserted alley and waited in the shadows. She was on the verge of attempting to go in on her own, when she saw a group of women and girls being herded toward the gate. Briar darted out and joined the end of the line. One of the guards waved the women in, indifferently. The other leered.

"Save some of that for us."

Inside the camp, Briar felt overwhelmed and disoriented. Smoke from small fires filled the air, mingling with a stench of strong drink and urine. Unwashed, unshaven men circled the women, catcalling, grabbing, sometimes breaking into fist fights. A few women managed to run to protectors; others waited, most frightened or resigned, a few seemingly eager or hopeful.

Sal was nowhere in sight, but Briar could pretend someone waited for her. Peering into the crowd, she waved and then sprinted as she had seen other women do. More than one man grabbed at her. She did not have to think what to do. Her foot tripped a man here, her hand parried there. Her fist found noses, her fingers eye sockets. And then, oh then, she realized there was someone at her back, back against back, four fists shot out, four legs and feet landed kicks. The two queens of the mountain together again, unbeatable.

At last the men retreated, some laughing, some shamed, some muttering threats. She felt a hand she knew as well as her own take hold of hers.

"Look at the midget!" a man called out. "Got himself a woman!"

"Sure you know what to do with her, son?"

"I could show you a few tricks."

The jeers and cheers faded away as the men lost interest and went to look for other sport. Still holding tight to her hand, Sal led Briar away, past tents and sleeping rolls, to the other edge of the enclosure, where they sat down and huddled together.

"Do you have anything to eat?" Sal asked.

Briar always carried food if she could, not for herself, but as a bribe, if needed, or a gift to someone hungrier than she was. Briar reached into her pockets and found a crust of bread and, even better, a boiled egg. She handed these to Sal, who ate with intensity, just stopping herself before she finished to offer the rest to Briar.

"No, no," Briar said. "It's for you."

She waited until Sal had finished every crumb and scoured the eggshell.

"Are the rations short?" Briar asked.

"No more than anywhere else," Sal said. "Just enough to keep us alive and working. But I'm always hungry. I've never been so hungry. I feel like I could die for food, die happy if just one time I ever had as much as I wanted."

"I know," Briar said.

But maybe she didn't. Even hungry, she had never known the hunger Sal described. There was something changed in Sal.

"Is it all right? In the mines, I mean?"

Sal didn't answer for a moment. And in the silence Briar's mind filled with pictures, darkness, torch light, and what looked like rivers of stars in the rock.

"It's not for you, beauty singer, what comes from the mine. It's not for us," said Sal. "None of it is for us. The miners, they're a rough lot, but not so bad as you might think. We look after each other. I think some of them may know . . . about me, but they don't ask. I'm just one of them."

Briar waited for Sal to go on, but she didn't.

"Any sign of a way out yet?" Briar asked.

Sal had always had a plan. Before Briar put forward her own plan, she needed to know about Sal's. She turned to look at Sal, her profile just darker than the darkness. Sal did not look back. She was looking at something intently, something Briar could not see.

"There is no way out," Sal finally spoke. "We dig and dig, farther and deeper, narrower. I've been to the end of most of the tunnels, because I'm small. When I'm inside I forget there is any outside, any anywhere."

Briar reached for Sal and pulled her close. How could anyone think she was a man? She was so soft, even with her tough wiry arms, her bristling hair, so soft.

"Sometimes, not very often, when I'm left alone, I feel so tired, I curl up and fall asleep. It's probably only a dream . . ."

Sal's voice trailed off. Her head rested on Briar's shoulder.

"Go on," Briar prompted.

"Do you remember the night when the bee woman hid us in the hive?"

"I remember," said Briar. "I remember waking up at dawn."

"Do you remember the dreams?" asked Sal.

Briar felt a sudden confusion, a pang of loss. Had there been dreams? She heard a low humming, she felt it. Bees in the roses, bees in the hive. There had been dreams, terrifying, sweet. But she could not remember. A piece of her memory was missing.

"I didn't remember," Sal was saying. "Not at first, not for a long time. Then the dreams came again."

"Tell me," Briar whispered. "Tell me."

"Huge women, huge as night, dancing. Their hair is the moon and stars, snakes and roots. There is one who comes most often. She is darker than me, dark as earth. I dream she holds me. She rocks me, like the whole ground is rocking and spinning. And then I wake up again, or someone shakes me awake, and it's dark and narrow with squeezing walls, and I have to shovel again. I feel, sometimes, I feel like I'm hurting her. I know that doesn't make any sense. And sometimes, I feel so sick, I can't keep down what little I have in my stomach, and then . . . "

Briar waited, the sounds of drums and fiddles, songs and shouts in the distance, Sal's ragged breathing, her heart beating under Briar's hand.

"And then?" Briar prompted

Sal began to hum, so softly at first, so low, Briar could feel the vibration more than hear it. She felt the humming go into her own body, into her own bones. And they hummed together, rocking gently.

"That is the sound, only it's stronger, deeper. So I know I'm not alone, whether I live or die—"

"Shh," said Briar. "You're not going to die. It's just a dream."

All at once, Briar remembered the moan of wind, the shadows swaying against the wall, enveloping her own small shadow. Surely she had been awake, the night she had almost been caught by the Guard. The night she had found the crack.

"Listen, Sal," said Briar. "I know a way out. We've done it before, we can do it again."

"Do what?" Sal drew apart from her.

"Climb the wall."

Briar pictured the wall, stark in the moonlight, with the shadow snaking its way up. They would wait till the dark of the moon and feel their way, dodging the searchlights, the Guard, the dogs. They would climb into a dark night, to a sky full of stars vast as the desert beyond the wall. They would wait till the dimmest dawn light and then find a way down. She filled her mind with pictures, so sharp, so vivid, Sal would have to see them, too.

"We climbed the wall when we were children, Briar," said Sal. "And now there's no cover. No briars, no bees, no protection. I pass by the wall on my way to the late-night shift. If ever there was any magic there, it's gone."

Briar had never heard Sal sound defeated, Cutlass Sal who'd hacked off her hair, bound her breasts. Sal who was always ready to fight and win.

"Then you didn't look closely enough," Briar said. "I went right up to the wall one night. I found a crack left by a vine. We could climb, you and me and Jack—"

"You and me and Jack," Sal repeated, as if it were an incantation, a magical incantation. "You and me and Jack. But Jack is with the Guard now."

"I know, Sal," said Briar, impatiently.

What were the Guard or the mines to the magic of the three?

"Sometimes he's with the squad that takes us from the camp to the mines," Sal went on. "But he never looks at me, he never speaks to me. You know what they do to the ones they take, Briar. Jack might have forgotten everything."

She was wrong. She had to make Sal see.

"He is still Jack, our Jack. The night I found the crack in the wall, the Guard went right past where I was standing. He saw me. He knew me."

"How do you know?"

"He protected me, Sal. He spoke up to the captain. He said I was only a shadow, but he would go look to be sure."

"And did he? Did he come near you? Did he speak to you?"

"The captain ordered the guard to move on. They're afraid of ghosts, Sal. Everyone thinks we're ghosts. They think we died in the fire."

"If that's so," said Sal slowly, "then Jack's plan might work."

"What plan? I thought you said he hadn't spoken to you."

"Don't you remember, Briar? Jack wants to turn outside world in and inside out. He wants to lead a revolution."

Sudden anger took Briar by surprise.

"You and Jack and your plans. You wanted to tunnel to out there. And now you say there's no way. And Jack who used to somersault in the sky, marches and marches in those awful boots. Why didn't you, why don't you, either of you, listen to *my* plan!"

Sal moved closer again and laid her head on Briar's shoulder.

"Oh, but I do listen, Briar. Every day."

"What do you mean?"

If they had listened to her plan, they would have gone over the wall that day the bees flew away. Whether they lived or died, they would have been together. It would be better than being apart, alone.

"Every day at dawn, I listen, beauty singer. Even when I'm in the mine, I can hear your voice. And Jack, if he's still Jack, as you say, he must listen, too."

Briar was taken aback. All those bitter dawns, the beauty of the song, of her own voice, had left her unmoved. Although she had listened to the beauty singers all her life, she had forgotten . . . listeners.

Sal. Jack.

"You always said you would be a beauty singer," Sal reminded her. "That was your plan."

"But Sal, that wasn't, that's not a plan, that's just—"

"Who you are," said Sal. "Whereas Jack and I, with our plans, we are in disguise."

"We're all in disguise," Briar insisted. "I wear a veil. I don't even believe anymore what I sing. Don't you see, Sal? Who I am, who you are, who Jack is, who we really are, is the three. The way we always have been, the way we were . . . that night."

Neither one spoke for moment. Was Sal remembering, too, how they turned into one sweet tangle?

"That night," said Sal, "everything changed that night."

Briar put her arms around Sal and drew her close, as if their closeness could conjure Jack, complete their embrace.

"Nothing has changed," Briar whispered.

"I've changed," Sal insisted. "Don't you see? If you can't see, feel!"

Sal took Briar's hand and placed it over her breasts, straining through their binding. Then she moved it down to the small swell of her hungry belly.

"Tell Jack," she whispered. "If you see him, if you speak to him, tell him."

"Tell him . . .?" What was Sal saying?

"You know, Briar, you *know*. I wish it had been you instead. You have a place to be, a mother—"

Now she understood, how could she not understand?

"You have a mother, too," she told Sal. "My mother said so. She raised you, Sal!"

Then a whistle shrilled.

"That's for the next shift," said Sal, getting to her feet. "Go, Briar. You don't want to get locked in here."

Sal pulled Briar up.

"Sal, you have to come with me. You can't stay here. Not now. Take off your men's clothes. I'll wrap you in my cloak. We'll leave with the women."

The whistle blew again.

"Whores out!" a voice ordered. "Men to the mines."

"Quick!"

But just as she reached for Sal, two guards searching the perimeter saw them.

"Time's up."

One grabbed Sal and shoved her toward the swarm of miners. The other dragged Briar away with a show of roughness that belied the gentleness of his hand.

"Don't come back here," the guard whispered in her ear. "It's too dangerous. They are still looking for us."

Jack's voice. Jack.

"Jack, listen," Briar whispered. "Sal told me, she told me to tell you, she's—"

The gate was opening for the women.

"Go!" Jack pushed her away. "Go!"

And he fell into formation with the Guard who were flanking the miners.

As she went out the gate, surrounded by the other women, Briar looked back. Sal and Jack were somewhere behind her in their disguises, leading their harsh lives, listening for the beauty singers, listening for her.

All at once she knew what she would do.

✳   ✳   ✳

The next day at dawn, as always, the beauty singers wound their way through the alleys, past the embers of scant fires, past the small dark mountains of rubbish and rubble, past the rats that watched from the sewers, and the forbidden roosters who could not keep from crowing. The women sang their chorus, lifting their voices to the fading stars.

come the sorrow, come the pain
come the sun, come the rain
come the toiling all day long
come the night, come the dawn
beauty will go on, go on, beauty will go on

Sometimes the beauty singers sang messages over the chorus—green seams in the dome where water sluiced down, secret stores of stolen grain. They sang of babies born, of old ones dying, of young ones taken. Now Briar began to sing her own message.

over the edge of the world we go
over the edge of the world we fly

The song of the three, the song they had sung together as children, spinning and laughing. Each day she added more.

over the edge of the world we go
over the edge the wall
in the cracks of vanished vines
we climb without a fall

As the moon waned day by day, dawn by dawn, Briar sang on, weaving in directions.

dark before dawn, dark of the moon
where roses once perfumed the noon

come to be parted nevermore
one and one and one makes four

Each night after everyone slept, Briar crept out of bed and made her way to the alley where she and Sal and Jack would soon meet. When she was sure no one would see her, she would trace the crack with her fingers and begin an experimental climb. One night on her way back, she sensed she was being followed, though she could hear no other footfall. She had almost reached her shack, when someone grabbed her and spun her around.

"Why are you changing the song?"

Briar recognized the voice of the most ancient beauty singer, expert at giving the guard the slip, taking the others with her into invisibility.

"I am only adding to it, grandmother," Briar answered, using the title of respect.

She could feel the old woman looking at her, her eyes keen as a bird's.

"Who told you to do that?"

"No one," she said. "It just came to me."

"Beware, youngest beauty singer, before adding becomes taking away."

She let go of Briar's arm and slipped into the darkness so silently that, if not for the lingering pressure of her bony grip, Briar might have wondered if she had been there at all.

✳   ✳   ✳

After that night, Briar did not sing the words again, just a high tune, wordless, beautiful as a lone bird soaring, weaving in and out of the clouds. With all her might, she wished on the vanishing morning stars for Jack and Sal to hear and understand.

The night of the dark moon, Briar kissed her mother goodbye. Her mother stirred and reached out for Briar, holding her close. Then she sighed and rolled over. Briar would never be sure if her mother had been awake or asleep, if she would feel betrayed, or if she had chosen to let her daughter go.

It was cold where Briar waited in the alley, even wearing all the clothes she had. She was hungry, but she did not want to eat even a crumb from the bread she had in the satchel. Nor would she drink a drop of water till she and Jack and Sal were safely over the wall. So she crouched and waited. And waited. She could see a sliver of stars above the alley, moving imperceptibly but all too quickly. There were only a couple of hours before dawn. At last she heard the sound of swift, surreptitious feet creeping down the alley. And then she was enclosed in a double embrace. Triple when she hugged them back.

"No time to lose," one of them said; or maybe they all did.

They got to their feet, pausing at the opening of the alley, looking and listening, then dashing over the charred earth to the crack in the wall.

"Here," Briar whispered. "Who goes first?"

"You, of course," hissed Sal.

"Sal in the middle," insisted Jack. "So I can catch her if she falls."

Jack knew. Sal must have told him.

"I'm not going to fall," huffed Sal. "Just because—"

"Hurry," urged Briar. "Hurry."

And she began to climb.

Noone

He could not sleep. No, he had chosen not to. He did not need to sleep. He was not like other mortals—and soon he would not be mortal at all. Oh, but the night was long; he watched the stars slowly processing inside the dome, inside his crystal ball. When he was immortal, maybe time would also stop, all this tedious repetition. There would only be select moments, whichever ones he chose, each one eternal, for as long as he liked.

But what were his feet up to now, his legs? Who told them they could leave his chambers, seek those infernal stairs? Well, he had of course. He was in control. He could not help himself. Here he was again, climbing, climbing to that round room that did not exist, with its cracked window looking out on a world he would soon unmake forever.

It must be very late out there where time ran amuck, where sun could burn, rain drench, and wind whip, where mud and sewage met, where moon and stars kept track of themselves. The hooting and howling had died down to sighing, an occasional moan. The footfall of the night guard kept a steady beat. But wait! What was that?

Soft, purposeful panting, now and then a grunt, the sound of loosened mortar falling. He closed his eyes, so he could see.

Three children dancing on a rubbish heap.

Three youths tangled together in the briar roses.

Three runaways climbing—

He opened his eyes and fled the room, forgetting to close the cracked window in his haste to sound the alarm.

All the grannies woke from dreams they could not remember. One by one and all at once they went outside. Granny Sweep to her lookout, Granny Spark to the top of a tree, Granny Dirt out the door in the toe of the boot, Granny Brine onto the deck of the ship.

Something was happening, far away, yet no distance at all.

Briar was more than halfway up when the siren sounded, and the searchlights began to sweep the night.

"Here," she said to Sal below her, "where my foot is. I'm going to lift my foot, then you grab hold."

Sal reached, but she must have lost her own foothold. Briar heard Sal muffle a cry as she fell, taking Jack with her. Briar looked down and saw them in a dark heap.

"It's all right," Jack called to her. "We're both all right."

But it wasn't all right. Light sluiced down the alley. Dogs bayed. Then came the heavy footfall of guards and the dragging song of the miners.

Don't know why, don't know why. Got to dig until I die.

"Run!"

Briar didn't know if she called aloud or if Jack did. They both meant Sal. And Sal, the scrappiest, feistiest of the three, who would have been the last to run, somehow understood. She made as much a dive as a dash toward the miners. A big man, twice Sal's size, scooped her up and hid her in the miners' midst.

Briar began scrambling and slipping down the wall.

"No!" Jack called to her. "Keep going!"

Then the attack dogs burst out of the alley.

"Run!" Briar shouted to Jack.

And Jack did, not away but straight toward them, scattering the pack as he tumbled into the air, somersaulted so high it looked for a moment as though he would fly. A flock of small birds tore up into the blood-stained sky. For a moment Jack floated, suspended.

Wings, he had wings.

Then he fell, spiraling down, a stray feather, his feet never touching the ground.

The Guard bore him away.

we sing the dawn the dawn the dawn
beauty will go on, go on, beauty will go on

The voices of the beauty singers, high as fading stars, came from everywhere and nowhere. One lone voice rose higher.

over the edge of the world we go,
over the edge of the world we fly

"There's one of them, up against the wall!" cried a guard. "Not just a runaway, but one of them singers. Our lucky night."

"We were supposed to get three runaways."

"Two's better than one or none."

"Seize her."

Seize her, shouted Noone, hands over his ears, to shut out the sound of the song, spilling through the crack of the window, down the hidden stairs that did not, could not, must not exist.

Granny Sweep leaned out over the edge, her arms still outstretched. He had tumbled so high, how had she failed to catch him?

Granny Spark saw the dawn fiery as her hair. From far away came a voice, piercing as stars, fierce, burning, then lost in the light.

Granny Dirt closed her eyes and hugged the girl she had dreamed close to her heart. For now the child inside her womb was safe. For now.

Granny Brine watched stars and birds drift over the cliff. The bells rang, the bones of the temple rattled. Queens and king.

When would they have wings?

Rose

The room was almost silent, as silent as it could be. Even the aunties tried to sniffle quietly. My mother held her breath, then let it out, like a wind from far away, wind I had never known in my little inside life. I opened my eyes, not knowing till I did that I had closed them. I saw the room that had been my whole world, false planets and stars moving across an unreal sky.

"What happened?" I formed the words, but it was like trying to speak aloud in a dream. "What happened to Jack?"

My mother's head was bowed. I couldn't see her eyes.

The aunties sobbed and hiccupped.

Then I remembered something I hadn't fully understood before. *The baby*. Jack had shouted to Sal to run. *Because of the baby*. I didn't know anything about babies. I had never seen one, though of course I knew I had been one, had grown from one into the girl I was, a girl old enough to hear this story.

"What happened to Sal?" I asked. "What happened to . . . the baby?"

My mother wept silently, her face covered with her hands.

"That's enough questions, Rose," said Auntie Vinda, "enough questions for one night. It is time for you to go to bed."

"I am not a child," I objected, even though of course I was.

"I don't know, Rose," my mother lifted her head at last. "I don't what happened to the baby. And Jack . . . I don't know . . . I will tell you what I can."

"Not tonight," pleaded Auntie Aloe. "I can't bear anymore tonight."

"Let your mother rest," said Auntie Vinda.

"Before she tells you the rest," said Auntie Aloe.

"Tomorrow," said my mother, "I will tell you the rest tomorrow."

A new question rose, one that couldn't wait. I had never wondered before how babies were made. But all at once I could smell the roses, see the stars, real stars, overhead. I could feel the tangle of arms and legs, hands and lips, Briar, Jack, and Sal all tangled together.

"Am I," I hardly knew how to form the question, but I was determined to find a way. "Am I Jack's baby, too, and Sal's and yours?"

In the silence I heard the flames roaring, the smoke, just as if I had been there that terrible dawn.

"Say yes," whispered Auntie Aloe.

"Just say yes," echoed Auntie Vinda.

My mother took a deep breath.

"I don't know," she said on a gust of bitter, cindered wind.

"Whose baby am I?" I whimpered, forgetting I was not a baby at all.

"Mine," she said firmly. "Mine."

She held out her arms for me, but for the first time in my life, I didn't go.

What happened to you?

I had not even asked her.

PART FOUR

Briar Inside

Rose

There were many tomorrows before I heard the whole story. Time and place got tangled up. My life and my mother's, what she told me, what she did not. I did not rest much between tellings. I was restless. But I did not try to get out of the room again. I would not go out again without knowing everything I could know. So I spent my days dreaming and drawing. Jack spinning in the air, the wind reaching out to catch him. Sal rocking in the arms of the earth. And each night my mother returned to our room, our womb, the safety I had breached. Head bent, voice low, she told me more and more, while my aunties rocked back and forth and moaned softly.

What happened to my mother I could not draw, could hardly imagine. And yet imagining was all I could do.

Briar

The sound of water.

Briar heard it even before she opened her eyes. She did not recognize what it was at first, coming from a world where water trickled, ran in muddy ditches after rain, fell into buckets. This water moved, somewhere over her or under her. And it stank of rotten eggs, sewage, a familiar smell in an unfamiliar place, cold, damp, and, except for the water, silent.

She opened her eyes, closed them again in terror. Then she opened them again. It made no difference. There was no light; this was not night. No dung fires burning in yards, no scrap of moon, no stars. The air was colder and more still than any dawn, as if it was holding its breath against the stench. There was no breath, except her own, and she hardly dared breathe. No one stirred, no mother, no dog, no bird, or rat.

What had happened to her, where was she?

Sal's face lost to her sight, Jack tumbling into the sky.

Her arms, she could feel them now, sore. Feeling was coming back into her body, bruised, scraped, a sharp ache in her ribs.

She closed her eyes again and tried to imagine falling, flying over the edge of the world. You weren't ever supposed to reach the bottom, but somehow she had. For this must be the bottom of the world.

The bottom of the world, cold, damp, with the sound of a sewer flowing on and on.

I sing the dawn. She tried to make a sound, but her throat wouldn't open. *Beauty will go on.*

But it wouldn't, it hadn't, it didn't, it couldn't.

Beauty had abandoned her.

She should try to get up, she told herself, find a way out, up. When she tried to move, something stopped her, something colder than the cold of the air. Shackles. She was shackled to the ground.

How long she lay sleeping, waking, shivering, sweating, she did not know. She hoped she would die. She hoped she was not dead already. If this was death, it brought no ease. If this was death, then there was no escape. She did not know what could be more terrible than this place.

Until the huge door swung open and light glared in. A figure stood in the doorway.

"Clean her up and bring her to me in my private chambers."

She could not tell if it was a man's voice or a woman's. It sounded dead and still as the air. It held no emotion. It terrified her.

The figure moved away, taking its shadow with it. Then the doorway filled with two larger figures. They approached her and knelt down, one on either side.

"Where's the key?"

"I thought you had it."

"No, you had it."

"I never did. You better not have lost it. He'll have our wigs, and then our scalps."

"The vat; we'll be tossed into the vats."

"No, he wouldn't do that. We're too useful."

"Wait, here it is."

"I told you, you had it."

"Stop fussing. Here, I've unlocked this side. You do the other side."

These voices sounded like men's voices, but whoever these hulks were, they smelled sweet, like pie, like roses.

Tears sprang to her Briar's eyes.

"All right, up you get, sewer rat. By the dome, the stench on her! I can hardly keep hold of her for needing to pinch my nose."

"She's limp as a ragdoll."

"Can you walk, little rat?"

"Can you stand?"

She could not.

"They probably broke both her legs."

"And ripped her tongue out."

"Can you talk?"

"No," she croaked.

"Well, you will soon. A few minutes with him, and you'll sing, all right."

Sing?

"Come on, then."

"Come on, first things first."

"No one wants to probe someone who's pissed themselves."

"Got to be fresh for the next round of torture."

"Ups-a-daisy."

And the two gigantic beings lifted her up and made a seat for her with their huge arms.

Briar had never had a hot bath before. There was never so much water at once in outside world, and no one would have used the fuel it would have taken to heat it. How could she be a prisoner and then treated to such luxury? For she must be a prisoner. The giants, who wore dark, plain uniforms that contrasted with their bright towering hair and painted faces, stood guard by the door. The small room was dimly lit by some source she could not see. She was grateful that they hadn't taken it upon themselves to scrub her. One had drawn the bath, while the other had stripped her of her torn, bloody rags. Then they had lifted her, not quite tenderly, but carefully, and lowered her into the tub. The water was so comfortable that, for a moment, she forgot to be afraid. She closed her eyes and leaned back.

"Does the chief want us to feed it first?"

"It's not an it, sister. Very clearly a she. Why do you always call them it?"

"You know why. It doesn't do to get attached. But you do anyway, you always want to turn them into pets, even the rats."

"There were never any rats."

"Not inside, but before."

"We're not supposed to talk about before."

"We're not supposed to talk at all."

And for a moment, they didn't.

"But as to my question—"

"I don't know anything more than you do, sister. We were both there. He said to clean it up and bring it to him in his private chambers."

"He said *her*. Bring *her*. Poor little thing."

"Don't get attached! Well, I suppose we better get on with it. I'll fetch it some clothes."

"Won't stay on long, poor dear."

"That is none of our business."

"It's all our business. We have no other business."

"We have no business."

"Hush. Then don't talk about it. Fetch the clothes."

The clothes were soft and clean, not fancy clothes, like the dress she had seen floating around the lady when she was child, but they were inside clothes. She had seen garments like them when she worked in the laundries. The plain white tunic fell over wide, flowing pants that tied at the ankle. Why were they giving her nice clothes?

Only so they could be taken off.

"Undress her."

Those were the man's first words.

"And put her on the examining table."

The gigantic women, with the voices like men, did as they were told and soon she was naked on a table in the glare of light, bright but without warmth and without a visible source. A white ceiling curved like the sky it was not. Something like clouds or smoke drifted across it, not gray or black or even brown, no color. She managed to turn her head away from the man. Across a room that was bigger than she had first thought, were vats of something that bubbled and steamed but gave off no smell. The strange fog came from there. She thought she saw shapes, of animals mostly, but the shapes came apart as if something or someone she could not see tore at them.

"You are dismissed," said the voice that also seemed to have no shape or color.

She looked up at the giant beings, one at her head (she could see inside the nostrils), the other at her feet, the one with the bright red wig and green on her eyelids. Something flickered in this one's eyes (was she the one who got attached?) and then went out.

"I said, dismissed."

They lumbered away, and Briar felt panicked. In that short time, whether they meant well or ill, they'd been her caretakers; like a kitten being cared for by dogs, she had imprinted on them. Now she was alone with someone who could command them to come or go, fetch, lay her broken body out on a table.

"Now," said the man, walking once around the table, looking at her from every angle before he stopped at the foot. "Let's find out what you are made of."

He regarded her, his face like his voice, smooth and unreal. Was he wearing a mask? What was *he* made of? She didn't know, and it frightened her. She could not tell what his body was like either. He wore a dark robe that was more like a shadow than a color. It gleamed a little when he moved.

"What are you feeling?"

She did not know what he wanted. No one had asked her that before. Her mother might have asked, how are you feeling, if she was sick. But mostly people didn't ask questions in outside world. Everyone knew the answers.

"Fear?" he prompted. "Are you afraid?"

He did not sound concerned, only precise. He needed a point of information. In outside world, no matter how afraid you were, you would never say so. Everyone was afraid, the same as everyone was hungry. You didn't talk about it. So she said nothing.

"What are you feeling?" he asked again, patiently, insistently. "Are you in pain?"

Pain, another thing never to admit, though her pain was becoming excruciating. Why ask someone who was bruised all over, whose bones had been broken?

"What are you feeling?" he asked again.

His face came too close to hers. His breath was cold.

"Cold," she said. "Cold."

"Good."

The mask of the face stretched into what she supposed was a smile. She wondered if it would split open, fall off. What was underneath?

"Good," he said again. "Then I shall warm you."

He parted his robe; she thought for a moment he was going to take it off and cover her with it, but before she knew what was happening, he covered her with himself. She struggled the way she'd seen beetles struggle on their backs. No, not even that much. Her legs would not move, her arms were pinned by his hands. And then he was inside her, sharp, quick, cold.

"There," he slid off her. "Now you are no longer cold."

But she was cold, colder than she had ever been, except for something scalding between her legs.

"What are you feeling now?"

His voice had become more insistent.

Dead, she wanted to say, but that wasn't what she meant.

"Killed," she whispered. "Killed."

"What did you say?"

She wanted to shake her head, but she couldn't move. She bit her tongue, till it bled.

His face receded; it looked as though it floated on the ceiling, a malicious moon. His hand flew toward her face. She closed her eyes against the coming blow. But it never landed, he stroked her cheek, his hand cold, so cold.

"We shall make great discoveries together," he told her.

Then he reached into his pocket for a bell; when he rang it, the sound buzzed in her bones and teeth. The giantesses appeared, almost fluttering like huge moths.

"Dress her wounds, set her bones, feed her. Next time I see her, I want her in one piece."

As if she weighed nothing, Briar was borne away in the arms of the huge women, one of them reaching down to scoop up the soft, fallen garments.

Dreams and Delirium

Inside and outside kept changing places. That's how it seemed to Briar as she moved through unmarked days, in and out of delirium. Inside world, if that is where she was, surrounded her. It was gray and close and blurry, when it was not bright and hard and glaring. Her body had been broken and invaded by this strange, horrible world. Yet if she went inside deep enough, she found vastness, skies without walls, water that roared and swelled and went on and on. And huge plants with roots that held the earth. And fire that turned into stars.

Waking and sleeping changed places, too. Waking was nightmare and sleeping was dawn and her old place among the briars, birds nesting and singing in the thickets. Sleeping was a piece of honeycomb held out to her by a brown hand. Sleeping was when she turned and there were Jack and Sal, children again, their hands sticky with honey, too.

One night, she dreamed of the old bee woman, made of a thousand translucent wings, her touch a tingle, her voice a humming, taking them into the hive. This time Briar could see and hear and smell and taste. This time she would remember the dreams. There was Sal curled in a tangle of loving roots; there was Jack catching hold of the wind. There was the dung fire with mothers and children gathering round. All around them, in the hive and beyond, the scent of roses and salt, the music of bells, the rattle of bones . . .

Then faint and faraway came the voices of the beauty singers.

gone the light of moon and sun
but beauty cannot be undone

beauty will go on, go on
beauty will go on

Let me not wake up, she pleaded, *let me stay with you. Don't let me wake up*. The voices of the beauty singers faded away into the sky she could no longer see.

✳ ✳ ✳

"Its fever has broken."

Someone laid a huge hand on her forehead, one of the giantesses, whose faces and voices blurred in her waking nightmares. Briar kept her eyes closed.

"She's going to live."

"At least for now."

"What does he want with this one?"

"What do you think? Same thing as all the others."

Briar felt the hovering giantesses stand up. She opened her eyes to a squint.

"Immortality," they sang, "pie in the sky, he always thinks it's drawing nigh."

And as they sang, they danced a sort of jig, swinging each other round and round, laughing till they cried. Then they pulled up chairs, one on either side of her, and sat down. Briar closed her eyes again. If she had to be awake, she might as well eavesdrop.

"Do you think he'll ever get the potion to work?"

"Well, until he does, the crocodiles won't go hungry."

There was a pause. Briar resisted the temptation to open one eye.

"If he succeeds, do you think he'd ever offer it us, the immortality?"

"Offer's got nothing to do with it."

"It's selection, election, all based on perfection," they chanted together.

"And aren't we perfect, sister? The most successful experiment ever?"

"Brother, we are freaks."

"Don't call me brother."

Briar cracked an eye open. Just over her head, the giantesses were doing some sort of play fighting with their immense pinky fingers.

"There," said one, dropping back into her seat, "I've vanquished you again."

"Haven't."

"Have."

"Have it your way."

Another ponderous pause.

"But seriously, he does seem more intent on this one than on the others."

"Poor thing, poor thing."

"Don't get attached, sister. He's scheming something."

"I think . . . he might have heard her singing."

"Everyone heard it singing. Even down here."

Briar's eyes widened.

"Hush, sister, she's awake. Come on, darling," said the one with the damper eyes, the one whose hair was a soft shade of blue.

"Let's get you dressed and fed," the orange-haired one stood up. "He wants you wide awake today."

Briar closed her eyes again. One of them pinched her cheek, gently, if a pinch could said to be gentle.

"Come now. We know you're awake. You can't sleep forever. Not yet anyway."

"Up then. Your legs have mended nicely. We know you can stand."

There wasn't much use in falling down. She was already at the bottom of the world.

"Today you'll walk on your own, there's a lamb."

"If you can walk, then you can run."

"Plenty to run from, but nowhere to run to."

"Sit down at the table, there's a daisy."

She sat and they set down a bowl of gray porridge in front of her.

"If we have to eat this slop, I'd hope he succeeds in doing away with the stomach."

"It's not the stomach that suffers, but the nose, the tongue."

"Has it got one? Open up!"

The red-haired giantess pried open her jaws and reached in to grab the tongue she tried to retract.

"It's there. A word to the wise, you'd better start using your tongue or it'll be the worse for you."

"And for us. Come now, one word, and I'll give you a sweet."

She clamped her mouth shut.

"Come on then, you've got eat."

The blue-haired giantess put some gruel on a spoon, then reached into the recesses of her uniform and brought out a bright red glistening berry.

Outside world, outside world.

She placed it on top of the gruel. Briar's mouth opened, the berry went in, and she savored it. Sun and sweetness on her tongue, outside world inside.

"It didn't speak. You're spoiling it. You're getting attached."

"Thank you," Briar whispered.

"She spoke! She spoke!"

And the two giantesses danced a jig with their pinkies linked.

What She Sees in his Eyes

"I'm glad to see you are feeling better," said the man with the mask for a face.

She was not feeling better. Not after walking past the cages, men, women, and children. Some curled into balls, some shouting for help, people who had been arrested for thieving or black marketeering or more likely for nothing at all but being in the wrong place at the wrong time. Or for trying to escape . . .

Jack might be one of them.

Stop. She must not think of Jack or Sal in this man's presence, Briar told herself. She must keep her face as masked as his. At least she was seated today, not stretched out helpless on the table. At least she had her clothes on today. She had the power of her limbs. Her will. She could run. (*Plenty to run from but nowhere to run to*.) If she could not run, she could—

"I have been waiting," he interrupted her thoughts, "waiting for a long time."

She waited for him to go on, but he didn't. Was he waiting for her to speak? Well, he could just keep waiting then. She looked down at her feet, in the soft, felt slippers she'd been given, she who had never worn real shoes, whose feet had always been dirty. She curled her toes, feeling their unfamiliar cleanness.

"Look at me," he commanded. "Look into my eyes."

No, she resisted silently.

"You will look. There is something you need to see."

Was it her own curiosity, or did he compel her?

She looked up at his eyes. At first there was nothing to see. They were empty, lightless. They could have been made of clouded night sky or a dull puddle. Then shapes began to form, chaotic shapes, wind and dust, torrents of muddy water, fire and smoke. Then nothing again, nothing. Out of the nothing rose something smooth and glittering and shining. And inside the shining thing, bright as a drop of dew, she could glimpse a world, gardens, fountains, richly dressed people. She could no longer see the man or his eyes, only the shiny world, small as a bauble. She could not stop herself, she reached out . . .

And the beautiful world dissolved into darkness, but not empty darkness. It was a hovel, like any hovel in outside world, and a woman inside wailing as she gave birth. No sooner had she swaddled her baby than it turned into a corpse wrapped in a shroud, and there was more wailing. She saw the rubbish heap, where she and Jack and Sal had played, all its stink and treasure, bone and rough stone. She saw them, the three, sinking, sinking, down into the mud and dirt where they couldn't breathe.

And then, bobbing up out of the muck, the beautiful world. This time she was inside the world, bathed in light that came from everywhere, among the richly dressed people, murmuring and meandering by the gardens and the fountains. But something was wrong, horribly wrong. Inside the dazzling clothes were skeletons, eyes sockets and nose holes, gaping and empty.

Like his eyes, his eyes that would not let hers go.

"You see," he said.

His voice broke the hold of his gaze. She squeezed her eyes tight shut and did her best to see nothing. But behind her lids, the darkness sparked and sparkled, the way Sal had described the veins of magic in the mine.

"So you see, you must see," he went on, "it all means nothing, the magic that made the beautiful world of the dome, it means nothing if we cannot conquer death."

Death. Jack spinning into the air. What happened after that?

"Open your eyes," he commanded. "You can't shut out the truth by closing them. Though most people's eyes are closed even when they are open. Their whole life is only a dream, a pretty dream or a nightmare, it doesn't matter which. It all ends the same way."

What was waking, what was dreaming? She didn't know anymore. She kept her eyes shut.

Open your eyes, open your eyes, whispered different voices, a voice like wind, a voice like water. And other voices, bees in their hive hidden in the stone. *Keep your eyes open, keep them open.*

And so she let her eyes fall open, like petals loosened from a rose, and there she was in that room at the bottom of the world, with the strange fog from the vats and the stranger man, who'd pinned her to the table when she could not move.

Killed her, but she was not dead.

"It was necessary," he said.

Was he speaking about what he had done to her? Could he read her thoughts?

"It was an initiation, a commingling of our mortal essences to ready us for immortality."

She felt her mortal essence rising to her throat. She wanted to be sick.

"We need not repeat that spell, unless for pleasure. Pleasure."

The word "pleasure" had a substance; it oozed around the room with the fog, swirling around her feet, creeping up her legs. Her whole body shuddered.

"That's right," he said. "You see? Pleasure."

No, she cried silently. Pleasure is honey and sun, roses opening in the full moon light, Jack, Sal. *Stop*, she told herself. *Don't think of them here. Not here.*

"You and I have other work to do. I've been waiting, waiting for a long time."

He was back where he'd started. And she still did not know what he meant.

"For you."

She tried again to look anywhere but at his face, and she failed. Her throat tightened; she didn't know if she could breathe.

"Go on, speak or you'll choke on your silence. Don't be afraid, speak."

Was she compelled or did her own will rise up?

"I don't," she began, "I don't know what you're talking about. You're making a mistake."

There, those at least were her words.

"You don't know what I am talking about," he said in that voice that was as expressionless as his face. "That is true. I don't expect you to understand yet. How could you? But I am not making a mistake. I don't make mistakes. I experiment, I observe. I wait. I conclude. I begin again, but I don't make mistakes. I am not mistaken in you."

You are, she wanted to say. *I am no one. I am a raggedy girl from outside world who has never had enough to eat or warm clothes. I have scrubbed shit out of insiders drawers, stains from their gowns. I've sweated in the sun and shivered in the cold and played on a rubbish heap. I've licked water dripping from stone. I have seen people die of fever and hunger. I've seen the old driven out, and the brave marched away to the edge of world . . .*

She was clinging to all she knew, to who she was, because she could feel it slipping away, seeping away.

"Noone heard you singing," he said.

Everyone heard her singing, even down here, according to the giantesses. Now he said no one had. What did it mean? Why did it matter?

"Noone heard you singing."

She felt herself growing dizzy. She just wanted to go to sleep again. Curl up in a corner somewhere and sleep.

"Noone heard you singing from high in his tower. It disturbed him; it terrified him. He came to me. He always comes to me. He is the one who dreams. I am the one who knows. I am the magician, the one who makes magic real. I've been waiting, waiting all this time."

Waiting, her eyelids were heavy, so heavy, weighted. *Keep your eyes open.* But she was so tired.

"Waiting for the sound, *the* sound . . ."

His voice was in her ear, inside her mind, and also far, far away.

"Sing, beauty singer, sing."

Suddenly she was on high alert. She opened her eyes and saw the man, and at the same time she heard the rush of wings, the scattering of feet when the beauty singers ran from the Guard.

"No singing," she told him. "It is against the law. Anyone caught singing is sent over the edge of the world."

Then why not sing? she asked herself. *Over the edge of the world we go, over the edge of the world we fly.* Why not sing? Why not fly, or die?

"I am the law," he said. "I am more than the law. I am the below to Noone's above. I am the hope of no tomorrow. For there will be no time when death is dead."

"I don't know what you're talking about," Briar said again.

"Your voice. Your voice is the one I have been waiting for. Everything else is in readiness."

"Well, you can't have it," she snapped. "It's *my* voice. You can't force me to sing."

For a moment his face almost had an expression, but she could not say what it was.

"Oh, but I can," he said.

A few minutes with him, and you'll sing, all right.

"But I think I will not need to."

Was he smiling? Could his mask stretch that far?

"Immortal life. No death. What if you could give immortal life to Jack, to Sal?"

How did he know about them? (Her thoughts; she had failed to hide them, her thoughts.)

"I don't know what you're talking about," she said for the third time.

"No, you don't," he said again. "Not yet. For now, sing for me, beauty singer. Sing. I will know the note when I hear it."

Unbidden by him, she closed her eyes again. *What do I do? What do I do?* Who was she asking? She saw her mother's face. She saw the beauty singers, tiny as a flock of birds etched against the dawn sky, their voices as far away as stars. She saw the crooked, crowded streets of outside world, children climbing and tumbling on the rubbish heaps. She heard the bees in the roses and something deeper, underneath everything, thrumming. *What do I do, what do I do?*

Briar did not know who she was asking.

Granny Sweep gazed out from her promontory. She thought someone had called to her, someone no bigger than a cricket, no bigger than a minute, but with a voice as bright and piercing as stars. For a moment she almost remembered what she had forgotten.

"Ah," Granny Spark sighed her pleasure. And then she stopped. Someone was calling, and it was not her latest lover. "Speak again," she whispered. "I almost hear you. I almost remember."

"Hush children." They tumbled to a halt around Granny Dirt's feet. Even the fussy baby she'd been rocking ceased squalling. She cocked her head like a robin listening for worms stirring in the dirt. But it was gone, and so was what she had almost remembered.

The sea was in Granny Brine's eyes, flowing down her cheeks. "I hear you," she whispered. "I will not forget you. Sing, not for him, sing for us."

*   *   *

Briar did not know who answered.

Almost before she knew it was happening, she heard her own voice, the voice she'd taken for granted, soaring, swooping, weaving in and out of the other women's voices, finding its way everywhere, into the mines, the barracks, the dungeons, singing beauty, bringing ruin . . .

"Stop!" someone spoke, a dried leaf scuttling on stone, a rotted door rasping open; that's what the voice sounded like. "Stop!"

Briar opened her eyes and saw a man standing before her, holding his face in his hands, an ancient face, dry as his voice, veined as a skeletal leaf, wisps of beard like lost trails of clouds overflowing his hands, tears standing at the rim of reddened eyes.

"Stop!" he said again, though she had stopped. "Send her away, send her over the edge of the world with the other rebels."

Please, Briar thought, *oh please. Send me. Let me go.*

"Noone," said the man who called himself a magician.

What did he mean by no one?

"This is the ingredient we've been waiting for. This sound is what we need to complete the work."

The ancient one turned toward Briar's tormentor. He looked so slight that a wind could lift him, if there were a wind in this still place. In contrast, the magician seemed dense, immovable.

"This is *my* world," said the old man. "From the dung heap I have created the world, I have created *you*. Without my dreaming, your magic has no power. The unborn star floating in the darkness of the vats remains sterile."

"Your dreaming alone has failed to call it forth," countered the magician. "Why are you so afraid of your dream coming true?"

The two men stared at each other with the intensity of two alley cats before a spat or the air before a storm. Then the magician broke it by looking away. His glance swept over Briar as if she were something inanimate, incidental that had gathered a sheen of dust. He reached for his bell and rang it. The giantesses appeared.

"Take her away till I call for her again."

"Wait!" commanded the old man.

He approached Briar and bent close to her. His breath felt like spider webs on her face.

"Where are they?" he demanded. "Where are the other two?"

Briar kept her eyes open, but she tried to close her mind. *Over the edge of the world, we go, over the edge of the world we fly.* Briar could still hear their voices.

"Why do you ask me?" she managed to say.

It was not her will that had separated the three, not her will that had lost her Sal and Jack. The old man peered at her, his face not a mask but a parched, barren landscape.

"Take her away," he said at length, running his hands over his eyes. "Take her away until *I* decide what shall be done. Until *I* know how the dream ends."

Briar and the Giantesses

Briar barely felt her feet touch the ground as the giantesses, holding an elbow each, skimmed her along through the corridors, and then down the skyless courtyards lined with cells where the other prisoners cursed and moaned. They paused by the room where she'd been fed and tended.

"Let's not put it back yet," said one giantess to the other.

"Let's not, not yet. Too boring just to stand guard. Or sit. "

"They won't miss it for a while."

"They'll be going on for hours, those two. Last time they argued for seven progressions of light and dark."

"Let's have some fun." Fun with the huge beings, their deep voices, their alarming faces, sounded frightening. "I know. The closet!"

"Oh, sister, really? The closet? Our precious closet?"

"Nothing else is ours. There's nowhere else to go. Just this once."

They held Briar suspended between them. She swayed back and forth as if she were a scrap of laundry caught in a breeze.

"Well, all right. Just this once."

"The closet, the closet, take her to the closet."

They began to chant, "a tisket, a tasket, better than a basket."

And still holding her elbows, they danced one of their jigs.

"I bet it's never seen a closet."

They resumed their progress down the corridor.

"Of course not. There are no closets in those shanties."

"There are no clothes, except the rags on their backs."

"What fun we shall have with our live little poppet."

And they stopped and twirled her in the air, making her feel dizzy and faint.

"Wait till you see!" Setting her on her feet again, they finally addressed her, their low voices squeaking with excitement.

"Our closet is not like other closets."

"It is a secret closet."

"It is a magic closet."

"No one knows about it, not even Noone."

"Not even the chief."

They dropped their voices to a whisper as they turned from one corridor into a another that began, so it seemed to Briar, to wind upward.

"You must promise not to tell."

"Never, ever tell."

"Why would you show me?" Briar asked. "If it's such a secret?"

She had once had a secret way through the briars. She had shared it with Jack and Sal. They had never told; none of them had ever told. And yet someone had found out. Noone, the old man called Noone. *Where are the other two?* He knew about the three, he knew. Even secrets, especially secrets, were not safe. Telling them or keeping them.

"That's right, sister. Why *are* we showing her?"

They paused and spoke over her head to each other.

"It's because it's pretty, isn't it?"

"You're pretty," they said together.

You're too pretty, Briar, Sal had said.

"Yes, pretty, pretty, pretty."

"Is that a good enough reason?"

"It is."

"Isn't."

" 'Tis."

" 'Tisn't."

Their back and forth went on and on. They began to propel her forward through a series of twists and turns that there was no danger of her remembering. They appeared to have forgotten that she had never promised not to tell. At last they came to a broader corridor filled with that strange light that came from nowhere. The floor sloped gently upward, and the walls were empty and smoother than any surface Briar had ever seen. She wanted to touch the walls, but she was still held firmly between the giantesses. They stopped and faced a blank curve of wall.

"Here goes nothing."

"Here goes everything."

Without knowing how—at least not then—Briar found herself on the other side of the wall. A scent of mustiness and sweetness washed over her. There was almost but not quite a breeze moving through a room that was bigger than any dwelling in outside world, as big or bigger than the chief magician's chambers. But instead of gray fog, there were colors everywhere, more colors than Briar had ever seen, except perhaps in a dawn or dusk sky. Even though she could not see where the movement came from, the colors swished against each other, floating yet substantial.

"Come," said the giantesses, "feel, look, breathe."

They led her through what she might have thought of as a forest of gowns if she'd ever seen a forest. It would be easy to get lost in the rows upon rows of gowns, some smooth and shiny like water, others loosely woven with dozens of different colors, some the color of moon and night, others as light as sunlight.

"Why do you have so many gowns?" Briar wondered.

"We collect them."

"Where did you get them?" she asked.

"We stole them."

"Fair and square."

"When we were slaves to the fine ladies."

"Before we became bodyguards."

"Bodyguards?" Briar asked, vaguely, focused on a gown that held the colors of rose petals and stone and honey all at once.

"You see, we got caught stealing."

"Red-handed, our hands in the most beautiful red satin . . ."

"But they never found our stash."

"No, they never found our stash."

"What happened to you?" Briar wanted to know.

Thieves that got caught in outside world were jailed or beaten or both. She had heard of servants to insiders disappearing and never returning.

"They sent us down."

"Down to the dungeons."

"We thought we'd be sent over the edge of the world. Or boiled in the vats."

"But the chief decided we could be useful."

"You see. We can be dainty and strong."

"Manly and womanly."

"Versatile, that's what we are. Tricksy."

"But why would the . . . chief need bodyguards? Isn't he a magician?" Briar wondered, holding the fabric against her cheek. It felt warm, as if the sun was shining on it.

"Oh, he has enemies, the chief does, inside and outside, upstairs and below."

"Hush, we're showing it the secret closet, not telling it state secrets."

"Come on, poppet. There's lots more to see."

And they tugged at her elbow, but she held on to the fabric.

"You can take the dress with you."

She slipped it off a hanger and folded it into Briar's arms.

"You can try on as many gowns as you like."

"Try them on?" She was amazed.

"Oh, yes! By the dome, don't you understand? We are playing the game, the best game!"

"What game?"

"Dress up! Have you never played dress up?"

"Of course it hasn't. Not outside."

"Neither had we."

"That's why we became . . . well . . ."

"Thieves," said Briar.

"Harrumph," they both grumbled.

"Well, you said you stole the dresses."

" 'Thieves' is one word, and 'going incognito' is another, we had to—"

"Hush, sister, remember, we said no state secrets."

"The bell could ring any minute."

"The blasted bell."

"The dread bell."

"That infernal bell."

"That tolls for our toil."

✳   ✳   ✳

Briar stopped paying attention to the giantesses' babble, and soon they stopped paying attention to themselves as they wandered through thickets of gowns, heaping garments into Briar's arms and then moving on to another wing of the closet, where voluminous dresses matched their size, to find outfits for themselves.

"Maybe that's enough for now."

"It's so hard to stop."

"I know, let it pick one last gown for each of us."

"Oh, yes, choose, poppet, choose."

And they gestured around them at dresses still floating just above the floor. She had never chosen a garment for anyone else to wear. With a decisiveness that surprised her, she selected a flame-colored gown with hints of blue and green for the blue-haired giantess, and for the fiery one she chose a deep blue with swishes of silvery gray. They eyed her choices dubiously.

"Shouldn't it be the other way round?"

"No," said Briar. "Try them on and see."

"All right, to the dressing room! What followed might have been called a storm if it had happened in outside world. Garments in a gale wind, swirling, flying on and off, landing in heaps, like petals, leaves. The giantesses laughed and shrieked and swore. Overwhelmed, Briar kept her eyes closed much of the time, lifting her arms when told or bending her head, getting stuck inside some many-layered construction. She could never have guessed dressing could be so complicated.

At last a silence fell, a calm, as if the wind had stilled, the clouds parted, the sun come out.

"Look," the giantesses said. "Look!"

And they led her toward a shining wall where Briar saw a girl standing before her, wearing the dress she had wanted, the one the color of rose, stone, and honey. How had that girl gotten her dress? Where had she come from, and why were the two giantesses standing there staring at the girl, wearing the dresses she had chosen for them?

"By the crocodiles down below! I do believe it's never seen a mirror!"

"They don't have mirrors outside, remember?"

"It's hard to remember ever living without a mirror."

"Poppet, this is a mirror. That's you. You! Do you see?"

Briar shook her head, and the other girl shook her head.

"Your reflection. Surely you've seen reflections in pools of water."

"Puddles. They only have puddles in outside world."

"Or in a rain barrel."

Briar remembered gazing at the sky pooling on the ground, how she would see the mud one minute and, by shifting her focus, a cloud the next. She and Sal had squatted and leaned over the puddle trying to see their faces, but they laughed so hard, the puddle would ripple with their breath and they would go back to splashing each other instead.

"But that's not water," Briar said. "The mirror. What's it made of?"

"Magic," they both answered at once.

What is magic? Briar did not ask aloud.

"Look at yourself, little one. You're not just pretty . . . you're—"

"Lovely."

"Lovely. And look at us!"

"Magnificent!" they told each other. "Magnificent."

"The child was quite right about the gowns."

"It has taste."

"Such a shame to keep us to ourselves."

"We ought to be seen."

"She ought to be seen."

"Dare we be seen?"

"Perhaps not as ourselves, not quite as these gloriously revealed selves."

The two giantesses in the mirror who had been admiring themselves now turned again to the girl, who was apparently herself, a girl with golden brown skin, hair the color of honey and eyes a mixture of both. *Too pretty*, Sal had said. Briar longed to see her tough dark friend with the black, tangled, flyaway hair. She wished she looked like that, someone who could pass for a miner.

Tell the truth Briar, she heard Sal whisper, *you always wanted beauty.*

"I know! we shall be ... "

"Her aunties."

"Her highly respectable aunties."

"I'm her Auntie Aloe," said the blue-haired one.

"I'm Auntie Vinda," said the orange-haired one.

"Taking her on the grand tour all around the dome."

"That's what we'll say if anyone asks."

"We're taking our little niece— "

"What is its name?"

"What is your name?"

Briar was taken aback. She still did not recognize the girl in the mirror. What was her name?

"I don't know," she whispered.

"What's that?"

"I don't know who I am. I am ... I am no one."

"You are not no one, that is one thing for certain."

"Only Noone is Noone."

"She might have forgotten her name, poor mite, in all the horror."

"We must name her."

"You know, in that dress, she puts me in mind of the roses. Do you remember? Where we used to play? Before."

"I hardly remember before, but I remember the scratches and our knees all dirty."

"When we were grubby little boys."

"We never were."

"Before. Before we were—"

"Snatched, sold, stolen."

It was impossible to picture the giantesses crawling through the tunnels in the briar patch, her briar patch where only she ever went, until she brought Sal and Jack there, too.

"Gone," Briar whispered, hearing again the flames pursuing them, crackling with heat, and then the charred remains, the shadow in the wall.

"It spoke! What did it say?"

"Don't call her 'it' anymore, not in that dress. Come, let's name her. She is our little niece—"

"Rosa. Rosa Rugosa."

Briar shook her head. The dress shimmered, rose, honey, stone.

"Briar," she said. "You can call me Briar."

Her eyes filled and everything disappeared.

"There, there," they scooped her up, "don't cry. Don't spoil your pretty face, little Briar Rose. Miss Rugosa."

"Now if we're going out to promenade . . . "

"As aunties, highly respectable aunties . . . "

"We shall need to look the part."

"It's a shame to take these off."

With a sigh, they shed their brilliant gowns down to elaborate undergarments, the like of which Briar had never seen. The bodies underneath were also confusing, muscles rippled, and breasts swelled.

"We shall set aside these gowns to wear for her coming-out ball."

"Don't! It's only pretend."

"Our grand tour, the ball, our pretty niece . . . "

"She might not live so long."

"*We* might not live so long."

"Slaves and prisoners, slaves and prisoners."

"But we can pretend."

Rummaging about in the heaps on the floor they re-clothed themselves in browns and blacks.

"Now. Pots and potions!"

The closet that seemed a world unto itself opened onto another room with more mirrors, where her self-appointed aunties seated themselves and stripped their faces of paint as surely as they had stripped themselves of their bright gowns. Then they lifted their mountainous hair from their heads and set it aside.

"Sit down, little Briar."

"This could take a minute."

Briar sat on a stool and watched what appeared to her to be myriad giantesses, in surrounding mirrors, transform themselves into severe-looking older women, elegant and refined. They rummaged in drawers and took out brooches which they fastened to their gowns. They chose dark wigs with streaks of gray and topped them with darker hats, decorated with subdued plumage.

"My dear," they said to each other, "you are looking very well."

At last they turned to Briar.

"Dear niece, you don't need much improvement."

"Let's keep it looking fresh and maidenly."

"Her, not it, her."

"Just a modest jewel or two."

They found a gold necklace with a luminescent stone that rested in the hollow above her collar bone. Tenderly they brushed her hair.

"If only we had fresh flowers."

"We can pluck one from one of the gardens when no one's looking."

"Are you ready, niece?"

She nodded, hardly knowing. She had been in a dungeon, then in a room with vats, now a secret closet, strangeness upon strangeness.

"Wait, it, I mean she, needs slippers."

"I've already got slippers," Briar pointed out.

So soft and warm, she never wanted to take them off.

"No, no, no!" cried her aunties. "Those are bedroom slippers."

Not that she'd ever had a bedroom.

"You need slippers to go with your gown."

The aunties scurried, if such huge beings could be said to scurry, into the deep recesses of the closets and came back with armfuls of shoes, gold, silver, jeweled, all with spikes. Like the ones she and Sal had glimpsed on the inside woman long ago.

You could kill someone with those heels, Sal had said.

The aunties took off her soft slippers and took turns cramming her feet into shoes they pronounced too big or too small, until they found a pair the color of moonlight spilled onto stone bright and dim, opaque and translucent all at once.

As soon as she stood up, she began to tip over. The aunties caught an arm each.

"We'll have to teach her to walk in these."

"We can't have her tripping."

"They could shatter."

 "What about us?"

"We can't wear our bodyguard boots."

"Crocodile shoes. That's what respectable aunties wear."

"We'll be right back."

Briar sat down and slipped off one of the shoes.

You could kill someone . . .

A weapon, now she had a weapon.

She put the shoe back on and waited for her aunties.

Rose

My mother lapsed into abstracted silence. I feared today's storytelling might be over, all without a hint of what I most wanted to know. What magic made the wall open? The magic I had worked that one time without knowing how? Where did my aunties learn it? How did they teach it to Briar? And if the three of them had such powers, why were they still here, hiding in the closet?

For that's where we were. That's the one part of the story I already knew. They'd moved the mirror room and the pots and potions into the recesses of closet to make room for our living space. But this was where we lived, where they retreated each day, their refuge from a perilous, public life I knew nothing about.

"Poor dear, you're tired," said Auntie Aloe to my mother.

"Beddy-bye for you, little miss," Auntie Vinda did her best to look severe.

How could they still treat me like a child? Did they think I did not understand the horror of my mother's story? Well, maybe I didn't. Not fully. But I knew what had happened to her was terrible. Not fit for a child's ears, not a bedtime story, so how dare they suggest I go to bed. I had to distract them, which in my aunties' case was never difficult.

"Just a little more," I wheedled, like any child from any time and place. "Tell about the promenade."

"Oh, how resplendent we were! How I wish we could be that carefree again."

"Sister, you know it was only ever pretend."

"But still, we cut quite a figure—"

They were off and running, bedtime forgotten. I turned to my mother.

"What did you think when you first saw inside world, I mean the real inside world, not the prison part?"

"Inside world is not real," said my mother. "It is all pretend, all a prison, all of inside world."

"So is outside world, dearie," said Auntie Aloe.

"The only difference is it rains there, and it's hot and cold," said Auntie Vinda.

"No shelter. Unless you count those dark, stinky, leaky hovels."

"You always say you don't remember outside world," my mother reminded Auntie Aloe.

"We don't," they both replied. "Except when we do."

"Tell me," I prompted my mother. "What did it look like to you?"

"In some ways it looked bigger than outside world . . ."

Promenade

Briar had seen the sky, but she had never seen wide streets or fountains. She had never seen people strolling, talking in murmurs. She had never seen people sitting at tables, sipping out of pretty cups, delicate cups with no chips or dents in them. Everyone was clean and dressed almost as beautifully as she, even the men, most of whom wore robes or suits that reflected the light, light that slowly climbed the high curved walls, yet still seemed to come from nowhere or everywhere.

There were gardens with flowers that did not look real to Briar. Surreptitiously one of her aunties broke off a blossom and stuck it behind Briar's ear.

"Promenade," said one auntie to the other.

"Promenade on!"

As they passed people, the aunties would nod and offer pleasantries.

"Do you know all these people?" Briar asked.

"No, but they think they know us—or ought to know us."

"Because we look so splendidly respectable."

"So respectably splendid."

"We are welcome at all the finest houses." They went on with their game. "Of all the first families."

"What about the second families?" Briar asked. "Or the third?"

"There are no seconds or thirds."

"Only the first families live in inside world, descendants of the founding families."

"Though some are more firstly than others. No one is second. Duels have been fought over such slight slights."

"Innuendos and implications."

"Do they kill each other?" Briar asked.

People did fight to the death in outside world.

"Of course not. Death would be in unforgivably poor taste. Removing a handkerchief is victory enough."

"It shows skill."

"Whereas ripping a sleeve is gauche."

"Clumsy and gauche."

"Speaking of gaucherie, niece, don't keep staring and gaping as if you've never promenaded before."

"Fresh and innocent does not, should not, mean unschooled and barbaric."

It was difficult to resist craning her neck. The dome of inside world seemed as high as the sky to Briar. It was hard to tell that it was not the sky. Parades of what might have been clouds passed by, and the shadows of what might have been birds. But the sky Briar had known was the source of weather. There was no weather in inside world, no changes in temperature, no cold, no heat, no rain, and no wind. There was no ground either, not as Briar had known it. No dirt, no mud, no straggling weeds or patches of parched grass, just something smoother than stone and shinier. Briar's feet hurt in the strange shoes, and her back and legs ached. Once she slipped and stumbled, but the aunties caught her and skimmed her along through squares and streets, past shops and tall buildings where people had what the aunties called chambers, and meeting halls, and houses with turrets and gable roofs and gardens full of impossible shrubs and blooms.

"Stop that!" Auntie Aloe slapped Auntie Vinda's hand when she attempted to snap off a large, luxuriant bloom. "She's fine as she is."

"I want this one for myself!" protested Auntie Vinda.

"No, we don't want to attract attention. Respectable aunts do not deck themselves with flowers!"

Reaching across Briar, she pulled Auntie Vinda away from the garden that surrounded a house decorated with intricate trim.

"Why do people in inside world need houses and halls," Briar wondered, "if it never rains or freezes?"

"Privacy, child," said Auntie Aloe.

"They have to have somewhere to lead their petty little lives."

"Secrets. They have to have secrets."

"Or pretend to have secrets."

"So that there's something to gossip about."

"Affairs, intrigues, scandals, plots and counterplots."

"It keeps them entertained while they wait."

"Wait for what?" Briar asked.

"That would be telling."

"We must not tell her."

"We can't tell her.

"For the simple reason that we don't know ourselves."

"No one knows."

"Noone knows. And so does the chief."

"We do know, we do, sister, you know we know."

"Hush. We are not supposed to know."

Briar began to feel tired and dizzy. She couldn't follow the back and forth of the aunties. They always seemed about to say something and then managed not to. She felt homesick, for Jack, for Sal, for the briars, the bees making honey in the wall. Her eyes begin to close . . ..

"It's falling asleep on its feet."

"She, remember, she. Our little niece, Miss Briar Rugosa."

"Let's stop and get it, her, an ice. I bet she's never had one."

"And cake. She must have cake."

"Let's stop and have a highly respectable tea."

"Splendidly respectable."

"We haven't eaten for ages. What hour of the dome is it?"

They looked around, and Briar also noticed the light shifting, turning thick and golden.

"High time for tea."

"Time for high tea."

"I think the Crescent is just at the end of this street."

Her aunties bore her along, and turned into one of the places she'd noticed where people sat in delicate-looking chairs. She did wonder if they could accommodate the aunties' bulk. But they sank down gracefully as if they were feathers or petals coming to unhurried rest. A slender man in flowing white clothes that reminded her of the ones she'd put on after her first bath, approached their table with a bow and asked how he might serve them.

A servant. Briar tried to look at him without looking, wondering if he had come from outside. If he had, it must have been long ago. His skin was so smooth. His eyes had no squint lines.

"If you please, bring us a platter of your finest cakes and a selection of ices."

"And tea."

"What kind of tea, madams?"

"Why, your finest tea."

"Your most refined."

"And delicate."

"Subtle, aromantic."

"She means aromatic."

"Of course, madams."

He bowed again and went back into what looked like a tent to Briar, but one made of fabric so thin it looked like light.

"Oh, what fun to treat our little niece."

They looked at each other and then looked at her fondly. A look Briar had seen on her mother's face only when her mother thought she was asleep.

Don't get attached, Briar warned herself. *This is all pretend, more pretend than playing king and queen of the rubbish heap.* The aunties were, by their own admission, tricksy.

When the cakes came, she hardly dared touch them at first; they looked no more real than the garden. Then all at once she felt overcome with hunger. She had often been hungry in outside world. She'd been nearly starved during the early time of her imprisonment. Now she felt a hunger that made her think of plants reaching for light, bees diving deep into the heart of flowers. She picked up a cake and breathed its scent, felt its moist stickiness on her fingers, then her lips, her tongue. Her teeth barely touched it and the cake fell apart, dissolved as she swallowed. Her stomach rose up and roared. More!

She reached for another cake and another. She felt as though she were devouring life itself and if she stopped she would die.

"Slowly, niece!"

"You are not a rat on a rubbish heap."

"Hush, sister. She was never, ever! Don't even think it."

Briar did not care what they thought; she did not care what she was.

"I am so hungry, I am so hungry."

Tears sprang to her eyes and flowed down her cheeks, salt cutting into the sweet.

"There, there," murmured the aunts, dabbing at her cheeks with their splendidly respectable handkerchiefs.

"You haven't tried the ices yet."

Auntie Aloe picked up a long-handled shiny spoon and slipped cold sweetness into her mouth. Auntie Vinda followed suit, and they took turns, feeding her tenderly as if she were a baby bird just hatched. She might have resisted such odd attentions if she hadn't been so hungry, so very hungry and so...she did not know.

"Now," Auntie Aloe said, "take a sip of tea. It will calm you."

She handed her one of the delicate cups, and Briar pressed it to her lips and sipped. The fierce hunger inside her backed away a bit and subsided into a soft growl.

Before she could take another sip, there was a change in the sound around her, as if the fountains were louder, the other people's voices softer but more excited. Something was happening. She held the delicate cup so tightly it might have shattered, but Auntie Vinda wrested it from her hand and set it down, slowly and carefully.

"Look to starboard, sister," said Auntie Vinda in a low voice. "Or rather, don't look now."

"How should I know where starboard is. We're not on a ship. We were never on a ship."

"We're on the ship of state, and unless we want to go overboard, we'll need to get below deck."

Briar didn't need to ask where starboard was. She turned as others turned. There he was, walking down the avenue in his dark cape, sober as the mask of his face, except for the purple band around his waist. He'd added a tall, shiny black hat, and when he lifted it from his head in greeting to the people who bowed and curtsied, white doves flew out. Next to him walked a portly man in rich garments of red and blue embroidered in gold. Instead of a hat, he wore a crown on his head, so heavy it squashed his brows into his cheeks. He kept talking and waving, now and then tossing a coin or a flower to the onlookers. But it was the darkness of the chief magician that drew people's eyes, including hers. And then, something else caught her attention. On the other side of the magician, a flicker of shadow and light, a hint of bones and wild hair and beard. For a moment the figure took form and then vanished. There was no one there.

Noone.

"Look down," hissed Auntie Vinda. "Keep your head down. He mustn't see you."

"It will be no good for you if he does."

"And no good for us."

"What are we going to do, sister?" Auntie Aloe's trembling began to shake the table. "What are we going to do?"

"Hush! Sit still, very still, until he passes."

"Statues, I remember that game, statues."

Briar remembered, too, she and Jack and Sal, becoming still, blending into the crumbling walls of an alley. Sometimes their pursuers would walk right by them, not seeing. And sometimes . . .

It was their stillness that gave them away, set them apart from the others who waved or rose and bowed, or sent up refined, decorous cheers. Briar could feel his eyes on her, the eyes that had forced her to look at terrible things. She could feel them commanding her now.

I won't, she answered silently, *I won't.*

And then she did. Just before he passed them, he caught and held her eyes. She was no more than a rabbit in a snare. His mask of a face stretched, but not into a smile. And then he moved on, his cape floating behind him, obscuring his companion—or his companions. For at the edge of him the shadows of birds still dove in and out of light.

"He's past," said Auntie Vinda. "Let's skedaddle."

He saw us, Briar wanted to say, *he saw us.* But her throat wouldn't open.

"Sister, we haven't settled the bill," Auntie Aloe fretted.

"They'll put it on our tab."

"Do we have a tab?"

"They'll think we do. Come on."

While the eyes of everyone were still on the passing dignitaries, the aunties got to their feet, whisked her down a side street, and then turned into the closest thing to an alley she had seen in inside world.

"Yo ho, yo ho, below, below we go."

"We were never sailors."

"Doesn't matter. Two, four, six, eight, now it's time to navigate."

And before Briar could understand how it had happened, she was back in her cell, the aunties hurriedly stripping her of her finery and tucking her into bed.

Briar Dreaming

She is crawling deep into the briars. How can she have believed the briar patch was burned? That was just a dream, just a bad dream. On and on she goes. Then without warning, the dense thicket ends. She crawls out into nothingness, no wall, no nothing. Only wind, sky, the sun, a giant star, burning through the mist, hard, bare earth under her feet. Far away, she hears something soft, repetitive, *whoosh, whoosh, whoosh*. She takes a step forward and stops. She is at some edge, *the* edge. Below is so far below, there is no below.

over the edge of the world we go
over the edge of the world we fly

Children singing, three children dancing in a circle on a dung heap. Who are they? Where are they? Birds take up the song. Everything is singing. If she just takes another step forward, she will . . .

Summoned

"Wake up, wake up! You are summoned."

Briar opened her eyes and found herself looking up at two huge faces, familiar yet skewed. Crooked wigs, smudges around their eyes, lips like wounds, red and purple marks on their cheeks.

"It's awake."

"She's awake, our niece."

"She's not really our niece."

"Whose idea was it to pretend she was?"

"We both wanted to take it upstairs and show it off. You're the one who wanted to play auntie."

"Well, it doesn't matter now. We'd better hurry up or the next round will be worse."

"What happened?"

Briar sat up, reluctantly leaving the vastness of her dream. How she could still be here? When she was just about to fly . . .

"He saw us, yesterday."

"You mean he saw *her*, we were accessories!"

"To the crime."

"No, not the crime, to the beauty."

"Beauty?" Briar echoed, the songs still sounding in her memory.

"You, he saw you!"

"I know," said Briar.

Both the pretend, giant aunties took a step back, put their hands on their hips, and glared.

"You knew?"

"Why didn't you tell us?"

"We had you all tucked up safely in bed."

"And then—"

"And then—"

"And then?" Briar asked.

"It doesn't bear thinking about."

"Sordid, disgusting."

"You could have at least warned us that he spotted you."

"I'm sorry," Briar said.

And she found that she *was* sorry, sorry for them, these big, strong, strangely tender (even if it was only pretend) beings. They worked so hard to put themselves together, and someone, some *ones* had tried to take them apart. On Auntie Vinda's face there was a dry tear track, like a gully after a flash flood. Auntie Aloe's eyes wet and muddy as puddles.

"I was so scared," she whispered. "I am so scared of—"

Briar felt her throat closing up.

"We can't blame her for that."

"No, we can't blame you for that."

"Not your fault he—"

"Well, never mind about that. It doesn't matter now."

"The thing is, he liked what he saw."

"And why wouldn't he?"

"He would, of course he would."

"Don't fret, child. We're all right."

"And at least he still doesn't know about the closet."

"We think he doesn't."

"We didn't tell, not even when—"

"Don't talk about it," Auntie Aloe shuddered.

"You were tortured!" said Briar.

"Well, that is putting it crudely."

"It was crude, sister. What do you call it when they—"

"Don't talk about it."

"I'm sorry," said Briar again. "I'm so sorry. I won't tell about the closet. I—"

"No need to promise, child. You never know—"

"Don't talk about it!"

"It'll all be all right."

"If he is pleased with you."

"He wants you dressed up."

"Just as he saw you yesterday."

"Ups-a-daisy."

They pulled her out of bed. The room began to whirl around her. If they hadn't been holding her up, she might have fallen.

"It looks a bit green about the gills. We might want to add a little color to the cheeks."

"She, she!"

"And perhaps we should feed it—her."

"He didn't say we couldn't."

"He wants her looking her best."

"Her best for the—"

"Hush, we don't know what he wants."

"Best not to know."

Briar closed her eyes again. It was better that way, the dizziness eased, and she did not have to see the ruined faces of the aunties, she just felt their hands, competent, gentle, doing what they had to do. They had no choice; she had no choice. All she really cared about was breakfast.

Strawberries and cream.

She opened her eyes and ate.

They wiped her mouth as if she were an infant.

Then they stood her up. Painstakingly, with no trace of yesterday's giddy joy, they dressed her in the beautiful gown, the color of honey and stone and roses. It might as well have been a rag. She wished it was; at least the clothes she wore outside were not stolen—or scrutinized. The giantesses brushed her hair and fastened the golden necklace with its shining stone that nestled in the hollow of her throat. They held her elbows while she stepped into the luminous spike-heeled slippers.

When they fetched an oval mirror and held it before her, she turned her face away. She never wanted to see herself again. *You're too pretty, Briar.* She wanted to see Sal and Jack.

"Look, just look," they pleaded. "Just once."

Because they had been kind to her, and suffered because of her, Briar did as they asked.

She had not noticed yesterday. She had not known her eyes were the color of the sky before light. She had not known she could look through her eyes to the edge of the world.

You Could Kill Someone
with those Shoes . . .

"Stand. Stand and let me look at you."

The giantesses had left the room. Briar was alone with the chief magician, face to face, with enough space between them that he could scrutinize her full length. She kept her eyes down. Through the low, creeping mists, she could see the pointy toes of her slippers.

"Look at me," he commanded. "Look."

Don't look, she told herself, even as she complied. He was not much taller than she was (in the shoes, she was taller), and perhaps not much heavier. She stared at him with wide-angle vision, doing her best not to look at his immobile face, his eyes that could force her to see things she did not want to see—where his power resided, his will, his power to take away her will. She hated him looking at her; she hated looking at him. He was about the same distance away as the mirror where she had seen herself for the first time yesterday. She shifted her weight from one leg to another, and he shifted, too, just as her own image in the mirror had mimicked her every motion.

"Perfect," he pronounced.

Then he took a step toward her. She took a step back, wobbling as the height of her heels threw her off balance. He caught hold of her wrist, his hand cold as frozen ground, and held her steady, held her fast.

"Noone won't interrupt today. He understands now what's at stake. Come."

Still holding her wrist, he led her through the gray, swirling fog past the vats. She could hear them now, gurgling, breathing, as if they were alive.

Beyond the vats was an archway framing the darkest dark she had ever seen, darker than the dungeon, darker than a rainy moonless night. He led her into a stillness so still she forgot for a moment how to breathe.

"Look," he commanded, coming to stand behind her, his hands on her shoulders. "What do you see?"

Was he mad? How could she see in a darkness that swallowed up even the eerie half-light of the outer chamber?

"What do you see?" he asked again, his breath cold on her neck.

"Nothing," she said. "I see nothing."

The grip of his hands was hard and soft at the same time.

"You are correct," he said. "Here is what lies beyond the edge of the world. Here is where whole worlds are made and unmade."

No, she said silently, her dream coming back to her, surrounding her. *The edge of the world is not like this, the edge of the world is . . .*

Alive.

She could hear the birds singing, the beauty singers bringing the dawn.

"Sing, beauty singer, sing," the cold of his breath went into her ear, hollowed her out. "Sing!"

She could hear the children, singing on the dung heap, singing at the edge of the world.

over the edge of the world we go
over the edge of the world we fly
queens and kings
when we have wings
we all have wings
over the edge of the world we go
queens and kings, queens and kings

The words sang themselves in her, through her, sang and sang until they disappeared. Her voice was not hers anymore, just sound, a falling star, a bird with flaming feathers, diving, swooping down into the nothing, and then there was nothing but light, obliterating light, light exploding.

When she woke, if it was waking, she was on the floor, her feathers—her feathers?—singed, her blood burning. Gray fog still swirled around her. But it could not obscure a brilliant light above her.

"I have done it! I have made a new star, a captive star, more concentrated, more dense, more powerful than the sun! Get up!" he commanded. "Look!"

She rolled over onto her hands and knees, her body felt so heavy, her muscles so weak, but at last she stood, wobbling on the knife-thin heels. In his hands the magician held light trapped inside a glass dome. With great tenderness and care, he set the dome in a stand on a table. Then he reached into the pocket of his robe for his bell and rang it. The giantesses appeared. Their wigs now straightened but their faces till smeared with paint and tears.

"Fetch the candidate," he ordered.

"The candidate?"

"Which is to say, the candidate?"

"She means which candidate?"

"Idiots," he said mildly, almost gently, his face twitching as if something alive was trapped under his skin. "The prisoner, the chief prisoner, the guard who tried to escape."

Jack, Briar thought, forgetting the pain in her limbs, the burn in the veins, *Jack!*

"That one!"

"Ah, that one."

Did they sound fearful or sorrowful?

"Of course, that one."

"Oh, now we know who you mean, chief, *that* one."

As they turned to leave the room, their eyes darted to Briar, almost communicating something. Sympathy? Warning? Briar held onto herself, willing her knees not to buckle. She shifted her gaze to the floor, shutting out the chief magician and his burning glass ball. She just had to keep breathing. She just had to stay alive. Jack was coming. Jack.

It felt like forever, longer than her whole life. At last she heard footsteps. She turned back toward the entrance to the once dark, now blazing, room.

There was Jack, supported on either side by the giantesses, just as she had been, his feet only skimming the ground. His cheeks were so gaunt, she could almost see the bones beneath them. His clothes hung on him like the last leaves on a skeletal tree. But his eyes were alive. She could see the sky in them, sun and storms, dusks and dawns, all the places they had wanted to go, all the places they might have gone.

What did he see when he looked at her, dressed like a rich insider?

"Ah, here he is." The magician came to stand next to her. "A little the worse for wear, but still alive."

Neither she nor Jack spoke. Did he even know her? She couldn't tell from the way he looked at her and then looked away, his glance falling on the trapped star.

"What would you do to keep him that way?"

What way? Imprisoned, starving, his mind dazed?

"What do you mean?" she managed a whisper. Her throat felt dry, charred.

"It is within your power to give him life, not just life, but the life of a prince, first among the elect. Riches and ease. No hunger. No want. No suffering. No death."

The magician's voice no longer seemed to be coming from him, but from everywhere, inside her, around her, even from Jack himself, who turned his gaze from the star to look at her again. His eyes wide, his mouth twisting, as if trying to speak, or not to speak.

"What would you give to give him life?"

She opened her mouth, but her words felt trapped in her throat, in her heart.

"Or perhaps you no longer care for him. Perhaps you would rather see him dead?"

"I would give anything." The words flew out, birds released from a cage. "I would give everything. I'd give my life. Let him go, let him live."

Jack alive, Jack free.

"It is within your power, yours alone."

She saw Jack crossing the vast plain to the faraway pinnacle, or the forest.

"All you have to do is give your hand in marriage."

Tears blinded her eyes. Marry Jack? Marry Jack!

We'll both marry him, Sal had said. They would find Sal and—

"No, Briar!" Jack cried out. "No!"

"Yes, Jack, yes!" She smiled at him though her tears. "Yes! Here is my hand!"

She reached for Jack, and the magician closed his hand over hers.

"My bride," he said. "My wife."

She tried to pull away, but he held tight.

"You tricked me!" she screamed. "Jack! Jack!"

Jack struggled with all the might that was left to him, but the giantesses restrained him.

"No trick," said the magician. "You said you would give anything, everything. Even your life. And so you will. You will give your life, to me, to our work together."

She stared into the magician's eyes, into that emptiness that could make and unmake worlds.

"You promised me Jack's life."

"And I shall keep my promise. You will give him the life I promised. Come."

Holding tightly to her hand, he led her to the table where the star blazed inside the miniature dome world. Reaching into his robe he took out a wand. At the lightest tap, the dome trembled, expanded, and just as it seemed as though it would shatter, a chalice, an almost invisible chalice appeared beside the small dome, brimming with light.

"Inside this chalice is one single drop of the new star you and I have brought into being. One single drop is all it takes to make a mortal life immortal. At your hand, Jack shall be the first to drink life everlasting."

Still holding on to her wrist, the magician placed the chalice in her hands. It had no weight. She could hardly believe she held anything at all.

"Take the cup and give him to drink."

Did she move of her own volition or at the magician's command?

As Briar lifted the chalice to Jack's lips, the giantesses held him fast, but he turned his face away. Then he looked at her again. In his eyes she saw the roses against the dusky sky, she felt his warmth and Sal's. He would live. What did it matter what happened to her? Jack would live. She lifted the cup to his lips again.

He shook his head.

"Remember, Briar, remember," he said, his voice so weak she could hardly hear him.

"Remember what, Jack?"

Briar wasn't sure he had spoken aloud, but all at once she is back in the dream, Sal among the roots, Jack riding the wind, her own mother holding her close as the sparks of the dung fire turned into stars, and far away the sound of bells, the scent of damp and salt.

"Give him the drink," came the magician's voice came from behind her. "Unless you want him to die."

"I'm not afraid to die," said Jack.

Briar's hands trembled, but she held fast to the cup.

"He is near death," said the magician. "He won't last much longer."

She could not bear it, a world without Jack, all the life would go out of it.

"Drink, Jack," she whispered to him. "Please. You need to live. Find Sal and the baby."

Jack still hesitated.

"If you value *this one's* life," said the magician to Jack, "you will drink."

The magician did not have a name for her. He did not know who she was. But Jack did. Briar stilled her hands. The magician was willing to kill her to force Jack. He did not value either of their lives.

"I'm not afraid to die either, Jack."

Maybe it would be better if they both died. Together.

"Give me the cup, Briar."

He leaned his head toward her.

"But Jack, what if—"

"I'll find Sal. We'll come back for you."

Still she hesitated, her hands trembling, light darting wildly over the walls.

"Give me the cup."

Jack parted his lips. Briar lifted the light of the star to his mouth. He drank.

When she lowered the cup, he looked at her, his eyes widening. She could see the whole sky in them for a moment, stars, sun, moon, and then . . .

Nothing, nothing.

Nothing.

His body sagged between the giantesses, his head lolled forward.

Dead.

When the chalice fell to the floor, its shattering seemed to go on forever, spreading out beyond the room over the earth; light leapt in shards, wind rose, carrying the scent of salt, the sound of bells and rattling bones.

over the edge of the world I go
over the edge of the world I fly

Someone was singing. Jack. Jack.

Briar rounded on the magician.

"You lied."

The gray snaking fog at her feet flickered and hissed; the trapped star flared. How could the magician still exist? How could he still be standing there, his face unmoved, his eyes empty?

"I did not lie," the magician's voice cut through hers. "If the experiment had succeeded, all I promised would have come true. He would have lived forever."

"You killed him."

She had killed him.

Briar looked back at Jack. The giantesses still clutched at him, but his body was fading, disappearing, a glimmer of light, a shadow, the rags he'd been wearing more substantial than his body.

"What did you do to him!"

over the edge of the world I go
over the edge of the world I fly

She could hear the voice, Jack's voice fading, vanishing.

"You sent him over the edge of the world," Briar accused. "He's gone. He's gone into that horrible nothing of yours. Send me, too. Make me a chalice, I'll drink every last drop. Send me, too. Do it now!"

She took a step forward.

"Ah, my bride, that I cannot and will not do. We have work to do, you and I. We have worlds to make and rule. Worlds beyond anything Noone ever imagined. He is only an old fool, a dreamer, a tool. It is a pity about your Jack. But his demise need not be in vain. We will perfect the elixir. Next time or the time after that, we will succeed. There are plenty of other candidates, perhaps none so worthy, but they will suffice for trial and error. And when we succeed, death itself will die, and the elect will live in perfect peace."

Not peace. No peace. Pieces. She would smash that ball into pieces. She slipped off her shoes, picked one up and took aim.

"No! Don't touch it, don't go near it. You would destroy us all, the whole world!"

She didn't care. Let the whole world fly over the edge of the world! The magician leaped, placing himself between her and the ball.

You could kill someone with those shoes.

She lunged for him, grabbed his arm and drove the heel of her shoe into his temple. His mask, for an instant, looked like a face, startled, terrified, human, then he crumpled at her feet. Beyond his body, the star she had sung into being still burned inside its glass dome.

For a moment there was no sound in the room, no motion; even the gray fog stopped swirling.

Then one of the giantesses sucked in her breath.

"She's gone and done it."

Briar turned around to look at them, shoe still in hand.

Jack, where was Jack? There was nothing left now but his rags lying on the floor between the two giantesses who had held him, held him while she gave him the cup, killed him.

"Where is he? Where is Jack?"

They shook their heads and trembled.

"He got lighter and lighter."

"Then he was gone."

"Gone."

"Wish the other one would disappear."

"The other one?"

Briar felt confused, dizzy.

Jack! Where did you go? Come back!

"That one, on the floor, at your feet."

"The one you just brained. With your slipper, oh that beautiful slipper."

"It's all right, sister, the heel didn't break! Almost as good as new. Just a smidgeon of blood . . ."

"Blood."

"Blood."

They sobered up.

"Do you think he's . . . "

"Dead?"

"We'd better be sure."

As if they were oversized, timid mice, they tiptoed toward the body on the floor, the body at her feet, his face staring, blood oozing from his temple.

They crouched down. Auntie Vinda felt for a pulse in his neck. Auntie Aloe reached into her pocket and drew out her a tiny mirror, which she held up to his gaping mouth.

"Dead."

"Dead."

"Dead beyond doubt."

"Dead beyond compare."

"Murdered."

"Completely."

"By our niece."

"Our pretend niece."

Slowly, Briar began to comprehend. She had killed him, the chief magician. The chief, the giantesses called him.

"Please," she said, not knowing what she meant.

"Please?"

"Please what?"

"Please," Briar said again. "What will happen? What will happen now?"

If she tried to make a run for it, would they stop her?

"Is it up to us?"

"I think it is up to us, sister."

Briar began to back away, hoping they would not notice. They moved more nimbly than she would have imagined possible, and held her between them, just as they had held Jack.

"And don't think the heel will work on us."

"Our skulls are much too thick."

"And don't think you are going to leave us with this mess."

"*You* killed him."

"Yes," Briar said, "yes. And I'm not sorry. Go ahead and kill me or turn me over to the Guard, send me over the edge of the world. Please. Please."

"Hush, niece."

"Pretend niece."

"Give us a moment."

They stood there, gazing at the body.

"No one must know he's dead."

"No, no one must know, especially not Noone."

"If Noone found out—"

"It doesn't bear thinking about."

"But we must think."

"Think of a plan."

"A plan."

It almost seemed as though they had forgotten about her, as she hung suspended between them, in suspense.

"First things first, we have to get rid of the evidence."

"Totally, utterly, and completely destroy it."

"Come, niece."

"Pretend niece."

"You must help us. Quickly."

"Help you what?"

"Feed him."

Briar looked in horror at the dead magician.

"What do you mean?"

"Feed him. To the crocodiles."

"Now."

The sound of water.

The smell. Rotten eggs, sewage, a familiar smell in an unfamiliar place, cold, damp.

Now she could also see. She held the lantern to light way for the aunties (pretend aunties) who carried the body of the magician. They wound down and around dark passages, the underworld of inside world. There was no edge to this world, seemingly no end, until they came to the water, the river she had heard when she lay chained in the dungeon.

The giantesses laid the magician's body beside the water that looked all the darker for the flickering reflection of the lantern.

"Shall we say a few words?"

"You mean the way we did for all the others?"

"The ones who died because of him."

"The ones he killed."

There was a silence as they pondered.

Suddenly the water churned, the flow interrupted by splashing. In the lamplight, Briar glimpsed flashes of teeth in wide jaws, small glinting eyes, as a float of crocodiles circled and snapped.

"Step back from the water, niece!"

"The crocodiles like living flesh as well as dead."

"Quick, toss him in."

"No ceremony, sister? He did us a good turn once."

"For a price, sister, for a price."

The jaws snapped, the tails thrashed.

"Bye, chief!"

"Bye-bye!"

Briar watched as the giantesses picked up the magician's body and tossed it toward the water. A crocodile caught him in its jaws and dragged him under.

"Quick, let's go."

One of the aunties took the lantern from her. For a moment Briar was terrified they were going to leave her in the dark with the crocodiles. Then she felt their familiar grip, one hand on each of her elbows.

"Come on, niece."

"Pretend—"

"No, just call her niece. She's ours now."

"Where are we going?" asked Briar, too exhausted to protest.

Not that it mattered much. Jack was gone. At least the crocodiles hadn't eaten him.

"Why, to the closet, of course."

Of course, the closet.

"The closet, the closet."

The secret closet.

✳   ✳   ✳

Hours later—or was it days, or nights, there was no time in here—Briar sat in a chair in the innermost chamber of the secret closet, with her eyes closed while the aunties clucked and fussed and pinched and massaged her face.

"No, don't look!"

"Not yet!"

"It's going to work."

"Yes, I think it's going to work."

"Wait! Smooth it again."

"There."

"That's it."

"Now!"

"Look!"

Briar opened her eyes and found herself face to face with the chief magician. She fought back a scream. He was dead, he was dead. She had killed him. He'd disappeared into the jaws of a crocodile. How could be here in front of her?

She was going to die. She wanted to die.

She closed her eyes again and waited.

"It's no good closing your eyes."

"You've got to get used to it."

"We've got to get used it."

"Look!"

"Look again."

Briar looked. This time she saw that the magician was flanked by the giantesses. He was wearing . . . her clothes. He was, she was . . . him, her.

No! A silent scream rose in her throat. *No!*

"Stand up, niece."

"You mean, chief, we've got to call her chief now. At least when she's wearing his face."

"Stand up."

Briar stood. The chief magician stared back at her.

"What have you done to me?" she whispered. "What have you done? Take it off."

She began clawing at his--her—face.

"Don't ruin all our hard work!"

"Give me back my face!"

Briar's stomach rose into her throat, the mirror blurred and spun, and she felt herself falling over the edge of the world.

✳   ✳   ✳

She did not want to wake up. She did not want to exist. But they would not stop talking. Even with her eyes closed, she could sense them hovering over her, giant moths.

"We should have talked to it first."

"She, our niece."

"He, the chief."

"Wake up, wake up."

"It's no good fainting all the time."

"We can't always catch you."

"There, there," they murmured and clucked.

Briar opened her eyes and let them prop her up.

"Drink this!" One of them handed her a cup.

"And have a little nibble." The other handed her a cookie.

Though she was still dizzy, she found she was ravenous.

"By the dome, she's got an appetite."

"Starving for years, no doubt."

"But look, is she getting plump around the middle?"

"And what shall we do with these?"

One of them lifted one of her breasts.

"Do you think—?"

"I do. They're bigger than they were!"

"Stand up, niece."

"Yes, let us have a good look at you."

They got her to her feet.

"Steady, steady."

They stepped to the one and then the other side and studied her. Briar wanted to close her eyes again. But sheer horror compelled her to look. A man's face, that man's face, above a woman's body. Hers.

"Where is my face?" she demanded. "What did you do with my face!"

"It's still there."

"Underneath."

"It's a mask."

"A clever well-made mask, if we do say so ourselves, a tricksy mask."

"So no one will know."

"So Noone will never know."

It had to be a nightmare.

"The real question is—"

"What will she wear, I mean he wear?

"Especially since . . . oh, sister, I'm afraid it's, she's—"

"What?" demanded Briar. "What!"

"Dear niece, you are . . . we believe you are going to make us great aunties."

"Not that we aren't great already."

"What are you talking about?" Briar demanded.

"Haven't you guessed?"

Briar shook her head, her face smooth, unfamiliar, grotesque.

"We think . . ."

"We suspect . . .

"We're almost certain . . ."

"You're going to have a baby."

Briar closed her eyes to shut out the magician's face.

A baby. Just like Sal. Sal's baby, Jack's baby, her baby.

"A baby?" she whispered. "A baby!"

"But not to worry. We'll dress you in robes."

"Of course! The chief always wore robes for important meetings."

"Robes will hide everything."

"Splendid, glittering robes."

"Rich, velvet robes."

"Your disguise will be perfect."

"No one will ever know."

"Noone will never know."

"Come, sister, let's see what we have that will suit."

"Sit down again, niece."

They lowered her into the chair.

"No more fainting."

Their voices faded as they disappeared into the rows and rows of clothes.

She closed her eyes to shut out that face. She was still herself, alone in the dark of her own body. No, Not alone.

She was going to have a baby.

Grannies

Granny Sweep stood on the edge of the promontory. A strong wind could have blown her over, but the wind was coming from the other direction, from dome world. It had been a long time since that wind had carried the scent of roses, not since the night of the smoke. The scent was both soothing and stirring. Something was changing, something was coming. She unwound her braid and let it down over the edge. It was almost long enough, almost. Someone or something was coming. Were they close or far away . . .

Granny Spark felt a rumbling in the roots of the trees, and the branches swayed as the leaves roared and whispered. Was it time to move again? It was usually she who saw the signs, who rhymed and sang the forest into motion. Now it felt as though the trees were talking among themselves, with the birds eavesdropping and the squirrels quiet for once. What were they saying? A black bear, with two cubs in tow, stopped and lifted her head, sniffing at the wind. Honey. Granny Spark smelled it, too, the scent as close as her own skin and at the same time far away . . .

Nestled in one heel of the old boot, Granny Dirt woke and sat up; when she rose, babies and children tumbled about her but came to no harm, the bed was soft, and the blankets bountiful, the whole old shoe was soft and worn. She felt around for her own shoes, her bag with its teas and tinctures and scented oils. She must have it at the ready. None of the mothers in the shoe were near their time. She never knew when she might be needed or where, near or far away . . .

It was Granny Brine who saw him, the first spark from the sun, a cinder on the wind, flying over the dark rock cliff. She watched him fall, and then . . . he didn't. The light turned lighter, the cinder burned brighter, the tatters of his flesh caught the wind. High over her head, he flew, a bird with sky-colored wings. One moment he was near enough for her to hear him sing:

over the edge of the world I go
over the edge of the world I fly

Then he flew, far away.

PART FIVE

Rose and the Grannies

Rose

"Me!" I said, interrupting the silence that had come over my mother and my aunties. "You were going to have me!"

I waited for the story to go on, for my story to begin. My mother looked at me and smiled. Why did her eyes look sad?

"You were having a baby, too, just like Sal."

Not just like Sal, I realized as soon as I spoke. She had already told me, not as clearly as I have told you. But suddenly I knew, something that was almost beyond my comprehension, and I felt sick.

"Rose!" my mother cried as I scrambled to my feet.

I ran to the mirror where the aunties spent so much time preparing themselves. I had seen myself many times. I used to pretend the child in the mirror was not a reflection, but a playmate. Now I was done with that game. I was done with games. The aunties were fond of saying how much I looked like my mother, how I would grow up to be beautiful like her. Now I looked and saw my mother's other face, the mask the aunties recreated every day to change my mother into the chief magician. How I feared that face. Now I saw it, just a hint, the curve of the brow, the set of the jaw.

My mother had killed him. The crocodiles had eaten him. But he lived on, not just as a clever mask. He lived on.

In me.

My mother came to stand behind me, placing her hands lightly on my shoulders. I was still a child, not as tall as she was. Did she guess that I would have pushed her away if she had put her arms around me? The aunties stood on either side of us, so large their reflections did not fit in the mirror.

"You are Rose, my Rose," said my mother. "That is all that matters."

But I had never seen a rose, or smelled one. Never felt the wind or the rain or the sun.

"Our Rose," echoed the aunties.

"Our sweet Rose."

"Our beautiful Rose."

"It was not her fault," said the aunties. "It's not your mother's fault."

It was his fault then, I was his fault. I was a fault.

"Everything she did, everything we've done, we've done to keep you safe."

Safe from what? Safe *for* what?

I did not speak, just kept looking at my face, wishing I could disappear, like Jack had, leaving only my clothes behind.

"Where is Sal?" I spoke at last. "What happened to her baby?"

"I don't know," my mother said.

How I hated those three words.

"How can you not know?" I demanded. "You are the chief magician. People have to obey you. You have power."

I watched in the mirror as she shook her head.

"It's only pretend, Rose," she said. "Surely you know. I am not, not . . . him."

I looked up at her reflection, her soft, lovely face, the one that had bent over me, kissing me goodnight, the face that had been for me the sun and the moon, as she cradled me, sang to me, the face that was the most beauty I had ever seen, the face that was erased each day when she turned into someone else, someone who had left his trace in my face.

"I *don't* know." I spat those words back at her. "I don't know anything. You've kept me hidden in here my whole life. You've made me a secret, a terrible secret."

She looked stricken, and the aunties made their sad whirring, clucking noises.

"Not a terrible secret. A beautiful secret, my best secret."

I pondered what it meant to be a secret. Secrets were kept, and I had been kept hidden in this room, the antechamber of a secret closet.

"When will I be told?"

"Told what?" my aunties asked.

"We've just told you all there is to tell."

"And maybe we shouldn't have."

"She's so young."

"Too young."

I turned away from the mirror to face them.

"*I* am a secret. When will *I* be told? How long will *I* be kept a secret? And why?"

I folded my arms around myself and resisted as best I could, but my huge aunties scooped me up and settled me in the familiar nest they made with my mother. Would I ever fly?

"We didn't think."

"We never thought."

"None of us ever thought that far."

"We only wanted to keep you safe."

"Safe, safe."

My mother stayed silent as the aunties' voices twittered around us. It had been their idea to disguise my mother, their idea to hide what she had done—killed the man who had killed Jack and maybe many others. Killed the man who was my . . . I couldn't even think the word.

"The prisoners," I said to my mother. "What do you do to them when you pretend to be him?"

I meant, do you hurt them? Do you kill them? But I was too scared to say it, terrified to think that my mother might have to do terrible things to keep me safe. The silence that came over my aunties frightened me even more.

"Mama!" I cried out at last. "Tell me. You have to tell me!"

"Can you keep a secret, Rose?"

I *am* a secret! I did not say it again. I just nodded.

"Briar, no!" said Auntie Vinda.

"It's too dangerous for the child to know," agreed Auntie Aloe.

My mother didn't listen to them, just looked at me.

"When I can, when no one is paying attention, I let them go, one at a time."

I pictured my mother—was she my mother then or the chief magician?—unlocking the cells in the dark, damp places where she had once been a prisoner.

"Go where?" I whispered, as if I were with her, as if I too had to be silent and on guard.

"I can't tell you, Rose," she said at length.

"She can't," chorused the aunties. "She can't."

"She can. You can," I insisted. "You know!"

"No, Rose." She looked at me, then away, far away. "I don't know where they go."

I saw, as if it were my own memory, as if I could see through her eyes, the three, Briar, Sal, and Jack, on top of the wall, gazing at the vast expanse of the out there, all the way to the edge of the world.

"Why can't you let us go, too? Why can't we go?"

"Oh, Rose." Her voice sounded thick, heavy, as if it was too hard to lift into words.

"She can't."

"We can't."

"You can't."

My aunties' voices spiraled to a shriek.

"If Noone found out—"

"If Noone knew—"

"We'd be sent—"

"Pitched, hurled, flung—"

"Over the edge of the world."

Like the ones you let go? I did not ask.

"I *want* to see the edge of the world," I said instead. "I'm not afraid. You weren't afraid before, when you were with Jack and Sal!"

My mother looked at me again. Her eyes were so sad, I could not keep the tears from mine.

"But I lost them. I lost Sal and Jack," she said. "And it was my fault. I don't want to lose you, too, Rose."

"Don't get lost again, Rose," the aunties sniffled. "You frightened us so."

Had I been lost that day, the day Noone found me?

"You mustn't be lost."

But you can't keep me here, I did not say, you can't keep me here forever. You can't keep me in this tiny, skyless world where I'm a prisoner. Yes, a prisoner, their prisoner, her prisoner, and, even though he was dead, even though she had killed him, *his* prisoner.

"I won't get lost," I said, careful not to promise anything more.

I had too much to find.

✳   ✳   ✳

Life went on as it always had, or it appeared to. My aunties selected their gowns and wigs for the day and painted their faces, softly or loudly bickering, a sound that could be comforting or irritating, but always a background. They were far more serious when they helped my mother into her suit and robes, then molded her face into the mask. Although I had seen this metamorphosis daily, I found myself watching, pretending to be reading a book, so no one would take note of my new scrutiny. I wanted to catch the moment her eyes changed, how it happened. No amount of makeup could account for how they went from bright to opaque, full of life to empty—or not quite empty. I sensed that if I ever stared into those eyes, I might glimpse horrors, whether suffered or perpetrated. But whenever she turned her gaze on me, they became her eyes again, bright and tender, reassuring but also disturbing, looking out from that awful mask, that face where the ghost of my own features flickered in and out.

As always, I paid covert attention when the three of them—my protectors, my captors—parted the wall and went out into the vast, dull beauty of inside world. Meetings, they murmured, whenever I asked what they did all day, applications, reviews. No further mention of prisoners. It did not sound as though the magician's underground chambers came into their daily rounds at all. I pictured the fog left to its own devices, the vats hissing in a desultory fashion, spitting aimlessly. Aimless as the ladies and gentlemen at their teas, or the children in their pods at school, never racing and climbing or scrambling as my mother, Sal, and Jack had done. As I had never done.

Everything behind the wall, inside the dome or out, was a prison, my mother had said. Which made our rooms the smallest, coziest prison of all.

✳   ✳   ✳

And of course, I was determined to find a way out, especially after my overt appeals got me nowhere.

"Couldn't I go with you to work?" I asked one evening during our supper (which was always brought from inside world; we had no kitchen of our own.)

"Of course not, Rose. Our meetings are top secret. Children don't attend them. Only the foremost of the most first families. And the king, of course."

What about Noone? I did not ask.

"Then couldn't you send me to school with the other children?"

This seemingly sensible suggestion met with silent consternation as my elders pondered again my one break, where I had gone, what I had discovered. They didn't like to think about that day, but they began to realize they had to.

"No one could explain your existence, Rose," Auntie Vinda explained.

"Every child is carefully catalogued—" Auntie Aloe broke in, and they both began speaking at once.

"From before birth—"

"And assigned to a pod—"

"According to descent from which first family—"

"It is all very complicated and tedious, Rose. It's not like—"

"It's the complete opposite of—"

"Outside children playing on a dung heap," I finished their sentences.

There was another silence. I looked at my mother, back in her own face for the evening. Did she regret all the stories she had told me? She never said much now. She left the protestations and explanations to the aunties. I wondered if she did that during the day, too, retreated into remoteness and mystery. How else could she have passed as the chief magician all these years, unless the aunties covered for her?

"Couldn't I be adopted?" I asked.

"What on earth do you mean?"

"Adopted," I repeated, "like you were, aunties."

"Well, as to that—"

"We weren't adopted, that is, not to say *adopted*."

The aunties were flustered. Auntie Aloe's eyes flooded, and Auntie Vinda gave a series of snorts.

"They don't like to talk about it," said my mother quietly. "And you know I couldn't . . ."

Her voice trailed off, and she looked away, hiding her own tears. My own mother could not adopt me, because she was a secret, too. She did not exist any more than I did. And I did not want to be adopted by the chief magician, even if she—he—was only pretend.

My questions put them on high alert. There were whispered conferences at night. They made the mistake so many adults make of assuming a child is asleep.

"We can't leave her alone so much. Not since she got out."

"Not since Noone saw her."

"It's not safe anymore."

All through my infancy and childhood, I had played alone much of every day, content with toys, pictures books, paper and paints. They had made our tiny world inside inside world soft and secure. It was still safe, but *I* wasn't.

"Even if we can't send her to school, I suppose she does need to be educated. We'll give her lessons."

"In what? She can read. What else does she need to learn?"

"Mathematics?"

"Geography?"

"Astronomy?

"Do *we* know those subjects, sister?"

"We know magic."

"No, no magic," my mother spoke up.

"Oh, quite." There was a pause. "And . . . no art?"

"No art."

Why not art? I might have demanded if I hadn't been eavesdropping. But of course I knew. The day I'd gotten out I had babbled about painting on the wall.

"History?" suggested Auntie Aloe.

"Not history," countered Auntie Vinda. "It's being abolished. Remember?"

"Science?"

"That's the same as magic, isn't it?"

"Well, education isn't the only thing that matters," declared Auntie Aloe.

"Tasks," said Auntie Vinda. "She must be given tasks, useful tasks."

"Children needs chores."

The aunties were in rare accord.

"I know! She can sort the closet."

"Put everything in order of size."

"No, color!"

"Or seasons."

"Are there seasons in inside world?" my mother ventured.

"Of course there are seasons," the aunties both insisted. "Parade season, ball season . . ."

"And then, of course, there's always mending."

"It's high time Rose learned to sew."

"How can we have been so lax?"

"She loves buttons and sequins. We'll start with those . . ."

I went to sleep to the sound of their whispered plans for the disruption of my own unformed plans, such as they were or weren't.

True to their word, my aunties began spending far more time with me than they ever had, and never on any predictable timetable, which I suspect was deliberate. My paints had indeed been confiscated. If I had been younger, I might have asked where they were, demanded them back, but I did not want to rouse suspicion.

The day the wall had opened and let me out, I had also sung songs and spun in a circle, dancing with the women on the walls. More than once, I tried again this method again.

over the edge of the world I go
over the edge of the world I fly
open the way and set me free
take me to my destiny

I would sing and sing, spinning and spinning. Then I closed my eyes and pictured the huge figures dancing with me, circling and circling. I circled and sang till the whole room, the whole world, spun with me. I felt myself falling, collapsing on the floor, such a soft floor. Everything was soft in my world, the floor, the beds, the pillows, the light, the dark, the rows of clothes, the powders and ointments in the pots. I wanted something sharp, rock, thorns, wind. I could almost feel it. . .

Then, inevitably, an auntie would interrupt.

"What are you doing lying on the floor, Rose? Have you finished sorting the front left closet? And what about your times tables, have you memorized them yet?"

And the next few hours would be taken up with some sort of instruction, though the aunties could be easily distracted, and often ended up giving me lessons on what color lipstick went with which gown, and how to apply glitter to false lashes.

"Oh my! What a mess we've made," said Auntie Aloe. "How about you tidy the makeup tables and drawers. And then, well, when I come back, we'll turn to whatever subject you like best."

"Geography," I said, a useful subject for a would-be escapee, which I hoped would not occur to my aunties.

"Well, dearie, dome world is quite vast. I'll see if I can find any books about it."

Of course, I didn't mean dome world, but I knew better than to say so. Auntie Aloe left me to my task, blowing kisses and making vague promises. For once instead of shirking, I started putting the makeup in order and rummaging through the overfull drawers. That is how I discovered a notebook the aunties had used for sketching clothes and then apparently forgotten. It had quite a lot of blank pages left. In the same drawer I found some discarded pencils, perhaps once used for eyebrows, worn down but still serviceable when sharpened with a nail file.

And so in my rare moments of solitude I began my own geography lessons, making a map of the world beyond from my memories of what Jack, Briar, and Sal had seen from the top of the wall. The drawings gave me a way to escape, however briefly, from my tiny world, and the notebook and pencils could be easily tucked out of sight under the bedclothes whenever an auntie appeared.

I drew the pinnacle first, rising into a sky higher than the dome. Next came a dense darkness. As I added more detail, it turned into a forest, trees and birds and even a bear, based on my childhood storybook illustrations. Then I sketched—I didn't know why, because they hadn't been able to see that clearly—a strange, oversized shoe, with its laces coming undone and little faces peeking out. The hardest to draw was what Briar, Sal, and Jack had never seen at all, their view blocked by the dome. There lay, in my imagination, the edge of the world, the endless falling into nothing. But how to draw nothing? How to draw the sound of bells, the scent of salt? I experimented with color and shape. On the borders of all the pages, I drew roses, as my mother had described them, blooming amidst a tangle of briars, with bees at their heart.

I knew there was something missing. Or some *ones*. The old ancient women with the wild hair, white, bright, black, blue-green, that I might have painted—or might not have painted—on the walls the day I got out. Where did the ancient ones come from? Could my maps ever help me find them? For I sensed the old women held the answers, not only to how to escape our rooms, but to everything.

There was no one to ask.

Noone. Did Noone know who they were?

Yes, my stomach gave a little twist as I thought of the old, old man (older than Father Time) with the twisted beard and sharp eyes. Somehow I knew I could not ask him, if I ever saw him again. I could not tell him. I must not.

There was no one to tell.

I went back to drawing the maps, filling them in with imagined details. When my mother and aunties came in for the evening, I tucked the notebook under my pillow.

✳   ✳   ✳

That night, I lay awake for a long time, watching the aunties and my mother sitting together, the aunties embroidering gowns or mending tears, my mother staring into space instead of looking at the papers in her lap. At last they went to bed, too. The ceiling's night blue fell and folded around us. My aunties snored and wheezed, my mother sighed. Everything as it always had been.

Except for the wind.

How had it found its way inside this closed and secret world? Invisible, but cold and sharp, circling my bed. I don't even know how I knew it was the wind, but there it was, wild air in motion. It beckoned me. I left my bed.

After all my efforts, all my scrutiny of my elders' comings and goings, that night it was so easy: walking through the tatters of the wall, a shredded garment or cobweb. I did not do anything but follow the whistle of the wind. I did not look to see if the wall closed behind me. When I had gotten out before, I had followed the downward slope of the hallway. Now the wind pushed and tugged me upward. I could almost see the wind, as if it had borrowed moonlight, taken on cloud to make it visible. Up and around, up and around I walked; the slope turned to stairs, and I climbed until I came to a door cracked just wide enough for me to slip through.

I found myself in a small room with round walls. On the other side of the room was something I had never seen before: a window. An open window. Air, outside air, poured through it. Beyond the window, real darkness and a naked moon, starker and more terrifying than anything I had ever seen. I don't know how long I stood transfixed, almost frozen in the presence of night and cold and moon. At last I took one step on tiptoe toward the window and then one more before I froze again.

I was not alone.

In a shadowy curve of the room sat . . . someone. Noone? I forced myself to turn and look. Not Noone. Someone just as old or older, long hair, hair the color of moonlight, enough hair to cover the floor, except that it floated, rising and falling on the gusts of wind that came through the open window. The ancient woman, for so I took her to be, sat in a chair and rocked in and out of the light, her face as startling as the moon's face.

"Here you are," said the woman, her voice like the wind, or maybe the wind like her voice, but softer, almost sweet, as though it held sunlight in it, not just cold and night. "I've been calling you. Or have been calling me?"

I had seen her before; I had never seen her before.

"Who are you?"

As I spoke, I knew: she was one of the women I had painted on the wall, who would not fit on the page of my sketchbook. Not a drawing or a painting now but fully alive, more alive than anything or anyone.

"Ah," sighed the woman, a long sigh. "I was hoping you could tell me."

I gazed at her moonlit face, intricately lined and creased, as if someone had tried to draw a map there.

"Don't you know who you are?" I asked.

The woman sighed again. And I could see shadows cast by her hair rising and falling on the round wall.

"Perhaps I knew once," said the old woman. "But I have forgotten, long since, long ago, forgotten."

"How old are you?" I wondered, aware of an echo. I had asked that question before. "Are you as old as Father Time?"

The old lady took so long to answer, I wondered if she had heard.

"Older," she said at last, "much older."

"Older than Noone," I said.

"Older than everyone," she said. "Except perhaps my sisters. I am not sure about them."

"Who are your sisters?" I asked.

The wind lifted again and circled in the room, almost moaning.

"I don't remember!" the woman cried. "I don't remember!"

For a moment on the walls of the round room, figures glimmered, dancing, swirling, like the ones I had painted on the wall that day. Then they faded again, and the moonlight dimmed.

"Rose," she said, and then as if she hadn't made herself quite clear, she said again, "Rose."

"How do you know my name?" I asked. "When you don't know your own?"

"Odd, isn't it?" she agreed. "I'm not sure how I know. There was a briar patch once. . ."

Her voice trailed off, the rest of the sentence forgotten as she gathered her sky-full of hair. From her hair, she took a comb, white and gleaming, and ran it through her drifting clouds of hair, so rhythmically I fell into a trance watching her; the room filled with a fragrance I could not name. Then she tucked the comb back into hair. Deftly and swiftly, she began to braid it, little breaths of air helping her to gather and lift the strands.

"But where is the other one?" she asked abruptly.

"Who?" I breathed.

"The other one. There is supposed to be another child. One and one and one makes two. Isn't that how it goes?"

I didn't know what she meant and yet I did. My body did, tingling all over, hot and cold at once, scared and excited, sure.

"Jack," she said. "That's right. I seem to remember, there's always a Jack. Where is he?"

And she started on a second braid of her impossibly long hair.

"I don't know," I cried. "Can't you tell me? Tell me, please!"

She sighed and rose from her chair, her moonlit braids sweeping the room.

"You must find him; he must find you. Then . . ." She paused for a moment. "Yes, then you must come and visit me. Both of you. My braids; my braids are almost long enough . . ."

Her voice now came from beyond the room, from outside.

"Where do you live?" I cried out, hardly expecting an answer.

"Look out the window, Rose."

I tiptoed across the room and caught a breath of sharp cold air as I gazed out and down at outside world for the first time in my life. It was night there, real night. I could just make out figures of people huddled around fires. I was high, high above the ground, but now and then I could hear a shout or laugh, a snatch of song. I lifted my eyes to look for the wall that my mother and Sal and Jack had never gotten over. At first I couldn't see it, but then I realized the vast darkness in the distance surrounding the fires and smoke and hovels was the wall, a high wall that would have blocked out the whole sky if it were any higher.

"Farther, Rose. Look farther."

The old lady's voice was distant now, a wisp of cloud, floating beyond the wall. Disappearing into whatever vastness lay beyond it. Then I saw it: a moonstruck pinnacle.

Just as my mother had described it, just as I had drawn it on my map.

How could I possibly get there?

I did not ask aloud, for fear she would not answer. I did not want to turn around to see what I already knew. The old lady was gone.

Then I heard the sound of footsteps, the door I had slipped through creaking open wider.

Down, Rose, a voice spoke in my head, soft and somehow bright.

I didn't know whose it was, not the old woman's. I had never heard this voice before, yet in an instant, I trusted it. I had to. There was no time to lose. I dropped to the floor just as someone stepped into the room.

"Who opened that window?" muttered a voice, one I *had* heard before.

Press yourself against the wall, said the inner voice, *inch away from the window. Don't make a sound.*

The other voice, the one that came from outside of me, kept muttering.

"For that matter, who opened the door? I gave orders for it to be sealed. I told the chief magician, it must disappear."

The speaker stepped into the room, into the shaft of moonlight, his long white beard forked and bright as lightning.

Noone, Noone.

"How dare she come in, how dare she?"

Did he know about me? My I could hear my heart pounding in my ear.

Keep moving toward the door, Rose.

"I banished her, her and all her kin. I rule here, there is rule here. Unruly, unruly. They are all of them unruly. Nevermore, nevermore will they come here. Never."

He was at the window now, reaching to close it, but then he paused.

"Ee oooh ahh. Eee, ooh."

His moan rose to a scream.

Out the door now, Rose, run! The voice somersaulted over me, bright, blue.

I did not know how I managed to make my legs move, but I did, down the stairs, down and around. Our secret chamber opened and took me in, as if it were my mother. And then I was back in my bed, my aunties still snoring, my mother whimpering in her sleep.

I closed my eyes, then opened them wide.

It was a dream; it wasn't a dream.

"What happened?" I asked silently, hoping the inside voice would answer.

But it was quiet, so quiet, except for a faint moan, almost too far away to hear.

✳   ✳   ✳

"Wake up, Sleepyhead!"

I opened my eyes to the sight of the aunties dressed for the day in their full regalia, brilliant colors draping the considerable expanse from their towering hair to their impossibly pointy-toed shoes. I squeezed my eyes shut again.

"Are you feeling well, Rose?" asked Auntie Aloe.

"We couldn't rouse you before," Auntie Vinda almost accused.

"Did you have bad dreams, Rose?"

I wished I could shut my ears to their twittering chorus, too.

"We let you sleep late. Your mother's already gone to work."

"She wanted us to stay till you were awake, but—

"We have to catch up with her."

"She needs us."

"We left breakfast for you."

"And your mathematics homework to finish."

"One of us will be back soon."

"Very soon."

Their voices hushed to whispers as they moved away.

"She's getting to be that age."

"Remember when we were girls?"

"I remember when we weren't."

"Hush. Don't talk about that."

✳   ✳   ✳

Once they were gone, I stared at the smooth, sealed wall, trying to picture it gone, open to the cold wind. Had my night adventure been a dream? An old woman who came and went with the wind? But Noone had been real, his rage, his menace, real. If what happened was a dream, then it must have been his dream, too.

I got up, put away the pretty clothes my aunties always laid out, and found the one outfit I preferred and they grudgingly allowed, a sort of flowing overall. I ate my now cold egg and tough toast. I did my math homework quickly, filling in random answers to complicated word problems involving different kinds of garments and hangers with recipes for stain removal thrown in. Right or wrong was moot, since the aunties seldom agreed on the answer and argued with each other instead of correcting me.

Then I felt under my pillow for my sketchbook. I filled one page with swirling windblown hair. Then I drew the ancient woman in the rocking chair. There she was, in my sketchbook now, where I could see her and remember her. Next I drew the dark wall and the moonlit peak beyond it. At last I drew the top of the peak as I imagined it. Patchy grass, twisted trees, a cow, a cat, chickens. I found that I could draw the old woman as well, now that I knew where she lived. I drew picture after picture, the old woman feeding the chickens, milking her cow, sweeping dust from out the doorway of her hut, and then lifting her broom to sweep a cobweb of stars.

"Granny Sweep!" I said out loud.

I drew one last picture of the whole peak, rising out of an empty land riddled with cracks, into a sky that would never fit on any page or inside any dome. Down the length of the peak hung two long white braids. At the top of the page I wrote:

Here lives Granny Sweep.

"Who is next? " I spoke to the silence of my small, soft world.

Wait and see.

A voice spoke in my mind, the same one I had heard last night.

Was it real? I asked silently. *Did it really happen?*

Wait and see.

From the edges of my vision, I could almost picture the voice, tumbling into a wild blue sky I had never yet seen.

The days passed, my aunties instructing me with as much strictness as they could muster. I was careful to put up just enough resistance to chores and schoolwork. Docility might have aroused suspicions. They thought, or pretended, they knew what they were doing—keeping me out of harm's way while seeing to my education. I knew that my mother was troubled, at a loss for what to say to me, now that she had no more pretty stories to tell. Her life as Briar, who ran wild with Jack and Sal, was long over. How could she endure her double life as my real mother and the false chief magician? How could I endure it, now that I knew who he was, what he had done? My feelings for her were all mixed up. I loved her; I was furious with her. I never wanted to leave her; I was determined to get out, not just out of our rooms, out to the world beyond. The world I was secretly mapping.

One night I woke in a sweat. I looked to the wall, and was not as surprised as before to see an opening, this time a dark, velvety green, shimmering with sparks. Up and down they flew, flickering on and off. The rest of the room was dark, and my mother and aunties audibly asleep. Without hesitation, I freed myself from my tangled sheets and stepped into the sloping hallway. This time I followed I followed a warm breeze. This time I knew where I was going, up and around, up and around. Again I found the door cracked open; from inside came flickering light.

"Come and find me," called a voice.

I slipped through the door, and there, sitting in the chair where the white-haired, moonlit woman had sat before, was a wizened woman with hair blazing around her, echoing the flames in the fireplace. I had only seen fire once, when Noone took me to his chambers, but that fire seemed tame compared to the one that crackled and leapt, throwing its light all around the round walls. Light and heat came equally from the old woman rocking in the chair, fixing me with eyes dark and shining as blackberries.

"Do you know who I am?"

That question again.

"Do *you* know who you are?" I asked. "Because the other one didn't."

"What other one?" She sounded cross.

"The other one who sat in that chair," I said. "The other one who knows my name, but not her own."

The woman stopped rocking and stared at me. From deep in her blaze of hair, she extracted a comb, also white and gleaming. As she combed her hair, it hissed and crackled, throwing off sparks, until she settled the comb back into the subsiding flames.

"You know more than you are saying," the old woman accused. "Tell me, Rose!"

Like the other old woman, she also knew my name.

"I think she is your sister," I answered.

"Sister, sister," she muttered and sputtered. "There was an old woman who missed her sister."

"Sisters," I said. For a moment I could glimpse them, four shadows dancing on the wall. "Can't you see them? There, look!"

But as soon as I spoke, the shadows disappeared. The light from the fire, from the woman's hair, flared as she rocked, keeping her eyes focused on me.

"Don't you remember your sisters?" I prompted.

"Long ago, long ago, there was a world and then there wasn't," she chanted. "Then there was, but it has to stay hidden. Run and hide, run and hide. That's all I remember."

She sounded sad, but her bright berry eyes were still merry, even young, younger than my mother's eyes.

"How old are you?" I asked.

"Older than the stars. At least I believe so. Everything was dark once. Then there was sun and stars and fire at night under the trees . . ."

Her voice trailed away, the fire burned low.

"Do you know about Jack?" I asked. "Do you know where he is?"

"Jack?" Her bright eyes dimmed a little, smoky with forgetfulness. "I believe I've known a Jack or two in my time. There's always a Jack. Now what's that tune my fiddlers play? Jack be Nimble, Jack be Quick . . . Why, Rose, have you lost your Jack?"

She peered at me, her eyes keen again.

"I haven't found him yet," I answered.

She paused to consider, the fire hissing and whispering.

"You will, Rose, you will find him. And when you do, you must come and visit me in the greenwood."

We both heard a step on the stairs and then another and another.

"Oh, oh, oh, it is time for me to go." The old woman leapt from the chair, leaving it rocking behind her. "Run trees! Run squirrels! Run bears! Run fiddlers! Run, Rose! Seek me, seek me when you can, and I'll hide you."

The fire roared, her hair turned into sparks. For an instant I glimpsed night, sheer night, black and bright with billions of stars.

And then it was dark, except for a few embers in the fireplace.

A moment later the door opened wide, and he came in, his forked beard catching the dying light.

Down, Rose, said the inner voice.

"Who left it open? Again! I told him to seal it once and for all. I smell smoke. Someone's been here, someone's lit a fire. Who, who!"

The door, Rose.

I crept toward it, silent as smoke.

"Living, dying fire. No! No! No! No! He promised me eternal fire. He promised me a living star. For years, nothing, years. No end of nothing. I'll end him. I'll send him over the edge of the world. Ee arr ohh eerr arr!"

He crackled and bellowed. I thought he would burst into flame.

Rose, now!

Still crouching, I made for the door, running on tiptoe down the stairs, around and down till the old man's roar was no more than an echo. I ran, wishing I could run away to the peak, away to the forest, but our wall opened and took me back in, safe from harm, safe and trapped.

❋   ❋   ❋

If it hadn't been for my secret notebook, I don't think that I could have borne the long days and the longer nights of waiting for something I could not will to happen, though I willed with all my might. Whenever I was alone, I took out my pencils and papers. Though I had never seen a tree except in picture books, I drew the forest, all the different greens and shapes of leaves. I drew squirrels and birds, foxes and bears. I drew the fiddlers by the open fire. Best of all I found I could draw the old woman, her legs kicking high as she danced, her hair bright as the fire, sparks rising to join the stars above the dark forest.

"Granny Spark," I said out loud.

Last I drew the greenwood rising from the dry, cracked plain. In the sky overhead, I placed the sun, as I imagined it, with a halo of flares. Under the sun and over the wood, I wrote:

Here lives Granny Spark.

❋   ❋   ❋

I was so pleased with my efforts that I put away my papers and pencils, did my homework and chores in record time, then set about tidying our rooms, setting the table for whatever my mothers and aunties would bring for supper. I wished I could decorate with green boughs and wild roses. I wished I could light a real fire in a hearth, but I did what I could to make our home beautiful, maybe because I believed I would soon leave it.

I was rewarded with pleased exclamations and lavish praise from all three.

❋   ❋   ❋

"Our Rose is growing up," remarked an auntie when they thought I was asleep.

"No, no. She's still a child," retorted the other.

"Our baby." They both sighed.

"Not for long, not for long."

"What shall we do, Briar, what shall we do?"

I held my breath, waiting for my mother's answer, but if it came I couldn't hear it.

"Do you think Noone knows? Do you think deep down he knows?"

"No one knows what Noone knows. Not even Noone."

"He has been acting strangely lately."

"He is always strange."

"We must think of a plan," my mother spoke at last.

"We have a plan."

"We've always had a plan."

What plan? I held my breath.

"A better plan. A new plan."

I have a plan, I almost said aloud.

But I didn't want them to know, not yet. And what plan did I have beyond my dreams, if they were dreams, and my maps? I strained my ears to hear more. But their voices had fallen to whispers, what I imagined soft wind might sound like in leaves. Soon they subsided into whistles and snores. We all slept.

✳   ✳   ✳

It was the scent that wakened me in the middle of the night, a dark, damp alive scent, not like anything I had ever smelled. The scent carried sound with it, rustlings, stirrings almost beyond the range of my hearing. I got out of bed and followed the fragrance, its warmth, its coolness. I could not see the opening in the wall. It looked darker and more solid than ever, yet I was not surprised when I walked through it into the hallway. Around and up, around and up, I went, the scent growing stronger and richer. When I slipped into the round room, I heard the sounds again. The room was full of growing things, vines, climbing through the window, green leaping in the fireplace. And there in the rocking chair was another old woman, brown and round and lumpy, with black hair twisting, twining in every direction. As she rocked, the vines kept growing.

"Rose," she said at length.

Of course, she knew my name, just like the others.

"Yes, I am Rose," I agreed. "Do you know who you are?"

I asked what had become a ritual question. She shook her head, and dug out a comb. With each stroke something shook loose from her locks and fell to the floor, all different shapes and colors. I was not familiar enough with fruits or vegetables to recognize all of them.

"Not at the moment," she said, burying the comb in her deep black hair. "I often forget. I am very old, very, very old."

"How old?" I asked.

"As old dirt, as old as dirt, as old as dirt, maybe older."

I waited for her to ask me if I knew who she was. I looked at the walls to see if I could catch a glimpse of their shadows, the dancing women. The leaves rustled; the vines were heavy with blossoms and fruit of all kinds. The old woman kept rocking. It was hard to tell if her tiny eyes were open or closed.

"Rose!" she cried out suddenly. "Help me remember!"

I was more certain now of my answer.

"You are one of the ancient ones who dance in a circle. I have met two of your sisters here." I hesitated, not sure whether to call them by the names I had given them.

"Not them!" She shook her head, releasing pods of beans. "I do remember I've forgotten them. Not them."

She must mean Jack, I thought. They all wanted to know where Jack was. So did I!

"Not them," she repeated.

"Jack?"

She stopped rocking.

"Not Jack. Jack's mother. That's who. Jack's mother."

Tears started to flow out of her tiny eyes, cutting rivulets in her dark face.

"There was an old woman who lived in a shoe, with so many children and their mothers too. But she did not come to me there, like the other mothers. I found her, far away inside the earth. In the dark, deep place where the stars are buried."

The mine. Could she mean the mine?

"What happened?" I prompted.

"I don't remember, I don't remember. Help me remember, Rose."

Help her remember something that might have happened before I was born? Yet I knew, of course, I knew, or guessed, what she had forgotten, what my mother had never found out.

"Her name is Sal," I told her. "She's a miner. She had a baby."

My heart beat so wildly, I thought it would break open and grow into something wild and green.

"Yes, yes," said the old woman. "She had a baby, a son. I helped her, just as I help all the mothers. Before she died, she named him Jack, Jack Quick, the son of Nimble Jack."

Sal? The room blurred; the vines swayed as if they were underwater in a strong current. Sal dead?

"But Jack, Jack Quick is alive," I willed it so. "Jack Quick is alive."

The old woman rocked again, her arms across her chest, as if she cradled a child. Her tears stopped, leaving her face muddy and streaked.

"Find Briar, give him to Briar, that's what the mother said, what Sal said. I tried, Rose, I did try. I kept asking everyone: where is Briar?"

Of course she couldn't find Briar. When Sal gave birth to Jack Quick, Briar was deep inside inside world, in disguise, hiding another baby under her false magician's robes.

"I wanted to take him home, the sweet baby. I wanted to take him home to my shoe to be with all the other children. But a woman took him from my arms and wouldn't give him back. He's mine, she said. I've lost all the others. He's mine. She took him away with her. That's all I can remember, apart from the crocodiles on the way out of that world, back to my home."

The crocodiles in the dungeon, the crocodiles who had eaten . . . I could not even think the word.

"Where is Jack, Rose?" the old woman asked again. "Where is Jack Quick?"

"I don't know yet," I said, though now I had a better idea. "But I am going to find him."

Outside, outside.

"When you find him, Rose, come find me. In the shoe. Old and muddy it may be, but you'll be safe there, you and Jack."

Then, just as twice before, came the tread on the stairs. It was not safe here. It would never be safe here.

Down, Rose, said the warm, blue, inner voice.

The door opened so wide, I thought it would tear off its hinge. I looked to the chair, but the old woman wasn't there, just a pile of dirt.

Noone stood and stared.

"Who did this! Who let the outside in? Someone is conspiring against me. Is it him? Is it him? Aarrgh grrrrrrrrrrrrrrrr ee aayyy."

Noone roared and tore the tattered vines from the wall, threw them out the window and slammed it shut, not noticing that the latch didn't catch. Then he sat down in the chair, buried his face in his hands, and wept.

Now, Rose, said the inside voice.

And I crept out of the room and ran away to the embrace of my soft, dangerous world.

After that night, it was hard for me to concentrate on anything. Jack must be in outside world, the world I had glimpsed from the window, the world where Briar, Sal, and Jack had ruled the dung heap and hidden in the briar patch.

But the briar patch had burned, and Briar and Sal's Jack was dead or gone or both. And Sal, Sal was dead, too. I could not look at my mother without thinking, *she doesn't know*. Should I tell her? But what would I tell her? *Your best friend is dead. An old woman with a face like a potato told me so. I found her in a tower where the walls were overgrown with vines. . .*

It was a dream, Rose, only a dream, I could almost hear her trying to comfort me. But she would find no comfort herself. Her heart would break. Yet it wasn't only fear of not being believed or of causing grief that kept me quiet. Secrecy had become habitual for me, maybe even essential, like air.

Don't forget your map, an inner voice spoke, but it was a different voice, not edged with blue, but dark with seams of light shot through. *You need to know where they are; they need to know who they are.*

Who are you? I did not ask, because whoever had spoken was already gone. I guessed whose voice it might be, but I did not say so, even to myself.

I got out my sketchbook, and I drew the old shoe again, an ankle boot, muddy, worn, with children inside and out, peeking through the holes for the laces, using the laces as a rope for sliding or climbing. All around the boot I sketched gardens, overflowing with ripe vegetables and berries. Best of all I could now draw the old woman, sitting outside, leaning against the boot's toe, her arms and lap full of babies and children, her face and feet, dark as dirt.

"Granny Dirt," I said out loud.

Last I drew the old muddy shoe, in an island of green, rising out of the empty cracked plain on the other side of the map from the forest, the pinnacle at the top of the map. Over the shoe I wrote:

Here lives Granny Dirt.

My mother and aunties grew worried about me.

"She hardly speaks anymore," fretted my mother. "Sometimes she looks like she's about to cry. And other times she can't stop smiling."

"Young girls are like that," said Auntie Aloe, trying to soothe her. "They cry over nothing."

"They keep secrets," added Auntie Vinda.

They were getting too close for comfort.

"But what secrets could she possibly have, safe in this room?" said my mother. "Unless, unless . . . But she's never alone for more than an hour. You promised me. Never more than an hour."

"That's right, Briar."

"We take turns."

"Never more than an hour."

"I try to talk to her," said my mother, "but she pushes me away."

My mother sounded so sad, I almost went to her, but I didn't want them to know that I was listening. I would be nicer to her, I resolved. I would say something, anything . . .

"Oh, Briar, young girls are like that," Auntie Aloe sounded her refrain. "We remember..."

"We don't remember," contradicted Auntie Vinda. "Not exactly."

"We do!"

"Well, you were a young girl, Briar. Don't you remember?"

"No," she said sadly. "I wish . . . "

She never finished the sentence.

Should I tell her? I asked the inside voices, the bright blue one, the dark shining one. *Will one of you tell her?*

Neither voice answered.

Jack, I told myself, *find Jack. Jack Quick. That's all you have to do. Find Jack.* But how, how would I ever get out of here?

✳ ✳ ✳

And I was not the only one my mother and aunties were worried about.

"He's getting more and more unhinged," said Auntie Vinda.

"Fit to be tied," added Auntie Aloe.

"I wish we could tie him up in his chair, lock him in his room," said Auntie Vinda. "Do you think he sleepwalks?"

"He's having nightmares," said Auntie Aloe. "Old man's nightmares. There are no cracks in the dome, no windows that open on outside world."

So, they didn't know, none of them knew.

"Whether there are or not, he's blaming you, Briar," said Auntie Vinda. "I mean, he's blaming the chief magician."

"I'm not a magician," said my mother. "How much longer can I fool him?"

"You know, Briar, we've never said this outright—" began Auntie Aloe.

"But it is time for plain speaking."

"Not that we know, sister," cautioned Auntie Aloe.

"We don't know, but we suspect."

"We've always suspected," they both said.

"What!" cried my mother in frustration; I almost echoed her. "Say it."

"The chief wasn't a real magician, either," said Auntie Aloe. "It was all Noone."

"It's always been all Noone," said Auntie Vinda. "The chief just persuaded Noone that he couldn't do without him."

"So if Noone says there's a leak in dome world . . ." said Auntie Aloe.

"It might be a leak in his own brain," said Auntie Vinda.

Now I felt confused and frightened. Did they mean the room wasn't real? The room I'd found, the room Noone wanted sealed off forever, was only Noone's . . . madness?

"But what about the star, the elixir?" said my mother. "The star is still there!"

"You sang the star, Briar. You called it forth with your voice. That's why the chief wanted you."

I could hear my mother's breath catch.

"But the elixir killed Jack, I killed Jack . . ."

I wanted to go to my mother then. I wanted to tell her it was not her fault. That Jack, her Jack, was a bright somersault of blue, and Sal had a dark voice streaked with gold. I wanted to tell her the room was real, and that Noone's rage was real and dangerous. That we must escape. But I did not know how to unseal my secrets.

Or maybe I didn't want to. Not yet. I hadn't met all the old ones yet, the old ones who did not remember who they were. When I had, maybe I would know what to do.

✳   ✳   ✳

Not many nights later, I woke up with cold, salt tears on my face. I wrapped my covers round me, but my teeth rattled. Despite the chill, I threw off my blankets and walked through a veil of mist, fine droplets beading on my face. I knew what to do, I knew where I was going, and could have found my way even without the whoosh and roar, the smell of salt, the sound of bells.

When I stepped inside the round room, I almost lost my balance. The floor rose and pitched, tilting this way and that, never lying flat.

"Find your sea legs, Rose. Widen your stance, always know where center is."

I saw the old woman, not in the rocking chair, but standing on the deck of what I did not know then was a ship. The walls had turned to sails, snapping and billowing. Then everything quieted; the floor stopped pitching. She stood, dark and shining, beside the wide-open window, beckoning me to come and stand beside her. I took in her blue-black skin and green-black hair, gleaming with shells and bones.

She took a comb from her hair—the same gleaming white as the others. Bone, I suddenly understood: the combs were all made of bone. When she combed her hair, the room came alive with scents and sounds I had never known; shells and shiny-scaled fish leapt and dove. Then everything quieted again as the comb disappeared under her undulating hair.

"Look, Rose." She pointed to the window.

As I had the first night I came to the tower, I saw the moon, waning now, but not like the picture-book moon on the ceiling of our chamber. It was wild, farther away and nearer at once. Then a dark cloud came to cover it. The air grew heavy and dense.

"Reach your hand out the window, Rose. Cup your palm."

I did as she said, and in a moment felt water falling from the sky, drop by heavy drop, till a small pool filled my hand.

"Drink, Rose."

The woman put her hand under my hand and guided it to my lips.

I, who had never been outside, except in my dreams, drank the rain. I reached out my hand again into the wet, wild night, longing for a way out. I looked down at the narrow streets, the sputtering torches of outside world. People laughed and cursed and took shelter under dripping eves. *Jack*, I thought, *Jack Quick*. He was out there, down there, somewhere.

"You will find him, Rose. Or he will find you."

She meant Jack, even if she hadn't said his name.

"And when we do?" I prompted, waiting for her to tell me where she lived.

She didn't answer. In the silence I heard bells and a faint rattling sound almost as musical as the bells, and the room filled with a sweet scent that met and mingled with the salt.

"Who am I, Rose?" she asked.

Of course, I needed to answer that question first.

"You are one of them, one of the four sisters who dance in a circle. You are all old, so old . . . older than Father Time, old as the stars, old as dirt . . . "

"I am as old as the sea," she took up the chant, "maybe older. Older than life, older than death. Yes, it's coming back to me now."

The silence rolled in again with a sigh and a whoosh.

"Where do you live?" I asked her.

Her answer was a long look. I could almost see a landscape reflected in her eye, an intricate, vaulted structure, open to the air, made of bone, clattering and swaying in the wind.

over the edge of the world I go
over the edge of the world I fly

She sang or someone sang. Maybe I sang.

The rain fell harder, so hard I could barely hear the sound of the tread on the stairs.

"Rose," said the old woman, "there's someone coming."

The door crashed open, a darkness flowed in, and the old woman rode it out the window into the night.

Noone's white forked beard flashed as he rushed toward the window and pulled it shut.

Down, Rose, came the inner voice. I dropped down, trapped between Noone and the wall.

"Who is it, who does this, who lets them in! I will have his head. I will gouge the eyes from his skull. Over the edge of the world he will fall, forever, a clattering heap of bone. Booooooooooooone," he bellowed, "boooooooooooooooooooooone."

Now, Rose.

There was no way out but between his knees. I crawled away and sprang for the open door.

"What was that! Someone was there! Who's there?"

His voice followed me down the stairs; I heard his feet stumbling on the narrow steps. And then I was being lifted, carried, by a huge force, strong and sure, through the wall that closed behind me, to the safety of my bed.

✳ ✳ ✳

In the morning, I was still chilled, and I could taste salt on my lips that felt dry and parched. I was a child who had lived all her life inside rooms, inside a world where the outside was forbidden. My brief exposure to a wide, wild world had been a shock.

"She's got a fever," fretted my aunties.

My mother, still unmasked, bent over me and kissed my forehead.

"There is no fever in inside world," said my mother. "How could she have caught cold? Even if she—"

"You haven't, have you, Rose—"

"She couldn't have. We've checked on her every hour."

I knew what they meant. Had I gotten out again, the way I had before, when they found me in Noone's chambers? Well, I hadn't. I tried to shake my head. It felt so heavy. I closed my eyes again.

"Let her sleep," whispered my mother.

And I did. When I woke again, they were gone. One of them would be back soon. I wasted no time on eating or getting dressed. I got out my sketchbook.

I found I could not imagine where the old woman lived, the way I had with the others. I tried to draw the clattering bones, gleaming in the dark, but they wouldn't stay still. I drew the round room as I'd seen it last night: the slanted floor, the walls that had billowed with wind. I drew the sliver of moon, and the clouds, the rain falling down into my cupped hand. I did manage to draw her, her darkness, her shine, the bones and shells in her hair.

At last I got out the map with the peak, the forest, the shoe. Across the emptiness from the peak, at the edge of the paper, I found myself at a loss. Where did she live, the woman who was older than the sea? I found myself drawing a jagged line at the very bottom of the page. Something wet and salty rolled down my face. I remembered my mother's description of a soup they made when they didn't have much soup. Brine, they called it. Salt and water.

"Granny Brine," I said out loud.

I looked at the line I had drawn. Though I could not see what was on the other side of it, I wrote:

Here lives Granny Brine: over the edge of the world.

I slept on and off much of the day and went to bed early after supper, not even bothering to eavesdrop. The next morning I got up, dressed, started doing my homework before breakfast. Everyone had to feel my forehead and comment on my appetite—good. Reassured that I was fully recovered from whatever had ailed me, all three went off to work.

"I'll be back in an hour," Auntie Vinda promised and threatened.

And I was on my own. Out of habit I felt under the pillow for my sketchbook, but I did not get it out. I had nothing more to draw. My map was as complete as I could make it. I sat and stared at the wall, as I had so many times before, and all at once I saw. It was not just the four ancient grannies who danced. It was everything. Nothing was still. And nothing was solid. I just had to find the rhythm, follow my own steps, and I'd be—

Through. I was through the wall, by myself, with the daytime light all around me in the corridor. Before I did anything else, before I went anywhere else, there was something I had to know.

"Let it be real," I whispered. "Let it not be a dream."

I followed the corridor up and up and found the winding stairs. There was the door. Noone must have slammed it shut so hard, the hinges had come loose. I slipped through the gap where the door hung open. By daylight (real daylight!) the room seemed empty, almost ordinary, except for a whiff of stale magic. How to describe what I mean by that; it wasn't just the smell of a fire stamped out, a wilted vine on the floor, a cup that had spilled its contents, or the rocking chair, dusty and motionless. Then I knew what it was. The window was closed; the room needed air.

Trembling yet full of purpose, I crossed the room and undid the latch, pushing the window wide open.

PART SIX

Rose and Jack

Granny Sweep

Granny Sweep stood at the edge of the pinnacle unwinding her braids, testing their length, as she had every day since her dream of the round room and the girl, Rose, who knew more about her than she knew herself. Every night she waited and willed to dream again, until sleep gave her the slip, and she left her hut to gaze at the spiders weaving cobwebs in the sky.

When would they come, the girl and the boy, when would they come?

"He has to find her first!" The raucous voice of Nightwing the raven rang out, her shadow circling the pinnacle. "Come to the lookout, old woman. Send your wind eye out."

Granny Sweep reeled in her braids, coiled and pinned them hastily as she climbed to the peak of her pinnacle. The morning light bounced back from the bright, dark opacity of the dome, making it hard to see anything at all.

The raven flew down to perch on her shoulder.

"Look low, not high. Not big, small."

Granny Sweep sent her wind eye out over the emptiness below, over the wall, where the bees no longer hummed and the briar roses had burnt to cindered shadows. Her wind eye became a subtle breeze, soughed over ragged fields, blew through breathless alleys. The closer she looked, the more vivid and chaotic the world she saw, people swarming, dust swirling, ragged children climbing on a mountain of rubbish, oblivious to flies and rats.

"Pay attention," said Nightwing.

And so instead of rushing past the filth, she sharpened her focus. Then she saw him, a merry-faced boy atop the heap, with dark skin that was also somehow rosy and hair like the fleece on a black sheep. He appeared to be laughing as smaller children flung themselves at him. He would swing them and send them spinning into the air. They always seemed to land safely, rolling down the heap, then climbing up for more.

(But where were the other two; hadn't there been three, once? Time was so confusing. Whose idea was time? And memory, what she had of it, was so mocking.)

A mob of larger boys began to mount the hill, sneers on their faces, sticks in their hands. The other children scattered.

"Run," she cried to the black-haired boy, whether or not he could hear her. "Run!"

Just as the bullies were about to beat him with their sticks, the boy somersaulted into the air, landed nimbly on the other side of the heap, and disappeared into an alley. He was so quick, her wind eye couldn't keep up with him.

"Jack!" she called after him. "Jack!"

For so he must be Jack; there was always a Jack.

Granny Spark

Granny Spark slept as late as she could in the darkest chamber among the roots of a huge old oak, but it was no use. Night after night, no more dreams of the round room or the girl, Rose, who knew things Granny Spark did not know, things she needed to remember. She climbed out of bed, out of the tangle of roots, out to stretch her arms beneath the canopy of leafy green, the play of light and shadow as lively as a fiddler's tune. The squirrels and birds had been awake and busy for hours. A bear sat with people gathered round a cheery breakfast fire, downing a bowl of berries. One of the fiddlers called out a greeting to Granny Spark and brought her a cup of honey ale.

All was well in the greenwood, far away from harm. Far, far away the girl Rose lived in in another world behind high walls under a vast dome of false sky. Outside the dome, behind a wall, an unkind world where briar roses had burnt to cinder (who had stolen fire and used it that way?), where the bees no longer hummed and made honey in hives hidden in the wall. The forest folk had fled that world, arriving in ones and twos, dazed and confused by their long journey through the wasteland. Granny Spark fed them mashed nuts and seeds, gave them teas and tinctures, and the sweet, merry oblivion of mead. And soon they forgot that they had ever lived anywhere but in the greenwood.

That morning Granny Spark found herself gathering her sturdy oak walking stick, a satchel of nuts and berries, a flask of mead and one of water. Only when she stepped out from the shelter of her greenwood did she know what she intended to do. She would find anyone coming her way before they retreated into the forgetfulness of the forest. She would sit down with them and share her food. She would ask questions while they still had answers. They would tell her what she needed to know. How to find the girl, Rose, and the boy, what was his name? Jack, of course, Jack.

There was always a Jack.

Granny Dirt

Granny Dirt had been up all night with the latest birth, in the clean, soft, secluded nest she made for laboring mothers in the hollow of the giant big toe. The baby had been born just when the dawn light spilled through the lacing holes. A fine plump newborn, soon suckling at his mother's breast, her face already smoothed of effort and pain. The other mothers could take over now, clean her up, see to it that she ate and drank and rested.

Dropping kisses and patting small heads as she went, Granny Dirt climbed out of the shoe and went to the place she always went when she needed to weep: a weeping willow by the winding stream that kept the shores green and the gardens fertile, fertile as the mothers that somehow found their way to her.

Granny Dirt stepped through the veil of leaves and climbed into the arms of the tree that held her as if she were a child. Had she ever been a child? She had so many children, so many mothers and children, she was always busy, always knew what to do. Except when she didn't. She had not dreamed again of the girl, Rose, in the round room. The girl who knew the name of the mother who had died, and the name of the baby boy Granny Dirt had left behind.

Granny Dirt let the tears fall. She knew about death as much as she knew about birth. There was no reason to cry, and no reason not to. The tears rolled in rivulets down her lumpy cheeks, into the ground, underground, where that mother had died; it was all the same ground, all one web of root, rot, and seed, life and death, the same dirt.

"Jack is alive," the girl had said. "I'm going to find him."

There was always a Jack; and now, a Rose.

Granny Dirt swung down from the tree. She felt in her apron pockets, full of seeds she'd saved. Yes, there were apples, too, and a loaf of oat bread. She always had food. She was food; it spouted from her willy-nilly; it tumbled from her. The starving mothers who came to her shoe could hardly believe it. That there was enough. She was enough. She had enough.

There were no babies due till the next moon; the children were plump and happy. She would follow the stream back. Maybe she would remember along the way, one step and another on the soft earth, what she had forgotten.

Granny Brine

Granny Brine stepped out of her coracle and pulled it up on the shore. She had come every day since her dream of the girl in the round room (so strangely familiar to her), the window almost off its hinge, the rain blowing in, the rain cupped in the girl's hand.

Drink, Rose.

How did she know the girl's name when she didn't remember who she was herself? Rose knew, Rose had been trying to tell her. Then the old man came in, the old man who was terrified of bones, his own bones. The old, angry man who had sent so many people flying, falling over the cliff.

Granny Brine stood looking up and up and up the cliff into the clouds that obscured the top. She watched them lighten, then turn golden. Soon the sun would spread light to the farthest reaches of the sea. The water would sparkle and glint. Dolphins and whales would leap and dive. But for now she stood in the shadow of the high cliff, the world's edge, her own bones cold enough to rattle with the rest.

No one had fallen over the edge in some time, whatever time was. Oh, she knew well enough, moons, tides. Pull and sway. Some of the fallen bodies got taken by the tide, but their bones would wash back up. And she would find ways to fasten the bones together. The seagulls helped her, flying the bones to the places higher than her reach, Captain squawking commentary and giving directions.

"Jack, Jack!" Captain had cried when the last one over the cliff had gone flying by, somersaulting into blue.

But he had never landed; he had left no bones.

Granny Brine stepped into the temple, walking through its arches and chambers. There was a new scent in the air, not just salt and seaweed, not just the memories held in the bones, hearth fires, bread, thin bean stews, and bitter tea, sweat, the blood of birth and death. The new scent was sweet and spicy. No, not new. She remembered from a time she could not remember. Roses growing wild along the cliff, roses.

"Come find me," she whispered. "Bring the others, show them the way."

She did not know what she meant, exactly, but as she walked along the shore, she bent and pick up here a fallen bone, there a shell of a razor clam. She made her small repairs to the temple, as Captain perched and prophesied: "Jack, Jack, he'll be back."

There was always a Jack.

Jack

Jack Quick, as people called him, went his merry way scrambling over battered fences, through hidden yards of chickens and goats. He could hear his pursuers' pounding feet, their huffing, puffing breaths, but he had no fear. It was all a game for him of you-can't-catch-me. He almost always won. He liked narrow escapes. Today he ran out into the open and almost let them catch him before he darted into an alley and leaped into an empty rain barrel. When they had passed by, shouting and enraged, he crawled out and decided to climb a rickety watchtower the Guard no longer used, because of all the missing slats in the ladder that no one had bothered to replace. It was one of his favorite perches. He could look down and see his opponents running in circles till they were winded. From the highest point he could look over the hovels and fields all the way to the wall. In the other direction, he had a view of the dome. He liked to watch it changing color with the sky, the reflection of clouds rolling over it. He was even willing to get drenched to watch the storms inside world never knew, the water sluicing down the sides of the dome, the women running with buckets to catch every precious drop.

Today the air was almost sweet, sweet as the briar roses his grandmother muttered about in her sleep. When he asked Bramma (for that's what he called her),about the roses, sometimes she would refuse to answer; sometimes she would weep. The place where the roses had once grown was haunted. People had died there, or disappeared. No one knew for sure. The place was bad luck; everyone gave it a wide berth. Except Jack. Whenever he needed to get away from everyone, his feet would take him there, almost before he knew where he was going. He never once felt afraid in that place. He would lie down on the hard stone that paved over the dirt, so that nothing could grow again, and he would imagine he could smell the roses, hear the buzzing of bees. Though he often searched, he could never find the honey they'd hidden in hives behind the stone. Maybe he would go there again today, scavenging along the way to bring back something for supper. How surprised Bramma would be if he brought her back a piece of honeycomb. Maybe she would cuff him for going where she told him not to, but maybe she would scrape together some flour and make him a cake.

The wind picked up (his Bramma had told him insiders never felt the wind) and the lookout tower swayed. Jack looked around to make sure the bullies had given up. Just as he was about to climb down, he heard a sound.

"Jack!"

The voice came from far away. Maybe it was the wind or the cry of a bird. And then he heard it again.

"Jack!"

Briefly he glanced down, but he already knew the voice wasn't coming from the ground. His eyes climbed the smooth dome, where his feet could never get a purchase. Then he saw something he had could swear had never been there before, a tiny tower rising from the round surface of the dome, and someone leaning out a window, hair the color of light on stone, blown by the wind. And a face, a girl's face, a sweet face, a serious face, gazing down . . . at him.

"Jack!"

The girl leaned out further, what might have been a foot appeared, a hand grabbing for a purchase.

"Careful," Jack cried out. She was so high above the ground; there was no way to climb down. "Wait, I'll come to you!"

How, he did not know, but he would find a way. He began to climb down, forced to watch where he was going, so he wouldn't fall through a gap in the steps.

"I'm coming," he called.

When he paused to look up again, the girl was gone. And even the tower seemed to waver, as if it could disappear into a passing cloud.

Rose

Someone had pulled me away from the window.

Flying and falling are not the always same. I should know.

I whirled around, but no one was there. I felt a hot prickle of mixed terror and relief. Noone was not there. I turned back to the window that had closed except for a crack and opened it again. I searched for the boy I'd seen on the top of the rickety tower. He was gone.

But I had seen him. He'd looked up when I'd called his name. Jack.

I looked all the way down, a long dizzying way down, all the more disorienting for a stray wisp of cloud passing by. I thought I could just see him, an upturned face in the crowd of milling people.

Close the window, Rose.

I did not turn again. Now I recognized the inside voice, the one that tumbled into my mind in a blaze of blue, the one who had helped me escape Noone.

"Who opened the door, who opened the window?" I remembered Noone muttering as he climbed the stairs. "I gave orders for it to be sealed. I told the chief magician, it must disappear." Then inside this very room, Noone had howled; his rage still rang in my bones.

The inside voice might have a point. Reluctantly I closed the window.

Now what? I asked silently. *Jack is out there. I'm in here. Now what?*

Your maps, Rose. It was the other inside voice, the dark voice, veined with light. *If you're going to set out on a journey, study your maps.*

I cast a last glance at the closed window, then crossed to the door, turning back to look at the room. Was the chair rocking slightly? Was there an ember hidden in the ash of the fireplace? What was that faint rustling sound? How strange it was to leave the round room, slowly and deliberately, not fleeing in heart-pounding terror. Gently, I pulled the door shut behind me, checking to make sure it would open again. The door, the window, a crack in the dome Noone wanted sealed. For me, they opened. Now I knew my way here, by night and by day. I had seen Jack. And he had seen me.

I made my way down the stairway into the daylit hall, slipping through the wall as easily as if I had been doing it every day of my life. Our rooms were silent. The aunties had not yet come to check on me, or surely they would have sounded the alarm. No, they couldn't do that. I was a secret. Still they would have been panicking and searching for me high (as high as the tower?) and low (as low as the dungeon?). But first they would have ransacked the closet. I went and did a thorough check. No sign of disruption; all the gowns as I had last been assigned to rearrange them, this time by color. In our small, secret world, not an auntie in sight.

I had gotten away with it, escaping the room again, by day. Even though I'd just retraced my steps, there was no turning back from whatever adventure I had begun. Out of our rooms, out of the dome, over the wall. I went to my sleeping nook and got out my maps from under my pillow. Sitting cross-legged on my bed, I leafed through the notebook to the map I'd made of the whole vast beyond, right up the edge of the world. As I gazed at the map, at the empty expanses between the pinnacle, the forest, the shoe, I thought I saw miniscule movements, someone or something making a line, two lines, new cracks or paths . . .

Wandering Grannies

Granny Spark was tired, and she had forgotten what she set out to do. Why had she wandered so far away from the forest? Why hadn't the forest followed her? Or she, the forest? They moved together; that was the usual way of things. What was she doing on this naked earth with the blaze in the sky glaring down at her, making her head a tangled nest of flame? She should go back. She turned around, or at least she thought she turned around, but she could not see the forest, not a tree in sight. No shifting shadows to tell her where she was or what to do. Even her own shadow seemed to be hiding at her feet. She felt so lost, she wanted to cry, but her eyes were too dry.

She closed her eyes and a memory came back to her. (Was it a memory or was it a bad dream?) Fire all around her, trees falling, animals running, people screaming, smoke choking. And three people crawling along the ground trying to escape.

I didn't mean to, I didn't mean to.

Then silence, except for the sound of bees making honey in a stone wall. And three children hiding nearby under a thicket of wild roses.

She opened her eyes. A shadow passed over the sun, over the earth. She followed it with her sight to a pinnacle, earth rearing into the sky. Maybe it was a sign. She would go that way. If she could climb the pinnacle, maybe she could see where the forest had gone, maybe she could remember what she was doing. Better to go that way than to the strange, distant dome catching all the light, giving back nothing but glare.

She was used to walking on leaves, pine needles, moss. Her bare feet, knobby as tree roots, recoiled from the hard ground, but she walked on.

✳   ✳   ✳

Granny Dirt looked around in confusion. Looking for surer footing, she'd lost the stream. The narrow band of green banks had disappeared. Everywhere she turned, the earth was parched and cracked.

She closed her eyes, but what she saw with her inner eye was worse. (Was it a memory or a bad dream?) The earth shaking, cracks opening into chasms, towns (she vaguely remembered them) falling, people and animals crushed, trapped.

I didn't mean to. I didn't mean to.

Then silence, except for the sound of bees making honey in a stone wall. And three children hiding nearby under a thicket of wild roses.

She opened her eyes, a shadow inched over the dry earth, creeping toward her as if it wanted to overtake her, take her in. The shadow of dome world, doom world. Is that where she was going? What did she intend to do there?

She had left a child there, hadn't she? Two children, three . . .

Turning away from the shadow, Granny Dirt saw a pinnacle, pink at the top in the afternoon light. In the distance, she spied a lone moving figure, the only living thing for miles, the only living thing she could see in the world. Granny Dirt began to walk towards whoever, whatever it was. Maybe someone who could help her find her way, back to the stream, back to the green banks, and towards whatever she had set out to do.

The earth was so hot and hard under her sore feet. How was it that someone who lived in a shoe had no shoes? (Or was the old shoe just another dream?) No help for it now. She walked on.

Rose

"Rose?"

I snapped to, shoving my notebook back under the pillow.

"What are you doing, Rose?"

It was Auntie Aloe, lucky for me. Her eyesight was not so keen, and she was more inclined to be vague about the rules. Unlike Auntie Vinda, who made them up as she went along and enforced them strictly, however unreasonable they might be, until she forgot them again.

"Nothing," I answered too quickly.

"Well, weren't you supposed to being doing *something*?"

"I'm sorry, Auntie. I think I must have fallen asleep."

Maybe I had. What I'd seen on the map had been more vivid than a daydream. The more I had gazed the more I could see. Granny Spark, far from her forest, looking grumpy. Granny Dirt, who always knew what to do, confused, lost from her shoe. Both of them frightened and out of their elements.

"We didn't mean to leave you alone for so long," Auntie Aloe was saying. "It was hard to get away. Noone is in a foul temper today."

Now she had my full attention. It was rare for any of them to speak of work, and rarer still for them to mention Noone. At least to me.

"I didn't like to leave your mother. I thought both of us should stay with her, but of course one of us is needed here, and sister is fiercer than me."

I must admit my first thought was for my own purposes. The more they stayed away, the better for me.

"I'm all right alone here, Auntie. I promise, I will do my chores and my homework."

Did I sound too eager?

"I mean, maybe you should go back to my mother," I paused for a moment. "And protect her from Noone."

Auntie Aloe gave me sharper look than usual and glanced around the room, as if looking for evidence, of something. I did the same. I saw nothing to arouse suspicion. My math book and worksheets waited for me on the table.

"What do you know about Noone? Has sister been talking?"

No, *you* just talked, I did not say out loud. Maybe, alone without her sister contradicting her and my mother casting anxious glances, I might get her to say something more. I changed tack.

"Now that you're here, why don't you sit down?"

As big and solid as she was, I could see her wavering, as if her legs were tired of holding her up.

"I could give you a foot rub." Something my aunties always welcomed after teeter tottering, sometimes for miles, they said, in their glamourous, precarious shoes.

"Oh, Rose," she sighed. "Dear, sweet girl. How thoughtful of you."

Apparently she suspected nothing. And she went to her favorite chair and did not so much sit as drift down as if she weighed nothing. I fetched a cushioned and removed her glittering shoes with care, setting them upright by the chair. I had been taught to treat shoes with reverence, though I rarely wore them in our thickly carpeted rooms. I thought of Granny Spark and Granny Dirt. In my dream, if it was a dream, their feet had been bare and blistered, as if they needed a foot rub, too.

"Ah," Auntie Aloe, sighed and closed her eyes.

"Why is Noone so angry today?" I asked, hoping to catch her with her guard down.

"That bit of whiskered bone and gristle?" she said with mild indignation. "He's always been angry. Since long before sister and I were born, before and after the disasters, despite the beautiful world he made out of nothing but magic dust. Nothing is enough, nothing is ever enough for him. He was angry with the old chief, too."

My begetter. And now he was angry with new chief, the imposter, my mother.

"Is it because the elixir still isn't ready?"

"Hush, Rose, your mother wouldn't like us to talk about it."

"But she told me about it," I pointed out. "I know the elixir killed Jack or anyway made him…disappear."

And Noone didn't know. I knew more than Noone. So did my mother and aunties. Did he suspect?

"And maybe we never should have told you. Your poor mother, Rose. We told her to tell you, sister and me. We thought it was best…."

I knew without looking that her eyes were misting, forming salt pools that threatened to overflow. I rubbed her feet, firmly, tenderly.

"No matter," she took a ragged breath. "Noone's been going on about the awful old elixir forever and ever. I don't know what he needs it for. If he was going to die, he'd be dead by now. Death doesn't want the old fool. No, something else is bothering him lately."

"The leak."

I bit my tongue, but it was too late. Auntie Aloe struggled to sit up, but I kept hold of her feet to keep my hands from trembling.

"How do you know about the leak, Rose?"

I shrugged, trying to think of way to avoid answering.

"Rose! Look at me!" She took my face between her huge hands. "Have you been eavesdropping?"

There. She had given me a way out, a partial truth I could admit.

"Sometimes, I wake up at night. I hear you all talking. I can't help it."

Auntie Aloe held my face, her grip turning to a caress, then she settled back down.

"Well then, you know as much as we do, which is nothing. There is no leak in the dome. The Guard has searched high and low. But Noone doesn't believe it. He rants on about secret doors and windows, evil forces infiltrating. The man is mad, and he thinks your mother—Gently, Rose!

Don't dig your in your nails. Oh dear, I have frightened you. Sister always says I talk too much. Ha! She's one to talk. There's no need to fear, dearie, come to auntie."

She reached down, lifted me as if I were still a small child, and gathered me into her lap, pressing my face into her colossal bosom.

"There, there," she crooned.

Should I tell what I knew? Should I warn them? But if I told, I would never be left alone again, never get out again. The open door, the open window, the crack in the dome, my way out into the rain, the sun, into the world where Jack waited would be closed to me. Forever.

"You're safe, Rose," Auntie Aloe was crooning. "We'll keep you safe."

Safe inside these tiny rooms, inside inside world

"We'll keep your mother safe."

Abruptly, I sat up and pulled away.

"Go back to my mother, please, Auntie Aloe. Stay with her. I'll be all right."

I didn't say where. I didn't say how.

"Child," she said. "Sweet Rose."

Auntie Aloe reached for her shoes. I helped her squeeze her huge feet into their narrow confines.

"Just for a little while. We'll all be back tonight. Promise. Do your homework now. What is it, algebra, geometry?"

Geography, I did not say.

"And arrange the clothes, by, let's see, I know, size this time."

Since both my aunties wore the same size, that wouldn't be hard.

"Promise."

And she held out her pinky to mine. We linked and danced in a little circle.

Jack and Bramma

No matter how far he roamed during the day, Jack always returned to his Bramma's hearth at dusk. He had to keep a close eye on her to make sure she didn't give him all the best morsels of whatever there was to be had. She declared she could live on rain and air and the light of dawn. But Jack made sure crusts of bread found their way into her soup. He kept her distracted with his tales of besting the bullies and hiding from the Guard. Bramma often clutched his arm, asked anxious questions or gave him more and more serious warnings. For Jack was nearing the dangerous age. Boys like Jack disappeared all the time into the mining camps or into the underground barracks of dome world.

Jack supposed that's what happened to his father, though Bramma never spoke of his father or his mother. When he was younger he thought Bramma was his mother, but when he tried to call her Ma or Mama, she shook her head.

"My own dear boy, I am not your mother."

"Are you my grandmother?" he asked, for many children had those.

It took her so long to answer him, he thought she hadn't heard him.

"I am your Bramma," she always said. "And you are my dear boy."

Jack knew he was lucky; there were many children who were dear to no one. Bramma, like some of the other mothers and grandmothers, tried to feed as many as she could, but only he belonged to her. Most of the time that was enough for him. Every now and then, when they were alone in the hut, and he was falling asleep, he would ask.

"Who is my mother? Do I have a father?"

"Hush," she would say. "It is best not to say their names."

"Why?"

But she never answered. Instead she would sing softly a rhyme that children sang on the dung heap until the Guard came out of nowhere, spears pointed, and sent them scattering. When Bramma sang, the song sounded different, beautiful, near and far away at once.

over the edge of the world we go
over the edge of the world we fly

And he would fly into dreams, only to waken to Bramma crying out in her sleep. *Briar*, she would said over and over. *Briar, Sal*, and his own name, *Jack*.

"What mischief have you gotten into today, my boy?" Bramma asked him as she did every night when they sat outside the hut before the fire.

As usual he launched into his tale of narrow escape and daring aerial feats, but he found himself trailing off midsentence.

"And then what happened, my boy?" prompted Bramma. "You climbed the old watch tower, which I've told you isn't safe time and again. What happened then?"

Jack turned toward her, coming back from where his thoughts had taken him to the tiny high tower, the girl leaning out, her hair floating on the wind, the flash of her face. The bare foot on the sill. Her voice calling his name.

"I . . . I don't know," he said, truthfully enough. For what *had* happened? Had he really seen what he had seen? Or was it a dream? "I just climbed down again, I guess."

He did not tell her that he had climbed down to try to find a way to get to the girl, or that when he looked up, the girl and the tower were gone.

Bramma peered at him intently, as if she could see in his eyes what he had seen, as if she suspected something.

"What did you see, boy?" she asked softly, sharply. "Who did you see?"

He just shook his head. Silently he answered, *It's best not to say her name.*

Then he remembered. He did not know her name.

Bramma nodded her head as if she had heard, as if she understood.

Grannies

Dark

Granny Spark and Granny Dirt walked until they each disappeared from the other's sight into darkness. They wrapped themselves in their cloaks. The bare earth, still sun-warmed, softened, and the two grannies lay down and fell asleep. The moon rose, and the shadow of the pinnacle stretched across the emptiness.

Unable to sleep, Granny Sweep stood on the pinnacle toward the dome, trying to send her sight beyond its deceptive reflections, but finding herself blinded and caught.

Granny Brine lay on the deck of her ship looking up and up and up to the top of the cliff where the moon would rise late. Far away in another world, something was happening, with her, without her.

One day she would remember.

Dawn

Granny Spark and Granny Dirt woke suddenly. The air was bright with sound. The stars were singing. No, it was birds, flying among the stars. Then they heard the voices, women's voices.

come the sorrow, come the pain
come the sun, come the rain
come the toiling all day long
come the night, come the dawn
beauty will go on, go on, beauty will go on

They rose to their feet, looked across the expanse and saw.
Each other.
Step by step by step, they walked, closing the distance between them. From her pinnacle, Granny Sweep watched, unpinning her braids, letting them fall and fall. The sun began to rise, casting the shadow of the pinnacle toward dome world.

Just below the pinnacle, Granny Spark and Granny Dirt came face to face.
"You," said one.
"You," said the other.
"I didn't mean to," said one.
"I didn't either," said the other.
"Didn't meant to what?"
"I don't know."
"I don't know either."

"Sister," said one.

"There was an old woman who missed her sister."

"Then she kissed her."

They came closer and disappeared into each other's cloaks.

I am not the only one," Granny Sweep whispered to herself, and then she shouted. "Sisters! Sisters! Come up!"

She loosened her braids and flung them over the pinnacle.

Beyond the edge of the world, Granny Brine stood on the deck of her ship, riding the swells, waiting for sunrise. The wind picked up; the bells rang and the bones rattled. Flocks of birds flew over the edge of the world, singing with women's voices.

Rose

I woke from a deep sleep. The dawn light was just coming on, paling our walls, turning them some delicate, nameless color that did not come from the sun outside, just as the circling, fading stars had no sky but the dome. My aunties snored softly in their beds, their bulk a familiar geography. But my mother was not in her bed. I sat up, alarmed, curious, wondering if she had gone out, alone, early. But it took both my aunties to transform her into the magician, and I had never known her to leave our rooms in her own form.

I got up and crept out of the sleeping nook. Then I saw her, on the far side of our rooms, standing alone, still in her robe, her lips moving, her arms outstretched, and tears coursing silently down her face.

Mama, I did not say.

For the woman before me was not my mother, not the woman who sat patiently every day while her face was molded into another's. She was not even the one who told me stories of the three, roaming wild in outside world.

She was Briar herself. Alone.

I am very old now, children, but I still wonder what would have happened if I had gone to her then, slipped my hand into hers, led her through the wall to the tower room, and showed her the window. Instead, one auntie stirred, and then another, and the day began like all other days, and yet not like all other days. For I had my own secret life now, and I decided to keep it a secret.

Jack

As usual when Jack woke early, his Bramma was already gone. Though she would never tell him, he knew she was a beauty singer. All the voices blended into one voice. As much as people loved to gossip, no one ever spoke the names of the beauty singers. It was considered the worst of bad luck to tell anyone their names. Bad luck for the teller and worse luck for the beauty singer, who could be arrested, tried, and sent over the edge of the world, though it rarely happened; the beauty singers were adept at dodging the Guard, disappearing with the last morning stars into the bustle of the day. By the time Jack got up and stirred the embers of the fire, his Bramma appeared as if she had never been gone. Together they ate whatever breakfast they could scrape together, before they went their separate ways: Bramma to work in the fields or the laundries, Jack to scavenge and dodge.

Or to race to the rickety tower and climb it as high as he could, high enough to hear if the girl in the tower called his name.

Grannies

Winded from their long climb up the pinnacle and weary from the even longer tramp across the emptiness, Granny Spark and Granny Dirt sat at a table beneath Granny Sweep's apple tree drinking chamomile tea, with honey from Granny Sweep's bees, and eating strawberries with fresh cream from Moo-n. Granny Sweep kept her guests company, now and then patting her head where she'd rewound her braids. Her scalp was a bit sore, but the braids had held. They would be ready for . . . who was it she'd invited?

"Rose," she said out loud.

It was the first time any of them had spoken in some time.

"And Jack," added Granny Dirt.

"Rose and Jack," put in Granny Spark. "I've heard those names before."

The three grannies looked around at each other, surprised, pleased but a bit baffled.

"One of us is missing," said Granny Sweep after a moment.

"I believe you are right. There are supposed to be—" Granny Dirt paused to count. "Four of us. Who is not here?"

"Hard to say," said Granny Spark, "since we don't know who we are."

They fell silent again; the sun warmed the earth and stirred a breeze that carried a sweet, spicy scent.

"Rose knows who we are," said Granny Sweep.

"And she knows who Jack is," said Granny Dirt. "She knows who Jack's mother is."

"And . . . Jack's father. There were three children once," said Granny Sweep. "In a briar patch. Then there was a fire—"

"I didn't mean to," said Granny Spark.

"None of us meant to. Not even—"

"Before."

"I don't remember," they told each other. "But I can't forget."

They fell silent; in their lost memories, they could hear the wind howl, the rush of huge water, the boom of quaking earth, the roar of flames.

"What do we do now?"

"Find Rose."

"And Jack."

"Help Rose find Jack."

"And Jack find Rose."

"And then what?"

A cloud passed over the sun; a few drops of rain fell on them.

"No one knows," came a soft whisper. "Not even Rose."

"Who spoke?"

"Was it . . . ?"

"Rose said there were four. Four old women dancing."

"Are we old?" they asked each other.

"We are older than old," whispered the voice.

Older than time.

Older than stars.

Older than dirt.

Older than . . .

Far away they heard something soft and loud, rhythmic and wild. Bells and bones. Then came the unmistakable, raucous cry of Nightwing the raven.

"Come on, old girls, come to the look out! Time to send your wind eye out!"

The three Grannies climbed to the very tippy-top of the pinnacle, holding on to each other to keep from being blown over the edge by the strong wind. There was a rickety railing surrounding the lookout, little more than a reminder to stay back from the edge.

"What does the bird mean by a 'wind eye'?" demanded Granny Spark.

"If I send my sight out, I can see the streets and the alleys, the dung heaps, the children."

"What about inside the dome?" asked Granny Dirt. "Can you see inside?"

"I've never seen inside, except . . . except in the dream," said Granny Sweep. "The window, the tower, the rocking chair, Rose . . . "

There was a pause, as they stood together gazing out, gazing in.

"I've had the same dream."

"And I."

"We've all had the dream," said the one they couldn't see. "And the nightmare. Part of each of us is trapped inside."

"Send out your wind eye," cried Nightwing.

"Tell us, sister, tell us what you see."

"See with me, sisters! Send your eyes out, too."

With the sun, with a blade of grass, with a bead of dew.

Jack

Jack climbed the old watchtower as high as he could. In the tiny tower near the top of the dome, the light caught the windowpane, and then the window opened.

Her name is Rose, the wind whispered. *Rose,* said the touch of the sun. *Rose,* the word rose from the very grass in the cracks between stones.

"Rose!" Jack waved and called her name.

"Jack!" the girl called back.

Neither of them knew until it was too late that a passing contingent of the Guard had heard Jack's voice and caught sight of him.

"There's the one we've been trying to catch!" shouted one.

"We've got him now."

The guards began to shake the foundations of the lookout. Jack peered around as if there were somewhere to go but down. He took a last look at Rose and smiled, hoping she could see, not wanting to risk another wave of his hand in case it drew dangerous attention to her.

"All right, all right!" he grumbled to the guards. "I'm coming."

He began to climb down, unhurriedly, seemingly without fear or concern. When he was just above their heads, he made a leap. Caught up in a flash of blue, he somersaulted into the air, once, twice, three times, landing lightly on his feet beyond their reach.

A cheer went up from the passersby who had stopped to stare. In the roar of the crowd he thought he could hear words:

Jack Quick! Son of Nimble Jack! Run, boy, run!

Jack ran as he sometimes did in dreams, the earth making each step buoyant, the air catching him up. He ran faster than he ever had before, the Guard in pursuit. He ran past a crew of miners on the way to their shift. The miners cheered, too, as they surged forward, blocking the path of the Guard. In their voices he heard words:

Run, son of Sal, run!

Jack ran on until he found himself surrounded by the silence and light of the burnt-out briar patch. There he threw himself down and waited for his breath to catch up to him, the words *Nimble Jack* and *son of Sal* echoing with his heartbeat.

Finally. He knew their names.

Grannies

Just as breathless, the Grannies found themselves back on the pinnacle.

"No one will follow him to the burnt briar patch," said Granny Sweep. "He is safe for now."

"For now," said Granny Spark.

"But he needs help; they need help."

"Getting up, getting down, getting in, getting out."

"He is very good at tumbling, just like his father, but he can't quite fly."

Granny Spark and Granny Sweep stood and dusted themselves off.

Granny Dirt still sat of the ground.

"Not very good topsoil here, but there, I wonder . . . "

Granny Dirt stood up and dug in her apron pocket. From its depths, she extracted something.

"I think I might know a way."

She held up a bean for all of them to see.

Rose

Even after Jack had disappeared from my sight, I stayed at the window, as if my watching could protect him, when in fact it had endangered him.

He's safe!

I recognized the inside voice, blue at the edges of my vision, the same blue that tumbled with Jack through the air.

He's safe. But you're not. Close the window.

I was and was not surprised that the window disappeared, leaving a shimmer of daylight behind. The rocking chair was still. Nothing moved but me. I closed the door, looking back once at a seamless wall. Had the whole tower disappeared?

I had no time to wonder.

"It better be sealed, it better be gone as if it never was. Never will be!"

Noone, still out of sight but coming closer. I sped down the corridor, and pressed myself against the wall.

"I told him. I warned him. No cracks, no cracks in dome world, no cracks. No cracks in my skin, no cracks in my skull."

Just in time, I slipped back into our rooms, into my safe little world, trying to hold my breath, as if he could hear me, or worse, see me through the wall. I could hear, or rather not hear, when he stopped where the stairway should have been. Then I heard him again, coming back down the hall, muttering.

"No crack, no cracks. No way for the terrible old women to escape, no way for them to get in. Did he heed me, or is it a trick? Is he a fraud or a traitor? Am I mad or am I dreaming? And what happened to that little girl?"

He paused, just on the other side of the wall from me. Surely he could hear my heart pounding.

"What did he do with her?"

He, the magician, my mother.

"Is he a fraud or a traitor? Am I mad or am I dreaming?"

He took up his litany again, his voice and footsteps disappearing as he walked on down the hallway.

When I could breathe again, I went to my sleeping nook and got out my notebook of maps. I had to find a way out of dome world before it was too late. Flipping through the pages, I found myself at the drawing of the pinnacle. *Here lives Granny Sweep.* Peering closely, I saw not one but three Grannies, making their way down from the lookout. A huge black bird circled over their heads and then flew away. Granny Sweep, white braids windblown but still pinned haphazardly to her head, led the others to the grassy shade under the apple tree, where they lay down, toes pointed skyward, and closed their eyes.

All at once I was overcome with drowsiness myself. I remembered to hide the map back under the pillow before I fell asleep.

Jack

Jack lay in the sun that touched his skin like the warmest, softest blanket he had never known. He heard a sound he had never heard before, a rustling, not made by an animal or by a breeze. The air grew heavy and sweet, filled with a humming that was not quite a song. He found himself looking up into a tangle of green he had never seen, full of flowers that he somehow knew were roses.

Rose, he thought. *I wish Rose were here.*

He tried to call her name, but no sound came out.

Rose is still inside the dome. We're with her; we're with you, whispered two voices. He could not see who spoke, but he had an impression of blue the color of sky and of a dark voice streaked with light. *We're everywhere. We're here.* Slowly a rose petal spiraled down. Slowly his heavy eyelids closed.

Hours later, Jack woke suddenly, chilled, as shadow slowly climbed the high, bare wall. No trace of the briars, no murmuring voices, the air empty of humming sweetness. Then he heard the rhythmic thrum of wings beating the air. A large black bird landed, somewhat ungracefully, beside him.

"Jack!" it croaked.

Something dropped from its beak, but Jack didn't notice. He was too busy staring into the bright eye of a bird who seemed to know his name.

"Jack Quick!" said the bird unmistakably. "The bean, boy! Pick it up. I've carried it a long way."

Jack looked around and saw a rather ordinary-looking bean lying on the stone in front of him.

"You mean this?" Jack held it up.

"Of course, this! I carried it all this way for you."

"You really can talk!" marveled Jack. "How do you know my name?"

The raven ruffled its feathers.

"Everyone knows your name. Or at least the old girls do. Do you know my name?"

Jack felt embarrassed that he hadn't asked.

"I don't," he admitted. "What is your name?"

"Nightwing," the bird answered. "At least that's what my old girl calls me. Kind of obvious, but with a poetic ring."

Jack wanted to be respectful, as his Bramma had taught him to be.

"Thank you for the bean, Nightwing."

He kept it between his fingers not knowing what else he should do.

"Don't tell me you don't know what to do with a magic bean, boy!"

A magic bean? He held it closer and looked at it tentatively

"It's not to eat!" squawked the raven in some alarm. "It's for planting."

Jack looked around at the empty, burnt-out briar patch. Could a bean grow roses?

"Follow me, Jack Quick. I'll show you! Hold on to the bean."

And Nightwing lifted herself into the air. Jack followed as best he could on foot, as the bird led him through a maze of the most deserted alleys, right to go left and left to go right, round and round, always closer and closer to the great, shining dome.

Noone

The state dinner had been tedious, as always. He ought to abolish banquets, except he hadn't given himself that kind of power. Or rather, he'd given it away to keep the so-called king happy and busy, and distracted from the real source of power. The king had become more and more insufferable, bloated, balding beneath his pompadour, insistent on giving speeches, overly fond of his own jokes. Was that the sort of person he would choose to make immortal or to have in charge, even nominally, of making the selection?

Noone opened the door to his solitary chambers, flung off his formal jacket, loosened his tie. He poured himself an amber drink from the magic decanter, set the glass on the table and sank into his chair, closing his eyes, waiting for the scenes of the evening to fade. All those fine citizens, dressed in colors and jewels never seen in nature (what was nature? He despised nature, at least in its raw form. He had conquered it, refined it, made it beautiful, lasting).

The citizens of inside world, the scions of the first families, could not get enough of their king. They vied for his attention, groveled before his wrath, danced to his tune, falling in and out of favor so quickly they didn't have the time or inclination to revolt. (Was he the only one who found his puppet revolting?) There weren't any real consequences to losing the king's favor (apart from seating arrangements or the withholding of invitations to banquets and balls). No one from the first families had been sentenced to outside world, much less sent beyond the edge of the world, in a generation or more. (Would this generation be the last, the one that would last forever?) There was only one real consequence.

Not being selected. For immortality.

No one wanted to die. It still happened in inside world, but it was considered rude and in poor taste, a soon-to-be antiquated primitive custom. Those who committed this faux pas were quickly removed from sight and mind. Not like—

(Women wailing, skirts dragging in the mud, rain falling—why was there always rain—clods of earth thrown into a hole.)

He stood for a moment, shaking the memory from him, as if it were that cold rain, that stinking mud that he had escaped, that he had abolished. Forever. As soon as the formula was perfected. Forever. Then he sank into the chair again, heavily, as if his body were far more substantial than it really was.

Damn the chief magician. Damn the man.

He had been seated opposite the magician at the dinner, that strange, slight man with his still face and his watchful, hypnotic eyes. Anytime Noone ever called him to account, the magician just gazed at him, speaking softly, monotonously. Had his voice always had that tone? Had it always been ambiguous, not male, not female? There was something wrong about his eyes, too. Sometimes they were opaque, almost flat, like a snake's. Then sometimes, alarmingly, only for an instant, they stood out from the rest of his face, as if they did not belong there. As if they had seen things that they should not have seen.

Unbidden, an image came to Noone: rose petals loosened in the wind, falling, falling . . . on his face.

He took out his handkerchief and wiped his brow, though of course he was not sweating. He never did. Then he took far more than a sip of his drink.

He had never trusted the magician, or those painted eunuchs, his body guards, his dungeon keepers. Why did he put up with the bizarre trio? The potent fire of the drink spread out through his limbs. And a thought occurred to him, not for the first time: what if he no longer needed the magician? What was a magician but a grandiose technician? The real magic was Noone's. His mind, his imagination, his determination. The magician could be tricking him, endlessly working on the formula for immortality, maundering on and on about distilled stars. Making everyone wait, making Noone wait for something—could it be?—something that was already his.

"Are you Father Time?"

Who had asked him that question?

"Are you Father Time?"

A child's voice, the girl's voice.

The chief magician had whisked the girl away. As Noone had ordered him to. Whenever he demanded to know what had become of the child, the chief magician's face went blank, as if he had not heard him, as if Noone had not spoken. Was the man mad? Or was the man trying to drive him mad? Well then, he would fail.

"My dear," he spoke aloud, as if the girl were sitting in the chair opposite his. "There is no time. I am abolishing time."

And memory. Without time, there would be no memories. There would be no more suffering. No death. Why was it taking so long to end time?

Damn the chief magician. Damn the man. He should put an end to *him*. He didn't need the watchful, elusive wraith of a man.

What he needed, he suddenly realized, was the girl, her vibrance, her candor. Her youth. Somehow she held the secret.

Noone stood up and began to pace in widening circles.

He must find her. He would search from the deepest dungeon to the crown of the dome. He would find every crack and seal it himself. The terrible old women would never get in; they would never get out. The girl would be his. Forever.

"No cracks," he heard some madman muttering, some old man with a tattered beard and sharp bones. "No cracks in the dome, no cracks in my skull."

Grannies

"Listen," said Granny Sweep to Granny Dirt and Granny Spark.

The wind stilled, and they all heard the sound, close and far away at once, of something splitting open, through the crust of the earth, rising. Behind them, the full moon rose, casting the long shadow of the pinnacle across the emptiness, toward the wall, the dome, toward twining tendrils, and unfurling leaves that climbed toward a tower.

"But what if someone who shouldn't see, does?" worried Granny Spark, feeling responsible for the bright light. "Maybe we should have waited till the dark of the moon."

"Magic beans only grow by full moonlight." Granny Dirt spoke with authority.

"What if someone hears what we hear?" fretted Granny Sweep.

"They won't see," Granny Brine murmured, not knowing who she answered. "They won't hear. They don't know where to look. They don't know how to listen."

"Did you hear that?" Granny Sweep asked the others.

They nodded.

"She knows."

"She's with us."

"Whoever she is, whoever we are."

"Time to go," cried Nightwing.

She rose into the sky, hoping someone would admire her silhouette against the moon, and her fleet shadow sweeping over the empty expanse as she flew toward the dome—and beyond.

From the deck of her ship, Granny Brine looked up and up at line of silver light in the mists at the edge of the world. Far, far away, something was happening, a vine was thickening, climbing to meet the moon.

"Time to go!"

Granny Brine caught a glimpse of black wings, moonlit, wheeling in a circle, high above the temple of bone. Her parrot woke and shrieked indignantly. "It's all right, Captain," said Granny Brine. "Stay with the ship."

It was time for her to go, find the others, whoever they were, meet and merge with them, remake the world.

Jack

"Time to go."

Jack did not know who spoke, but he woke and sat up, disoriented for a moment by the shards of moonlight coming in through all the cracks of the hut, lying scattered on the floor. Careful not to disturb his Bramma, he rolled off the pallet and stood up, pulling on his leggings and his only shirt. He stopped still when Bramma rolled over.

"Bring me back a rose, Jack," she murmured from her dreams.

Yes, thought Jack, that is exactly what he would do, and he slipped out of the hut, following a thread of moonlight, a whisper of wind, a dark, shining flash of wings. He knew where he was going, but he was still astonished by what he saw when he got there.

"I told you," whispered the raven, in so far as a raven can whisper. "Now do you believe me?"

"Ssh," said Jack, glancing around to make sure there was no one looking.

"Climb, boy, climb. We've got all night, but that's it."

Jack took hold of the thick, strong vine.

Rose

It was not the light of the inside moon moving across our ceiling that woke me, a display I had seen all my life, coming and going along with the sun and stars. It was the shadows of something I had never seen, except once on the walls of the tower room: leaves and twisting vines, blown by a wind I longed to hear and feel. Inside our rooms, the air was still as always, the only sound the syncopated wheeze and snore of my aunties. My mother slept quietly, unaware of the light and shadows moving over her face.

I had made up my mind to tell her when she got back from work. Exactly what and how much, I was not sure, but something. She and my aunts had come in late from the state banquet, bringing me dainties and desserts as they always did. I could have spoken then, but I didn't. The chief magician's shoulders drooped, the mask looked more mask-like, old, wrinkled, cracked. When it finally came off, my mother's face seemed just as tired, almost as if she couldn't cast it off and return to herself. Leaving the treats untouched, I went and stood next to her, looking at her face in the mirror. She tried to smile and meet my eyes, but she kept looking down.

"Your mama's tired, dear," said Auntie Aloe. "The windbag king went on and on."

"Someone should pull the plug from his arse," declared Auntie Vinda, "and let all the hot air out at once. And then stuff it in his mouth to shut him up."

"Don't be crude, sister. You set a bad example for Rose. People will wonder who raised her."

If I am ever around "people."

The aunties went on bickering and trading recriminations, as they removed their eyelashes, then loosened their corsets. But I knew it wasn't the king's speeches that had tired my mother.

"Was Noone there?" I asked.

My aunties fell silent, my mother looked up at my reflection in the mirror.

"He is always there," she said, her eyes flat for a moment, like the chief magician's.

Now, I thought. *Now I should tell her. You're in danger. We're in danger.*

"Did he speak?" I said instead.

"Noone hardly ever speaks," said Auntie Vinda.

"Just watches," said Auntie Aloe.

"He wants people to forget he's there."

"Most people don't even see him. It's as if he vaporizes, like some nasty green mist from the vats."

"I see him," said my mother. "I always see him."

"But does he see you?" I managed to ask.

There was a moment of silence as everyone understood what I meant, and then decided not to.

"Of course he does," sputtered an auntie. "He sees his chief magician."

"He'll never see through our clever tricksy disguise."

"Never ever, ever, ever, ever."

"Don't you worry, Rose."

"Don't you fret."

"Your mama is safe with us."

"You're safe, too, Rose."

"Safe, safe."

My mother, I noticed, said nothing. Just lifted her eyes to mine and this time let them linger.

I knew I should say more, but if I did, they would know I had gotten out of our rooms again, put myself—and them—at risk, done all the things they had forbidden me to do. I would have to tell my own hard-won secrets, the room that appeared and disappeared, the grannies rocking in the chair,

Jack waving to me from outside world. And if I told, would they believe me? And if they believed me, would they want to escape with me, or would they keep me under constant guard?

Ask me something, I pleaded with my mother silently, *ask me*. Because if she did, I would have to tell her.

"It's time for bed, Rose," was all she said.

Reluctant, relieved, I went.

Now I slipped out of my bed and went to stand beside hers. I looked down at her sleeping face. In the shadowy moonlight, I could see that the magician's face had finally disappeared. She looked young, as young as the Briar in her stories, rose petals falling on her face, loosened by a soft breeze, the same one that touched my cheek.

For the air had come alive around me, the leafy vines now more than shadows. They had overgrown the wall, they were opening the way for me.

"It's time to go," I whispered to myself, to her.

She stirred in her sleep but did not wake. I turned and went through the wall, not stopping to see if it closed behind me.

I had never seen the tower room quite like this, cozy and inviting, strange and exciting all at once. The rocking chair was empty, but still in subtle motion, as if someone had just gotten up from it. Two low stools I'd never seen before waited by the hearth where a fire blazed, casting its patterns on the curving walls. From the corners of my eyes, I could see them, the women dancing, but when I looked directly, they were gone.

Then I turned toward the window.

It was opening—or being opened—by a leafy vine growing before my eyes. And then—

One hand, and another.

A dark, bright face.

One leg, and another, swinging into the room.

A whole boy, standing.

Jack.

❋　❋　❋

My children, we were children. For a long while, we just looked at each other without saying anything. Then all at once, we both laughed, and we starting jumping up and down and twirling; we clasped hands and swung each other round and round until we were dizzy. While we weren't looking, someone had laid a small table before the fire with a plate of cakes and two steaming mugs. Jack gazed at the table in wonder and then looked at me.

"For us?" he said.

In his voice, I could hear a crackle of blue and a hint of dark gold, but also it was just his voice, a boy's voice, a boy who had grown up running and jumping but rarely having enough to eat, an outside voice, hushed with wonder.

I nodded.

"Not a trick?"

He was right to ask; as I knew from my storybooks, magical food was often used to lure children into a trap. Yet somehow I knew Noone had nothing to do with what had been set out for us. The food had appeared silently, without any stomping or muttered threats.

"It's from the grannies," I guessed, and as soon as I spoke, I knew it was true.

"Your grannies?" he asked.

Shyly, warily, he sat down, and I sat next to him.

"That's what I call them," I said. "I don't think they are mine, exactly, not only mine. After I met them one at a time, here in this room, I gave each one a name."

Jack looked hungry. Of course he was hungry. I knew from my mother, they didn't have cakes like this in outside world. But he hadn't yet reached for one. I took a cake and handed it to him. He hesitated, then divided it and gave half to me. We each took a bite. For a moment we just savored the sweetness. Though I'd had plenty of cakes from dome world kitchens, this one tasted like it was made of the outdoors, the sunlight, rain, dirt, air, I had glimpsed only in dreams, the scent of the roses I had never breathed.

"Why did you name them?" Jack asked. "Didn't they have names?"

He picked up a mug and handed it to me and took the other for himself. I sipped the warm red drink, sweet and tart.

"They don't remember who they are," I explained. "I call them Granny Sweep, Granny Spark, Granny Dirt, and Granny Brine."

As I named them, a gust of air rustled the vines; the fire crackled and leaped, from far, far away came the sound of bells. Shadows swayed on the wall, and I thought I could see the grannies again circling, dancing. But I kept my gaze on Jack. All of the grannies had known about Jack.

"Have you ever seen them?" I asked him. "They know who you are."

Jack wasn't as surprised as you might expect.

"I haven't seen them." Jack set down his mug, breaking another cake in half for us. "But I think I might have heard of them. Nightwing calls them the old girls."

"Who is Nightwing?" I asked, holding my piece of cake suspended before my lips.

"Nightwing is a big black bird. She came and found me when I ran away from the Guard, after I saw you again, to the haunted place where the briars burned."

I had never seen that place, but I had more than heard of it. It was in my bones; it was in my name.

"Nightwing can talk," Jack went on. "She knows my name. She brought me the bean. Do you know about the bean?"

I shook my head and finally managed another bite of cake. It was so strange to have Jack here, to talk to another child my own age about things I could never have imagined speaking of to anyone. Not just any child, practically my brother.

"The old girls sent Nightwing with a bean, a magic bean, for me to plant right at the bottom of the dome. And so I did. That's how I got up here, to the tower. The bean grew into a huge, tall beanstalk, and I climbed it."

He turned and gestured toward the window. The wind got stronger, the shadows wilder. Then he looked at me again.

"I climbed it to find you, Rose."

"Who told you my name?" I asked. No one in outside world knew my name.

Jack looked confused for a moment, as if the question had taken him by surprise and he wasn't sure of his answer, then he shrugged.

"It must have been the grannies," he decided.

"I thought you never saw them."

Jack smiled, a big broad smile that spread to his ears.

"You don't have to see to hear," he pointed out.

As I knew very well.

"How do you know my name?" he asked.

I smiled back at him; my cheeks ached with the smile.

"The grannies of course. They said I had to find you—"

"But I found *you*," Jack interrupted.

"I found you *first*," I said. "That's why I was looking out the window that day. That's why I called your name."

Children, we were children.

"All right," he agreed, grudging and merry at once. "You called my name, and I looked up, and saw you in the window, that window."

We both turned toward it. The vines whispered and seemed to beckon.

"What else did the grannies tell you?" he asked.

I thought back to those nights, so vivid, so strange. Granny Sweep, Granny Spark, and Granny Dirt had all described where they lived.

"They told me when I found you, or when you found me, we should go and visit them."

Jack stared around the room, from the door to the hearth to the window.

"Where?"

I thought of my maps hidden under my pillow. Granny Sweep's pinnacle, Granny Spark's forest, Granny Dirt's shoe, and Granny Brine beyond the edge of my map, over the edge of the world. And yet, weren't they here, too, stirring the vines, dancing in the light and shadows on the curved wall of the tower room?

"They live beyond the wall, Jack. Or at least that's where their homes are." I paused. "But I've never even been outside."

"I've never climbed the wall," he confided in turn. "I don't think anyone has. The ones who get sent over the edge of the world are taken out through the gate."

My mother's stories came back to me now as vividly as when she told them to me.

"Your mother and father climbed the wall once," I said slowly. "My mother did, too."

Jack stared at me, his eyes filling with tears that did not quite spill.

"How do you know about my mother and father? No one talks about my mother and father. Not even Bramma, the old woman who raised me."

"Sal and Jack," I said softly. "Nimble Jack, they called him."

"Who told you their names?" he demanded, almost angrily, knuckling back his tears, "if you've never been outside? Was it the grannies?"

I shook my head. What to tell him, how much?

"Not the grannies," I said at length. "Briar, my mother, told me. Briar, Sal, and Jack. They were the three. Does anyone outside ever talk about the three?"

"Briar," he repeated. "My Bramma cries out Briar in her sleep. Briar, Sal, and Jack."

Then he began to sing, "Over the edge of the world we go."

"Over the edge of the world we fly," I joined in.

And we sang the song of the three until we were silent again.

"Do you have a father?" he asked, as people outside did, because so many did not know their fathers.

"The man who was my . . ." I couldn't say the word. "He's dead."

"Oh," said Jack. "I'm sorry, Rose."

Both of us were silent for a moment.

"I don't know if my father is alive or dead," Jack said at length. "Or my mother. I've never seen them, but I think, I might have heard their voices."

The blue voice and the dark voice, shining with gold.

Could I ask him? Could I tell him?

"I am glad my father is dead," I finally said. Then all the waiting words tumbled out at once. "He was the chief magician. He forced my mother to give your father a potion. She thought it was the elixir of immortality, but it might have killed him. Or anyway, he disappeared, right in front of her eyes. And then, my mother, Briar, killed my father and disguised herself as the chief magician. No one knows."

No one knows. Noone knows.

At those words, the air stilled, the fire stopped crackling; Jack and I stared at each other, waiting for something to happen. We didn't know what.

Suddenly the vines shook.

"Jack, Jack Quick!"

A huge black bird landed on the window sill.

"Nightwing," I guessed.

"Yes," said Jack.

"You've only got all night," croaked the bird, "and it's almost over!"

And the huge bird flapped away, leaving shadows in her wake.

"Are you ready, Rose?" asked Jack.

Ready for what? I tried to say, but my heart was pounding so hard in my throat. Jack stood up and gave me his hand, leading me toward the window.

"I'll go first." He swung one leg over the window. "Just do what I do."

What I had been waiting for, dreaming of, all my life, now that it was here seemed sudden, terrifying. For I moment, I didn't know if I could move.

"Come on, Rose," called Jack. "I'll be right ahead of you. I won't let you fall."

Briar, Sal, and Jack, climbing the wall, risking not just a fall, but everything.

"But where are we going?" I asked, though I knew and didn't know.

"To find the grannies, of course."

Of course.

I crossed the room to the window, swung a leg over and another. I grabbed hold of the stalk.

✳   ✳   ✳

Oh, children, I had looked out the window before; I had felt the wind; I had tasted the rain. But now I was all the way out, under the vast dome of sky, in the coldest, darkest time of night. There were stars over my head that I could sense rather than see, because all I could do was cling to the stalk, really more a vine that matched my own trembling.

"Don't look down, Rose," called Jack from below. "Just keep moving, one hand, one foot at a time."

I was clinging so tight to the vine, movement seemed impossible at first. It meant letting go, while holding on, letting myself fall, a little at a time. First one hand held, then the other, one foot, then the other, till movement was all there was. I did not notice the sky pale, hardly registered that I could now begin to see as well as feel the stalk. And then—

come the sorrow, come the pain
come the sun, come the rain
come the toiling all day long
come the night, come the dawn
beauty will go on, go on, beauty will go on

I stopped, mid-step, hearing the beauty singers for the first time, not for the first time, hearing my mother's voice singing me awake, bending over my cradle, my bed.

honey in the stone, rose in the dawn
beauty will go on, go on

Then from inside the dome—and inside my head—came another sound:
"Ee oooh ahh. Eee, ooh."

The howl grew louder and louder. I knew what it was; I knew who it was.
I will kill him; I will end him, endless, bottomless death.

"Hurry, Rose," called Jack. "It's almost day."

Jack! I tried to speak, but no sound came out. *My mother, my mother—*

I needed all my breath and all my strength to climb back up the beanstalk,
back through the tower window, back inside the dome to save my mother.

Jack

"It's all right, Rose," Jack kept saying, "it's all right. You can do it."

He was halfway down when he realized she wasn't there.

"Rose? Are you coming? Where are you, Rose?"

He started to climb back up when the stalk broke and began to crumble. Magic can be like that. It comes, and then it goes, and there you are, dangling over the world, holding on as best you can to what's left. Down and down Jack half slid, half fell, clinging to the last tatters of the stalk.

come the terror, come the dawn
beauty will go on, go on, beauty will go on.

As the beauty singers wove their song into the rising day, a flock of bird in full cry caught the light on their wings. Jack landed more softly than he might have, on the remnant of the stalk, the leaves already wilting.

"Rose!" he called aloud. *Rose!* he screamed inside his mind.

He had to find her again.

He had to find her.

Grannies

Granny Sweep, Granny Spark, and Granny Dirt waited atop the pinnacle, gazing toward dome world as the sun rose behind them, sending their shadows out across the emptiness. A blackness moving toward them grew bigger and bigger, till her wings took over their sight.

"Jack," squawked the raven. "Rose!"

The raven landed by their feet, folded her wings and began to make liquid, brooding noises.

"What is it?" implored the sisters. "What happened?"

"Lost," mourned Nightwing. "Lost."

Lost, the waves sang, the bells rang, as the cliff disappeared into red-rimmed cloud.

Granny Brine felt herself rising, drawn up by fire, into air, gathering herself into more than herself.

"I will find them," she whispered, she wailed. "We will find them."

PART SEVEN

Trials

Rose

Once inside, I ran through the rising half-light, blinded by tears and terror. At times I thought I heard other footsteps, breathing; or maybe it was only my own, echoing, made loud and monstrous. It seemed as though I ran for a very long time, much longer than it had ever taken me before, down endless stairs and a corridor that wound around and around. It felt as though I ran for hours, for years, forever.

I will kill him, I will end him.

My heart hammered with those words.

I had to find my mother. I had to save her.

Rounding yet another bend, I ran smack into something huge and solid. It toppled over. They toppled over, and I went down, too, landing on top of two immense, stiff bodies that rolled to either side of me. I scrambled up and back. In the false morning light creeping up the walls, I saw them, lying inert, wigs askew, their mouths and eyes open in horror, their arms frozen in the act reaching out, one coiled in a fist.

My aunties.

Someone was screaming, screaming so loud, I put my hands over my ears, I closed my eyes.

But the screaming went on.

283

Grannies

The three grannies remained rooted at the edge of the precipice. Nightwing settled into grooming her feathers, as if she had not just delivered the direst of messages. Meanwhile Moo-n took up her own lament; it was shockingly past milking time.

"Lost?" Granny Sweep said one more time, stirring the air into little eddies.

"But they just found each other," Granny Dirt insisted one more time.

"Things are never what they seem," Granny Spark observed, but no one knew what she meant, least of all her.

Puss meowed and rubbed against Granny Sweep's leg, sharing Moo-n's concern. But the grannies continued to gaze toward dome world.

"Send out your sight," said Granny Dirt. "What are you waiting for? We've got to find them!"

"Why does everything depend on me?" objected Granny Sweep. "We've all traveled to that room."

"'Traveled' may not be the right word," said Granny Spark.

"And we don't all see, not exactly," added Granny Dirt. "Not my first sense."

"This is your precipice," pointed out Granny Spark. "We're your guests."

"All right," sighed Granny Sweep.

And she sent her sight out on a breath of wind, on the morning light.

"Jack!" she said after a moment. "I've found Jack!"

"We see, too," said her sisters. "We're with you."

"But I don't see Rose," cried Granny Sweep.

"Jack can't find her either."

"She must have turned back!" said Granny Spark. "Why, oh why didn't she stay with Jack?"

"Oh, no," cried Granny Dirt. "Look the magic bean stalk. It's collapsed. It's all in a tangle; it's all in a heap."

"Won't it grow again?" asked Granny Spark. "Don't all things grow again? Acorns and maple whirligigs."

"They do, they do," said Granny Dirt, "but never the same way twice."

"He's trying to straighten it; he's trying to make it climb again," cried Granny Spark. "Oh, Jack, Jack."

"Tell him, someone tell him!" cried Granny Sweep.

"Tell him what?" said Granny Spark.

"Don't you see? Follow the wind, look with me!"

However they saw or sensed, however they traveled or didn't travel, the grannies rose to where the tower had been, the secret opening to inside world, where each one had sat and rocked a while, where they had set a table for Jack and Rose. Had it been a dream? Was everything only a dream? Were they only Rose's dream? Was she theirs? For there was no window. There was no tower. The last crack in the dome was sealed.

How had he done it, after all his railing and slamming and smashing? By whose power, by whose strength had he shut them out—and locked them in? For they sensed that they were cast out and trapped inside at once, slaves, wraiths of themselves, forced streams, forced air, false suns and flower beds.

And Rose, the only one who knew who they were, who knew what to do. Rose was trapped there, too.

"Old Man!" Granny Sweep's voice rose. "Father Time. Noone. Noooooooooone!"

The wind howled around the huge dome; black clouds rolled in from the edge of the world. Rain came in waves; lightning hurled itself in bolts, and hail pounded and battered the dome.

"Noone! Let us in, let us out!"

"Stop!" Nightwing screamed over the noise. "Stop, you crazy old women. Do you want to destroy the world again? What's left of it? Stop!"

They came to the selves they knew and did not know, wild hair battened down, dripping, clothes tattered.

"Maybe we got a little carried away," said Granny Dirt.

"But we were all together again," exulted Granny Spark. "Lightning and rain, wind and hail. All of us! I had forgotten, forgotten...."

She trailed off, as the memory lifted and dispersed with the clouds.

With one exasperated squawk, Nightwing flew away, her shadow sweeping the empty world below.

Rose

"Stop, Rose, stop it at once!"

"You could wake the dead with that caterwauling."

And it appeared I had. I opened my eyes and saw my aunties, getting to their feet and straightening their wigs. I flung myself at them, nearly knocking them over again.

"Gently, Rose, gently."

"There, there, don't cry. It's all right. Everything's all right."

For a moment I believed it, but not for long.

"Then why were you lying there in the corridor, frozen?" I demanded, drawing apart from them. "Where is my mother?"

My aunties looked at each other and then back at me, confusion giving way to alarm. In the distance coming closer, and closer, I heard the sound of marching feet.

"The Guard!" whispered Auntie Vinda.

They turned to the wall, and I saw that the opening to our secret rooms was no longer a veil of water, a cloud; it was slashed, tattered.

"Quick!" the aunties pushed me through first.

"Seal it, we've got to seal it before they get here."

They worked frantically, and the wall cohered again, looking almost as it always did, but with a hairline crack. We could still hear the sound of the marching feet from beyond. Their hands shaking, the aunties smoothed the cracks as best they could. Then they each grabbed one of my hands and pulled me deeper in, closing the door of the mirror room, locking it.

The room was a shambles: shattered mirrors, overturned chairs and stools, spilled make-up, my mother's dressing gown pooled on the floor. And the face, the mask my aunties made into the chief magician's face each day, had been flung against the wall. It stuck there, stretching out of shape, dripping, oozing.

"Further in," they pulled me toward the deepest recesses of the closet.

"Where's my mother?" I balked. "Where is she?"

"Hush, hush. We've got to hide!"

They pulled me into the dark forest of gowns, deeper and deeper. They gathered garments as we went on and on, farther than I had ever been. At last we stopped and huddled together underneath a mass of heavy velvet.

The sound of marching feet had stopped. There was a muffled scratching and scrabbling, a distant banging.

"It's going to hold," whispered Auntie Aloe.

"Of course it is," Auntie Vinda hissed back. "The Guard have no magic. He's a fool, an inept fool."

I did not need ask who. I knew, and suddenly I was so sick with fear, I could hardly speak.

"My mother," I got the words out. "My mother."

My aunties began to cry, quietly at first, then with gale force.

"Stop it! Stop it!" I grabbed hold of whatever part of them I could find in the dark and shook them, digging in my fingers. They stopped wailing abruptly.

"Where is my mother? Where is my mother!"

"We don't know," one said.

"We do know," said the other.

Then they both spoke together.

"We think, no we suspect, no we—"

"Noone took her." I spoke the words.

In fits and starts, with disputes and interruptions, my aunties managed to get the story out. My mother had been getting ready to go to work. I was not awake yet, or so they thought. My mother had put on the chief magician's robes but not the mask. If she had time, she liked to wake me before she put it on. When I was half asleep, I would reach for her as I used to when she was the sun and the moon to me, when she was the world to me, beyond inside or outside. So she came to my bed in the cozy alcove and found it . . .

Empty.

"Rose? Rose!"

In my mind, in my heart, I can hear her voice still, joined by my aunties' voices.

"Rose! Rose! Rooooooooooooose!"

"She must be hiding."

"Just to scare us."

Something I had not done in years.

"Check the closet."

"She loves the satins."

While my aunties squawked and bustled, my mother must have stood stricken, staring at the wall. Could she see the echo of moonlight that had opened the way out? Could she trace my shadow? Maybe she did not have to part the veil. Maybe the wall gave way and she rushed through just as Noone, muttering and cursing, rounded the corner.

My aunties did not tell me this part; they were still ransacking the closet. But I can imagine it. My mother standing there, exposed, her hair loose over the chief magician's robes, her beautiful face, bare. And there was Noone, his ancient body skeletal, hardly more than a twig on a tree branch, trembling, his beard and hair flying out from the astonished fury of his face.

Did he accuse her? Did she answer?

Maybe they were both beyond speech. Noone knowing in a flash that he had been deceived. My mother knowing she was undone, all her life-saving secrets exposed in an instant. The wall gaped, open as a wound. There was nothing to keep him out.

According to my aunties, they emerged from the closet and tried to block his way into the mirror room. Despite his seeming frailty, he grabbed them and sent them reeling, as if they weighed nothing, and stormed into the room.

"This is where you did it!" he screamed. "Spies, false females. Grotesqueries. This is how you covered up treachery."

He turned and pointed at my mother.

"And murder."

Somehow he guessed or maybe in his nightmares he had always known: this woman, whom he'd last seen as a tortured girl, one of the three whose voices he'd vowed to silence, was not just an imposter, but a killer.

Turning back, he proceeded to the makeup table and picked up the chief magician's mask. He held it away from himself, gingerly, as if it were something disgusting and dead. Then he hurled it against the wall, and began smashing mirrors and throwing pots and combs and brushes, while my aunties righted themselves, took hold of my mother's arms, and started to back away.

"The child. Stop, Noone, stop," he ordered himself. "Nothing else matters. The child!" He rounded on them.

"What have you done with the child!"

They froze. Rose. It was true. Nothing else mattered.

"We didn't—"

"We haven't—"

The aunties sputtered, covering their panic and my mother's.

"She must be hiding in the closet."

"From all the ruckus."

"You've frightened her, sir, with all your rampaging."

If he had fallen for their trick and delved into the closet, they might have locked the door and had a chance to escape. Instead, he pushed past them out of the mirror room into the chamber where we had lived our little secret lives together, eating, playing, singing lullabies. When he came to my sleeping nook, he sank down on my unmade bed, picking up my pillow and clutching it to his chest. Then he saw: the notebook I'd hidden underneath. Casting the pillow aside, he picked it up and began poring over it— my maps, my drawings of the place where each granny lived, with the signs declaring their names. My mother and aunties stood horrified and transfixed by this evidence of my own secret, a secret life that they had altogether missed.

"You!" He roared to his feet, grasping my notebook with one hand and pointing his finger at my mother. "You! You let them in!"

"I don't know what you mean. I don't know who you mean."

And if she knew once, long ago, when she had dreamed inside the beehive, she had forgotten.

"The terrible old women. You let them in."

He dangled my open notebook, but of course my mother had never seen it before. No one had. No one but Noone.

"You let them in. I told you to seal it. No cracks in the dome, but you let them in!"

He began ripping out the pages.

"She didn't!" my aunties shrieked. "She never!"

Page after page, he tore.

"You let them get to her. You let the terrible old women get to the child. Where is she? Have they taken her? Have you given her to them! Tell me!"

He flung the leafless notebook from him and advanced on her.

"Tell me where she is!"

"I don't know," my mother broke down. "She was gone when I woke up. Help me find her, please. She's a child, my child. I only wanted to keep her safe. Noone, help me!"

Did she really believe she could make common cause with him?

"Oh, I will find her," he said. "But you will not. You will never see her again."

And before my aunties could make a move, he had my mother's arms twisted behind her back. He dragged her through the gash in the wall, my aunties bounding after him. Still holding onto my mother, he stretched out his fingers toward the aunties.

"Horribly long fingers," said Auntie Vinda. "Bony, a skeleton's fingers."

"It wasn't the fingers that did it," said Auntie Aloe. "It was the eyes. Bottomless, like falling over the edge of the world."

They became so still, I was afraid they had fallen under his spell again.

"But where is my mother?" I grabbed them and shook them. "Where did he take her!"

"We don't know!" They began to sniffle and hiccup. "That was the last thing we knew till you started to scream."

"We tried to stop him."

"We tried to protect her."

"You know we did, Rose. We would give our lives—"

"But we failed, we failed."

And they gave way to their grief. The more they carried on, the quieter I became. It was my fault. If only I hadn't left the room, if I only I had gotten back in time, as I always had before, Noone never would have found her.

But this time had been different; this time I had met Jack. I stayed away too long. But If I had kept going down the vine with Jack, I never would have come back, I never would have—

I'll end him, endless, bottomless death.

I had turned back without one word to Jack. (Oh, Jack, Jack!) I had left Jack climbing down the vine alone, thinking I was right behind him, so that I could warn my mother.

And I had failed.

"Quiet," I said to my aunties.

And to my surprise they stopped mid-hiccup.

"We have to save her."

"How?" they both asked. "How can we hide from Noone anywhere in inside world? He knows our secrets now, all our secrets."

We couldn't hide inside. Or at least, I wouldn't hide. Noone wanted me, only me. If he had me, no matter how furious he was, surely I could persuade him to let my mother go. I had to go to him. But I couldn't tell my aunties my plan. They would do whatever they could to stop me—and they were much, much bigger and stronger than I was. I would have to deceive them. (Hadn't my life, all our lives, been one long deception?) I would be deceiving them to good purpose. Even if they did not understand how or why, they would help me, they had to help me.

"We won't hide inside. We have to go outside. To find Jack."

"Jack? What can you mean? Jack has been . . . well . . . gone since before you were born. You know what happened, Rose."

"Vaporized, so to speak."

"Vanished."

"Without a trace."

Not so completely as they thought, but there was no point in contradicting them.

"Not Nimble Jack, his son, Jack Quick."

Calling on the spirit of Jack's fleetness, I gave the quick version of the story, how I had almost followed him down the stalk, but turned back for my mother.

"We have to find him," I said. "He'll help us."

"I don't see how." said Auntie Aloe.

"Isn't he just a boy, a raggedy, outside boy?"

"Living in the rubble like all the rest?"

I didn't know how either, but I knew one thing for certain.

"He's not just any boy," I said. "He Jack's son. And Sal's son."

The aunties were uncharacteristically quiet for a moment. They knew the story, too. They knew Briar had been there, that night. Jack was the son of the three.

"If he is who you say he is—"

"Then Briar might want us to—"

"She would," I said. "You know she would."

I tried to hurry them.

"Now wait just a minute, missy. There are other things you haven't told us—"

"A lot of things."

"What about those drawings!"

"Why did you hide them!"

"From us!"

"From your poor dear Mama—"

A storm of tears threatened again.

"Who is being blamed—"

"For something she never did."

"Rose, did you let them in?"

"These terrible old women—"

"Who are they, Rose?"

"Don't you dare keep any more secrets from us!"

"Who are the terrible old women?"

"They aren't terrible," I began. "They are just . . . very, very old. So old they don't remember who they are. I call them the grannies. And they're not exactly, well, not only, women—"

"You're not making any sense, Rose!"

I wasn't. I didn't know how to.

"I can't explain any more, and there's no time. We can't hide in here for long. Noone knows about our rooms now."

"She's right about that, sister."

"And since we don't have any other plan—"

"We might as well—"

"But how do we get outside without being noticed?"

"Stopped."

"Interrogated."

There was a silence, and I quailed at the thought of what could happen if they were caught.

"Oh, sister!" Auntie Vinda clapped her hands. "It's Tuesday. We can join the ladies' benevolent society's guided tour of the outside."

"Yes, yes! But we must dress!"

"In our very best!"

"We will make ourselves impeccable, respectable!'

"Above reproach and beyond question!"

Forgetting their sorrows for a moment, the aunties set about choosing just the right clothes and jewels. I quietly backed out of the closet before they could turn their attention to my outfit. I found myself praying, to Jack, to Sal, to the grannies: let them believe I've gone outside ahead of them, impatient to get to Jack. Let them follow their plan to go outside and find Jack, believing they will find me with him.

And if I can find my mother, if I can save my mother, maybe . . . I could not finish that thought. While my beloved aunties bickered over feathers for their hats, I was off and running, trusting my feet would remember the way.

Jack

Jack crept out from under the ruined stalk where he had sheltered from the sudden storm. The vine was sodden, sinking into the mud. He stepped away from the dome where water still sluiced down. He jumped the little rivulets and streams that ran in through the alley, though it was too late to avoid getting wet. His feet were bare, his clothes and hair, drenched. But the sun was coming out again, and so were the people, emerging from their leaky shacks, almost as wet as he was. They shook their heads, shrugged, and began to go on with the day. Life was like that, violent and unpredictable. But the drudgery beneath it all was always the same.

Not that Jack knew about drudgery. He was too quick; he had managed to dodge it so far. And besides, he was in the middle of a perilous adventure. It could not be over, not yet. He climbed the watch tower where he had first seen Rose. His eyes swept as much of the dome as he could see in case, by some desperation or magic, Rose had managed to cling to its impossibly smooth surface, or had found some remnant of vine. But the dome was smooth as ever, except for the drops of water that caught the light. Then he saw something—or rather he did not see something.

The tower was gone, and with it, the window where he had first caught sight of Rose, the window they had both climbed out.

Had it all been a dream?

He looked down again; the stalk had almost disappeared. The shadow of wings swept over the dome.

"Jack! Jack!"

There was the big black raucous bird, landing next to him. At least Nightwing was real.

"Have you brought me another bean?" he asked.

But then he remembered: the tower was gone, and the window as well.

"Jack! Jack!" said the Raven again. It sounded like she was laughing, laughing at him. "Magic never works the same way twice. Rose knows, Rose knows."

Rose was real. Rose.

"Where is Rose? I've got to find her!"

The raven lifted into the air.

"Don't go," said Jack. "I don't know where Rose has gone. She's gone! The tower's gone. The vine's gone. Everything's gone!"

The raven balanced her wings and circled him.

"Come on, Jack! See if you're as quick as me."

Jack climbed down far enough and leaped to the nearest rooftop. Jumping and scrambling, Jack followed the raven's flight until he found himself outside his own shack. With one more cry, the raven flew higher and higher till she was no bigger than a cinder flying from a cook fire.

"Jack."

There was his Bramma, stirring the coals under the pot. She said nothing more, but gazed at him with her eyes that still held traces of dawn, gray flecked with gold, and flocks of spiraling birds. Then she handed him a bowl of porridge, sweetened with the honey she saved for rare occasions. He spooned it all down, and she did not scold him when he licked out the bowl.

"I'm so tired, Bramma." For suddenly he was, his eyes heavy as stone, impossible to hold open. He'd just close them for a minute and then he'd find Rose . . .

As if he was a much younger boy than he was, Jack's Bramma took his hand, got him into dry rags, and tucked him under his blanket and hers. Jack fell asleep, dreaming of the vine tumbling from the sky, the raven's wings turning day to night. Rose calling to him. Two strange, familiar voices, one bright blue, one dark, gritty yet golden, threaded in and out of his sleep, half waking him, half soothing him.

Grannies

"That is a very odd looking cloud," remarked Granny Dirt. "It's headed this way."

"What we need, after that storm, is some warm sun," said Granny Spark.

"Look!" Granny Sweep pointed. "The cloud is following Nightwing. Or Nightwing is following the cloud. She keeps moving in and out of it."

"Do clouds ever get snagged on your pointy little pinnacle?" asked Granny Spark.

"Nothing I can't clear with my broom," said Granny Sweep.

"Though rain clouds can be useful for watering plants," put in Granny Dirt.

Nightwing flew clear of the cloud and landed with a self-satisfied croak on the top of the wind-twisted oak. And then the cloud was upon them, dark swirling, smelling faintly of salt. When it lifted, there she was, the one they'd been missing. Never mind they still weren't quite sure who she was, who any of them were. They were all here. All four. They stood and stared at each other for some time, as the sun shone, and a soft breeze sweetened the air.

"Rose knows," they whispered to each other. "Rose knows who we are."

And they took hands and danced in a circle, to an old, old song, older than time, older than stars, older than dirt, older than the sea—and just as new, a song they had made up that moment.

sure as the wind blows
Rose knows

sure as the fire glows
Rose knows
sure as the grass grows
Rose knows
sure as the water flows
Rose knows

Aunties

"Do you think we've taken a wrong turn?"

"How would we know? All the turns look the same to the me. Besides, it's not as if we know where we're going."

"I don't remember it being so dirty."

"You always say you don't remember anything at all."

"I don't. Who wouldn't want to forget?"

"Me. I've never forgotten."

"It's so smelly and crowded. And the sun . . . it's just there, the sky, it's indecent."

"We should have brought our parasols."

"We left in such a hurry. I told you not to hurry."

"But we had to. We had to catch up with Rose."

"How did she get away so quickly, how did she get out?"

"Leaving us to chase after her without accessories or other necessities."

"Like sensible shoes."

"Do we own any?"

"Now look at us. We stick out. We stick out like huge, throbbing thumbs in these tiny alleys."

"We dressed for the ladies' guided tour. We blended in fine with the ladies."

"Says you. Didn't you see the side-eye they gave us? And what happens when they notice we're gone? People know who we are, they *know*."

"We should have thought it through; we should have come up with a plan."

"This *is* the plan. Searching for a ragamuffin boy without a clue how to find him."

"I wish she had at least given us directions."

"How could she? She's never been out before."

"Or has she, the deceiving little—"

"Oh why, oh why, didn't she wait for us!"

"She jolly well should have. It was her idea."

"We should have put her on a leash."

"Handcuffed her to us."

"Do we have handcuffs?"

"Of course we do. In the dungeon. We should have gone out that way."

"Too late now."

"Why didn't we just follow her?"

"We did. We are!"

"Drat the child. Who knew she was such a brat."

"Don't say that! Never say that. She's our Rose. No matter what she's done."

"How will we find her? We don't even know where she is."

"We do know. We just have to find the boy."

Jack

Jack opened his eyes. Late afternoon light shone through the cracks.

"If he even exists, her little beanstalk-climbing friend. He might be some imaginary—"

"Jack. She says his name is Jack, Nimble Jack's son! Let's ask someone. There's no harm in asking."

✳ ✳ ✳

Jack sat up. Who was looking for him? Those were men's voices he was hearing. The Guard? But how did they know about Rose? What had they done to Rose?

"There might be harm, if he is who she says he is, but we don't have much choice. How else will we find him?"

"And if we find him, we find Rose!"

"That woman, out in her yard. Let's ask her."

"Pardon us, madam."

Who was madam? He had never heard anyone called that.

"We are inquiring for the whereabouts of a boy named Jack. Might you be able to assist us?"

"There are many boys named Jack," came the answer. "A very common name."

His Bramma. That's who madam was. And she did not want to answer the men. They must be the Guard. Rose had given them the slip. He had to find Rose. He couldn't let himself be caught.

"I believe this Jack is known as Jack Quick."

"Son of—" came a second voice.

"Hush, sister."

Sister? Was one of them a woman? Jack crept to the entryway and pulled aside the heavy blanket that served as a door. There was Bramma, sitting cross-legged on the ground picking stones out of dried beans. Before her stood two huge, fantastically dressed ladies with equally fantastical shoes, one pair blue, one red, at least, what you could see of them under the mud. They looked even taller because of their hats, one blue, one red, matching the opposite shoes, decorated with a garden full of flowers that didn't look real, and topped with feathers that shimmered and changed color like rainbows.

"Most boys in these parts are quick," Bramma shrugged. "They have to be."

"I'm sure they are," said one of the fantastical creatures. "Believe it or not, we ourselves were once—"

"Please be assured, madam," the other one interrupted, "that we mean the boy no harm."

Bramma tossed aside a pebble and then looked up—and up.

"And if I should happen to come across such a Jack, who might I say 'inquired' for him?"

The old woman mocked the visitors' mannerisms. Did they notice?

They were too busy looking at each other, exchanging questions and answers with their plucked and painted eyebrows and giving way to frantic whispers.

"You may tell him—"

"Be sure to tell him—"

"Rose," they both spoke at once."

"Rose sent us."

"Or rather we were following her."

"Rose is, well, a friend of Jack's."

"Or he's a friend of hers—"

"Rose," the old woman bent her head over the beans, so that the tall creatures could not see her face. "Rose."

Jack started to emerge when Bramma caught his eye and shook her head at him.

"Well," said one lady.

"Well," said the other.

They had another whispered conference, he only caught fragments.

"Remember Briar's stories. King of the mountain. Other children might . . ."

Then they turned to Bramma again.

"Perhaps you could direct us to the . . . um, rubbish heaps?"

For a moment it seemed as if Bramma had not heard or would not answer. Then she just pointed, her head still bowed.

As the two enormous ladies wobbled on down the muddy alley, Jack crept out of the shack. Bramma looked up, and he saw the tears she'd been hiding from the visitors.

"Rose?" Her hand closed on his arm. "Rose?"

"Rose," he said. "I've got to follow them, Bramma. They said Rose sent them—"

"Rose. Whose daughter? Whose granddaughter?"

She held him still with her eyes.

"You know, Bramma, I think you know."

Slowly she nodded, releasing his arm.

"Go, Jack Quick, go."

Jack rounded one corner, then another. The next alley opened onto the rubbish heaps where he found the giant ladies surrounded by a mob of boys. Other children watched from the mountain of garbage, their cheers mixed up with jeers. The bullies leaped and feinted, trying to grab at the ladies' finery. The giantesses were giving as good as they got, bellowing and shrieking, as they landed punches and kicks. Such a ruckus would soon bring the Guard down on them, and that would be no good for anyone.

Jack moved back as far as he could and then took a running leap, somersaulting through the air over the assailants and landing in front of the beleaguered pair.

"Can you run?" he asked them.

"Not in these shoes, honey," said one of them.

"Take them off," said Jack, blocking an attacker.

"Hey, Jack. Come off it. These are inside birds, fair game! You gone soft?"

And the bullies piled on him.

"Jack?" said one giantess to the other.

"Jack!"

Just as he started to go under, the boys let go, guarding their heads as the ladies rained down blows with the heels of their shoes. At last, bloody and bellowing, the attackers peeled off.

"Run," said Jack. "Quick!"

Without looking back to see if they were following, he took off.

"Oh my, he is quick," one of them panted.

"It's so muddy. My stockings will be ruined."

"Hurry up, sister, don't be such a girl."

"We *are* girls!"

Breathless and bickering, they followed him, holding on to their hats with one hand and their shoes with the other, as he led them through a warren of streets, rubble-strewn alleys, scaling fences, leaping rooftops, not stopping until they came to the far place, the haunted place, the charred place, where the sky rose blue and empty over the high wall with it memory of vines. All three flopped down on the ground, the two ladies lying flat on their backs, gasping for breath. Then one them sat up.

"Is this where—"

"It is," said the other, also sitting up, and looking around.

"I don't remember, but—"

"It must be."

"Who are you?" demanded Jack. "What do you want with Rose?"

"You see? He knows Rose. He must be Jack, Rose's Jack."

"Then it must all be true, what she told us."

"All that folderol about climbing out a window down a beanstalk."

"I am Jack!" he said impatiently. "Rose was climbing after me. And then . . . she was gone."

Everything was gone, the window, the tower, the stalk, but it wasn't a dream. Rose was real; these two fantastical creatures were looking for her.

"Jack," they addressed him directly at last. "We are Rose's aunties."

"We raised her from a—"

"Helped raise her."

"She came back to us, Jack."

"Not just to us, sister. To Briar."

"Her Mama, but Briar was already gone."

"Taken!"

"Rose said we had to go to you, Jack."

"She said you would help us."

"Help us rescue her mother."

"Will you help us, Jack?"

"Of course, I'll help you. But if Rose came back to you, where is she now?"

"We thought she had come to find you!"

"Do you mean to say—"

"You don't know where she is?"

"At all?"

Jack shook his head. "I haven't seen her since the night."

"Then where can she be?"

"Where is Rose?"

"Where is Rose!"

"She can't have gone to Noone."

"She must have gone to Noone."

The two giant ladies began to wail.

Granny Sweep kept watch from her lookout on the tippy- top of the pinnacle. Her magical wind eye widened as it took in two enormous women, sitting on the ground, legs splayed, with Jack in front of them.

Hardly knowing what she did, she sent a breeze to right their towering hair, which looked as though it was about to topple from their heads.

"I've found Jack again!" she called to the other three.

Granny Dirt had been digging potatoes, while Granny Spark tended the cooking fire, and Granny Brine filled a kettle with fresh rainwater. They left their tasks to climb up and stand beside Granny Sweep.

"See!" Granny Sweep invited, commanded. "I'll lend you my eye. See!"

It took them a moment to catch up with her vision, but then they saw, too.

"What in the world or beyond its edge are *those*?" asked Granny Spark.

"Are they real?" wondered Granny Dirt "Will they hurt Jack?"

"I don't think so. It looks like they're weeping enough to fill buckets!" said Granny Brine.

The wind began to circle.

"I can't hear what they're saying," grumbled Granny Spark. "Why do none of us have a magical ear?"

"Hush," said Granny Dirt, lying down and putting her ear to the ground. "Listen."

"Rooooooooooooooose!"

"Where is Rose?"

No one knows, moaned the wind.

Noone knows.

Rose and Noone

Maybe there was a world beyond this chamber, so silent I could hear each soft breath of the old man who sat and held me fixed in his gaze. The fire in the hearth made no sound, the flames did not flicker but glowed dull and red, unmoving. I did not move. The air did not move. I thought it would be better if I did not breathe. Perhaps I had stopped.

The old man—had I known his name once?—kept his eyes on me. He sat in a wingback chair, and I sat across from him in its soft red twin. He had his hands clasped, just inches from his chin, where a beard cascaded all the way down his chest. He tapped his forefingers together. I could not hear the tap, but I could see it, feel it, keeping time, going on and on, tapping, tapping as if he would never stop.

Time, Father Time, that was his name. Long, long ago (I strained to remember) I had been in this room with him. Someone had knocked on the door, someone—

"Have you," I spoke as if I were dreaming, the words straining to come out, "are you going to summon your chief magician?"

I will tell my chief magician to take you down to the dark place—or perhaps to cast you out.

Out. Through the dark place, where the crocodiles waited for the bodies of prisoners, for the body of—

"The chief magician," the old man repeated. "Tell me, child, who is or was the chief magician?"

She is my secret, my best secret. He is my secret, my worst secret, I did not say.

He waited, his tapping fingers almost making a sound, his black eyes almost seeing my secrets. Then, without warning, he got to his feet, pacing in circles, pulling at his hair and beard.

"It's all her fault," he growled. "It's all his fault. I told him to seal that room, but she cracked it open. I'll kill him. I'll kill her."

For a lightning, darkening moment we were both back in the round room with the broken pane, night and moon and wind pouring in. But there was nowhere for me to hide now. No Nimble Jack whispering in my mind, guiding me to escape.

"No!" I got up. "She had nothing to do with the round room or the cracked window. She knows nothing about it."

He looked down at me, startled, and everything stopped again. Maybe he had turned us into statues, as he had my aunties.

"Was it you then?" he spoke at last. "Was it *you*, is it *you* who let them in? Is it *you* who let them out?"

I did not know how to answer him. Had I let in the night and the wind and the rain, the vines and the flickering fire, the grannies who sat and rocked? They were so much bigger than me, and yet they had sought me out, then vanished, leaving me to run back down the twisting stairs and halls alone.

"Who are you?" he said softly. "How did you come to have such power? Who are you?"

No one, I wanted to say, as I had once before. I am no one.

But I wasn't.

"My name is Rose."

Somehow I had answered both questions. I had been a secret. Now I was telling.

"You have heard my name in the wind and the rain, in the crack of a window pane."

Had I spoken or was it the grannies, whispering, singing through me?

"I am the one you want."

He peered down at me. I thought he was ancient, but for a moment he looked young, young and afraid. Then he took my hands in his, gripped them, hard. I could feel his bones, his flesh so thin and worn, it was barely there. I could picture the bones of his hands bleaching in the salt air, hear them rattling in the wind.

"Yes," his voice creaked. "You are the one I want."

"Then let her go," I cried out. "Let her go!"

"Let who go?"

He kept hold of my hands.

"You know who!" I did not want to say her name, not to him.

He released his grip on my hands, and sat again in his chair with its high back and its wings, as if at his command it could fly away with him.

"Yes." His fingers began their tapping again. "I know who she is. Murderess, deceiver. The one who killed my chief magician. The one who kept you a secret all these years, the one who kept you a secret. From me."

With every silent tap of his fingers, my legs and arms felt heavier. I sank down in my chair again, the soft red chair that seemed to want to swallow me.

"It wasn't her fault," I said, pushing the words into the air. "He tortured her. He—"

Killed Jack, I did not say aloud. But maybe Jack was still alive somehow, somewhere. I did not want Noone to know about Jack, any Jack, Nimble Jack or Jack Quick. They were secrets, but not my secrets alone. Even if they were only a dream, even if everything was just a dream.

"It wasn't her fault!" I got to my feet. "She just wanted me to live."

He came to stand before me, bringing his face close to mine, too close. His breath was hot and cold at the same time. A wisp of his beard brushed against my cheek

"You are life, Rose, you are the elixir. Through me you will live; through you I will live. Forever."

Noone

Noone kept talking to the child, Rose, his Rose, softly, rhythmically as waves lapping at a shore, kittens lapping at milk.

"You are life, Rose, you are life. You are my life, I am yours, rest now, Rose. I have you, I have you."

His own voice soothed him, soft as thistledown, as the eiderdown, soft as a mother's voice, his mother's.

"You are safe now, Rose, I have you, I will never let you go."

She began to sway on her feet, her eyes swimming under heavy lids. Just before she fell, he caught her in his arms. Long unused muscles sprang to life. She was life, she was his life. He lifted her, so warm and heavy, yet so light. She was light, his light. He carried her to his own bed. He covered her with a heavy, satin quilt.

"Rest now, Rose, rest. I will be your dream."

He stood over her, watching her. She was his now, no father, no mother. He willed himself to forget them; he willed *her* to forget them. They were forgotten. Her face was bright as a long afternoon, as the moon he had taken from the sky, as they sun whose warmth he commanded.

Rose, his life, his elixir. Now the work, the real work, could begin.

As she lay asleep, not asleep, entranced, he told the story of the world over and over and over again. How it began, how it was destroyed, how he was saving the world, how she would. Over and over and over, the world, rising, falling, rising again . . .

Rose

"Who causes suffering, Rose?" he sings over me. "Who destroyed the world beyond?"

"The terrible old women."

I don't name them, but I see them. He has shown me. He has taken me back to before time. He has taken me to the end of time. I see things I have never seen, walls of black water higher than the dome, wind with fangs, earth that gapes like a toothless mouth, and fire that leaves only ash.

He has shown me a woman dead, a boy weeping over her body. But no, he has not shown me that picture. He doesn't want me to see. He reaches out his bony hand and wipes away the scene.

"Fear not, my sweet Rose. Inside the dome, I have bound the wicked old women. Inside the dome, they do my bidding."

"Outside?" I force the question through my lips.

For a moment I see the sky and the moon. I smell salt and sweet, I taste it, I feel the air touch my cheek. My hand is heavy, but I lift it and cover my eyes. It would be dangerous if he knew, if he could see.

"Outside, ah outside. They have forgotten who they are."

Rose knows, Rose knows.

"They are just foolish old women now. Forgetting is their punishment. You must not tell them, Rose. You must never tell."

I never told. I will never tell. I missed my chance.

"Now then, Rose. Who destroyed the world?"

I know the answer. He has told me answer, over and over and over.

"They did."

Who are they? What have I forgotten? Forgetting is my punishment.

"And who saved the world?"

"Noone did."

"And who will save the world once and for all? Who will save Noone?"

"I will," I answer. For he has told me so, over and over and over. "I will."

"And how will you save the world, Rose?"

I know this answer, too.

"I will give my life."

I will die, I will die.

He hears me, even though I didn't speak, he hears me.

"No, Rose, no. There is no death." He says again. And again. "You will live forever. Now Rose, tell me again. How will you save the world?"

"I will give my life. I will give my life to you."

"That's right. And you will live forever. You will live forever. In me."

"I will live. Forever. In you."

My blood runs in rivers. My breath pours in and out of him; I live in him. I am him.

"Rest now, Rose. I have things I must do. Only for a little while. Soon there will be only you. Only me. Only you. Only me."

But once, there was someone else . . .

"Please," I gather all my strength; I struggle against the weight of heavy blankets, the weight of his weightless voice. "My mother, my mother. . . "

"Ah, Rose, remember? Remember. You have no mother, Rose. No mother, not anymore."

"M-murderess, deceiver . . . " I strain to remember, his voice accusing her.

"There are no more mothers," he soothes. "Now we need no mothers. You were never born; you will never die. You will live forever. In me. Say it, Rose."

"I will live forever. In you."

But what . . . what if I don't want to?

"Rest now, Rose. Just a little while, just a little while longer . . ."

Jack and the Aunties

When night fell, Jack led his two huge, conspicuous charges through the darkest alleys, which was tricky with a just-waning moon sending its probing light into every crack and crevice. The night Guard was on patrol. The taverns overflowed into the streets with brawling miners. Jack's route was circuitous and slow, with the two giantesses alternately hobbling in their heels or taking them off and yelping (in whispers) whenever their stocking feet encountered a pebble.

At last they crouched in the shadows by his shack. Bramma sat cross-legged before the fire. By moonlight and firelight her face looked like it was made of earth or stone. Signaling to the giantesses to wait, Jack crept toward the fire and sat down next to her.

"I found them. The ladies, the ones who came looking for me. They say they are Rose's aunties."

Bramma got up and stirred the fire. She looked straight to where the huge women waited. And then she sat down again, without acknowledging them.

"Rose," she said softly. "Where is Rose?"

"She might be inside, caught. Do you know who Noone is, Bramma?"

"No one knows who Noone is," said Bramma, staring into the fire. "He is older than the time Before. He made the world again from ashes. He is a trickle of foul water, a crust of moldy bread, a feast gone to waste."

"I should have stayed with Rose," Jack accused himself. "I didn't know she'd turned back till too late."

"What is too late is too late. What is not is not," Bramma said, and then she turned to the shadows. "Come out, little boys."

Little boys? To Jack's astonishment, the giantesses tiptoed into the firelight.

"We were never—" whispered one.

"We were, sister, we were."

They stood before Bramma, abashed, staying quiet for longer than Jack would have believed they could, swaying with uncertainty and fatigue.

"Sit," said Bramma. "Before you fall over and crush something."

The ladies did as they were told.

"Do you remember our mama?" one of them asked.

"We never saw her again. After."

Bramma looked from one to the other, then back to the fire.

"Everyone remembers your mother. When you disappeared inside and never came out again, she led an uprising. You were not the only children who lost a mother that day," she paused. "And she was not the only mother who lost a child inside."

Jack sat across from Bramma and the giant ladies, their painted faces streaked like a sunset sky fading into night.

"What happened to her?"

"Is she alive?"

"Tell us."

"Please, tell us."

Bramma began to sing, her beauty singer's voice, faint but true. The giantesses leaned in to hear her, their wigs slipping into her lap.

over the edge of the world she went
over the edge of the world she flew
when she had wings, now she has wings

The ladies wept again but softly, like a spatter of rain when a storm is already spent.

"We knew."

"We didn't know."

"We always knew."

"But how—"

"How did you know who we are, were?"

"We've changed."

"Changed beyond memory. I still don't remember."

"We used to be little boys with ragged clothes and dirty knees, and now we're—"

"Disheveled grown women, our shoes ruined, our stockings in shreds, our wigs—"

"You haven't changed that much," said Bramma. "You still talk and interrupt the same way. People used to call you the little bird boys."

Before they could start up again, Bramma reached out, taking hold of one massive arm each with her small, rough hands.

"Now it is your turn to tell me. About my daughter. About Briar."

Bramma, Briar's mother. Of course. Hadn't he known? Bramma had always known, even as she kept it secret from him, from everyone, that he was the son of the three. A breeze stirred the fire where a blue flame leapt and the embers glowed, dark, gritty, golden.

"We only meant to protect her—"

"And Rose—"

"Who wasn't born yet—"

"You see, Briar killed the chief magician—"

"With a spiked heel. We picked out the shoes for her, so I suppose we are accessories—"

"I'm not sorry, he deserved it; he made Briar give Jack that nasty potion—"

"That vaporized him."

"But once the chief was dead—"

"We had to think quickly—"

"Because of the baby—"

"Who wasn't born yet."

"So we disguised her as him—"

"Is my daughter alive?" Bramma cut them off.

There was a heartbeat of silence, and in the distance, the rhythmic tread of heavy boots.

"Last time we saw her."

"But Noone took her."

"Shh!" said Jack.

Right, left, right, left. The Guard was coming closer, a few alleys away now.

Quick, Jack Quick! the blue voice vaulted from the flames. *Now!* exploded an ember shooting a spray of golden sparks.

"We've got to hide them, Bramma. We've got to disguise them."

"Disguises, of course, we are mistresses of disguise, and we do need a change of—"

"But we can't be ladies, sister. They're looking for ladies. We've got to be—"

"Men, ugh! Not men. We wouldn't have the first idea—"

"I have no men's clothing," said Bramma, getting to her feet. "But you can wear rags, like the rest of us outsiders. Take them inside our shelter, Jack. Find some old blankets to cover them. Then slip out the back and bury their clothes and wigs in the rubbish heap."

The aunties sat up and clutched at their wigs.

"Hurry!" said Bramma. "For Rose's sake. For Briar's."

Rose

The sound of water in the dark. Coldness. Damp. The stink of something rotten.

I remember this part, when the story turned scary. When the story changed from three children, no longer children, running and dodging the Guard, lying together in the briar patch, to three children, no longer children, separated.

Because one of them tried to find a way for them all to escape over the wall.

That is the story the little girl wants to hear. The three children, no longer children, running free in the wide world beyond the wall.

But that is not what happened.

The sound of water in the dark, coldness, damp. The stink of something rotten.

Who am I in this story? Am I lying broken on the stone floor? Am I a rat invisible in a corner? Something heavy covers me; something holds me down. I can't move; I can hardly breathe. I can't wake up from this dream.

"Rose!" a voice calls out.

Who is Rose? I can't remember. There is only the sound of water in the dark. Coldness. Damp. The stink of something rotten. Broken bones lying on a cold floor. Pain.

"Rose."

Someone used to tell me about the roses blooming in the briars. She would try to describe the sky to me, and the air that stirred the petals, and the bees humming.

"That's why I named you Rose," she would say.

I am Rose.

318

"Rose!"

It's my mother's voice. She is my mother.

I've found her. I've found her!

I'm here, mama. I'm here. I call to her, but no sound comes out. I am not here. I twist and turn, trying to throw the blankets off me, trying to get untangled, trying to wake up.

"Rose, run away, Rose. Run."

I won't leave you, I say. *I won't leave you.*

But I can't hear my voice. My legs won't move.

A door creaks open. It stirs the stale air; it lets in light that frames a long, spindly shadow. The shadow falls across someone lying on the floor, her arms and legs shackled, needlessly, for she is too broken to move.

My mother. But where am I? Where am I?

"Murderess, deceiver."

I know this voice. I have to warn her. *Run away,* I tell her. But she can't run.

"You tried to destroy the world, my world."

Who destroyed the world, Rose? His voice whispers in my dream.

Where am I?

"You tried to keep her from me. The only one who matters, the only one who knows."

Rose knows, Rose knows

sings the dark water.

Rose knows, Rose knows.

sings the air that has never seen light,

Rose knows, Rose knows

sings the cold stone.

Rose knows, Rose knows

sings the light that never shone.

You are destroying the world! I shout, but again my voice makes no sound.

"And so my doomed dear, twisted, blighted briar that yielded my sweetest Rose, it is time for you to go."

And he begins to sing; it is an awful sound.

over the edge of the world you'll fall
into the endless deep
no more air to carry your call
no grave your bones to keep

Then she sings, my mother sings over him, her voice at first parched and broken, but growing stronger.

over the edge of the world we go
over the edge of the world we fly
queens and kings
when we have wings
we all have wings
over the edge of the world we go
queens and kings, queens and kings

Her voice soars over his, weaving in and out, always beyond his reach. Then I hear other voices, children's voices. I remember, I remember this part of the story, three children dancing for joy on a rubbish heap, all the others joining them, dancing and singing for joy—

"No," the old man howls. "Noooooooooooo!"

It is silent again. The sound of water. Coldness. Damp. The stink of something rotten.

"Guards!" the old man shouts. "Come. Prepare her."

Wait, I call to her. *I'm coming with you!*

I see myself running down corridor after corridor.

Wait! I shout.

My voice wakes me. I am not there. My eyes are open, but I cannot see. I try to stand, but there is no ground.

Rose, I whisper.

I am no one. I know nothing.

The Grannies

"We need to go."

One of them spoke, although they did not know which one. Maybe it did not matter. They were not separate anymore. Maybe they never were. The moon shone on them as it slipped down the starry dome of night, the round of sky that made dome world look like a small pebble.

"How do we get there without Rose dreaming of us?"

"Or without our dreaming of her?"

Any one of them could have asked the question. Any one of them could answer.

"Rose is dreaming."

"But her dream can't get out to us."

"We can't get in."

"We are in, inside the dome."

"We can't see us there."

"We can't be us."

"We can't remember."

"Are we dead there?"

"Can we die?"

"Are we alive?"

"We are outside of inside, too."

"Heaps of garbage."

"Narrow passageways in the mines."

"Sewers and crocodiles."

"I want to go home."

"We are home."

They sat quietly, their own songs singing around them, the wind, the crackle of fire, the stirring of seeds, and, from far away, the scent of sea.

"Jack," one of them said.

"Jack," they all said. "We must go to Jack."

They sat for a little longer, singing to themselves, singing to each other.

if we go
who will sweep the sky
who will catch the babies
who will tend the trees
who will gather the bones
if we go, if we're gone

Nightwing sang back, as she flew from the pinnacle toward the moon, her shadow winging behind her, her voice sharp as a thorn on a rose, wild as a bramble patch.

Rose knows, Rose knows
as the fire glows, as the wind blows
as the seed grows, as the water flows
go here, go there
you are always everywhere

"Rose," the voice came from far away, but it was one of theirs.

"What if Rose has forgotten? What if Rose has forgotten who she is?"

"Then we must tell her, tell her, tell her, tell her."

"It's time to go."

Jack

come the sorrow, come the pain
come the hunger, come the rain
come the darkness, come the dawn
beauty will go on, go on, beauty will go on

"Sister, wake up, sister, listen!"

One of the massive, shapeless lumps rolled over and shook the other. Jack woke, too. It was still night inside the shack, but his Bramma was already out and gone as she always was.

"Is it the stars singing?" the other one asked.

come the fever, come the cold
come the babies growing old
come the darkness, come the dawn
beauty will go on, go on, beauty will go on

Jack had heard the singing all his life, upon every waking. The voices did sound like stars, each one distinct, yet so many, so far away, yet so close.

"It's them, sister, it's them. Don't you remember?"

"The beauty singers, oh sister, I do remember."

Jack got up to go outside. He liked to have the fire going and something warm to eat or drink ready for his Bramma. He turned and cautioned the giantesses before they could follow him.

"Make sure there's no paint on your faces. And cover your heads with kerchiefs."

"Does your grandmother have a mirror, Jack?"

"We'd just like to see what we—"

"No, mirror!" he said, stepping outside. "Just make the best disguises you can."

come the silence, come the breath
come the birthing, come sweet death
come the darkness, come the dawn
beauty will go on, go on, beauty will go on

Jack listened to the last note lingering in the silence.

"Jack," someone whispered. "Jack, Jack, Jack."

The sound was lost in a murmuration of starlings racketing into the air to catch the first light. For a moment he glimpsed four old women, wavering in an uncertain knot, before turning into shadow and light.

Had he really seen them?

When Bramma returned, they all sat around the fire, the aunties silent for once, as they spooned the thin gruel that they must have remembered from when they were little boys. He did not think they were in any danger of being recognized as the two runaway inside ladies he'd rescued yesterday, except for their size. Their stripped faces didn't look male or female, old or young. Just tired and sad. They had covered their heads and fashioned skirts and shawls from blankets—rather cleverly, he thought. Now he just had to come up with a way to get inside. He would rather go unencumbered, but the giantesses knew inside world from bottom to top, and he had never been inside except for his climb up a now-ruined vine into a tower that had disappeared.

He was about to speak when they heard a loud, creaking groan, followed by the rumble of heavy wheels rolling over cobblestone. Then came a blaring sound, so loud that it caused waves in the gruel.

"What in the dome is that?" said one auntie.

Another blast came. They set down their bowls.

"You know what it is, sister."

"No!" She put her hands over her ears and squeezed shut her eyes. "I don't!"

The awful sound came again and jolted them to their feet.

"They are wheeling out the Judgment Seat," said Bramma, though they could barely hear her over the ringing in their ears. "Come."

Bramma took hold of Jack's hand, and he reached for the ladies' hands to keep from getting separated in the crowds that were all streaming in the same direction, answering the same summons.

The Judgment Seat was visible to the crowd, sitting high on the wheeled platform. It was crude and oversized, an intentional mockery of a throne. A crowd of insiders had gathered, too, on outdoor observation decks, roofed to protect the viewers from sun or rain. The insiders had seats on risers and cups of steaming drinks to warm them in the unaccustomed chill. They called greetings to each other, laughing as if gathered for an entertainment, which for them it was. Despite its size, the outside crowd waited in silence.

A contingent of guards carried portable steps to the platform, which served as a stage with the empty throne in the center. Then came the heavy-booted footfall of the Guard, marching in formation out of the dungeon to the Judgment Seat, the prisoner surrounded.

"Who is it?"

"I can't see!"

When they reached the platform, the Guard formed facing lines, leaving two of their number to drag the prisoner up the steps.

"Whoever it is can't walk."

"One of ours then. They always break their legs, first thing."

The guards deposited the prisoner in the Judgment Seat and bound him there. No, *her* there. A slight woman with a bruised face and long tangled hair. One of the giantesses shrieked.

The guards turned from the prisoner to the crowd, their spears and swords at the ready.

"Hush, sister! We've got to keep our wits about us."

"But it's our—"

"Shut up, you stupid cow," said a man standing near them.

Jack felt Bramma's nails digging into his palm. She kept gasping, and then holding her breath. And so, though he'd never seen her, Jack knew:

The woman was Briar, Rose's mother, Bramma's daughter. Briar on the judgment seat.

Jack stood as high as he could on his toes and scanned both the inside and outside crowds.

There was no sign of Rose.

Then came another blare of trumpets and the sound of more marching feet as a man strutted past the cheering inside crowd, down the staircase from the main entrance of the dome. The fanfare continued as made his way to the platform. He wore a gold crown on his unnaturally orange hair. A bright purple cloak decorated with peacock feathers trailed in the dust of outside world. A herald, carrying a speaking horn, followed the king to the platform. Standing on a step below, he turned to address the crowd.

"His Majesty King, King, um—"

The herald appeared to have forgotten the king's name. There were titters from the crowd, a couple of boos, and a raspberry or two.

"Silence!" bellowed the herald, and the guards menaced the crowd again. "His majesty...the King of the Dome!"

The king strutted in a circle on the platform, alternately raising arms in a victory stance and waving, now and then blowing a kiss to a pretty girl.

"His majesty will now judge and sentence the prisoner."

The herald passed a speaking horn to the king. The king continued to pace while he spoke.

"Ladies and gentlemen, first families of the dome, men and women of the walled world, whose purpose and honor is to serve those who will soon be immortal—and, ladies and gentlemen, there's been slight delay in those plans because of this sorry creature you see before you. She may look like nothing much, because she *is* nothing much, growing up on a dung heap...but I tell you she is a bad person, very, very bad...."

He rambled on, and people began to shift from foot to foot, losing their fear in boredom. Briar slumped in her chair, passed out or asleep.

"Your majesty, if I may suggest," interrupted the herald. "Just the crimes and the punishment. No one wants to—"

Or did he say Noone?

At the sound of that word, the king's red face paled, and he looked down at his hands, which apparently held notes.

"Assassination. Impersonation. Subversion. Perversion. Guilty! Let me hear you say it!"

"Guilty!" mumbled the crowd.

"It's not her fault—" shouted one of the aunties.

"Louder!" commanded the king.

"Guilty!" the voices rose.

"It wasn't her idea—"

"And what happens to traitors to the dome! I can't hear you! What happens to them!"

The guards pointed their spears again.

"Over!" someone shouted. "Thrown over!"

"Over where?" demanded the king.

"Over the edge of the world!"

"Say it again!"

"Over the edge of the world they go"

The voices rose; the crowd caught the rhythm and roared. The king paced, then danced a jig.

Before Jack knew what was happening, the giantesses plunged into the crowd, parting it with their double hugeness.

"Wait! What are you doing? Wait!" shouted Jack, but he couldn't hear his own voice.

When he turned to look for his Bramma, she was gone, too. Alone in the baying crowd, Jack dodged and squeezed his way to the front just in time to see the two aunties swing themselves up onto the platform—even in the chaos he admired their unexpected agility. They weren't just the inside ladies they appeared to be, with painted faces and ridiculous shoes. They were bodyguards, Briar's bodyguards. They punched and kicked and fought their way to her.

For one moment Jack had a wild hope. Maybe they could save her. One of them worked at untying her bonds, while the other auntie looked around for a way to escape. If only they could leap into the air over the crowd, over the wall. Jack could feel the trajectory in his own body. But in another moment, they were surrounded by guards on all sides, one rank facing in, the other facing out.

"Take them away!" sounded a voice, not the voice of the king, but instead a voice that came from everywhere and nowhere, a voice that rose with the wind that sprang up, a sharp cracking voice that struck like the lightning from the black clouds that rolled in.

It took several members of the Guard to subdue the aunties, who kept knocking them down till their hands and feet were bound at last, and they were heaved into a horse-drawn wagon, the kind used for hauling and dumping rubbish. Finally two guards lifted Briar from the Judgment Seat and carried her to the wagon, setting her down almost gently on the heap of aunties.

Jack ran toward the wagon, thinking to somersault into the air and do something, he didn't know what, there was no time to know. He just had to be nimble; he had to be quick. He backed into the crowd and prepared to make a running leap.

"No, Jack," the bright blue voice tumbled by. "Leave them to me. I know the way."

"Don't be sad, Jack," said the gritty, golden voice. "We're all together again, the three. If you squeeze your eyes almost closed, you'll see."

Jack did as the voice bid him. For a moment all he could see was rainbows, flying and darting all around the cart. Then he saw them, three children holding hands, shimmering, transparent, dancing.

over the edge of the world we go
over the edge of the world we fly
queens and kings
when we have wings . . .

Other voices soared, higher than the wind, more piercing than lightning, weaving in and out of the children's song.

come fall or flight, night or dawn
beauty will go on, go on, beauty will go on

"Round them up," shrieked the voice that came from nowhere and no one. "Take the beauty singers, too, over the edge, over the edge, over the edge of the world!"

Jack saw her, his Bramma, half-hoisted, half-climbing into the wagon along with the other beauty singers.

come fall or flight, night or dawn
beauty will go on, go on, beauty will go on
beauty will go on, go on, beauty will go on

"Bramma!" Jack ran after the wagon as it rolled toward the gates. "Bramma!"

Then he felt himself being pulled against the current of the crowd.

"Jack, Jack, Jack, Jack."

Someone, something was calling his name.

He turned and saw shadowy figures waiting by the unguarded dungeon door.

"Find Rose!" the raven flew low over his head. "Find Rose."

He followed the beckoning shadows. Four women, older than old, there and not there.

"Find Rose!"

And he followed his guides into the dome.

PART EIGHT

The Beginning of the End

Noone

Noone watched from the window.

His feet had dragged him there from the dungeon of the dome to the winding stair, to the round room that did not exist, the crack in the dome that he would seal forever. Himself. No one else. Noone.

This was the last time.

The end was beginning.

He watched the crowds surge toward the gate, following the wagonload of traitors. Really, he should let all the outsiders go, such dirty, ignorant people. They would not be needed much longer. It would be a mercy to send them over the edge of the world into the nothing they came from, back to the nothing they were.

The great gates groaned open, a laboring beast in the throes of a monstrous birth. Yet still he could hear the high sound of the women's voices.

come fall or flight, come dawn or night
beauty will go on, go on, beauty will go on

The gates thundered closed, and they were gone, the murderess, her unnatural accomplices, the treacherous singers. Let them sing as they fell forever, until there was no more air and no more breath. Nothing. Only nothing.

He would never hear their voices again.

He moved back from the window and raised his hands. With deft motions, sure magic, he smoothed away the window till there was no break in the wall. Neither the deceiver nor the magician she had impersonated had his power to make and unmake. He stepped into the corridor and pulled the round room after him, leaving the dome as it was meant to be: unblemished, perfect, impenetrable. This time it would stay that way. No more nightmares, no more empty rocking chairs, rain, moonlight, wind, or scattered leaves. No more entrance from outside for the terrible old women.

They had tried to lure Rose outside. But she had come to him, and he had saved her. Now she would see.

Inside, the terrible old women had no power. Inside, they were his slaves.

The Grannies and Jack

They were inside.

All four of them, not through the window in the high tower, but down deep, dungeon deep. The air was so still that Granny Sweep's hair dragged after her along the cold floor. Granny Spark's flaming hair flared and guttered. Granny Dirt sank her roots down, seeking something that wasn't there; she felt herself growing dry and brittle, full of cracks. Granny Brine wavered, threatening to dissolve into the sound and stench of fouled water.

Jack tiptoed down the corridor, though his bare feet made no sound on the cold floor. Eerie light came from everywhere and nowhere. On both sides, he saw locked cells, too dark to see inside, but he sensed they were empty; the whole place felt dead.

"Rose?" he whispered. "Rose!"

He looked around for his guides, sometimes ahead of him, sometimes behind, but growing fainter all the time.

"Don't disappear on me," he hissed. "We've got to find Rose."

Who are we? Jack heard them murmuring. *We don't remember. We don't remember.*

"Shh," cautioned Jack. "Just remember Rose."

Rose knows, Rose knows, Rose knows, Rose knows.

"Rose!" Jack called a little louder.

Then he heard the sound of the Guard marching back inside, still in formation. Jack started to run, not knowing where he was going. He glanced back and saw the Guard round a corner, so he flattened himself against the wall, but one of them spotted him.

"Who goes there!" the man shouted.

"It's an outsider trying to get in."

"Stop him!"

Jack took off again.

"I know who it is. He's the one they call Jack Quick. The one we've been trying to catch."

"We've got him now!"

"We'll run him down!"

"Rear Guard, block all the exits."

Before they dispersed, Jack turned to face them and did what he did best. Taking a running leap, he somersaulted over their heads. Their confusion, as they did an abrupt about-face, gave him a head start.

"Do something!" he called to the grannies.

Rose knows who we are.

Deep in the cavernous dungeon, the wind kicked up and pushed Jack forward. Behind him, the Guard shouted in terror as out of nowhere, rain sluiced down, lightning flashed, thunder crashed. Jack slipped through a door and started up a winding stair, the grannies ahead and behind, all of them emerging into the vastness of the great domed city.

Jack ran on with the wind at his back, his feet springing from the smooth paving stones and the unreal grass, through the parks, streets, and corridors of the dome, flashes of light shaped like birds or butterflies appeared at every turn. Fountains and streams flowed, covering the sound of his racing feet, his ragged breath. He had no time to wonder at the splendor of the domed city, or the crowds in their finery returning from the observation deck. He paid no heed to their cries of alarm at the sight of a ragged, barefoot boy, dodging and leaping. He ran on and on, up and up, into a winding corridor, finally stopping at a door, a plain door he could have missed, a door that was meant to be missed.

Open it, open it, open it, open it.

And Jack did.

Rose

I am dreaming. I am a dream. I am nothing but air and light, I am nothing but hard ground and driving rain. I rampage over the empty world where there is nothing but a cart making its way, rolling on and on. Toward the edge.

"Rose!"

What is a rose? Someone told me once long ago. Soft petals, sweet, spicy scent (how would I know, I, who never went outside), briars that can make you bleed, bees humming, their soft, relentless touch.

"Rose, wake up!"

I am dreaming, I am a dream.

"Rose, wake up! We've got to go."

over the edge of the world we go
over the edge of the world we fly

I hear children singing. I was a child once. Now I am a dream.

"Rose!"

The voices fade. Something is shaking me, the wind, the rain, a swarm of bees. The dark is coming down on me. I am back inside, inside myself, so small, so cramped.

"Rose, wake up. It's me, Jack!"

I opened my eyes and saw him, the boy I had looked for, waited for, his dark face and his wild curls tinged with red. I sat up, almost bumping noses with him. And then, behind him, in the glow of the unconsumed fire, in the shadows that no one cast, I saw *them*. One with hair the color of moonlit cloud, one with hair flaring like fire, one with hair dark and alive, and one whose hair smelled like salt and rattled with bones and shells.

Who causes suffering, Rose? Who destroyed the world beyond?

Walls of black water, wind with fangs, earth that gapes like a toothless mouth, and fire that leaves only ash.

"Come on, Rose!" urged the boy.

He tried to pull me to my feet, but I held back. They were there, they were everywhere, all around us. In the way.

The terrible old women.

"Why are they here? Why did you bring them?" I pointed.

Jack looked around him. Maybe he couldn't see them. They kept shifting shape, now shadowy, now clear.

"The terrible old women," I spoke aloud.

Jack turned in a circle, facing me again.

"They helped me, Rose. The grannies, that's what you called them before. They showed me the way inside. They led me to you."

"They destroyed the world beyond."

We didn't mean to, we didn't mean to, we didn't mean to, we didn't mean to.

All at once, the room was filled with moaning. And memory. But not my memories. How could I have seen the world beyond, overrun with people? How could I have seen forests cut down, rivers burning, air choked with smoke, the ground parched with thirst? They were not my memories. I was remembering for them.

They have forgotten who they are. They are just foolish old women now.

"I don't know anything about that," said Jack. "They gave us cake. Don't you remember? You know them, Rose. You know who they are. That's what they always say."

Rose knows, Rose knows, the old women whispered. *Rose knows, Rose knows.*

Forgetting is their punishment. You must not tell them, Rose. You must never tell.

I closed my eyes. I felt the wind on my face, the sun on my crown, I felt the water rushing around my feet. I breathed the sweetness of roses, heard the bees gathering nectar, tasted the sweetness of the honeycomb hidden in the stone. All things that had never been mine to know, except in my mother's stories.

My mother . . .

The dream came back to me, and I saw my mother in the cart, her broken body cradled in my aunties' arms. They were surrounded by other women, on their way to the edge of the world, all of them singing.

come fall or flight, night or dawn, beauty will go on

"Who will save her?" I spoke aloud. "Who will save them—"

"Who saved the world, Rose?"

I opened my eyes. Jack whirled around. Noone stood before us. Thin as a knife, his beard longer than he was, his hair a tangle. The old women receded, watchful, wary, but still there. Did Noone know? Could he see them?

"Who saved the world, who built it all again from nothing?"

"Noone did," I answered as he had taught me.

Then I spoke again. "No one did."

Did he hear the change in meaning? Did they? What did I mean?

"And who will save the world once and for all? Who will save Noone?"

I will. I knew the answer. *I will.*

It was hard not to say it.

"What is he talking about, Rose?" whispered Jack.

I couldn't answer him. Noone held me in his gaze. Beside me, Jack felt insubstantial as dust dancing in a shaft of light.

"Remember, Rose. There will be no more death. You will live forever. Tell me again. How will you save the world?"

I will give my life. I will give my life to you.

"Remember, Rose. You were never born; you will never die. You will live forever. In me. Say it, Rose."

"No one lives forever!" snorted Jack.

"That's right," Noone turned to Jack. "Noone lives forever."

Released from his eyes, I saw the old women, the terrible old women. The grannies of the world. One moment they looked frail and shadowy; the next I could see through them to the world beyond, a sky-high promontory, a band of green along a river, a thick forest, a temple of bone gleaming beside water that never stopped moving. Water beyond a cliff that disappeared into mist . . .

Rose knows who we are. Rose knows!

"Stop!" bellowed Noone, as the world beyond roared into his world. "Stop!"

He covered his eyes; he cowered.

"Run!" shouted Jack, grabbing my hand.

We ran down and around corridors, past tier after tier of houses. When we reached the huge central hall, with its dome-high ceiling, Jack and I ducked and weaved our way through crowds of people panicked by rain that began to fall from the no-sky, and wind that tore off their hats. Bells clanged, sirens wailed, and a voice boomed out a warning:

"Outsider in, outsider in! Invasion."

We held onto each other's hands. Where were we going? We had no time to wonder, no breath to ask.

Down, came the answer, not a voice so much as a tug on our feet. We slipped through a door to a narrow staircase winding down and down, to another door, which opened on the dungeon.

"I came in through the dungeon gate," said Jack. "The grannies led me through. This way."

But as we rounded a corner, we saw that the gates were now closed and bolted, with two of the Guard standing sentinel. Jack pulled us back before they saw us. Both of us barefoot, we ran soundlessly down another winding corridor, deeper and deeper. Around one curve we paused for breath. We could hear the sound of water somewhere and smell the stench of something rotten. We were in the deepest part of the dungeon, though the barred cells we passed were empty.

Because she let them go, I heard Nimble Jack's warm, blue voice. *Briar let all the prisoners go. I was the first.*

"Does he talk to you in your head?" I whispered to Jack.

Jack nodded as if he knew exactly who I meant. Then in a voice lower than a whisper, he said, "Someone's following."

I heard it, too: the sound of feet, not the heavy pounding of boots, but a whisper of feet, a scrabbling. We pressed ourselves against the wall and listened. Maybe it was only a rat. Then without warning, the wall gave way, hurling us into a chamber.

Jack and I stood and stared. Mists that glowed with their own light overflowed from bubbling vats and swirled around us on the floor. There was a bare, examining table on one side of the room, gleaming coldly. I shuddered. My body knew before my mind: my mother had lain on this table, helpless. I thought I would be sick. How could it be that my life had begun here, in this deserted place of foul, stale magic?

"Where are we?" said Jack, his voice flat and echoing at the same time.

It's his place, my father's place, I could not bring myself to say.

"Let's get out of here," I said aloud.

But the wall behind us had closed. Ahead of us, light glowed from another chamber.

"That could be the way out," said Jack. "Let's look."

I sensed something not right about that light. But I knew nothing but the light and dark of inside world, which followed each other across the walls and ceiling without casting shadows. Shadows were something I had seen only in storybooks and dreams—and for those brief moments when I glimpsed the real sun and the real moon through the tower window. This light was not like either. As Jack and I tiptoed towards it, I thought I could hear the light...singing.

Sing, beauty singer, sing.

All at once, I knew what made the light, *who* had made the light.

"Wait" I said. "It's not the way out. It's not the way anywhere. It's trapped, a trapped star. The elixir was made from a drop of that light, the elixir the chief magician made my mother give your father to drink."

"The drink that killed him," said Jack.

It was different here than when I had told him in the tower, the window open, our escape before us. Here, where it had happened. Here, where we were trapped.

Vaporized, the blue voice swooped in, mimicking the aunties. *I am still here, there, everywhere. Everywhere.*

"Did you hear him? My father!" Jack said with awe and pride. "My father."

Before I could speak, there was a blast of foul air; the dank mists swirled around us, and the blue voice tumbled away into the beyond.

"Your father." Someone behind us spoke.

We turned and there was Noone. The wall closed again.

"Your father. Looking at you, boy, I see him again." His tone was almost kind yet no less frightening for that. "King of the dung heap. He used to disturb me. The ruckus he made! I heard him through that window . . . That window, who kept opening it?"

His tone shifted; he muttered to himself.

"Them, them. I thought it was him, my cursed chief magician. He wanted to take over, he thought he didn't need me. Ha, ha! He got his comeuppance, didn't he? Killed by a girl. A filthy, ragged girl from outside world."

A girl, I did not say aloud, who had been arrayed as a bride in fine clothes, including glittering shoes with lethal heels.

"But it wasn't him," Noone went on. "It was them all along."

The terrible old women, came a whispering from all around us, *terrible, terrible, terrible, terrible.*

"How did they get in from outside, when I already had them bound inside?"

For a moment, Noone seemed to have forgotten about Jack and me. We took a step back from him, though there was nowhere to go. Then his hand flew out toward me—in that light it looked like sheer bone—and closed on my wrist, so tightly I could feel the pressure on my own bones. Jack took hold of my other hand. Even in this damp place, his hand was warm, warm as the blue of his father's voice.

"It's all coming back to me now," Noone went on. "The disturbance they made, the dung-heap king. And your prickly, tangled mother, Rose, before she became a murdering imposter. And there was another one. There were three, I distinctly remember three."

"Sal!" I breathed, before I could stop myself.

It's all right, Rose; no one can hurt me now, the gritty, golden voice thrummed through me. I hoped Jack could hear, too. *Noone can't hurt me.*

"I didn't know their names. I didn't need to, I didn't want to. They were the three. I just wanted them to stop! Stop!"

He dropped my wrist and held his hands to his ears.

"Stop that singing. Stop that ringing round and round! What did they have to sing about? I've put a stop to it now. Once and for all. Over the edge of the world. All of them. Gone."

Sal died in the mine, I did not say. And my mother, where was she now? How close to the edge? I closed my eyes, but I couldn't see anything but the glow of the star that seemed even brighter through my lids.

"But none of that matters. From that dung heap, that usurping traitor, that deceiving whore, has come the purest Rose."

I felt his cold breath on my face and opened my eyes to find him right in front of me.

"Go away now, boy," he said to Jack.

"No," said Jack simply. "Not going nowhere, Noone."

Noone tried to pry Jack's hand loose from mine. Then he shrugged and gave up.

"No matter. You do not exist. No one exists but Noone. Noone and his Rose. Come. It is time to go to the star, the star that your deceitful mother concealed from me all those years, just as she concealed you. She thought she was clever, doling out a fake elixir drop by drop, fermented honey, fiery and fake, laced with herbs to cloud my mind. Everything she did, false. All the tests for selecting who would join me in immortality, who must be cast out, all the schemes and conspiracies she fomented, all the meetings and banquets to attend, all the endless pomp and pompousness of the first families."

That's what my mother did all those days and years when she put on the awful mask and left me alone in our secret rooms. How tedious, how sad, how much sadder than whatever death might be, sadder even than falling over the edge of the world.

"And her grotesque attendants," Noone went on. "Not male, not female, always flanking her. How I loathed them."

My beloved aunties, my only playmates, how I missed them. Were they frightened now? Were they already gone? How could they not exist?

"Everything false, everything fake, everything but you, my Rose, you and the star you've led me to. Yes, my Rose, I followed your sweetness. Come, my Rose, lead me the rest of the way. Lead me to eternal life."

He took my hand again, his so cold, so old, and yet, and yet, he felt more like a child than Jack Quick, who kept my other hand in his warm grip. I turned to look at the old man I had called Father Time. He had closed his eyes, like someone too tired to see anymore. Then he squeezed them even more tightly closed, as I used to do when my aunties brought me a surprise.

"What do we do?" whispered Jack. "He's off his nut!"

Go to the star, said a new inside voice, *take him to the star.*

"Did you hear that?" I asked Jack Quick.

Neither the gold voice, nor the blue.

"I thought I heard something," he said. "Like the wind whistling around a corner."

Don't be afraid, go to the star.

"Come on then," I said.

And holding each of their hands, I led the old man and the boy to the chamber where the star burned.

And sang.

over the edge of the world we go
over the edge of the world we fly

"Who is singing, Rose?" fretted Noone. "Who is singing? Make them stop."

"It is the star, Noone," I said. "I can't make it stop. The star is made of singing."

My mother's voice singing. The voice that sang me to sleep every night, the voice that sang me awake.

honey in the stone, rose in the dawn
beauty will go on, go on

As we came nearer, my mother's voice became one of many voices. The song of the stars, the beauty singers' song.

world without edge, world without end
beauty will go on, go on, beauty will go on

"No," Noone whispered, and then he howled.

"Noooooooooooooooooooo!"

All three of us stopped before the star, which was trapped, I saw now, inside its own dome. The song shifted to softer sounds without words. Water lapping, wind rustling leaves, and, if I had ever heard the sound, I might have recognized the call of a mourning dove.

Jack and I looked at each other, and then looked at the star. Noone kept hold of my hand. We all gazed, separately and together.

"Do you see what I see?" whispered Jack.

"Yes," I said, though I did not know if he saw what I did.

The star was still there in the sky of a dark world, maybe at the edge of the world, the endless nothing stretching beyond, below, above. And then nothing became something, a world, worlds, I had only dreamed or heard about in books, mountains, forests, seas. Cities as vast as dome world but naked to the sky, plains where herds of animals thundered; I could feel that world shaking with the beat of their hooves. And people, more people than I had ever seen in dome world.

And terror.

People killing each other, people dying, people with no food, no water. Where did all the smoke come from? Who had let the fire loose? Why did the water sweep everything away before it? Then everything was dark again. In that darkness I heard the sound of a child sobbing, calling over and over again for his mother. Darkness gave way to an eerie dawn glow, and I saw her. She was dead. I had never seen anyone dead before. But that's what dead was: empty eyes, disjointed limbs, under glaring sky. Flies buzzing, birds circling, and a boy crying.

Then it all stopped. There was only the light again and the singing. And someone weeping, Noone weeping, still clutching my hand.

come fire and flood, come death, come dawn
beauty will go on

come the wind and quake, come death, come dawn
beauty will go on, go on, beauty will go on

Noone

He would put an end to that singing once and for all. He let go of her hand. Whose hand? Who was standing next to him? He turned and looked at the girl and the boy beside her. The dung heap children, the ones who mocked him. There had been three. Hadn't there been three? Hiding in a tangle of briars. Who let briars grow there, blooming with roses, buzzing with bees, making honey, the fermented honey the deceiver had dropped into his mouth?

Rose, the name came to him, a hint of sweetness with it. Now he remembered. He had thought she was his. He had plucked her. He would save her. No, she would save him. That was it. She would give him his life. She would give her life for his. He gazed down at her, perplexed. He remembered a little girl, lost in a corridor carrying with her a whiff of the outside, a whiff of danger. He had brought her to his chambers. Once, twice. He was going to keep her forever. Now here she was. Standing next to that ragged boy. She was a dung heap girl, after all. A rose sprung from filth. She would wither and die. She was no one.

He was Noone. He had remade the world.

For what? For what?

His mother was dead; she would never get up again.

come birth, come death, come the stars fading into dawn
beauty will go on, go on, beauty—

"Stop!" he whispered to the singing, the terrible, beautiful singing of the star. "Stop!"

He backed away from the star, trapped in its dome, trapped in its night, trapped in that song.

He was Noone, he had made the world, he had made a world inside a dome, a world without an edge—and they had broken in, the terrible old women. They always destroyed everything and everyone.

But not this time. He was Noone. He had remade the world. Now he would destroy it.

over the edge of the world we fall
over the edge of the world we fly

He ran, he leapt into the air, as nimbly as any Jack, he flew. This, this was what he had really wanted, not life, not death. Flying over the edge of the world, into the endless nothing. Then he fell. The dome over the singing star shattered. This time he had done it.

Noone.

Ended.

Everything.

Rose

Over the edge of the world, there was not nothing. There was glass flying, catching the light of a huge sun; there was the crash of waves, and the wind hollowing out caves in the rock. There was the shadow of birds' wings.

And Jack's hand still holding mine.

Then we landed back in the chief magician's chambers, the air dank and the green fog swirling around Noone's still form, among shards of glass that glimmered dimly.

"Is he dead?" whispered Jack.

I let go of Jack's hand and knelt down next to Noone. He should have been splayed out flat, but he lay on his side, his body curled in on itself, his long beard and hair wrapped around him.

There, there, I wanted to say, but I didn't. Everything's all right now. But it wasn't.

"Yes, he's dead."

No breath. Stillness. Still as fallen wind, still as any stone, still as ashes, still as cold. Everything felt still but my own heart, beating as if it was trying to flee my chest.

Rose knows, Rose knows, began the murmuring.

But I didn't know or hadn't known anything.

I felt the air stir around me, sweet, salt, alive, a hint of honey and light.

Stand up, Rose, stand back. We know who we are now. We know what to do.

I got to my feet and stood beside Jack.

"Do you see what I see?" This time I asked him.

I felt rather than saw him nod. The terrible old women, or their shadows, began to circle Noone. Faint sound came from somewhere—the star voices. The old women danced, faster and faster, till they became a whirling blur and sank down to the ground around him. Which one of them cradled him— or did they all at once? The terrible old women, the tender old women, and Noone, no one at all anymore. Older than time, younger than dawn. I don't know how else to describe it. They took him back, the turned him back into everything, bees, briars, roses, honey, day, night, and no time, no time at all.

Then, without warning, the shaking began. The ceiling loosed a shower of dust. The walls began to buckle. We could hear panicked shouts, stampeding feet.

"Is dome world falling down?" cried Jack.

No, said the inside voice, *just cracking open*.

Not the blue voice or the gold, a tangle of green.

My mother's voice.

It's time for you to go.

Where? we both cried out to her. *How?*

The grannies know, she whispered, and then she was gone.

We turned and there they were, a knot of grannies, a whirl of grannies, murmuring among themselves, no, arguing.

"I invited them first. They'll be safe on my pinnacle."

"Safer in the forest."

"Faraway, but safest of all with me."

"But I know the way, I know the way out right now. And remember what Nightwing said."

go here, go there
we are always everywhere

They chanted and circled, merging with one another.

Then Jack and I saw her clearly, waiting for us: Granny Dirt, brown as the earth I'd never yet stood on, her wild hair tumbling.

This way, she gestured urgently, this way. She led us past the shattered glass to an opening on the far side of the chamber. We found ourselves in a stone passageway, the smell and sound of water growing stronger and nearer.

We heard before we saw. A huge tail splashed. Dark water churned. A head surfaced, mouth wide open, displaying its gleaming teeth; another appeared beside it, and another. The crocodiles, who had eaten the chief magician and who knows how many others.

"Bye, bye chief!" my aunties had said as they tossed him into the waiting jaws.

"This is the way out, children," Granny Dirt urged us forward.

Bye, bye, Rose and Jack!

"Um," said Jack. "If it could be arranged, I'd rather go over the edge of the world. I think I might be able to fly, but I can't actually swim."

There was a peculiar sound. Rust and grit, the tumble of stones. Granny Dirt laughing as she bent down and picked up a chain attached to an iron ring.

"Pull, children, pull."

We pulled and pulled, lengths of chain piling on the bank, while the crocodiles swished and snapped and swam in circles. At last a little boat came into view, just big enough for the three of us.

My boat, said the green tangled voice. *For the freed prisoners.*

"Rub a dub dub," said Granny Dirt, helping Jack and me into the boat. She untied the rope that attached the boat to the chain and climbed in after us. "Keep your hands clear of the crocs. They're hungry, poor things. I'll just give them a bite to eat."

She shook her hair, loosing turnips, potatoes, rutabagas, berries, melons. And accompanied by the crocodiles, who snapped and swished, Granny Dirt rowed the boat down the dark river to the world beyond.

PART NINE

The World Beyond

Rose

Even in storybooks or dreams, or in the few glimpses I'd had from the window of the tower room, I had never encountered such bright light, the afternoon sun in its full force. I had to squint, using muscles I had never needed before, and shade my eyes with my hands, so that I could look at everything, as much as I could take in. The sky was a color I had never seen in all the ceiling displays of inside world. I had not known that color has its own light. I could feel it in my body as if it had penetrated my skin and flooded my blood. I did not at first know clouds for what they were. They seemed like magical beasts, alive, moving, changing shape, their shadows racing over land that at first looked brown and desolate.

Jack was also surveying the world beyond—and the world we were leaving behind.

"I didn't know the dome was so big!" he said, one moment. "But it's getting smaller and smaller!"

Granny Dirt rowed silently with the current of the river, resting every few strokes, letting the boat drift on water that gradually became clearer, brighter. Its scent changed. I could not say what it smelled like, but I associated it with the sky and the light, and the green plants that began to spring up along the banks.

In time (and what was time but light changing as the sun moved?) the sky began to soften. As dome world got smaller, its shadow grew longer, elongated, like a finger. I thought of Noone's fingers, more bone than flesh. Was I sorry for him? Sorry that he was dead? He hardly seemed real now. The world that had contained my whole life was beginning to feel like a story someone had read to me long ago. A make-believe story.

"We are beyond the reach of the shadow of the dome," said Granny Dirt. "We'll be home soon."

Home. In the hugeness of the world beyond, it was harder and harder to remember the secret rooms that had been my home. But I remembered, with a sudden sharp pang and a sting of tears, my mother and my aunties.

"I can't go home." Whatever that meant, wherever it was. "I need to go to the edge of the world. I need to find my mother and my aunties."

"And Bramma," Jack said.

No one added "before it's too late." How long did it take to get to the edge of the world? Were they still travelling in that little cart somewhere out there, under this huge sky? A wind swept over the emptiness, feathering the water. The huge black bird, who had come to Jack and me in the tower, flew overhead, making the strangest sounds I'd ever heard.

"That's Nightwing. She brought me the bean," Jack said.

"Yes," said Granny Dirt. "She'll make sure Granny Sweep "Nightwing. She'll make sure Granny Sweep knows you are safe, and tomorrow Nightwing will guide you. But tonight you shall rest and be merry with me. You'll see. Not long now. Around the next bend in the river."

As she promised, around the bend, rising up amid patches of green, I saw the old shoe, just as I had sketched it, just as Granny Dirt had described it, but still beyond whatever I had imagined. From a distance, it looked like someone had left it behind, stuck in the mud. Then we got closer.

"It's huge!" marveled Jack. "It must have been a giant's shoe! And it's got a thatched roof! And a chimney with smoke coming out. How many people live here?"

"I can never keep track," said Granny Dirt. "Oh, children, children. I have so many children, I don't know what to do."

No sooner had she spoken than we saw—and heard—hordes of children racing toward the shore.

"Granny! Granny!" they cried, waving and jumping up and down as the boat neared a sandy shoal.

Jack stood up and waved back.

"Sit!" said Granny Dirt. "Or we'll have to swim the rest of the way."

I felt shy. Or rather, what I know now as shy. I had never had a reason to feel shyness before—fear, perhaps, of Noone, and awe of the appearing and disappearing grannies. But I had never known that there were so many children in the world beyond. In my mind, there had been only Jack and me.

Now children waded into the water, swarming the boat as they pulled it onto shore. Granny Dirt disappeared into dozens of embraces as soon as she set foot on the ground. Other children took Jack and me by the hand and pulled us into a race up the hill toward the giant shoe. Mothers with squealing babies walked toward us.

"More hungry mouths for supper, mothers!" called Granny Dirt.

A woman, further up the hill, pounded with a spoon on an empty dented pot.

"Soo—eee!" she called.

Children and chickens, goats and pigs, ducks and geese, dogs barking and adding to the chaos, all joined us in a jolly stampede to the cooking pots where the mothers ladled stew into chipped, heavy bowls and handed out chunks of bread. Everyone sat on stone benches or on the bare ground and sopped their stew with their bread. I had always been well-fed, but except for the magic cakes the in the tower room, I had never eaten food that tasted so much of earth and sunlight, water and air, elements still new to me.

As soon as we were done eating (Jack marveled that he was allowed a second helping, and I took one, too), the children gathered us into a game that might have been tag or hide and seek. I had never played games before, except with my aunties. But Jack was perfectly at ease, enchanting everyone with his high, flying somersaults. I might have felt left out, but the other girls kept pulling me in whenever I hung back, putting their arms around my waist and kissing my cheeks. Just like Sal and Briar used to do, I thought, homesickness for a home I'd never had thickening my throat. We played till it was almost dark. A sudden hush fell. We could see birds winging home in a sky of changing colors I could not name. We could hear the birds, one after another, singing their last songs. One of the girls took my hand and pointed. At first I saw nothing, and then a light glimmered out into the darkening sky. The first star of the night. From the stillness came more singing.

birds in their nests, stars shining through
babies at breasts, children tucked in the shoe
the shoe, warm and safe, safe and warm
the whole night through, the whole night through

Mothers gathered the younger children; the older ones followed. Beside the door in the arch of the shoe, Granny Dirt waiting, taking each child in her arms in turn.

"There'll be beds for you," Granny Dirt assured us.

And we went inside with the others.

Children, I wish there was a storybook I could show you with a picture of what it was like in the shoe, which seemed even bigger inside than it had when we first saw it. The curve of the heel had a giant hearth where a fire crackled. Near the big toe of the shoe were chairs and cushions, cots and cradles and hammocks where the mothers stayed with the littlest ones. The rest of us climbed a spiral staircase. Starlight shone through the holes for the laces, and little bridges woven of lacing led to platforms with bunkbeds (and yes, if you're wondering, chamber pots tucked under the beds). Jack and I were shown to bunks about halfway up to the ceiling. Each bunk had a quilt and pillow filled with goose down.

"It's nice here. I wish. I wish we could . . ." he yawned.

I had been feeling drowsy myself, but all at once, I was wide awake.

"We can't stay," I said, sitting up. "Or I can't, anyway."

"I know," said Jack. "It's not our destiny."

Destiny? I had only been thinking of my mother and my aunties.

"What *is* our destiny?" I asked him.

"To find the edge of the world, of course, and rescue everyone before they're pushed over."

If we got there in time.

"But it's more than that," Jack went on. "I want to know what's *over* the edge. Don't you? Is it really nothing?"

My maps had always stopped at the edge, yet I knew . . .

"Jack?" I said. "I think I know who lives there."

He didn't answer. In a moment I heard his soft, deep breathing. I closed my eyes, too, trying to see where my mother might be under the beautiful, terrible sky. A sky that made the dome world seem like a toy, a broken toy, cast aside in the corner of the room where I had slept so long ago, surrounded by my mother and aunties. I followed the thought of the cart, rolling along through the emptiness, into my dreams.

✳ ✳ ✳

The sound of pounding on the door woke me suddenly. The shoe—I was sleeping in a shoe!—wobbled a bit.

"Help us!"

The bustle began downstairs.

"Coming!" Granny Dirt called.

Jack and I joined some of the older children on the staircase, peering down to the commotion below. One of the mothers opened the door, and a small huddle of people came in. I couldn't at first tell how many, but the one in the middle had a belly the shape of the dome.

"Where have you come from?" asked a mother.

No one spoke for a moment, and then they all answered at once, and I saw that they were women and children.

"Outside of the dome."

"What used to be the dome.

"The dome is cracking."

"The wall is crumbling."

"The mines are collapsing."

The mothers began to cluck and fuss. For the first time I wondered where all the shoe mothers had come from. Had they escaped, too?

Only Granny Dirt stayed silent. Her hands busy, feeling the newcomers for injuries, calming those who trembled, gathering the children into her arms.

"The world is ending," one of them whimpered. "The beauty singers were rounded up and sent over the edge of the world!"

No, I pleaded silently, they haven't gone over yet. They can't have gone over yet.

"Everyone is running every which way. Outsiders storming the inside. Insiders running outside. No one knows who's in charge."

No one had ever known. It had been Noone all along, and now he was dead. What had he done? What had I done?

"The Guard is divided against itself. Some killing insiders, some killing outsiders, killing each other. We climbed through a gap in the wall just as night fell."

"We heard the water; we followed the stream."

"We didn't know if we would ever find anyone, but we had to get away."

"Find somewhere safe. It's almost her time."

Their breathless account was broken by a wail.

"Please, can you help us?"

"Help us!"

If a mighty mountain could be swift, that was Granny Dirt.

"Some of you mothers, make our guests welcome, give the children milk, bread, and jam, then tuck them up in beds. The rest, prepare the birthing room."

Everyone bustled to their tasks. Granny Dirt supported the moaning woman with the huge belly, and they moved out of our sight into the toes of the shoe.

"That's where the new babies come from," one of the girls explained to us. "The big toe."

The mothers fed everyone, while rocking various cradles and hammocks, picking up a fretful infant here and there. Finally they guided the bewildered children, who were rubbing their eyes and stumbling with exhaustion, to the spiral stairs.

"Find them a bed since you're all out of yours!" ordered a mother.

And the older children took their hands as kindly as they had taken ours earlier, sharing beds and blankets. One little girl, they tucked in with me. My mother and aunties had cradled me, but I had never held a younger, smaller person. She nestled into my side, and we both fell into a sweet, deep sleep.

It was still dark when someone shook me awake.

"Granny Dirt says we need to go now." It was Jack, whispering so he wouldn't wake the others. "Nightwing is waiting for us."

I slipped out of bed and kissed the cheek of the little girl who was still fast asleep. Downstairs, mothers gave us a drink of warm milk sweetened with honey and pressed loaves of bread into our hands. From the toe, I could hear a sound I'd never heard before, but I knew at once what it must be.

"May I see the new baby?" I asked the mothers.

I could tell she was about to say no, but then she changed her mind and led me and Jack to the little toe, a cozy, nest-like room lined with soft, colorful quilts. The new mother sat propped up in bed, holding a tiny creature in her arms, with a face that was all closed up and scrunched. I tiptoed over, and the mother let me touch the baby's cheek.

Then Granny Dirt came to find Jack and me. She led us outside into the cold. Remember, I had never felt cold for more than an instant, through the window of the tower room. There was a line of red in one part of the sky. Stars glimmered on and off and on again. The raven circled slowly, making liquid clicking sounds.

"Nightwing will guide you to Granny Sweep's pinnacle," said Granny Dirt. "From there, you will see all you need to see."

"All the way to the edge of the world ?" Jack asked.

Granny Dirt was silent for a moment. We could hear the whoosh of the raven's wings, and I thought I could hear, though I couldn't be sure, the faint fading voices of the stars.

"Yes," she said at length. "And all that lies between."

The broken dome, the people running every which way.

"Will the shoe be safe, Granny Dirt?" I asked. "Will the mothers and children be safe?"

"We have our ways, Rose. If anyone comes to harm us, they won't notice an old shoe lying in a muddy field. "

"Is it the end of the world, Granny Dirt?" I persisted. "Like those people said, with every cracking and crumbling?"

Maybe she sensed my distress, my fear that I had caused the catastrophe.

"When seeds split open, it feels to them like the end of the world. Till they find the dirt."

She gathered us both into her arms, into the warm darkness of her, and she sang softly.

everything inside must go out again
everything outside must go in
in out, out and in, round and about again

"Go now, children, never fear. I remember now. I remember everything. I am with you every step you take."

"Even over the edge of the world?" asked Jack.

She released us from her embrace and pointed to the sky, where Nightwing circled.

"Go, children," she said. "Nightwing is waiting."

Then she sang:

seeds fly and seeds fall,
wind, water, dark, light
the earth will hold them all
Granny Dirt is under all

And her song followed us until it finally faded into the emptiness of the world beyond.

Sometimes Nightwing was just a speck in the sky. As the sun rose, she was also a shadow sweeping the ground. If we lost sight of her, she seemed to know, and let out a raucous cry. Even more than yesterday, when the river banks at least were green and gave some shelter, the emptiness overwhelmed me. Jack, too, seemed awed, accustomed as he was to walls, narrow alleyways, and crowds.

The raven's shadow was not the only one we saw. In that stark empty world, any shadow stood out. First a long, thin finger of a shadow pointed toward what we recognized as the dome. Its cracked surface mirroring the sky, as if the sky too were cracked, like the bare earth that surrounded us. With our squinting eyes, we followed the thin shadow to its source: a pinnacle rising up over the plain, seeming to pierce the sky. The raven was flying steadily toward it.

"How are we going to climb that?" Jack wondered.

I thought of my map, all my drawings of Granny Sweep atop the pinnacle.

"They're almost long enough," she'd said in the tower room as she braided her moonlit clouds of hair.

"Granny Sweep will help us," I said to Jack.

"Maybe Nightwing will teach us to fly," he said, sounding hopeful.

I wished we could fly now. How ill-prepared I was for life in the world beyond. Romping with my aunties had been my only form of exercise, unlike Jack, who spent his days running, leaping, and climbing. The soles of Jack's feet were tough as any shoes; mine were excruciatingly tender. I did not want to admit my difficulty keeping up, but Jack must have sensed it. He put an arm around me and took some of my weight.

Slowly the shadows reversed direction as the sun crossed the huge dome of sky, the shadow of the pinnacle receding, as if it were running away from the shadow of the dome, which advanced steadily across the plain. It was not only the shadow that advanced. We heard the sound of booted footfalls even before we saw: a contingent of the Guard marching, marching toward the pinnacle.

"We've got to get there first, Rose!" said Jack. "Can you run?"

He withdrew his arm and grabbed my hand. His wiry strength surged into me.

"Yes!" I said.

And we did. How could I have known before, having only run down a corridor, what running was really like? My body was heavy and light at once. My heart became wing beats. There were bursts of light behind my eyes. And the ground pushed back, propelled us into the air, caught each step where it landed, then sent us flying again.

The pinnacle loomed over us, and the Guard was gaining on us.

"Runaways!" someone shouted. "Seize them!"

As we ran toward the pinnacle, Nightwing gave a ringing cry and dove at the Guard. Behind us startled cries turned to screams of terror and howls of pain. We arrived panting at the base of the pinnacle, which was so high we had to bend backwards as far as we could to see the overhanging ledge at the top.

"Here goes everything," said Jack.

He backed up to take a running leap, when two long white ropes tumbled down the pinnacle brushing the ground before us.

"Up, children, come up!" cried a voice that sounded like the whistling of the wind.

We each grabbed a rope, a braided rope, made of hair white as the moon.

We climbed, hand over hand, bracing our feet against the side of the pinnacle. Then we realized we were also being pulled upwards. About half way up, we could hear singing, and then the words of the song came clear.

braids longer and older than time
threads swept from cobwebbed sky
I reel you in on the wind and rhyme
where stars spin and birds fly

At last we climbed over the edge, through the thorny thicket, into Granny Sweep's arms.

It was true. From the pinnacle, we could see everything, which was probably why the Guard hoped to climb it. Granny Sweep had wisely led us away from the edge and sat us down at her rickety table with the benches built in, so they wouldn't blow away. Even Granny Sweep's cow Moo-n looked as though she could sail away on a strong gust. The chickens held on to the dirt and clucked over their nests. The daredevil goats butted and pranced, teasing the sheep. Only Puss, Granny Sweep's calico cat, knew how to find the grassy hollows out of the wind and in the sun.

Granny Sweep ladled fresh milk into cups and gave us bowls of nuts, apples, and pears to eat. Nightwing landed on the table beside us, the closest we'd seen her. She had something in her beak. I'm afraid it might have been an eyeball. I looked away as she swallowed it whole.

"Routed!" she croaked.

"I'll send them a wind at their back, poor lads," said Granny Sweep, as she stood and whistled.

Wind is invisible, but I swear I could see her gather all the breezes swirling around the pinnacle and send them to the plain, where the Guard, tiny as what I would later know as ants, swarmed and fled.

"Why do you want to help them, Granny Sweep?" Jack asked. "They wanted to capture us. They called us runaways."

"Well, I suppose you are runaways—or runners toward. And as for the Guard, they were all just boys once. Even Nimble Jack was forced into the Guard. And you might have been, too, if you had stayed."

"No one could have caught me," Jack declared. "No one can catch me."

"Just as well, for you've a ways to go yet, children. Look! Look and you will see."

She took our hands and led us even higher, to the very top of the pinnacle.

"Here is where I send my eye out," she said. "Look, children, I will lend you my sight, look and see what you can see."

I thought I would see far away, everything small, swallowed up by distance and sky. But with Granny Sweep's eye, I could see close, too. The cracks in the wall surrounding dome world. I saw insiders in bedraggled finery wandering the streets, bewildered, begging a place at the dung fires, a bowl of food, a scrap of bread. I could see cracks in the dome, birds flying in and roosting on houses that had never known weather. I saw the huge gates, fallen and dangling on their hinges. With Granny Sweep's eye I kept going out the other side, following the rutted tracks that led to the edge of the world.

The sun travelled in the same direction and began to fall slowly down the sky toward the edge, the place where everything appeared to disappear. I was not used to seeing the sun of outside world. The sun that had sailed over the ceiling of our room had been pretty, the light rising and falling each day, reassuring. But the outside sun was fire, sometimes so bright and high in the sky, I could not see it, only feel it. The closer it got to the edge of the world, the bigger, rounder, and redder it looked. How near to it could I go, with the power of Granny Sweep's eye? Could I follow it down into darkness? Where did it go?

"Come back, Rose," Granny Sweep cautioned. "That's far enough."

As my vision swept back over the far plain beyond the dome, I glimpsed in silhouette a wagon with two huge figures dwarfing it. And a smaller one between them, holding something, someone in her arms. Riders on horseback galloped away from the cart back toward the dome, leaving the prisoners unguarded.

"They're still alive," I said. "They haven't gone over!"

Now that we were back on the pinnacle seeing with only our own eyes, the edge of the world looked so far away, farther than we could see. In between the pinnacle and the edge lay the whole of dome world, however ruined. As the sun disappeared, leaving night in its wake, we saw light flaring through the cracks of the dome. All along the top of the broken wall, torches burned. There were encampments inside and outside the wall.

"We have to find a way to get by all these people without getting stopped," said Jack. "We need to fly, Granny Sweep. Make us fly."

As if in answer, the wind that had been hovering and circling, blew stronger. Granny Sweep's braids lifted in answer, two white paths into the sky where the stars were just beginning to make a wavering appearance.

"I'm ready!" shouted Jack.

And then the wind softened to a sigh. Granny Sweep's braids pooled at her feet, and she began to wind them around her head.

"They are not long enough or strong enough yet for flying, I'm afraid. But there is a way."

She put a hand on each of our shoulders and turned us away from the dome. At first we could see nothing, but as the stars shone, surer and brighter, I saw the outline of the shoe, and fancied I could hear the mothers singing their lullaby. The sound faded and Granny Sweep kept us turning, until we faced the opposite direction from the shoe.

"What do you see, children?"

We peered across the plain.

"I can't see anything," said Jack. "It's dark."

"Look more closely. Look with my eye."

Our sight travelled again in this new direction, first seeing only the rise and fall of the empty land, the stars defining its darkness. Then I saw shapes against the sky: trees I had seen in storybooks and later drawn on my map. Some trees twisted as if in the midst of turning in the wind. Others stood straight, their branches falling around them, their outlines against the sky, so different from a wall or even a hill, intricate and varied. Flickering under the trees were little lights. I might have called them fireflies, if I had ever seen them before. Fairy lights.

"What is that place?" asked Jack.

The world behind the wall had few trees; the wildest place inside had been the briar patch, destroyed before Jack Quick and I were born.

"That's Granny Spark's forest," I answered. "Isn't it, Granny Sweep?"

Granny Sweep stood and stretched, the wind playing with the loose silver threads of her hair.

"Yes," she sighed. "I suppose it's her turn next for a visit from you two."

"But we are going to the edge of the world," objected Jack. "That's not on the way."

Granny Sweep didn't answer, not directly. She hummed a little hum, and then she sang.

On the way, in the way, up and down, in then out
sometimes you have to go around to find your way about

"Come children," she said. "I've shown you all I can for tonight. I need to rest my eye. I'll give you pastry made of the passing clouds, light as air, sweetened with berries. Then you can watch the spiders weaving their webs in the stars."

We sat and ate as many pastries as we liked, and Jack liked a great many. Then we lay in hammocks, swaddled in warm quilts, and gazed at the sky. My eyes were bleary with sleep, but I thought I could see the star spiders spinning their shining threads, holding the whole huge sky together. As I slept I could hear them singing, the spiders or the stars, their voices high and bright, thin and strong as the threads of Granny Sweep's hair.

Granny Sweep has done her task
Rose and Jack are here at last
rock-a-bye, fall or fly
cradles rocking in the sky

It seemed we had only just fallen asleep, when Granny Sweep gently shook us awake. The stars glimmered in and out of the brightening sky, and I could still hear their dimming voices. They sounded like the beauty singers, but even higher, wilder.

day and night, dusk and dawn
beauty will go on, go on

Granny Sweep gave us a drink of milk, still warm from Moo-n. She had packed a satchel with apples, pears, and nuts, bread, cheese, and hardboiled eggs from the chickens. Overhead Nightwing circled, making her clicking sound.

"Best go before it's full light, children."

We said goodbye to all the animals while Granny Sweep loosened her braids and sent them tumbling down the pinnacle to the ground below. I felt sad to leave her.

"Can't you come with us, Granny Sweep?" Jack asked.

"Now that would be quite a trick," she laughed, "climbing down my own braids."

"But Granny, don't you know yet who you are?" I demanded.

Rose knows, Rose knows, whistled the wind.

"I know," said Granny Sweep. "I know, and don't you forget. Go on now, my children, my darling bits of thistledown."

She gave us each a kiss, handed us a braid rope, and sent us sliding and swinging down the side of the pinnacle. All the way to the ground we could hear her singing:

air and wind, wind and air
blow a kiss, I'm hard to miss
invisible and always there
Granny Sweep is everywhere

It felt strange to be on the ground without a view. From here we could not see the forest. But Nightwing could. She kept us within sight and within sound, the shadow of her wings spreading wide over the ground as the sun rose.

When the sun was high and hot overhead, and our shadows shrank back into our feet—or that is how it looked to me—we sat down in the shelter of a boulder and ate some of our food, saving our water by quenching our thirst with the fruit. When we looked, we could hardly see the dome now, and the pinnacle faded into the noon. Then we saw in the distance, but too close for comfort, something or someone moving in our direction.

"The Guard!" said Jack. "We've got to run. Or hide."

But where? We leaned further into the scant shelter of the rock.

"Not so fast," croaked Nightwing, who flew off in the direction of whoever was heading our way.

We could only wait. Without Nightwing to guide us we could not be sure of our direction. There were no landmarks. Only sky marks, if you could call the sun a mark. The clouds were beautiful but changeable, flocks of them, passing over us, giving us the momentary relief of shade as they passed over the empty plain.

"Company coming!" croaked Nightwing on her way back.

And she flew ahead, just as the people behind us got close enough that we could hear the fall of their feet and their voices not so much singing as panting a chant to keep time:

out of the mine, into the sun
out of the ruins and on the run

Soon they came into sight, a band of people, mostly men with a few women, all covered with a sheen of dusty sweat that glinted in the sun as they moved. Some had pickaxes over their shoulders. Others carried rucksacks. I thought at first they would run right past us, like a flock of birds on foot.

At a sign from a man in the lead, they all dropped to the ground, panting, the sweat cutting channels in their dust-coated faces. The ones carrying bundles got out canteens and began passing them around. I wasn't sure that they had even seen us, but then the man who had called a halt offered us a drink, without wasting any breath on words.

"Thank you. We have water," said Jack. "We've got some food, too."

We got up and opened our own sacks. Walking into their midst, we offered apples and pears. Some people hesitated at first, but they were clearly hungry.

"Thank you," said the man, whose bare arms bulged with muscle.

No one seemed inclined to speak much. They huddled together, casting anxious glances at the sky.

"How did you escape?" Jack broke the silence. "We heard the mines collapsed."

The man eyed Jack, debating whether to answer.

"Not hard to tell we're miners, eh?"

Not even for me, though I had never seen a mine or a miner except in a dream.

"Her," said a woman. "We followed her."

"Right out of the mine."

"We came out way beyond the wall."

"She gave us a head start."

There was no breeze, but I felt the hair rise on the back of my neck.

"Never mind that." The man cut off the flow of information. "How did you come here? You're hardly more than children. But you're out here on your own, better provisioned that we are. Are you lookouts? Spies? Well, we're not falling into any traps. We're not going back. We'd rather go over the edge of the world than go back there."

"Speak for yourself, Digger!" another man said. "Maybe we were too hasty. And I don't recall us taking a vote or appointing you leader. Maybe we should go back. What's out here but hunger and thirst? We're armed. We could fight for our fair share of inside loot."

"Joining in the looting, raping," a woman spoke up. "That's what you want? Whichever way you go, I'm going in the opposite direction."

"What kind of a miner would walk into something that could come down on his head in a minute?" said another man. "That dome is riddled with cracks."

The miners began to argue among themselves.

Jack and I looked at each other. What to tell? Where to begin? We might be the only two people who knew what had happened. Maybe it was even our fault—or my fault, at least. Was it a good thing, a bad thing?

"We've got to say something," Jack whispered to me.

He scrambled to the top of the rock. I climbed after him. It gave us a small vantage point. I looked up and saw Nightwing, making wide circles overhead, unnoticed by the miners.

"We escaped from the dungeon when the dome cracked," said Jack, attempting to make it clear we were not on the side of the Guard.

We had their attention.

"The grannies helped us," I said. "They gave us food and shelter."

"The grannies?"

"What does she mean, the grannies?"

At the word, a doubtful wonder passed through the crowd of weary miners, like a breeze or a ripple. They sat up, and their dusty faces looked suddenly younger.

"Where are these grannies?"

"I never saw any grannies feeding people."

"Bite your tongue," said an older woman. "Who else but grannies ever fed anyone? Just because you don't see them don't mean nothing. No one ever saw the beauty singers neither."

"But we heard the beauty singers every morning, even in the mines."

"Well, they're gone now. Sent to the edge of the world with that murdering imposter."

My mother, they meant my mother.

"She's not . . . she didn't!" I cried out. How could I make them understand? "She was an outside girl who got captured, one of the three. Do any of you remember the three?"

"The three," the miners murmured and muttered.

"They're long gone, the three."

"No good ever came of them."

"No good ever came to them."

"Not true. You Know Who was one of them."

"And one of them is still alive," I jumped in. "The beauty singers are still alive! We're on our way to find them. We—"

Jack laid a cautioning hand on my arm. We didn't know yet if the miners would help us, hinder us, or harm us. Yet they had protected Sal, gathered her into their ranks, and hidden her from the Guard.

Then faint and distant, coming from nowhere and everywhere, I heard voices, more an echo than a song:

over the edge of the world we go
over the edge of the world we fly

I was not the only one. People looked around uneasily. Then another, clearer sound rang out. Nightwing flapping down, landing on Jack's shoulder. The miners took a step back from the rock.

"Bad omen," people muttered. "Bad luck."

They made signs for warding off disaster.

"It's all right." Jack spoke as clearly as he could. "This is Nightwing. She's a friend."

The raven began to vocalize urgently and then flapped up into the air, circling our heads.

"What's she saying?" demanded Digger.

"Guard," translated Jack. And he pointed. "Back there."

Everyone scrambled to their feet and looked back toward dome world.

"I don't see anything."

"It's a trick, I tell you. It's a trap."

Maybe I still had some of the magic of Granny Sweep's eye. There in the distance I saw them, the sun reflecting on their helmets and weapons. Nightwing cried out and began to fly ahead.

"Come on," I cried out, turning to the crowd. "She's guiding us."

"Why should we trust a bird?" someone shouted. "Why should we trust you?"

"They've gotten this far on their own," said a boy, not much older than Jack. "We can't just stay here."

Arguments began to break out again.

"Maybe we should give ourselves up. Better than dying of exposure out here."

"Where are we going, anyway? Where is there to go?"

Just then, at the edge of the crowd, I caught sight of a woman, not dressed as the other women were in ragged, bunched-up skirts. She was dressed like a man and carried a pickaxe over her should. Her hair was raggedy and wild. Her eyes gold, bright as the sun. She looked at us, no, not us. She was looking straight at Jack.

"Follow them!" she called out, her voice as golden as her eyes, dark as the mine.

The miners turned and stared. For a moment she was still there, shimmering in the light, then she was gone, leaving only a trace of shining dust.

"A ghost."

"Not just a ghost, it's her."

"The one who led us out."

Sal.

I looked at Jack. His eyes brimming with the light she'd left behind her.

Nightwing called again, her cry echoing out, filling the whole emptiness, even as her form got smaller.

"Come on, Rose," said Jack. "Let's lead the way."

We scrambled down the rock and took off after Nightwing, not looking back to see if anyone was following us. It wasn't long before we heard the steady fall of their feet.

out of the mine, into the sun
out of the ruin and on the run

We sang with them. The chant kept us going until nightfall.

Night fell. It did feel like a fall. One moment everything glowed red and the next, darkness and stars, Nightwing a small shape amid their glitter. And the cold came just as suddenly. We all stopped and moved into a huddle. Even if we had the means, we didn't dare light a fire. In the distance we could see the fires where the Guard had made camp.

"By the cracked and stinking dome, now what?" said Digger.

No one answered, which was more unnerving than grumbles and complaint. Nightwing plummeted, finding Jack's shoulder with ease, croaking what sounded like a command.

"What did she say, boy?"

"Jack," croaked Nightwing. "His name's Jack. Tell them to be quiet."

"She says to be quiet," Jack translated.

"Ha! She's one to talk."

"Yes, she is," agreed Jack. "And now she wants us to listen."

Everyone was too tired to do anything else. At first we heard nothing but our own sighs, which joined the night air that shifted and swirled around us, and then—

"Is that a fiddle?" someone asked.

"Would the Guard have brought a fiddler?"

We all listened more intently. Soon we could pick out the sound of more than one fiddler.

"It's not the Guard," said someone. "It's coming from the opposite direction."

The faint, bright sound of the fiddles was joined by something high and shrill: a piper. Then the drums started. Some of the miners began to tap their feet.

Nightwing lifted into the air again. By now everyone knew her call for *follow*.

"Can't see the damn bird."

"She wants us to follow the music," said Jack, getting to his feet.

"How do we know what it is?"

The grumbling began.

"Could be an enchantment."

"An entrapment."

"Fairies, witches."

"Renegades and thieves."

"Whoever they are," said the older woman, "they sound good to me."

But of course I knew where the music came from. With my wind eye, I could just make out the dark mass of trees, twisting and reaching into the starry sky.

"It's Granny Spark's forest," I almost shouted.

"You and your grannies," someone grumbled.

"I've heard stories," another person spoke up. "of people who escaped and ran away to a forest, even though we've hardly seen more than a few spindly trees."

"Maybe the stories are true."

"Maybe they're lies."

"Come on!" called Jack. "Quietly, so we can hear."

Spurred on by cold and hunger, we held hands with each other and ran on toward music that grew louder and wilder with every step. Soon we could see lights floating in the darkness of the forest, that rose higher into the sky the closer we came. At last we drew near enough to see lanterns, hung in tree branches. At the very edge of the forest, we stopped and peered in. Through the trees we could glimpse people dancing to the music—but not just people. Shambling bears, swooping owls, deer and hares leaping. No one spoke. Even Jack and I held back.

Sensing our presence, the trees began to talk. That's what it felt like. The branches of the canopy began to sway and brush against each other. They sent a breeze, one to another, farther and farther into the wood. Though I could not hear it with my ears, through my feet I could hear their roots thrumming. Over- and underground, the trees announced our arrival. All at once, the trees stilled again; it felt as if the air held its breath. Then out of the stillness came a creaking and gentle clattering, as the trees opened an arching pathway.

dead of night and blaze of day
falling star and leaping fire
flickering or steady ray
Granny Spark will light the way

I had seen Granny Spark before, but not like this. I could not tell if she was young or old, human or flame, or the forest itself in something like human form. Her hair blazed and sparked and leafed. Her skin looked both gnarled and smooth. She was robed in moss and fur and flowers. She was everything wild and unpredictable coming toward us. But Granny Spark stood on no formalities.

"On your feet," she said to the miners, many of whom had fallen to their knees. "Come with me."

Then she scooped up Jack Quick and me as if were much smaller and younger children than we were. Maybe to her we were all just children, all no more than babes in her wood.

My memories of that evening in Granny Spark's forest all flow together. The dance became a feast of wild, foraged foods, strong mead, stories turning into songs, and songs to stories, and back again. Lovers disappeared into the wood and then returned, casting their own glow.

As joyful as it all was, I found myself receding from the festivities, deeper into the listening silence of the trees. Well, they weren't all silent, and I don't just mean they creaked and moaned with the wind. They had a way of speaking that I found I could hear without translating it into words. An awareness I could sense, and, in the case of one huge tree with low-slung branches, a beckoning.

I pulled myself up into a lap of branches and let myself be cradled. Without words, although I have to use words to tell you, I told the tree some of this strange story, a life lived inside without sky or earth or other children, my mother and aunties doting and disappearing, my mother most of all, turning each day into someone I did not recognize—did not want to recognize. I told the tree about the forgetful grannies coming to me, asking if I knew their secrets when I didn't even know my own. And Jack climbing a magic beanstalk to find me. And how when I didn't follow him the first time, because I wanted to save my mother, I lost her instead.

Then the tree told me stories, took me right down into the roots of memories that were more than hers: dark earth, water, stone, how seeds split open and took hold and joined the song, warnings and secrets that traveled underground, the short life of each year's leaves, what sunlight and moonlight taste like. And she told me stories of terror, of what happened when a tree or a forest was felled, how you could hear the change in the root song, a dead silence coming closer. She told me how Granny Spark taught this last forest to protect itself.

As I fell asleep, all of it became one dream.

When I opened my eyes, the moon was bending over me the way my mother had. Granny Spark lifted Jack into the tree nest beside me, covering us both with a blanket.

"We have to go, Granny Spark," Jack murmured sleepily. "We have to find the edge of the world. It is our destiny."

"I know my little seedlings. I know . . . "

✳   ✳   ✳

Jack and I woke when it was still dark to the miners' panicked shouts.

"The Guard is coming! They've got torches. They're going to burn us out."

Though there was no wind, the leaves started murmuring in the canopy. The squirrels and birds chattered, excited, but, I sensed, not afraid.

"Old timers," Granny Spark called out, "you know what to do. Help the newcomers find a tree to climb."

Everywhere, people and other creatures were clambering into branches, our ruckus obscuring the sound of the approaching Guard and their heavy boots.

"If the Guard is planning to torch the forest, why are we climbing trees?" demanded Digger.

His question was echoed by other miners on the ground. But no one questioned the bears or the tusked boars that charged anyone who lagged behind.

"Hoofed and winged ones who can keep up, leave space in the trees for the slow-foots."

Finally everyone was treed, and Granny Spark hoisted herself up beside us.

"Climb higher," she urged us. "So you can see."

We followed her up. From gaps in the canopy of our beautiful tree (I later knew it as a beech), with its changeable green and purples leaves, I could see the torches of the Guard with my ordinary eye, some on horseback, all armed.

"Everyone ready?" called Granny Spark.

"Aye, aye," came a chorus not only from the people perched in the trees, but a sort of deep, excited, wordless rumbling from the trees themselves. Granny Spark climbed even higher.

"Right, greenwood. First we rush the plaguing Guard till they soil themselves and turn tail. Then you know where to go. On your mark, get set—"

up trees, make your roots strong legs and swift feet
up and away to find new earth, dark and sweet
away, away over the dry and thirsty ground
to a place near or far where we cannot be found

What is the sound of a forest pulling up roots all at once? Think earthquake, thunder, tidal wave, more. Scent: think darkness, depth, water, fire, stone. Motion: think a horse rearing and a ship pitching, more. Hold on tight to your tree, ride, don't fall, fly with roots turning into feet, branches into wings.

We could not hear the scream of the Guard over the roar of the forest. We could hardly hear own shrieks and, in the case of Jack and me, wild laughter. I can't tell you how long we rode the forest, the sun rising and racing along with us, sending tree shadow before us, then beneath us, then behind us, the large birds flying overhead adding their cries to the din, the small birds holding tight to their branches, scolding and singing. We shared our tree with squirrels as well as root-dwelling animals, badgers, hedgehogs, a rabbit or two. On we went, giddy and merry, until we were too tired for wonder or fear.

Then gently, so gently, it might have taken hours or minutes, the forest slowed, tiptoed to a stop. I have never heard silence like that before or since. Not a bird twittered, not a human spoke a word. Maybe all of us—trees, birds, animals, people—felt ourselves, still reeling, settle into some unknown beyond. Silently we reeled ourselves back to stillness. We breathed together. A wind from beyond came into the forest, reaching out to us, welcoming us.

Granny Spark swung down from the tree and began pacing the new ground, bare of needle and leaf.

"Roots down," she spoke at last, "but not too deep, just enough for rest and sleep and food. Birds and animals and outlaws, at ease. Fold your wings, find your feet."

At last she beckoned to Jack and me. We climbed down, our legs barely holding us up. Granny Spark took our hands.

"Briar's Rose and Jack Quick, son of Nimble Jack, come with me."

PART TEN

The Edge of the World

Rose

Here we are at last, children.

Close your eyes and imagine. See the expanse of empty sky on one side, the wide empty plain on the other. Hear, so far below it's almost beyond hearing, the heartbeat of the waves. Taste the faint hint of salt, feel the wind on your face and the light of the sun that has traveled all the way from the other side of Granny Sweep's pinnacle over the edge of the world. Breathe a sweet scent that drifts up in pockets of sun-warmed air. I have never breathed that scent before, but I know (*Rose knows, Rose knows*) that it is the same scent that drew my mother deep into the briar patch, where the bees hummed and sipped from roses, wild roses, the last and only roses inside the wall.

We walk slowly, our own eyes open wide, as close as we can to the edge of the world, not close enough to fall. Granny Spark keeps a firm grip on our hands. We look down as best we can. Clouds, which could be mistaken for sheep, flock below. All our lives we have all been told, there is no bottom. The setting sun is shining in the empty, endless distance, each day falling, falling into night, into nothing.

But not quite yet.

Granny Spark turns us away from the edge, facing us toward the land. The light is behind us; before us, our long shadows, stretching across the emptiness toward the distant broken dome. In the sky are wisps of cloud, coming closer, sweeping down. And there is Granny Sweep facing us. To one side of us there is a hill, shaped like an old woman bending over in her garden. Then she straightens up, Granny Dirt, with mothers and children tumbling around her, the shoe, small now, lying close by. On the other side is the forest, swaying gently. Granny Spark kneels down, embraces us and steps aside to the edge of the trees. Jack and I reach for each other's hands. Behind us, the scent of salt and roses grows stronger, the rattle of bones, the bells ringing, clearer, closer.

And then, even before we turn to look, I know Granny Brine, blue-black with seaweed hair, stands at our backs.

world's edge, edge of fear
salt and rose, bell and bone
falling, flying, shrouded, clear
Granny Brine is always here

One moment it seems all the grannies are close to us, the next far away. One moment they are grannies, with arms and laps, grannies who sing lullabies and give us warm milk to drink and nuts and berries to eat. The next moment they are so huge I can't see them at all, but they are here, there, over, under, everywhere. Sky, ground, light, leaves, the roar of wind and blood, the taste of honey and tears on my tongue.

Rose knows, Rose knows.

"What is happening, Rose?" whispers Jack.

Before I can answer, a tatter of blue flies over our heads on its way to the edge of the world.

Your destiny is here, your destiny, says the warm, blue voice.

"Did you hear that, Jack?" I whisper in turn.

He nods.

Then we see something coming toward us over a small rise, framed by the dusky sky. Soon we hear the creak of a wagon. Two gigantic beings pull in harness, while a dozen or so small birds fly in circles around the wagon, easily keeping up. We can hear their twittering over the sound of bickering voices. The wind stills and shifts, carrying the words to us.

"I say we stop here."

"You know she wants to go as close as she can. She wants to look over the edge."

"That's dangerous. I told her that's dangerous. I'm telling you—"

"It's dangerous, I know. Of course it is. That's the whole point."

"We should have gone back, taken our chances, when the big crash boom crack came."

"We are taking our chances. It was our lucky day when the Guard turned tail and ran away."

"Leaving us to die of exposure or, failing that, starvation."

"Well, if we're going to die, we might as well fly."

"Plummet you mean. You and I, we'd plummet. No thanks."

Jack and I looked at each other. Then we dropped each other's hands and ran as fast we could, running and flying toward the huge arms of my aunties.

After the aunties had removed their harness, then covered us with kisses and smothered us with hugs, sobbing the whole while, scalding us with tears, they finally calmed enough to speak.

"Should we tell them?"

"No need. They'll see."

"Must they? They're only children."

"We can't stop them."

They stepped aside, and Jack and I saw. In the wagon sat an old woman. She looked even older that the grannies.

"Bramma!" whispered Jack.

"Come up, Jack Quick, but gently. Bring my granddaughter with you."

Granddaughter. I looked around to see who she meant. Then I remembered.

Without shaking the cart, Jack climbed in. He reached out his hand to me. I didn't take it. I just stood, as if I had taken root like one of Granny Spark's trees. No one spoke. The birds fluttered down on the wagon's side.

"Rose," someone whispered my name. "Rose."

Strong hands lifted me into the cart. There was my mother lying on the bottom of the cart, my mother as I had never seen her. Had my aunties made her another mask? This face looked like hers, but her eyes were closed. Her head was wrapped in scarves. I could almost see her bones shining through, like the image of the daytime moon that traveled across the ceiling of our secret room.

"Rose," she said again.

"Mama."

I lay down next to her and held her in my arms.

"Is Rose's mother going to be all right?" Jack whispered to my grandmother.

I could not hear her answer, but I knew. I could hear the aunties conferring anxiously.

"Should we tell her?"

"Not yet, not yet."

You don't need to, I didn't say out loud.

In my dream, I had been with her in the dungeon, where she had lain with all her bones broken. I was with her now. I could hear the wheeze and whistle of her breath. I could see the shard of bone that had pierced her lung. Far away, over the edge of the world, I could hear the sigh of the waves and the rattle of bones in the wind.

My fault, my fault, the words rose and repeated in my mind. My fault, my fault. If I hadn't run away to the tower. My fault, my fault. If Noone hadn't seen me. if I had never seen Noone. My fault, my fault . . .

"If you had never," my mother murmured. "We would still be inside inside. I would still be *him* . . . "

Her voice trailed off.

"Noone died," I told her. "The dome cracked."

My fault . . .

Not your fault . . .
"Rose. I'm going to die."
No, no, no, no, no.
"Rose, listen to me. I'm going to fly."
As I held her close, I could already feel her leaving me.
"Sing to me, Rose. I don't have enough breath. Sing me the song . . . "
Of course, I knew which song she meant. I sang.

over the edge of the world we go
over the edge of the world we fly
queens and kings
when we have wings
we all have wings
over the edge of the world we go
queens and kings, queens and kings

"That's where I'm going, Rose. Tell them. Over the edge of the world."
Those were the last words she spoke.

* * *

I held her all night as the air and her body cooled. The aunties, my grandmother, and Jack slept close, our bodies, big and small, young and old, making a nest for my mother. Overhead the star spiders spun their webs. I did not wonder where the grannies had gone. I knew.

Dawn came. The little songbirds lifted their heads from beneath their wings and flew into the gathering light, singing.

come darkness, come the dawn
beauty will go on, go on, beauty will go on

come birth, come death, come silence, come song
beauty will go on, go on, beauty will go on

Keeping hold of my mother's cold hand, I listened as the beauty singers sang and sang, as the stars began to fade.

"Goodbye, Briar, Goodbye Rose, daughter of my daughter, goodbye Jack Quick, son of Sal and Nimble Jack."

Wings stirred the air and touched our cheeks as one more bird, small, with a golden breast, rose to join the flock.

come sorrow, come joy, come perilous dawn
beauty will go on, go on, beauty will go on

We watched until the beauty singers disappeared into the sun's full light. Then we turned our attention to my mother.

She was dead. I knew what dead was now. I understood why Noone had wanted to do everything in his power, beyond his power, to stop it. I also knew that he could not. No one could.

Rose knows, Rose knows.

My aunties looked at me. They had never been so silent. They even wept soundlessly. Jack still gazed at the sky, too astonished to cry. I turned my gaze to the edge of the world. The grannies were there, waiting for us. The grannies were everywhere.

I climbed out of the wagon. Jack leaped out. The aunties heaved their bulk over the sides and put on the harness. Jack and I led the procession, stopping just short of the edge of the world.

"No, Rose," the aunties wailed.

"We can't."

"How can we let her go?"

A voice louder than the aunties rang out. We turned and saw Nightwing leading a small band of outlaws and miners. They stopped at a respectful distance. Then Digger came forward.

"We heard there was a death. If there's anything we know, it's how to dig."

The aunties kicked over their traces and rushed toward him. He quite understandably backed up a step or two.

"How kind."

"Oh, how kind."

"Think of it, sister."

"A grave at the edge of the world."

"We can mark it."

"Tend it. Plant flowers."

I stepped between my aunties, took their arms and pulled them back.

"Thank you," I said to Digger.

"Least we can do. You and your friend, saving us from the Guard."

"Thank you," I said again. "My mother wants to go over the edge of the world."

There was a silence. The wind blew from the emptiness, salt, sweet, as the air warmed. Nightwing settled on Jack's shoulder. I turned back to the wagon, climbed in and slipped my arms beneath my mother's body. But of course I couldn't lift her alone. The sky became, as it so often had in my childhood, my aunties bodies bending over me. Now Jack was here, too, lifting her feet as I cradled her head. Soon we had her out of the cart. My aunties lifted her upright, as if she could walk, her feet skimming the ground.

"Um," one of them said.

"How do we—"

"Throw her over the edge—"

"Without falling."

"Not that I wouldn't do anything for her—"

"But."

"I'll do it!" I said. "I want to go, too!"

There was an outcry from the aunties, Nightwing, the miners and the outlaws.

"No," said Jack, taking my hand.

"What about our destiny?" I pleaded with him.

"Really, Rose. You're going to fling us over a cliff when you wouldn't even climb all the way down a beanstalk?"

There was another silence. Far below I heard the faint sound of rattling bones.

"Tell you what," said Digger. "We've got rope. How 'bout we anchor the heavers, so when they give the ho, they don't go."

Everyone began to confer. I went to my aunties and tried to pry them loose from my mother.

"I'm going to throw her," I told them.

"No, Rose."

"Absolutely not."

"We have known her."

"Loved her."

"Ruined her."

"Cared for her."

"Since before you were born."

"It's our job,

"Ours alone."

The kept protesting, even as I turned away and nodded to Digger. They subsided when the miners roped their waists and shoulders, leaving their massive arms free. They anchored themselves with their own weight. I stood to the side, as close to the edge as Jack would let me.

"Ready!"

"What do we do?"

"On the count of three."

"Give her a flying start."

Three times my aunties swung my mother back and forth, back and forth, back and forth, the way they used to swing me. And then . . .

They let her fly.

Sing, Rose!

over the edge of the world she goes
over the edge of the world she flies

I sang and sang as my mother's body spun up into a hurtle of blue and a shimmer of gold, and then down, down, down, until I couldn't see her anymore.

I don't remember much of the rest of the day. I think the miners, outlaws, and Granny Dirt's mothers tended us, bringing us food, kindling and wood for a fire, strong mead to drink. I fell asleep.

I dream.

Granny Spark sits crossed-legged before the fire; she is the fire. Granny Dirt holds me close; she is the ground. Granny Sweep sweeps the cobwebs into the sky; she is the sky. And then, as the waning moon rises, I see Granny Brine, a shining darkness, walking among the bones, the gleaming bones, till she comes to my mother's body lying on the sand covered with rose petals.

"Your daughter's coming," says Granny Brine.

Or it might be the rush of waves, the rattle of bone.

"I'm coming, mama, I'm coming."

My own voice wakes me as the first light touches the fading stars.

In the full light of day, my determination seemed preposterous. Then I saw Nightwing flying up from below the edge and dipping back down again. Jack watched the raven, too, as intently as I did.

"There's our destiny, Jack," I said.

He nodded.

"We're going to climb down."

Children, we did find the way down. Crack by crack, crevice by crevice, briar rose by briar rose. I went first this time with Jack right behind me, but we were not alone. Some of the miners and outlaws joined us, and a few mothers with their babies and children strapped front and back. And bringing up the rear . . .

"Help! My foot slipped."

"Careful, sister. If you fall, you'll crush everyone."

"If I fall, we all fall."

"We should have just jumped, gotten it over with."

"Can't you be quiet? I need to concentrate."

How long did we climb down, how far, through masses of cloud, and fierce splashes of hot sun, down and down, the scent of salt and seaweed growing stronger, the sound of waves going from murmur to roar, the bones rattling, the bells ringing.

At last we stood at the bottom of the world, gazing out at a new endlessness. Granny Brine's ship rode the swells as the sun turned red and the sea, gold.

Leaving the others gazing, I turned and entered the temple of bone where my mother waited, not just her broken body, her bones shining through, already part of the temple. No, children. I did not see her, not the way you might mean.

Just like the grannies, she was everywhere.

PART ELEVEN

My End

I was a young girl then, when I lost, and did not lose, my mother. Now I am the oldest of the old, though never as old as the ones who are older than time, older than stars, older than dirt, older than the sea where we have made our island homes.

I know you want to know. My aunties lived long lives. They died interrupting each other. In honor of their memory, people still debate which one had the last word.

Jack Quick also lived a long time, till his body slowed and his heart stopped, releasing his quickness into a flying somersault. I still hear his voice sometimes, dark blue, shot through with light. We had children, grandchildren, great-grandchildren; so did many of the others who climbed down from the edge of the world. All the children are my children, children. All the children are everyone's children.

The rain is stopping. Dawn light is seeping into the cave where I've sheltered as I've told you this story. Now I know that if anyone from the world at the top of the edge finds us, I will tell them the story, too: all the secrets the grannies once forgot, their nightmares and their nature, the adventures of the three, how dome world cracked open and the wall crumbled. Tonight I will tell the story to my children—grandparents now.

They will tell their children, who will tell their children, who will tell their children, so they will remember.

What Rose knows, what Granny Rose knows, what Noone did not know.

Life and death turn into each other, outside turns in and inside out.

The grannies are always with us, everywhere.

And beauty will go on, go on, beauty will go on.

I step out of the cave and join the song.

When I am done telling the story, I will take a small boat and row back from our islands to the temple of bone. If I have the strength—I know Jack Quick's bright spirit will urge me on—I will climb to the top of the bottomless cliff.

Once more I will stand at the edge of the world.

Then I will fly.

ABOUT THE AUTHOR

Elizabeth Cunningham is the author of ten novels, including The Maeve Chronicles. She lives in the valley of the Mahicantuck on unceded land that was home to the Lenape. For more, visit her website: https:// elizabethcunninghamwrites.com/

9 781944 190194